# UNDENIABLY CONVENIENT

## J. SAMAN

*This book can be read as a complete standalone. This family tree is simply a reference if needed.

# Boston World Family Tree

***This Does Not Contain Spoilers And Will Be Updated As The Series Progresses**

## Fritz Family

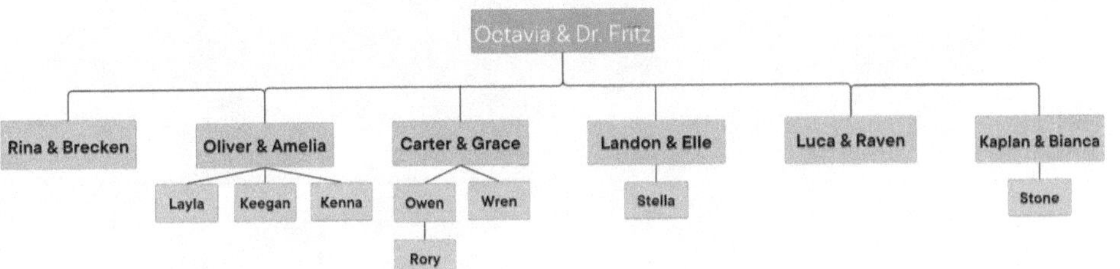


## Central Square

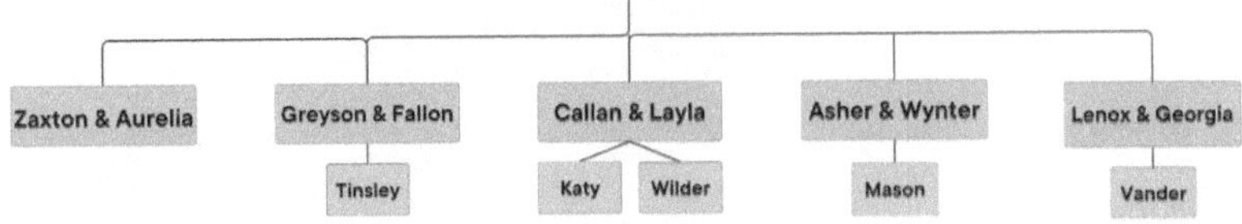


## The Edge

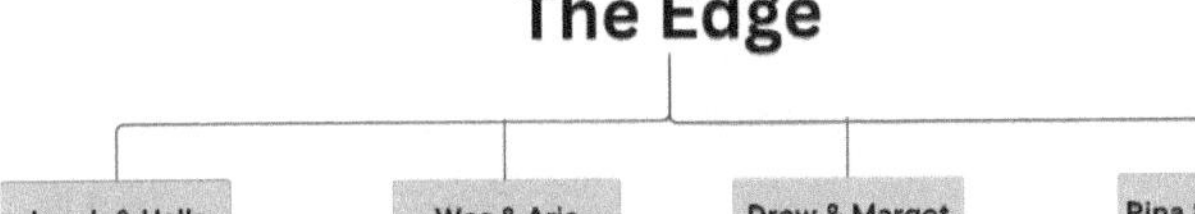

# Chapter One

## Katy

"Slow down!" my best friend and cousin Keegan yells to me as I blow past her.

When you work as a surgeon, every second counts. Every patient on your table is someone else's someone you're there to save. As a surgical resident, my ass belongs to the hospital. And as a resident who hopes to eventually become a trauma surgeon, when I get a stat page to the ER, I run at a goddamn sprint.

It doesn't matter that I'm wolfing down a protein bar mid-stride or that I haven't slept in far too many hours. I have another five to go on this bitch of a shift that doesn't seem to be quite done with me yet.

"Can't! Stat page to the ER. Something about a car accident and a family."

"Oh," she remarks with the same trepidation I have in my gut. She knows what happened to my parents when I was six. She knows they died in this very hospital while I was unharmed in the back seat and how every freaking car accident that comes in makes my stomach feel as shitty as if I just ate a chili cheese dog and chased it down with a sixteen-ounce Guinness.

People always wonder how I manage to work here. The weird truth is it somehow makes me feel closer to them. Like they're watching over me here. This hospital is part of my story, the tragic part, and I work as hard as I can to change that around and rewrite it.

"Yeah. Oh." My head flips to my left, catching her out of the corner of my eye because suddenly she's beside me. "The storms outside are causing all kinds of pileups. Why are you running with me? You're an OB."

"Because I have to tell you about the hot new doctor."

I roll my eyes and dodge a gurney, only to come to a halt as I reach the bank of elevators. "I don't care about a new hot doctor," I puff out, trying to catch my breath.

The side of my fist pounds into the button and I hold my ribs, wheezing while I also try to finish off my protein bar because eating time is precious. I tuck a loose strand of brown hair that fell out of my messy bun behind my ear only to think better of it and yank the elastic out to quickly redo it since half my hair is now plastered to my slightly sweaty forehead as the protein bar hangs from my lips.

"Yes, you do," she assures me, her hands on her narrow hips, all business.

"Don't you have patients?" I garble around my last bite.

She waves me off. "None past five centimeters dilated. I swear, the storm is making every woman go into labor. But like I was saying, you totally will care because not only is the new doctor hot, but you'll also be seeing a lot of him." She gives me a devilish smirk. "Since he's the new chief of trauma surgery."

"What?" My head whips in her direction, my eyebrows pinched tighter than a nun's ass. "No way. I haven't heard about any new doctor in trauma, and that's the sort of thing to hit the gossip mill at full speed. Not to mention Wes would have told me about this."

Wes Kincaid is not only the current head of trauma, but

he's also my mentor and friends with my uncles. I've known him my entire life. So again, he would have told me. Right?

She shakes her head. "It was hush-hush. Rumor has it the contract was just signed this morning. He's some hotshot from the Midwest. Maybe Mayo? Or was it Cleveland?" She tilts her head contemplatively before just as quickly waving that away. "I can't remember. I overheard my dad talking to Wes this morning, so you know it's no bullshit. But then I saw the new doctor earlier and whoa, holy hotness Batman. Like epic hotness. Like, I'd take you down in a cage fight over his hotness."

I stare dumbfounded at my friend. "I don't even know what to say. You're telling me I'm going to have a new boss soon? This isn't a small thing for me. You know that."

"Yep. But at least he's a hot new boss."

"You mentioned that already. About ten times now," I deadpan as I scrub my hands up and down my face, too tired to try and weed this out. "What's his name? This new hotshot you're already swooning over?" Just then the elevator doors open, and my phone vibrates against my hip. "Never mind. I don't have time. Tell me later."

I walk backward onto the elevator and hit the button for the ER, checking my phone as I do.

"Katy!"

"What?" I glance up at her just as the doors close to see her eyes wide with meaning as if she's trying to relay something to me. I tilt my head, following her as the doors come together, but they close before I can figure out what any of that is.

Weird.

But then again, so is Keegan.

I go back to the text on my phone.

**Wes: When you're done with the patient in trauma two, come find me. I have something I need to tell you.**

Wow. So I guess it's true. I'll have a new boss soon. And since I'm seriously hoping to secure a trauma fellowship here, I need this new hotshot guy to like me. Or else I'm going to be stuck trying to find an elite trauma fellowship elsewhere, likely outside of Boston, which considering all my family and friends are here, is far from my first choice.

"This seriously sucks."

"What does?"

"Ah!" I jump in the air and spin around, having been so preoccupied I hadn't realized there was someone else on the elevator with me. Only the second I start to get a good look at the man who was standing silently—and directly, I might add—behind me, the lights flicker and go out. The elevator makes a strange noise and then coasts to a stop.

What the fuck?

"Um." Fear ripples through me, and my instinct is to go to the panel and repeatedly smash the open button with my fist until the doors do just that. Or scream for help. Or generally lose my freaking mind. My lungs empty and immediately refill, but I can't seem to catch my breath.

"Don't move," the man demands urgently. "The power must have gone out. It's been going out all over the city today from the storms. It'll likely come back on in a second, or the hospital's generators will kick in."

"Right. And I should try not to panic, correct? Because I'll be honest with you, this is legit one of my biggest fears and a reason why I take the stairs whenever I can. Why didn't I take the stairs? It's only ten floors."

He chuckles. "Don't worry. We're perfectly safe. All modern elevators should have safety lights and the fan should keep going."

"I hate to be the one to point out the negative, but the lights are out, though bonus, I do hear the fan in the ceiling."

"Yeah, I'm noticing that. I take it this elevator isn't the newest?"

I snort. "It's been here since I was a kid, and I don't think it was new then. And not to be a total downer, but that generator you promised me isn't kicking in either."

He audibly sighs. "So it seems. Okay then. Plan B." I hear him move around, and then the screen of his phone lights up, illuminating his downturned face in weird shadows and a blue glow. "There we go." Turning on his flashlight, he flips the phone around and goes straight for the control panel which appears to be dead. "There has to be a maintenance or emergency number to call."

"How do you know so much about elevators?"

His head turns slightly in my direction, and I catch a hint of a smile before he turns back to the panel. "This is my third time being stuck in one."

"*Third?!*" I bark incredulously. "Who gets stuck in an elevator three times? Remind me never to get on an elevator with you again."

He laughs, the sound rich and smooth, and not the least bit ruffled. Unlike me. I'm a half-beat from hysterical. "When we get off this one, I'll be sure to remind you."

"I suppose I should be grateful you've done this as many times as you have and are alive to talk about it. And get stuck a third time." Before he can locate the number, my phone rings in my hand. "Even better than that number, it's my friend, Keegan."

I answer. "Hey, Keegs."

"Oh my god! There is no power. As in, the main generator isn't working and the backup generator is only powering the red outlets and necessary life-support systems. Please tell me you're not—"

"Stuck in the elevator?" I finish for her. "I am."

"Holy shit. I'm calling Bruce. He'll know what to do."

"Sounds good. Thanks!"

"Don't go anywhere." Then she laughs awkwardly. "Sorry, I'm flustered. I have laboring women here with minimal monitors and my best friend is trapped in a freaking hospital elevator. I'll call you back."

She hangs up on me, and since it seems I'm not going anywhere anytime soon, I take a seat, scoot my butt until I find the wall, and press my back into it. Gross or not, I'm too exhausted and scared to stand anymore. "Did you hear any of that?"

"Yes," the stranger admits. "Your friend is a phone shouter."

I brush some of my hair back from my face and draw my knees up. "Don't I know it. Bruce is the head of maintenance. Keegan knows everyone because her family more or less owns this hospital—well, and a few others in the area—but her family has been working here as doctors and nurses forever. Lucky for us, she's also my quasi-cousin, so she'll get this sorted even if my last name isn't Fritz like hers is."

"Quasi-cousin?"

"Don't ask. It's a long story. I should probably let my boss know where I am."

I text Wes, informing him I'm stuck in the elevator and that I won't be able to get down to the ER to check on the patient in trauma. I hope the patients are stable. It was a stat page, and that makes me uneasy. Plus, if any of them require surgery or other intervention, the elevators aren't working.

Thankfully, he replies immediately to let me know he's there covering, that the patients are, in fact, stable, and that help is on the way soon since Keegan already put out the alert.

"Good news. My boss says help is on its way. I'm Katy, by the way. I might keep talking because talking is keeping me from fully losing my shit over the fact that I'm trapped in a pitch-black elevator in a hospital with no power."

"It's nice to meet you, Katy. I'm Bennett," he says, taking a seat beside me, pointing his flashlight up at the elevator ceiling which gives me enough light to see him.

And when I do, I gasp. Out loud. Which admittedly isn't

my proudest moment, but it can't be helped. At least I don't cover my mouth with my hand or point like a loony at him. But still. Holy shit.

Bennett Lawson. Bennett fucking Lawson.

It's a good thing I'm sitting down, or I'd likely pass out. I haven't seen him in a long time—seven years to be exact—but the way my already wildly beating heart is now hammering in my chest, you'd never know it's been that long.

He was chief resident when I was a third-year medical student.

But more than that, we shared a very drunken, very hot kiss one night at a party. A kiss I'm positive he doesn't remember even if it made my toes curl. He left the next day for a fellowship across the country, and that was that.

But before the hot kiss, I idolized him. He was so smart and amazing with a scalpel. Undoubtedly, he was the best teacher I had as a med student. Residents, especially chief residents, never take time with med students, certainly not third-year med students.

They're the lowest on the org chart of the medical hierarchy. The scut puppies.

But Bennett Lawson taught me. He brought me into the OR and worked with me on cases. I learned so much under him.

The only memorable thing about me was possibly that kiss in a dark corner where no one could see us. We'd been talking a lot that night. I didn't even bother to flirt. He was a lot older than me, and again, I was only a medical student.

I told him the truth about why I wanted to be a trauma surgeon, explaining how my parents had died when I was just a little girl, and I was in the car with them when it happened. I remember I went to the bathroom, and when I came out, he grabbed my hand and dragged me into that corner, threaded his hands up into my hair, and then kissed me.

After a few minutes or so, he pulled back and murmured against my lips, "For luck." And that was it. He was gone.

But now he's here, in my hospital, and after what Keegan told me about Wes bringing in a hotshot trauma surgeon, I have a gut-sinking feeling he's my new boss. And judging by the complete lack of recognition in his eyes, I was correct in my assumption that he doesn't remember me at all. I do my best not to be disappointed by that.

I'm stuck in an elevator with my new boss, who also just so happens to be the man I made out with seven years ago. Talk about bad luck and timing.

"Are you okay?" he asks, taking note of the fact that all the blood has drained from my face and I'm making weird noises in an elevator as I blatantly stare at him.

I blink and look away. "Yes. Um. Just… nervous. Confined spaces aren't my favorite, and stuck elevators even less so." At least that's not a lie.

He smiles and I die a little. Keegan—as usual—wasn't wrong. Just looking at him I know exactly why everyone is swooning. His shorter on the sides and slightly longer on top dark, wavy hair flops in an almost Superman way on his forehead, making his startlingly blue eyes and black lashes that frame them stand out even more against the harsh flashlight. His smooth, sharp jaw was obviously hand-chiseled by God, and when he smiles like he is now, angels weep at the sheer perfection of his white teeth and fantastic chin dimple, giving this man a slightly boyish appearance.

"Don't be nervous," he says softly, though there is an obvious hint of humor in his smile and glittering eyes. "Despite the weird situation and lack of lighting, we won't plummet to our deaths or anything."

I shake my head at that, turning on my flashlight and setting it down on the floor so it also shines up. "You must give motivational speeches for a living. You're very comforting and inspiring, Bennett."

He laughs, rubbing a hand across his sharp jaw and bringing his knees up so he can rest his forearms on them. "Sorry. That probably wasn't the right thing to say. The last time I was stuck in an elevator, I was with two three-hundred-pound offensive linemen, and I was their quarterback's doctor. That time, I *was* worried that was a possibility. I'd happily be stuck alone with you over them anytime."

"Same. Definitely same. Though I won't tell my cousin Mason that. He's a quarterback, not a lineman, but still." I stare down at my hands, closing my eyes. Jesus, I need to shut up with the nervous talking.

"You have a lot of cousins," he notes, not commenting on my inane babbling.

"Yet another long story, but most of them aren't blood."

He reaches out, grasping my chin and lifting it until my eyes are back on his. "Are you doing okay?"

No. Definitely not. Not with his large, warm hand on my face making butterflies drunkenly zip through my stomach and chest. I lick my lips and manage a nod.

"Good. Keep looking at me. It'll help."

Is he kidding? That's making it harder to breathe, not easier.

He stares directly into my eyes for a beat, smiles, drags his thumb along my jaw, and then releases me, but I can't tell if that extra touch was an intentional move or not. "What kind of doctor are you, Katy?"

"How do you know I'm a doctor?"

"Your badge tells me so." He points a lazy finger at it. "It also says surgery."

And my last name, so now he knows it, and obviously, that did nothing to jog his memory. Again, I try to remember it's for the best if he doesn't remember the last time he saw me.

"I'm a trauma surgeon."

His head tilts in my direction, and his eyes dance about my

face. "Funny, so am I. And we happen to be stuck in the same elevator together. That's an odd coincidence."

"Well, you know what they say about coincidences, don't you?"

His lips twitch. "No. What?"

"They're coincidental," I deadpan.

He laughs at my corny joke and inches in closer to me. "So they are." He angles his head the other way, giving me a knowing smirk. "You didn't seem surprised I was a trauma surgeon too."

I shake my head, unable to stop my Cheshire grin.

"You know who I am, don't you? Even though you're not supposed to yet."

I fold my knees and lean forward, twisting so I can see his face. "Yep. That same phone-shouting cousin of mine was telling me about you before I got on the elevator. In addition to knowing everyone in this hospital, she also knows all the gossip before everyone else does."

"Ah." He shifts, extending his legs and crossing them at the ankles. "That explains the wild look she was giving you."

"A look I clearly missed since I didn't even register you were on the elevator with me. I thought I was alone."

"Instead of on an elevator with your new boss," he plays, shifting in even closer to me until his leg almost touches mine and his shoulder is only a few inches away. "I'm sorry you found out that way. I believe Wes was planning to tell each of his fifth-year residents individually before the announcement was made."

I shrug. "It's fine." It's actually not fine. Wes knows I plan to try and get pregnant on my own in the coming months, and he was on board with it. Who knows how Bennett will take to that or if it'll affect my chances at the fellowship I'm after? "He texted me right when I got on the elevator. I suppose panicking in an elevator isn't the best first impression a trauma surgeon can make on her new boss."

"The first time this happened, I panicked too. I think that's a pretty standard reaction." He leans in, his lips twisting into a wicked grin. "And trust me, Katy, you've already made a perfect impression on me."

My belly flutters, and I have to remind myself that he's simply being polite. Nothing more. "I likely should take this time to suck up to you. Tell you I'm the best trauma surgeon in the program. But that's not exactly my style."

He dips his head, almost as if he's telling me a secret, his mouth near my ear. "You don't have to. I already know you are. Wes speaks very highly of you. He tells me you're his ace."

I inch in too. I can't seem to stop it. The energy flowing between us is too electric, too delicious to resist. Even if I know I should. "Rumor has it you're a hotshot from somewhere in the Midwest."

"I came here from the Mayo Clinic."

A smile curls up my face. "You're not denying you're a hotshot."

"You're not denying you're an ace," he retorts, playing with me.

"Nope. I'm the best."

"Of that, I have no doubt," he maintains, tipping his head down and inching forward. His shoulder brushes mine, and my breath catches. I'm positive he hears it. "Still, I'll refrain from making a final determination until after I see you in action in the OR."

The air drifts out of my lungs as he tucks a strand of wayward hair behind my ears, making warm tingles skate across my skin and raising the hairs on the back of my neck. His touch is so unexpected, so intimate, it shocks me, making my heart lurch in my chest.

Like his hand on my chin or the brush of his shoulder, just as quickly as it was there, it's gone, his hand returning to his lap, but his magnetic gaze hasn't left mine, making the air in the elevator feel thick and intense.

But worse than that, he smells good. Not like the hospital —which is what I'm positive I must smell like—but like tea tree oil and musk. Like sandalwood and spice. Like men's bodywash, which in my humble opinion, is more delicious than cologne.

I'm not thinking about the fact that I'm stuck in an elevator or that he's my new boss. I'm thinking about that night so long ago. The one where he pulled me into a corner and kissed me like my mouth was everything he had been searching for his entire life.

And it needs to stop. Now.

That was a long time ago, and I'm not that girl anymore. Moreover, I refuse to ever be her again. My career and the things I'm trying for mean too much to me, and with him now running the trauma department, he holds my future in his hands.

I move to pull back, suddenly realizing our proximity when the lights pop on and the elevator bounces before it starts moving again. I shoot up to my feet, and he does the same, albeit at a slightly slower pace.

"Looks like the power came back on. And we survived without plummeting to our deaths," I tease awkwardly, my voice high-pitched. Mercifully, the elevator chimes, and the doors open. "Thank you for, well, I don't know. Making it so I didn't panic too much. I have to go check on my patient. See you around, Dr. Lawson."

I move to escape, needing to flee and get my head back on straight where it belongs when he reaches out and grabs my arm, stopping me. He steps in behind me, his mouth close to my ear, and he whispers, "It was nice spending time alone in the dark with you again, Katy. See you around."

He releases me, and I stagger out of the elevator, stunned speechless.

Son of a bitch. He does remember me. And our kiss.

# Chapter Two

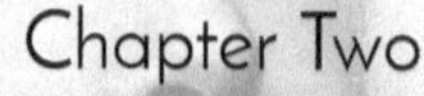

## Bennett

Katy doesn't know this, nor will she ever, but I knew she worked here before I even interviewed for the position. That morning, I was walking into the hospital on my way to the interview with Wes Kincaid along with the chief of surgery when I saw Katy enter ahead of me. I recognized her instantly. She was wearing scrubs and had an elastic dangling from her teeth as she ran her hands through her thick, brown hair, and I was immediately hit with the memory of doing the exact same thing to her once.

Her hair felt like silk beneath my fingers, and she smelled like fucking sunshine and vanilla. Tasted like it too.

Katy Barrows.

The young, bright-eyed, and bushy-tailed medical student who utterly captivated me. So much so that I spent extra time teaching her simply to have an excuse to look at her and talk to her while hoarding her attention all to myself. I had wanted to kiss her from the moment I first saw her, and I only did so that night because she was going into her fourth year of medical school, and I was moving across the country for a fellowship.

I had nothing left to lose.

I figured I'd never see her again, and that was my last shot to do the one thing—well, one of the many things—I had always wanted to do with her. Now she's even more beautiful than I remember, and that day in the lobby, I found myself following her, watching as she grabbed a coffee from the kiosk and then met up with a friend before climbing into the elevator and disappearing.

I knew she had planned to become a trauma surgeon. She had told me all about it that night at the party before I kissed her, and I wondered if I took the job, if she'd be working for me once again. I told myself it didn't matter. Despite the unethical quandary that comes with dating a resident, after what happened in Minnesota, I need this fucking job and have no plans to risk it. Not to mention, I have no interest in dating anyone.

Not after how badly my marriage to Lizbeth ended.

No. I moved back to Boston for one reason and one reason only. My mother. And the job, so maybe that's two. But my mother is my primary reason. She's sick and alone, and I can't abide either for her.

So Katy doesn't enter into my plans. Not even a little.

But I won't lie and say I'm disappointed that I'm going to be seeing her regularly, even if only as my resident.

She's everything I remember her being but with the added confidence and maturity of a great surgeon. I knew the second she got a good look at me that she remembered me, and sitting there in the dark in that stuck elevator, it was easy to suspend time and not think about the hospital beyond the four walls of the elevator or the reality of our situation.

Even if just for a moment.

I touched her. I teased her. I flirted. Though I did manage to keep it somewhat professional. That's where it ends. Toying with the line is dangerous and forbidden, even if she is alluring as hell.

I released her after letting her know I remembered her,

and in doing so, I vowed that was it. The simple truth is, I can't fucking touch her. From now on, we're chief and resident and nothing more.

I scrub my hand along my jaw and walk through the emergency department, watching her race toward the trauma rooms. Inwardly, I sigh. It's going to be a long fucking year.

Taking a left, I head out the ambulance bay doors and jog toward the garage in the sweltering heat and torrential rain of a Boston August storm. Instantly, my blue button-down is soaked, sticking to my skin as my hair drips water directly into my eye, making it harder to see. Overhead thunder rumbles loudly, followed almost immediately by a crack of lightning. If that, along with getting stuck in an elevator, are not ominous signs for my first non-official day, I don't know what is.

Wes is letting everyone know he's stepping down as trauma surgery chief, and tomorrow will be my first official day where I greet everyone. And hope that the rumors of why I left don't reach Boston. But today, I have somewhere more important to be, and as I climb into my car and drive across town, I do my best to focus on that. Not on what I left behind or the strings I had to pull to get this job after the way I left my old one or my ex.

And certainly not on the pretty brunette with eyes so blue they almost appear lit from within or the fact that she was so adorably nervous and unsettled in that elevator but seemed just as drawn to me as I was to her. Was it from seeing me again or the situation we found ourselves in?

I growl out a frustrated breath, running my hand through my wet hair and turning up the volume of the song playing through my speakers to drown out my useless thoughts. By the time I pull into the parking garage at Dana Farber, I'm centered on why I'm here and nothing else.

My mother.

After stopping at the restroom to use the hand dryers on my shirt, I weave my way through the building and take the elevator up to the infusion area, the bookstore bag dangling from my wrist. "Good morning, Kimberly," I greet the nurse in the front.

"Good morning, Dr. Lawson." She blushes as she did the first time I was here. "Your mother is just getting started. Would you like me to take you back to her?"

"Sure. That would be great. Thank you." I may be an angry, grumpy prick now, but I'll never be a dick to nurses, and certainly not nurses responsible for my mother's care.

She stands and swipes her badge on the wall and then leads me back to an open space that appears more like a lounge than a hospital with its large, comfy, reclining chairs and sweeping views of Boston out the large floor-to-ceiling windows. Patients can choose to be either in a communal infusion area where they can socialize or in a private space, and my mother has chosen the latter.

Likely because of the books I'm carrying with me.

"Ah, there you are," my mother announces when she sees me. "Perfect timing. They're just starting my infusion. Did you get the books I ordered?"

I hand her the bag and take the recliner beside her. Leaning back, I kick my feet up and toss my hands behind my head. "In all their smutty glory."

My mother and her nurse, Astrid, laugh. My mother is a dirty romance book junky. Minus the dirty parts, I always found her continued faith and love of romance to be a bit baffling considering my father fucked his assistant and then her best friend and left her with nothing except for me after telling her he never loved her. As far as I know, she never dated anyone after him, but somehow loves to live vicariously through the pages of books. I'm only too happy to supply her habit, occasionally being a sucker enough to read some of them to her if she's not feeling well.

My father, as you've garnered, was a class-A asshole to everyone in his life, including his only son and wife. He made all his money after my parents divorced, selling his first company for millions and then his second one for billions, only to divorce his second and third wives and eventually die alone of liver disease. Ironically, as his only surviving heir, I inherited everything and subsequently bought my mother the condo of her dreams, gave her enough money that she'd never have to work again, and sent her on a four-week cruise around Europe.

It wasn't until she returned home and I came to visit her that I heard her coughing. She blew it off and claimed it was just a cold and it would pass. Except it didn't. Finally, I forced her to get a chest x-ray and after that, a biopsy, and now here we are, treating her non-small cell lung cancer that has spread to her nearby lymph nodes.

Sometimes being a doctor sucks. Especially a doctor who currently doesn't have the happiest or brightest outlook on life. Actually, life deserves double middle fingers and can fuck off accordingly. The only thing that's managed to make me smile in I don't even know how long is Katy Barrows.

But despite my less-than-rosy disposition, there isn't anything I wouldn't do for my mother or to make her happy, so we don't talk about her cancer or prognosis, and I let her focus on me when she's not focused on her romance books.

Case in point...

"You're smiling," my mother accuses, and I close my eyes, pretending to rest comfortably and casually when her words make me feel anything but. I hadn't realized I was smiling.

"I got stuck in another elevator today." With a beautiful woman who now works for me though, I still remember what her kisses taste like.

My mother laughs because unlike me, nothing gets her down or holds her there long. "How many times does that make it now?"

"Three," I answer without missing a beat or bothering to open my eyes.

"Remind me never to get on an elevator with you," Astrid teases, and my stupid, traitorous smile grows. That's the same thing Katy said.

"See, and I was hoping that smile was because you were going to tell me that you've met a funny, vivacious, brilliant woman, and you're giving me a grandchild."

I groan. Loudly. "Please, don't start with that again."

"I'll be back to check on you in a bit." Astrid politely sees herself out, leaving me alone with my baby-hungry mother.

"Lizbeth called me."

"What?" My eyes pop open, and I jerk up, bringing the feet of the recliner back down as I sit up and glare at my mother. "Mom, what are you doing? You go from talking about new women and grandbabies to my ex-fucking-wife?"

She ignores the curse. For an Irish woman who grew up in South Boston and swears like a biker at a rally, she rarely tolerates that in me. "She said you're not returning her calls."

I blink at her, nonplussed. "I'm not. Why would I? We're *divorced*."

"She says she needs to speak to you. That it's important."

I roll my eyes derisively. "Oh, I'm sure it is. And I'm sure it has nothing to do with the fact that she wants a bigger bank account and a husband to rely on because her trust fund is gone." I raise a *you know I'm right* eyebrow at her. "Besides, I don't know why you're even bringing her up. You never liked her. She's a lying, conniving, backstabbing, life-ruining snake."

It's a fact my mother can't argue.

When Liz and I met, fell in love, and got married, we talked about starting a family one day. I wanted kids. I've wanted kids for a while. And not just to please my mother. I want to be the dad mine never was. But when I started bringing it up, Liz would always have a reason why it wasn't a good time. And for a while, with the hours I was working, I let it ride. Then I started to push because I was more than ready, we'd been married for four years, and I wasn't getting any younger.

Eventually, she relented, and we started trying and trying, but after six or so months of nothing, I was starting to get concerned. She blew it off, saying maybe it wasn't meant to be. More than that, she refused to go for testing of any kind and wouldn't even discuss fertility treatments. I suggested adoption, but she wouldn't entertain that either.

Anytime I'd try to talk about any of this with her, she'd grow angry and dismissive and blame me for a hundred things that were all out of my control and not related to starting a family. It was wearing on me and silently breaking my heart.

Then one day, after a particularly long, awful shift, I didn't want to go home. Liz was out late at a hospital administration dinner, and the thought of going home to an empty house was too much. I went to a local restaurant and ran into one of Liz's friends who also happened to be her GYN. We got to talking, and I confessed that I was stressed that we were having so much trouble getting pregnant.

She looked at me as if I had three heads and asked me when Liz had her tubal ligation reversed. Naturally, you could imagine my shock, and when I asked her what fucking tubal ligation, she turned pale and told me she couldn't speak further about it and had only mentioned it because she thought I knew. Of course she did. Because why wouldn't I know that while I was out of town at a conference a year prior, my wife went behind my back and had her tubes tied and never told me?

Only that wasn't the final blow. It was simply the tip of the iceberg, and things got worse from there. Much, much worse. So as far as I'm concerned, she's not owed me picking up her calls, and she has a ton of fucking nerve calling my sick mother.

"Fine. You're right. I fucking hated Liz." My mother purses her lips to the side in her universal display of I'm conceding the battle, but not the war. "But there has to be someone else who could do it."

"I tell you what. Instead of romance that doesn't exist in real life, why don't we read the literary fictional type?"

"If you read to me, that's a deal. There's rarely sex at the beginning of these books anyway, which frankly is a shame."

I chuckle lightly, knowing that's a lie and that often there is sex in the first few chapters of her books. I don't comment though, as I pull out the first book my hand touches. "Let's hope so. The last one started with a one-night stand, and I'm still scarred from reading those words to you."

She rolls her eyes. "When you get to be my age and are as sick as I am, you stop caring so much about words like pussy and cock and revel in the notion that someone's getting some good action."

I plug my ears. "La, la, la. Stop! You're still my mother."

"And you're my almost forty-year-old son. Grow up." She throws the wrapper from her straw at me, the white paper landing on my lap.

"Grow up? You're telling me to grow up when you're throwing paper at me?" I ball it up in my hand and chuck it back at her. "And I'm not forty. I'm thirty-eight."

"Excellent. You're still too old to play a virgin when I know you're not. Now start reading and stop being such a prude. No skipping words or scenes either this time."

I pick up the book and groan at the title before I flip the cover around and glare at her, shaking the book and making the pages flop around. "Are you trying to be cruel?"

"What?" She feigns innocence.

"*Surprise Baby for the Billionaire Doctor?*"

She blinks her wide blue eyes at me. "Is there a problem?"

"Mom." I groan her name, scrubbing a hand up and down my face. "You have the subtlety and grace of a head-on collision."

"You don't have to have love and romance to have a

baby," she presses. "With your kind of money, you can hire a surrogate."

"A surrogate?" I utter. "You do realize I need a woman's egg to fertilize and implant in said surrogate, right?"

"Okay then. Forget that. Find a woman who wants a baby too and is willing to have it with you even if there is no love or romance involved since I know you've sworn that off. I won't push that side of this. Yet." She gives me a meaningful look. "But there is no fucking earthly reason why you have to give up on having children, and I have to give up on my *dream* of being a grandmother."

I sigh, leaning back in my chair, losing steam with this argument. "You're really pushing it today."

She points to the machine on her right pumping chemo into her PICC line or peripherally inserted central catheter, which is a long-term IV site that allows the chemo and other medications to be given. "I'm having chemo for stage three lung cancer. Of course I'm fucking pushing it. Just think about that, okay? You can still have it all, even without the wife."

I grunt because as much as I hate to admit it, she's right. I could. And it's something I want. Not to mention, it is her dream to have grandchildren, and there is nothing more in this world that I want than to have my mom meet my children.

But it's also not nearly as easy as she's making it sound.

Adopting as a single man who works long hours and has no family other than a sick mother is nearly impossible. And it's not exactly like women are lining up to have babies with men without love and commitment being part of the equation. So that leads me back to square one, which is nowhere.

Thankfully, my mother grows tired, and the argument is left at that. I read the first five chapters of *Surprise Baby for the Billionaire Doctor* until it gets to a sex scene, and when my mother is done with her chemo, I drive her home and stay the night at her condo, making sure she has everything she needs.

Even if I can't give her everything she wants.

# Chapter Three

*Katy*

"I still don't know why you don't use a freaking pump like every other type 1 diabetic out there," my best friend—and yes, cousin—Owen comments, watching as I lift my shirt above my belly button and inject myself with my short-acting insulin pen. He winces, but I don't know why. I hardly feel the stick at this point, and he's a doctor who has seen way worse. Hell, he's seen way worse with me over the years. "They have some really good ones now."

I peek up at him as I close the pen and tuck it back in my purse. "I tried the pump, a few different kinds, and I had catheter kinks that led to crazy high blood sugars. The ones without catheters gave me site infections and made my skin break out in rashes. They were also big and a bit bulky on my skin. Remember?"

He makes a noise in the back of his throat, lifting his bourbon to his lips and taking a sip. "That was fifteen years ago, Katy."

"Yes, and I hated it then. I hated it even more when I was in college and then in medical school when I tried it again, thinking that would be easier given my hectic schedule. Do you know how annoying it is to have sex, or sleep, or even take a shower with a pump on you?"

"Thankfully, no."

"Well, let me tell you, it's not fun. Anytime I wanted to wear a dress—which you know I love wearing—I had to tuck the pump into my bra, which was no treat either, and that also meant I couldn't wear a dress without a bra."

"Can we stop talking about your bras?"

I give him a cheeky grin. "Besides, it's easy enough to control my sugars now that I have the continuous glucose monitor, and by this point, I'm used to giving myself a few injections a day."

I was diagnosed with type 1 diabetes when I was ten. Having two emergency medicine doctors as your guardians sometimes pays off because they recognized the signs and symptoms and caught it early before I got really sick with it, or even ended up hospitalized, which often happens to newly diagnosed diabetics.

That's not to say it's been all sunshine and roses for me, because it hasn't been. I've had my struggles, and those struggles have been real. But I've been in a good rhythm with it for the last four years after a terrifying near-death experience, and that's not a boat I want to rock. So for now, it's pens for the win.

"Fine. You know better than I do about that. I just hate having to see you stick yourself is all." He sets his glass down and cradles it in both hands as he scans the restaurant before turning back to me. "Where are you on picking a donor?"

"Nowhere yet. I have an appointment coming up with my endocrinologist, and once he tells me I'm good to go, then I'll start seriously digging into it. I don't want to find someone, get excited, and then be told I shouldn't get pregnant." Life isn't always the picnic we're promised. Sometimes it's gritty and messy, but I'd rather trudge through the sludge than never get the chance to play in the mud.

Owen leans over and kisses my forehead. "You'll get what you want, Katy. You will. When the time is right, you'll have everything you deserve, but no matter what, I'll be there with you every step of the way."

I start to get choked up and sniffle back the tears burning my eyes. "Thank you. I love you. You're the bestest best friend on the planet."

He sighs, worried about me because Owen is a natural worrier. "I love you too. Now, are you going to tell me what happened today? Or even better, have us order food and then tell me? I told my parents I'd pick up Rory in two hours, and I'm starving."

Rory is his five-year-old daughter, and despite the massive family we have who love to spend time with her, Owen doesn't relish being away from her when he can help it. He already works long hours as a pediatric surgeon, and since Rory's mom bailed on them when Rory was little, he always wants her to feel like she's his priority—which she is.

I shake my head, taking a sip of my lemon drop. "Not yet. I promised Keegan I'd wait for her and Kenna to get here so she could join in describing her trauma from the power outage."

"Of course she did," he deadpans. "Because no one is more dramatic than Keegan."

Truth.

"Still, you just took your shot," he maintains. "We should order food before your blood sugar gets too low."

I roll my eyes. "Okay, *dad*. Whatever you say."

He reaches over and pinches my side, making me yelp, but he signals our waitress and waves a hand for me to order. "We'll have one of every appetizer, please."

"Sure thing. Do you want me to bring Keegan and Kenna their drinks?"

I hold in my snicker. "Yeah. I have a feeling they'll be here—"

"Oh, my hell! My attending was such a jerk today." Keegan comes barreling in, dropping dramatically into the chair across from me.

"—any second," I finish, smirking at Jeanie, our regular waitress, because we obviously come here a bit too often. But in fairness, it's across the street from the hospital and has amazing food and drinks.

Jeanie gives me a wink and then goes off to get our order going.

"You know your attending is my father, right?" Owen points out, though I don't know why he bothers. Keegan always complains about her attending despite the fact that he's her uncle. I consider everyone here my cousins—my family—but I have no biological relation to them the way they do with each other.

When my parents died when I was six, my uncle Callan took me in. He met and fell in love with Layla who had a nearly identical situation to mine growing up, though it was her sister Amelia who took care of her and not her uncle. Amelia married Oliver Fritz, the youngest son in a family of famous billionaires, and together they had Keegan and Kenna. So my stepmother of sorts is the biological aunt of Keegan and Kenna, and Owen is Oliver's brother Carter's son, so, also biological cousins with Keegan and Kenna.

"Yes, and Uncle Carter was a total jerk," Keegan grumbles adamantly. "He made me run labs with the interns after the power outage. For no reason!" She slams her palm down on the table, rattling Owen's and my drinks. "He put someone else on two of my laboring women. All because I might have gotten a bit too hysterical about the power outage."

"You, hysterical? Never," Owen mutters dryly, making Keegan flip him off.

"The generators weren't working as they should have been, Owen. That's scary stuff."

"I agree. Think of the patients in the OR, or, I don't know the people trapped in elevators."

Keegan points a finger at Owen. "We all suffered the price. And scut sucks. You can't deny that."

"Are you doing laps in Greyson's pool tomorrow?" Kenna asks me, ignoring her twin completely as Keegan continues to go back and forth with Owen.

The Greyson she's referring to is Greyson Monroe, the famous rock star. My uncle Callan has four best friends—Zax, Greyson, Asher, and Lenox—who were all once part of Central Square, a wildly famous rock band. They broke up after four years of being on top, and now they all do different things but are still impossibly close, more like brothers than friends. And since Layla is a Fritz and some of the Central Square people are good friends with the Fritzes, we're now pretty much one big, giant family.

All the Central Square kids and the Fritz kids are my cousins. The only blood cousin I have—who is more like my brother—is Wilder because he's Callan and Layla's son.

I nod, sipping my drink. "That's my plan. I have to be at work by six though since I have a new boss to impress."

"That's fine. We can go at four-thirty. I have to be in early tomorrow too. But speaking of your new boss, are you going to tell us about the elevator?" Kenna bounces her eyebrows suggestively at me. "Keegan says he's who you were stuck with. And that he's hot."

Owen grunts, shaking his head. "Who cares if he's hot? How is that even important?"

"Oh, right. Like you guys don't comment on your female nurses, techs, and doctors' appearance? I'm so calling bullshit on that," I tell him.

"You know I don't. Dating someone you work with is about the dumbest fucking thing you can do."

I glare. "Ouch." Since that's exactly what I did and it didn't just end badly, it ended in disaster.

He sighs remorsefully. "Sorry. That wasn't a dig at you. You know what I meant. I don't look because there's no point for me."

I bat my eyelashes playfully at him. "You could try dating again. Meet a lady who sweeps the handsome, broody Owen Fritz off his feet."

He sips his bourbon, a grimace on his face. "Why do I spend all my free time with you? We need another guy here. Why isn't Vander or even Mason here? And why don't I hang out with people my own age?"

"You're old. We get it. But you love us too much to leave us. Besides, that won't change the fact that I speak the truth, oh hot, brilliant doctor of Boston Children's Hospital."

Another grunt because he knows I'm right. Every straight woman and not-so-straight man is after Owen Fritz. The fact that he's a single dad doesn't detract from that one bit.

"Anyway, I invited Vander and Stone to come," I offer, smiling smugly because he can't argue with me on his hotness. "Vander doing something I don't want to know about and Stone has a shift." Vander is Lenox's son and he's somewhat of an evil genius. A bit morally gray, especially when it comes to his hacking abilities, but he's as loyal as it gets. Stone is Kaplan's, Owen's uncle and godfather's, son. Owen and Stone work together and are very tight. "And you love me too much not to come out with me."

For how close I am with Keegan and Kenna—since I now sorta temporarily live with them—I am the closest with Owen and have been since we were kids. The moment I came to live with my uncle, Owen took on the role of big brother and protector. Now we're pretty much inseparable.

"Ignore Owen," Keegan says dismissively, waving him away. "You've evaded this long enough. What happened in the elevator with the hot doc? What?" Keegan blinks when Owen gives her a disgruntled look. "He's not *my* attending. I can say he's hot. Hell, I can even hit on him if I want."

I groan, picking at a few split ends before forcing myself back from that train wreck. "Who are you, Dr. Seuss? Stop rhyming about my new boss."

"Because you want him all to yourself," Kenna teases, playing with a cocktail napkin on the table and searching around for our waitress in the hope she'll deliver her drink.

I snort derisively. "No way. Absolutely not," I lie. Because I might. Just a little. But purely in a competitive, I-want-to-be-his-ace-way and nothing more. The fact that he once laid one of the best kisses I've ever had on me and his touches in the elevator today had my stomach feeling full and fizzy like I drank too much Diet Coke means nothing.

"Me thinks the lady doth protest too much."

I scowl at my friends, making Owen choke on a laugh. "As much as I hate to side with Kenna, she's right. You have a look about you and you're a horrible liar. What aren't you saying?"

Ugh. Having people who know your every expression and tone is both a blessing and a curse. "I know him," I admit, running my finger along the rim of my martini glass. "Or, I mean, I guess knew him might be the better way to put it."

"What do you mean?" Owen asks, dropping his elbow on the table and resting his head against his fist as he angles his head in my direction.

"He um…" Here comes my awkward, uncomfortable giggle. Shit. I clear my throat, willing it down as I stare at the pale-yellow liquid in my glass. "He was chief resident when I was a third-year medical student."

They all fall silent for a moment as Kenna and Keegan's drinks are delivered along with a first round of appetizers. I pick up a chicken finger and dip it in honey mustard before taking a crunchy bite.

"Okay. He was chief resident when you were a med student. So what?" Owen's eyebrows bunch together in confusion. "I was chief resident, and we had over a dozen medical students."

"Did he remember you?" Keegan presses, waving Owen away.

"Or not remember you?" Kenna jumps in.

"He remembered me." But I didn't know just how much until the very end.

"That's cool," Keegan exclaims, scooping up salsa with a chip and popping it into her mouth, talking as she crunches. "I heard he's a bit of a hard-ass and can come across as a jerk, so it's lucky that you already know him."

"Yes," I agree. "Lucky."

Owen is studying me. I can see him doing it out of the corner of my eye as I start attacking the spinach and artichoke dip with gusto. "Why are you still being weird? Was he a dick to you in the elevator or something?"

"No. He was fine," I remark brightly with a mouth full of carrots and dip. I never talk with food in my mouth, and everyone knows it, so I'm not helping my cause here. I swallow and wipe my lips with my napkin. "It was his third time getting stuck in an elevator and we joked about that a bit because, legit, who gets stuck in an elevator three times? We talked, and he did his best to keep me calm when I was anything but. He wasn't a jerk at all, and he wasn't when I knew him before, so I'm not sure why he has that reputation now."

"Again, what aren't you telling us? You're shit at hiding your thoughts and feelings, Katy."

I sigh, my head dropping to Owen's shoulder. I'm being weird about it, and I know I am. The truth is, it felt like he flirted a bit. Which I know is nuts. If we didn't have the past that we have, I likely wouldn't have thought twice about it. He was being comforting, not sexual.

My problem is I enjoyed it. The terrifying stuck in an elevator aspect notwithstanding, I enjoyed sitting in the dark with him and talking to him like that. It's been plaguing me all afternoon—more than the fact that I have now a not-so-friendly fear of elevators—because I shouldn't have liked it as much as I did. Not only is he my boss and quite a bit older than me, but there is also no room for those sorts of thoughts.

Not with him. Not with any man. At least not for the foreseeable future.

Owen blows out a breath. "What's up, Kit-Kat? Spill it already."

I look around the bar, making sure I don't recognize anyone since it's a popular spot for nurses and doctors to hang out. Especially on a Thursday night. "Back when I was a student, we shared a very drunken kiss one night at a party. It was his last night as a resident and my last night as a third year, and he pulled me into a corner and kissed me."

Kenna's eyes light up like sparklers, and she and Keegan exchange gleeful looks. "Oh. That's just too good. You kissed your hot new boss."

"Shhh," I hiss at Kenna. "Quiet your freaking megaphone voice down. I did not kiss my hot new boss."

Keegan cackles. "Ha! You just called him that."

I flip her off. "It was seven years ago, Keegs."

"Whatever. Tell us all about your *hot*"— She emphasizes the word while daring me to challenge her on it—"make-out session with him. Was he good? He looks like he'd be good. He has that tall, dark, and commanding thing going for him." She fans her face.

He was good. Very good. But that's neither here nor there and certainly not something I'm sharing with them tonight. "I didn't make out with him," I protest. "Not really anyway. It was a kiss and nothing more. He left the next day for a fellowship across the country, and that was that."

"Until now," she taunts.

That giggle finally breaks free.

"You're making your hyena noise," Owen accuses. "Why are you so nervous? Do you have feelings for him or something? Because I'll be honest with you, it was a kiss a long-ass time ago. You didn't fuck him, and if you think about the number of drunken kisses you've had in your lifetime, this isn't chart-topping significance other than the fact that he's your new boss."

He has a point. I've had a lot of drunken kisses. It was sort of my thing until my ex came along, and soon, I'll be trying to get pregnant, so it's definitely not my thing now.

So why does this one feel different to me when it shouldn't?

"You're right," I cede. "I don't know why I'm so nervous about it. It was just a kiss, and it was a very long time ago. My problem is that he's my boss. I think it's universally accepted that it's never a smart idea to have kissed your boss. This is a big year for me. I need him to recommend me for my fellowship and not care about the fact that I want to try and get pregnant and have a baby."

Owen sits up straight, forcing me to do the same. He puts his hand on my shoulder and gives me a stern, serious look. "Then forget about the kiss, shove it into the do not go there again drawer, and prove to him why you deserve that fellowship."

Again, he's right. I give him a sharp nod, determined to put my past with Bennett behind me. How difficult can that be?

# Chapter Four

*Katy*

"Good morning," Wes greets us just after the change of shift with a content smile on his face. "I know you've all heard the rumors, and if I haven't gotten a chance to speak one-on-one with you, I apologize. I tried to get to as many of you as I could yesterday. Some of you may feel as though this move is very sudden, but it's time for me to step down as chief of trauma surgery."

I take a sip of my coffee as I stand in the back of the pack, hating the bundle of nerves tightening my stomach. Cricket Peterson—my biggest competition here—is standing front and center like the suck-up she is. Part of my nerves come from the fact that I'm sad. Wes was my mentor. He's the one who brought me here to this residency program. I'm going to miss him and the trust we had with each other.

And obviously, the other reason for my nerves is standing just to the side of Wes looking like Superman in scrubs. Especially when he slides up the sleeve of his long-sleeved undershirt to reveal his powerful forearms. Damn. I clear that away and go back to listening to Wes.

"It's something I had been thinking about for a while," Wes continues. "It was a difficult decision. I've been here my entire attending career. With that, I wasn't going to leave this department to just anyone. Lucky for us, the perfect person fell into our laps. Dr. Bennett Lawson received his medical degree from Johns Hopkins, where he also did his residency before doing a trauma fellowship in Los Angeles. He's spent the last five years working as an attending and then chief of trauma surgery at the Mayo Clinic. Please join me in welcoming him. Doctor?"

Wes steps aside and Bennett, tall, confident, and sinfully fucking gorgeous, steps forward. His eyes instantly meet mine, as if he knew exactly where I was standing—and hiding—all along. I catch a curl of his lips that could hardly be called a grin before it disappears just as quickly, and he shifts his focus to the crowd before him, all business.

"Good morning, everyone," he says, and I swear, I hear two nurses nearby emit dreamy sighs. "I'll keep this brief since I know you have patients to get back to. As Wes said, this likely came as a bit of a shock to you. I realize I'm step-ping into some very large shoes, and I'll attempt to fill them as best I can. General and trauma surgery is what I've dedi-cated my life to, and I'm beyond thrilled to be working with such talented staff at one of the best hospitals in the country."

Bennett continues to speak, but I'm distracted by the two second-year residents near me. "How are we supposed to focus on patients when he's walking the halls?" one teases the woman on the other side of her.

"I know," the other resident whispers. "I heard he's divorced. You think he's looking for wife number two?"

They both snicker. "Gah, I can only hope so. Oh, but listen to this," her friend murmurs conspiratorially. "My cousin is an intensivist at Mayo and he told me that Dr. Lawson was forced into resigning. That's why he left there and came here."

My eyes bulge, but I do my best to hold in my reaction.

"*Forced* into resigning?" the other resident hisses under her breath. "For what?"

"No clue. But it has to be pretty bad to get fired, right?"

"For real. I'm shocked they hired him here if he was fired from Mayo."

"No joke. Whatever the reason, the hospital kept it quiet."

I return my attention to Bennett, not sure what to make of that.

"I appreciate your time, and I'm always available if you ever need anything," he finishes, giving a small but firm smile.

In a beat, he's surrounded by people welcoming him—naturally, Cricket is first—and I linger back, insatiably curious about what I overheard. I pull out my phone and do a quick Google search, but nothing comes up other than a brief press release from Mayo stating that Dr. Bennett Lawson has stepped down as the chief of trauma surgery. That's it. No reasons are provided, and it says he stepped down, but then again, I don't think press releases usually go into nefarious details about firings.

I glance back up at him, watching him from afar. This stiff man with his rough lines and stern voice is so different from the one I encountered yesterday. So different from the man I had known for a year of my life.

Whatever happened to him, whatever his reason for leaving or being forced out, he's different. Cold. Detached. Distant. Keegan said she heard he was a jerk. I haven't seen that from him at all, so I think that might just be a rumor and nothing more. Regardless, I think there's a lot more going on with Dr. Bennett Lawson than anyone here knows about.

Whatever it is, it doesn't matter, I decide. His personal business isn't mine to know, nor does it impact what I'm here to do. I make my way over to him once most of the crowd has dispersed. His cobalt blue eyes watch me approach, a smirk slithering across his lips.

"How'd I do?" he asks in a low tone now that it's just the two of us. "Did I sound like a total asshole?"

I can't help my snort. Or the fact that I love how he's still familiar with me. "I already told you I don't suck up."

He chuckles, gripping the back of his neck. "That bad, huh?"

I shake my head. "You're not fooling me, Doctor. Confidence isn't something you're lacking. You're fully aware they were eating out of the palm of your hand."

He wipes at the blooming smile on his lips and shifts until he's facing me head-on. "But not you," he surmises.

"I'm not so easily won over anymore."

"I'm not either, Dr. Barrows." Something crawls over his expression as he says that—something dark and haunting. He looks away and clears his throat. "We should get to work. I'm sure you have rounds."

I do have rounds and I do need to get back to work, but for whatever reason, I pause, tempted to ask about the rumors I just heard, but know I can't. I need to let whatever past we have stay there. Something about him is too tempting. Too familiar, even if it's been seven years.

Still, I find myself asking, "You good?"

His head whips back to me, surprised by my question. He stares blankly for a moment before his features soften, and he shrugs. "Not exactly. But hopefully, I'm getting there. I'll see you around, Dr. Barrows."

I take his dismissal for what it is and throw him a wave as I start to walk away. "See you, Dr. Lawson."

⬜

"MRS. JACOBS," I greet the anxious wife of my car accident patient. "I'm Dr. Barrows. I'm the surgeon who will be taking care of your husband today." I explain how we're getting a CT scan of his abdomen to know the extent of his injuries, but based on my initial exam and his current status, I'm having him prepped for surgery.

"You mentioned something about his spleen?" she murmurs, knotting her hands in her lap. I nod, and she gulps. "Do you think you'll have to remove it?"

I place my hand on her shoulder without squeezing it—this is meant to be comforting, not reassuring. "I won't know anything for sure until I get the CT results, and even then, I likely won't know for sure until I'm in there. But if I do have to remove his spleen, you should know there are many people who go on to live normal lives without it. They're nice to have, but not essential."

She bobs her head as tears leak from her eyes, and it never gets easier to do this part of the job.

I ask her questions about her husband's health and any medications he's taking, and then I instruct her and her daughter where the surgical waiting room is located and that I'll be back to update them as soon as I can.

But before I leave the room, I ask the question I ask of all family members and sometimes patients when I meet them. After she tells me what I want to know, I leave the room, ready to get into that OR and do what I do best.

It's situations like this that made me want to be a surgeon. I know what it's like to be the family member, the child, about to lose everything, and every time I step into the OR, I work my ass off to make sure that doesn't happen to someone else the way it happened to me.

I hustle my way to the elevator—because there is no way I'm jogging up eight floors before going into surgery—reading a text that tells me that OR three is being prepped for my patient when a shadow moves in directly beside me and two things I hate happen at once.

The first, my stomach does a somersault and my heart speeds up when I catch the scent of whatever soap, shampoo, or deodorant he uses that's so freaking heavenly. The second, the hairs on the back of my neck stand at attention when he accidentally brushes against me.

"Where are you headed to, Dr. Barrows?" Bennett asks, his voice low.

I blow out a silent breath, buzzing in a way I know better than to buzz. "The OR. I'm doing an ex-lap on a patient with a suspected splenetic laceration. You?"

"I was told you had a trauma down here, and then I saw you walking toward the elevator."

I twist to him. "Were you looking for me?"

His eyes dance about my face, and then he clears his throat and turns back toward the elevator. "I happen to have some free time this afternoon, and I thought I'd assist you in surgery."

I scoff. "Assist me, huh? I'm cute, not stupid, Dr. Lawson. I know full well you're here to evaluate my work as you are every other resident in your program."

He smirks but still doesn't look at me. "You're a hell of a lot more than cute, Katy, and I certainly never thought of you as stupid. But I don't remember you being this brave and bold with me the last time I knew you."

I dip my head to hide the smile the flutters in my belly are trying to spread across my face and press on. "The last time you knew me I was a third-year medical student. I was there to look but not speak or touch. If you want to assist me, be my guest. I'm not sure how much help I'll require with an ex-lap and possible splenectomy."

Just then, the elevator doors open, and he pans his hand, indicating I should get on first.

I shake my head in horror and take a step back. "No way. I'm not getting on an elevator with you."

He twists and starts walking backward, stepping onto the elevator and giving me a taunting look. "I thought you were brave and bold. A total badass trauma surgeon who never turned down a challenge."

Defiantly, I fold my arms. "Really? You're going to throw down the gauntlet like that?"

He shrugs nonchalantly, leaning casually against the elevator wall and holding the open button on the panel. "Hey, I'm the one who's been stuck three times, and here I am, tempting fate while making it my bitch. But you go ahead and take the stairs." He rolls his wrist and checks his watch. "I'm sure the patient is stable enough to wait for you to do that. Spleens aren't notorious for being bleeders or anything."

"Bastard," I grumble under my breath and reluctantly step on the elevator beside him, making sure I give him a wide berth.

"What was that? I'm not sure I caught it."

I rock back and forth from my heels to the balls of my feet as I stare straight ahead, trying to focus on my breathing. "Probably better that way. It wasn't particularly kind."

He smiles, making his dimple divot deeper into his chin. "Do you normally call your boss a bastard?"

My teeth sink into my bottom lip, and I pinch the inside of my palm to quell this... this feeling. "I thought you said you didn't hear it."

"No. I said I wasn't sure I caught it. I lied. I was curious to see if you'd admit it or try to cover it with something else."

My gaze stays trained straight ahead. Why did I get on this elevator? It's about to lock me in here and start moving. Especially since he finally releases the open button. "Yes, I normally call my boss a bastard. Just ask Wes. Though, in fairness to him, I only used it when he was being a particularly bastardy bastard and it was more a term of endearment since I've known him practically my entire life. He's good friends with my uncle, Callan."

"Bastardy bastard? Hm. That sounds a lot like me. At least as of late." Before I can question that, he continues with, "Your uncle works in the ER here. So does his wife, Layla, right?"

That catches me by surprise. My neck twists and my chin lifts so I can gawk at the side of his handsome face. "How did you know that?"

He doesn't so much as glance in my direction as he says, "I do my research." But then he does look at me, and something in his eyes glimmers. It makes my pulse race even before he adds, "And I remember the important things. You told me the night of the party that they worked here."

He looks back at the doors as they close, leaving me here utterly flummoxed by that. That was seven years ago. How in the hell does he remember—

"He's the one who took you in when your parents died?" he recalls, snapping me out of my thoughts only to have them nosedive into insanity land as the elevator starts to shoot up.

"You have an amazing memory. I can't believe you remember that about my uncle and stepmother." My voice cuts into a gasp as the elevator makes a weird noise. I swear on all that is holy if this fucking elevator gets stuck again…

He shifts in beside me when he hears it, his hands reaching out for me as if he's about to touch me, comfort me, only to catch himself and lower them to his sides. He's far more in control with his restraint and protocol than I am right now because reflexively I grip his forearm before I'm even aware of the motion. My heart is racing too fast, my head is spinning, and I'm a half-beat from hyperventilating.

"Sorry. I realize this is likely inappropriate, but it seems yesterday gave me a bit of a fear of elevators," I manage. "I didn't think it would be this bad, but here we are. If we get stuck, you might regret goading me onto it."

"Grip me as hard as you need to."

Oh, thank God. I do as he instructs, not even caring that he's my boss.

"I've got you," he soothes. "Just breathe."

"I'm breathing. A lot. Probably a bit too much."

"Okay, fine. Breathe less." Humor dances in his voice.

"You breathe less." I close my eyes. "Sorry, that was rude and also inappropriate."

He shifts closer to me until the side of his body is aligned with mine, the contact grounding me and making my head spin less.

"You have to get over the panic at some point," he instructs.

"I was planning to. Tomorrow."

He chuckles. "You're not working tomorrow."

"Oh, darn. Monday then."

"It wasn't so bad when we got stuck, was it?"

"Truth that you can't hold against me?"

His arm rubs against my shoulder. "Go for it."

"I was terrified."

His head angles and his eyes catch mine, sparkling rare blue gemstones. "You were fun. I liked that you were pretending we didn't know each other. Incidentally, you talk a lot when you're scared."

"I talk a lot all the time. I just tend to ramble when I'm scared. I did warn you about it."

"You did. That's true." He nudges my shoulder. "Truth that you can't hold against me?"

"Go for it." I throw his words back at him, clutching him a little tighter because he's here and he's letting me, and frankly, this elevator is no picnic.

"It was the highlight of my day."

A strangled laugh flees my chest. Partially because, even though I was freaking out and terrified out of my skull, in a weird way, it was for me too. And partially because I want off this elevator yesterday. Except my life never goes in a straight line, so we stop on a floor, and no one is there to get on. What is that bullshit?

"You're a liar," I challenge. Still, I like that he feels the same way I do about it.

"No. I swear," he promises. "Who knew I'd get trapped

with the student I made out with once? And what are the odds that she'd work for me again?"

He did not just say that we made out when I adamantly denied last night that's what we did. I squint accusingly at him. "Are you distracting me or flirting with me?"

"Both," he says plainly. "But don't worry, I'll only flirt with you on the elevator and only as a means to distract you until you're over your newfound fear."

"I'll remember that. If I ever get on one again after this. How slow is this elevator, speaking of which? This is a hospital. People's lives are on the line here." I shake my head in exasperation. "If getting stuck was the highlight of your day, your life must not be all that great at the moment." My eyes shoot wide, and I clap my free hand over my mouth. "Oh, shit. I'm so sorry."

His head tilts. "Don't be. You're not wrong."

"Why is that?"

"Maybe I'll tell you about it another time. We're here."

The elevator finally comes to a stop, and the doors mercifully open, granting me freedom. I take a deep breath, peeling my hand away from his arm. "I'm sorry if I hurt you. You have my nail marks on your skin. And yes, I get there's a joke in there."

"I wasn't going to go there even if my mind did. I may flirt and distract, but I do have boundaries."

"Sort of," I tease and step off the elevator. "Thank you for distracting me. Again. It looks like I survived without getting stuck."

"Maybe you're cured then."

"Let's not get ahead of ourselves here, Doctor. I'll see you in the OR. I'm going to check on the status of my patient and the CT results first."

Without waiting for a response, I start off at a good pace when he calls out, "I remembered you, Katy. Just as you were impossible to ignore, you were impossible to forget. But don't worry, that was the last time I'll ever bring it up, and I promise not to try to distract you like that again."

I turn back to him, the sudden change in his tone and demeanor surprising me a bit. "You were fine."

His face dips toward his feet. "As long as I didn't make you uncomfortable. I'd never want that."

"You didn't," I promise. "But I agree about us not bringing it up again. I work for you, and that was a long time ago."

He nods his head and slowly lifts his chin. "I'll see you in surgery, Dr. Barrows."

He stalks off in the other direction, and I stand here for a half-beat, our strange interactions leaving me perplexed. At least we're on the same page. No more flirting. No more discussing our past.

*I remember the important things. I remembered you, Katy. Just as you were impossible to ignore, you were impossible to forget.*

Ugh. No. Just no. I roll that off my shoulders and let it die on the hospital floor behind me. Nothing good comes from crushing on your boss. But more importantly, I don't want more from him.

I have too much at stake.

Too much to earn and prove.

So Bennett Lawson might be painfully gorgeous with a smile that makes angels weep and nuns want to sin and say the most perfect things at the perfect moment, but from now on, where he's concerned, I'll be taking the stairs.

# Chapter Five

## Bennett

There is something about Katy Barrows that immediately makes me lose my head. And considering one of the reasons I'm here and not still at Mayo, I need to get a grip on myself. It wasn't like this before. Seeing her makes me forget. She distracts me from my hard-earned rancor and teleports me back to a happier time in my life. She reminds me of the guy I once was—the guy before my life crumbled around me—and I react accordingly, desperate for any sliver of that I can get.

Even if it's wrong.

In the past, I never said inappropriate things to her. I never touched her unnecessarily. The only time I allowed myself to lose control wasn't even a loss of control. It was planned. There was no way I was moving across the country without knowing what it felt like to kiss her at least once.

But prior to that?

No. I never lost control with her—because I never lose control with anything, or at least that used to be the case—despite the massive temptation she presented. I saw her and we were alone again, and I didn't know how to stop myself. She was scared, and I wanted to make that better. My mouth just ran. My body moved in.

And it can never happen again.

I could lose myself in Katy Barrows. In the filthy, perverse thoughts I only allow to consume me at night. But I'd start to make mistakes if she became the star of my show, and mistakes are not something I can afford again. I'm not going to cross the line with her—there will be no more stolen kisses with Katy Barrows—so what good did all that flirting and touching do?

Other than tempt me to want something I can't and won't have.

"Dr. Lawson, there's a woman on the phone who says she's your wife," one of the nurses calls out to me as I walk by the station.

Christ, she is fucking relentless. How much of my blood is this woman determined to spill?

"I'm not married," I tell the nurse without any further explanation and continue down the hall toward the ORs, though my jaw is clenched tight. I went from smiling like a high school kid with a crush to practically cracking a tooth all in a matter of seconds. What a fucking day this is, and it's nowhere close to done for me.

"Hey," Wes says, coming in beside me. "How's your first official day, Chief?"

It was going well. Until I got in an elevator when I knew better and then heard my ex has now taken to stalking me at work.

"It's going. How's your first day as non-chief?"

Wes grins the grin of a happy man. He's pulling back his hours, and starting next week is going to be on sabbatical as he and his artist wife Aria travel around Europe for three months as part of some art tour thing she's doing.

"I can't say I miss the paperwork. Or the stress."

"That I can understand." I glance around, making sure we're alone. "Listen, I want to thank you again—"

He holds up his hand, stopping me. "There truly is no

need. I think you're going to do incredible things here, Bennett, and for what it's worth, I think Mayo was wrong to let you go. Especially the way they did it."

I sigh. I owe Wes and his son, Jack, everything. I did my fellowship in LA with Jack, and he happened to be in Minnesota one week and called me to grab a beer and catch up. I broke down and explained everything to him, and when he heard what Liz did to me and about my mom's cancer, he called his dad, who he knew was interested in stepping down, and everything fell into place.

"That said, Cricket Peterson is looking for you, and I'm glad she's now looking for you instead of me."

Ah, yes. Cricket Peterson. Annoying suck-up with a weird name. I watched her in the OR this morning. She's one of the other fifth-year trauma hopefuls vying for a fellowship here, along with Katy.

"I'm heading in to watch Katy Barrows do an ex-lap on a car accident patient, so Dr. Peterson will have to wait."

Wes glances around, ensuring we're still alone. "Cricket is very talented, but she is a win-at-all-costs sort of surgeon, whereas Katy does it with heart and passion. Katy is one of the best surgeons I've seen come through these doors in a very long time, and I'm not just saying that because I'm friends with her uncles and aunts."

I shake my head. "One of these days someone will have to explain the whole uncles, aunts, and cousins thing to me. She said she calls you a bastard as a term of endearment."

Wes laughs, leaning against the wall and folding his arms. "Katy is a pistol, and her mouth is loaded at all times. Sometimes she fires it without thinking through the resulting trauma. Still, you can't help but love her. She's a ball of sunshine. I hope she wasn't inappropriate with you."

*No more than I was with her.* "No. She was fine. In fact, I'd like to be there at the start of her surgery. I'll catch up with you." I smack his shoulder and head for the surgical part of the floor.

The moment I catch sight of Katy at the scrub sink, that's when it happens. The smile my ex wiped off my face curls back up of its own goddamn volition. Katy is wearing her mask and surgical cap, bopping her head back and forth, singing softly to herself as she scrubs.

*You can't help but love her. She's a ball of sunshine.*

And right now, I'm in the aftermath of a category-five tornado that could use a little sunshine in the worst of ways.

For a moment, I stand here, watching her, wondering what it is about her that makes her stick to me like glue. She's enchanting, distracting, and terrifying because she's both of those things. I'm her boss and she's my resident and that automatically makes her off-limits. Though neither my brain nor my body seems to care about that.

I slept in my mother's guest room last night and spent half the night helping her when she was sick, but no matter how hard I tried, Katy managed to flicker in and out of my thoughts on vicious repeat.

I told myself it was to be expected after what I've been through. With where I find myself now—miserable and alone, feeling wrecked and betrayed. Katy is a happier past, a breath of fresh air I can't help but want to inhale over and over again.

Something about her got under my skin almost immediately all those years ago and hasn't left. Something that drew me to her, that had me giving her time I didn't even give my primary residents. But now, she's nothing more than an inconvenient attraction.

I like the way she looks at me and talks to me. Not like I'm her boss or she's trying to suck up the way Cricket Peterson does. But like she has no filter and doesn't care. Like she's too good for me and she knows it, but she tries to rein it in when she remembers I'm her boss.

Fuck. I need to get a grip. And laid.

This isn't a bar, and Katy isn't just any woman I could lose myself in for a night. I haven't been single in over five years, and now I run into her. The girl I thought about more than I had any right to. But that was a long time ago, and our timing isn't any better now. More than that, I'm not looking for it to be.

I shake it off—I shake my ex-fucking-wife off—and get my ass back into what I'm here to do.

Surgery. Teach. Restart my life.

I head toward the sink and ask, "How's your patient's CT?" I don my mask and scrub cap and move to the basin beside her. Stepping on the water pedal, I slide up the sleeves of my shirt and start scrubbing in.

Katy gives a quick glance at my forearms and then returns to her sink. "He has a grade three, possibly grade four, laceration to the spleen and some bruising to the bowel without obvious signs of bleeding there."

"Your plan?" I watch her out of the corner of my eye as she scrubs her hands and forearms with precision, only to force myself to concentrate on what I'm doing.

Katy is all business as she answers. "Removal of the spleen and explore the bowel to ensure it's intact without any leaks. Then I'll explore the rest of the abdomen to make sure I don't miss anything."

I nod in approval. "Good. Show me how it's done, Dr. Barrows."

"I intend to, Dr. Lawson." With that, she pulls away from the sink, forearms wet and held out in front of her as she enters the OR backward.

A few moments later, I follow after her, and the nurse gowns and gloves me up. Katy is already at the table, talking with the scrub nurse and the intern who's waiting on her.

I linger back, watching how she works, how she commands and runs her OR. She conducts the time out and then orders, "Ten blade, please," without even acknowledging me. "Alexa, play Katy's alternative mix," she calls out, and some indie rock song that I'm not familiar with comes blaring from the speaker in the corner with a snarling guitar and upbeat, almost pop bass. "Yes. Good. Let's do it."

I'm not here to her. She's one hundred percent focused on her work and on her patient. She makes a perfect incision, packing off and cauterizing any bleeders she can, and then has the scrub nurse use the retractors so she clearly visualizes the field.

She pauses, tilts her head, and emits a rueful sigh. "Well, that sucks."

"Are you going to have to remove the spleen?" the intern whose name I don't yet know asks.

"Yep. Tell me, Dr. Fields, why is the spleen so difficult to repair once it's been lacerated?"

The intern falters for a moment. "Um. Because of its location beneath the rib cage? And because it's, um, difficult to stop it from bleeding once it starts?"

Those come out like questions, and Katy nods. "Yes. Good," she praises, and the guy preens like a show pony. "Both of those are accurate. But don't forget that the spongy nature of the spleen makes it difficult to suture, it has minimal regenerative capacity unlike the liver, and there is a higher rate of postop complications like bleeding, infection, and clot formation. See." She drags her instrument along the bleeding organ. "Once it starts, it doesn't like to stop. But actually, the reason I said that sucks is because of this."

"What is it?" Dr. Fields questions.

"Dr. Lawson, can you come here and give me a second opinion, please?"

I step forward and peer over the patient's open abdomen. "What am I looking for?"

"This," she tells me, briefly glancing up and meeting my eyes before returning to the surgical field. "Is this..."

I pick up the dissector and touch the small, firm mass on the liver. "It looks like your patient—"

"Mr. Jacobs," she inserts.

"Mr. Jacobs," I correct. "It appears as if he's very lucky he got into a car accident today. Though I suppose we won't know for sure until we dissect it and have pathology take a look."

"So that's…"

"A tumor," Katy tells Dr. Fields. "We'll remove it and send it down to pathology to see if it's benign or malignant, but the rest of his liver looks healthy and there was nothing on his labs that indicated it wasn't. Which means, if it is cancer, we hopefully caught this very early."

"Wow," the intern says, his voice laced with awe. "That's wild."

"We'll see. For now, let's finish saving his life. Thank you, Dr. Lawson."

I smirk beneath my mask at her dismissal of me. She wants to do this on her own. She wants to show off for her new boss, and I'm only too happy to let her.

Katy continues to work quickly and diligently, pressing her intern for answers to questions she continues to throw at him, and once the patient is stable and she's getting ready to close, the circulating nurse asks her, "What was his thing?"

"Alexa, stop." The music cuts out and Katy looks at her intern. "You can close. Have you ever done that before?"

He shakes his head.

"Okay. I'll walk you through it." She shows him how to staple and then steps back to allow him to work as she addresses the scrub nurse who asked her the question. "Mr. Jacobs trains service dogs. Every year or so, they bring a new dog into their home, and he trains it to be a good service animal for people with disabilities or medical conditions that benefit from them. That's where they were headed this morning," she continues. "To pick up a new dog to train."

"That's a really good one," the nurse says. "Way better than that guy from last week. What was his name? The one who admitted to collecting doll heads because they remind him of his ex-girlfriend."

Katy chokes on a laugh. "His name was Mr. Lawson." Now it's my turn to choke. Only I'm not laughing. Katy pins me with an amused stare. "I'm assuming they're not related to you, Dr. Lawson. Unless you have a brother or cousin, we don't know about."

"No. Definitely not." I hold my gloved hands up in surrender. "I'm an only child with no cousins, unlike you with your six hundred, and thankfully Lawson is a pretty common last name."

Katy gives me a taunting shrug. "If you say so."

*Brat.* "I definitely say so, Dr. Barrows." I raise a pointed eyebrow at her since that's all she can see of my face other than my eyes, but then I realize how harsh and stern I sounded and try to soften myself. "Doll heads? Really?"

"All the same type of doll too. The ones where the eyes open and shut with how you move the doll. He has a thing for blondes with blue eyes and has over a hundred he's collected. He was very proud of that when he told me, and I was very grateful my hair is brown and not blonde."

A small laugh ripples through the OR. "You and me both," the circulating nurse deadpans.

"And I assume he lives in his mother's basement and his ex has a restraining order out on him? What did he do with the bodies of the dolls, or do I not want to know?"

"I have no clue. I didn't get that far with my questioning, nor did I want the answer. I stopped pressing after he said doll heads."

I give an exaggerated shudder, making Katy laugh.

"Nice work, Dr. Fields," Katy applauds. "You can breathe now. Your staples look perfect. I'm going to speak to the family. Thank you, everyone."

We leave the OR as the nurses, along with Dr. Fields, finish up with the patient before they move him to the PACU or post-anesthesia care unit, and we go and scrub out. Katy is singing quietly to herself again. She did that a few times during the surgery and was doing it before while she was scrubbing in as well.

"That was excellent, Dr. Barrows. So far, I have to agree with Dr. Kincaid. You know what you're doing in there, and you do it with heart and passion." I shoot her an approving glance. She was great. A thoughtful and patient teacher. Calm at all times. Skilled at a higher level than her fifth-year peers.

The pleased smile on her lips makes me want to kiss it just so I can feel it for myself, and I clear my throat, shoving my fixation with her back into the recesses of my mind. How am I already so fucked with this girl? It's only been twenty-four hours.

"Thank you, Dr. Lawson. I appreciate that, and it means a lot coming from you. Wait till you see me kick some ass with a serious trauma."

I smirk at her arrogance. "What was all that about the patient's thing?"

She glances at me as she takes her foot off the pedal and dries her hands with paper towels. "Whenever I can, I ask either the patient or a family member something about them I should know. Something I can take with me into surgery. Something beyond the mechanics of what I'm there to do."

"Something personal," I contribute.

She removes her scrub cap and holds it in her hand, staring down at the pink fabric with what I think is a small blush tinting her cheeks. "Yep."

"What? What aren't you saying?" I dry my hands and lean my hip against the sink, facing her with my arms folded expectantly over my chest. "There's more, I can tell."

She puffs out an annoyed breath, making a few flyways of hair dance around her face. "I need to work on my poker face." She sighs, still not meeting my eyes. "Fine, but we're back to that no-judging, can't hold it against me thing."

"Promise."

She gnaws on her bottom lip, shakes her head, sighs again, and then utters what I think is "fuck it," only to quickly go on. "When I was a third-year medical student, the chief resident told me that surgeons like to cut and sometimes in doing so, we forget the person on our table is a person and not simply a patient there for us to work and learn on." She looks up at me, her stunning, bright blue eyes locked on mine in a way that makes me feel their intensity. "That stayed with me, especially as someone who has been through a similar traumatic event. So I ask that question because when I walk into that **OR**, I want to remember it's not just a cool case or another surgery. It's someone's someone I'm trying to save."

Fuck. I wish I hadn't asked. I wish I didn't know that. For a moment, I can't do anything other than stare unblinkingly at her. Taking in every perfect line of her beautiful face that easily outshines every other woman I've ever laid eyes on.

"Sounds like a good teacher," I quip, hating the thickness in my voice and hoping she doesn't hear it. Her truth is making me feel way more than I want to feel right now. The warmth flowing through my veins is like a drug made out of sweet, delicious poison, and I find myself once again staring at her lips, remembering just how equally sweet and delicious they were.

"He was." She pushes away from the sink, oblivious to my inner turmoil. "I'm going to update the family and then head out. I'll see you Monday, Dr. Lawson."

"See you Monday, Dr. Barrows."

She leaves me here, and I take a few extra minutes to get my head back on straight. Again. Something I seem to have to do with annoying frequency anytime I'm near her.

My phone vibrates against my hip, and I pull it out, read over the text, and then head for the computers so I can put in the order the nurse needs. I log in, reading through the patient's chart when I hear a squeal of delight followed by a loud laugh. When I look up, I see a little girl, maybe five or six, running straight for Katy, who crouches down and scoops her up into her arms, twirling her around the middle of the surgical floor.

The little girl wraps her arms around Katy's neck, and Katy kisses her cheek before a tall and good-looking man approaches her and snakes his arm around her waist, drawing both of them into his side. They talk, all smiles and laughter, and then the girl says something to Katy, who nods enthusiastically in response. After that, the three of them head for the exit together.

And that sweet, delicious poisonous drug I was feeling high on only moments ago turns corrosive, burning me from the inside out.

I'm an asshole.

A huge fucking asshole.

I never asked Katy if she was with someone. If she was married or a mother.

I never asked her anything personal about herself at all.

I just assumed she was single the way she was seven years ago. As if time hadn't moved for her the way it moved for me. I flirted with her. I made inappropriate comments. I touched her.

But the worst of it? That's not even what has me feeling like total and absolute shit right now. I'm jealous of that guy.

The one who gets to have Katy and their daughter.

The one who gets to have it all when I'm left with nothing.

# Chapter Six

## Bennett

*I move my hand slowly up her thigh until I find her soaking wet panties. "Mmmm," Catia moans. "Yes, Maverick. Don't stop." Before she can utter another sound, I grip the wet center and tear, sheering the soft fabric away and leaving her glistening pussy bare and exposed for me to devour.*

Yup. Definitely won't be reading this scene to my mother. Maybe the next chapter is... tamer. Or at least something that won't make my dick hard and my stomach curdle while reading it to my sick mother and reminding me of all the pussy I'm not getting. Besides, I can't get over that his name is Maverick. I still keep picturing Tom Cruise in *Top Gun*.

Not the mental image I want when he's talking about devouring a pussy.

This is why men watch porn and women read. Who cares about the build-up or their names? Just show me him eating her cunt without all the chitchat back and forth. Though, I'll admit, some of these scenes turn into fodder for my late-night fantasies. Especially the ones where he ties her up and spanks her ass till she's a moaning, writhing mess for him.

I sigh, rubbing a weary hand across my forehead and setting the book down on the cafeteria table as I take a sip of coffee. It's been a long fucking night, and I'm more than a little exhausted. I pick at the stiff piece of likely two-day-old blueberry muffin and toss it in my mouth.

"A little light reading there, Doctor?" comes a soft voice from behind me, close to my ear. A voice that starred in my dream just last night before I woke to a nightmare, but instead of moaning Maverick's name, it was moaning mine.

I bolt upright, flipping the book back over like a fourteen-year-old whose mother just caught him with a *Playboy*. But in the process of acting like I'm fourteen again, I swallow a bit too quickly and start to choke on the arid piece of muffin I had been forcing down.

I wheeze in, desperately trying to suck in air while simultaneously coughing as my body works to expel the lump of cake from my trachea.

Katy's blue eyes go from mischievous to wide and *oh shit* in a nanosecond. "Crap. I'm sorry! Don't die. Hang on."

She jumps into action, coming in behind me and slamming the butt of her hand into the space between my shoulder blades, and then moving in on a full-on Heimlich maneuver. Thankfully, the muffin chucks out of my mouth and onto the table, and I can breathe again. Not thankfully, it does it in front of Katy, my resident, and the girl I generally haven't stopped thinking about since I laid eyes on her again four days ago.

I've found myself lingering at the hospital well after my shifts end just to watch her a bit longer. Just to see her, possibly catch her smile, and feel that *feeling* she evokes in me before I go home and face the emptiness of my house. And now this. Perfect.

"Oh my god, I'm so sorry." Her hand meets my shoulder, and she crouches beside me, making sure I'm not turning the same shade as the blueberry I just expelled from my lungs. "I didn't mean to startle you like that. I mean, I did, but I didn't mean to make you choke. Are you okay?"

"Awesome," I manage with a harsh grunt as I take another

sip of my coffee to wash it all down along with my humiliation. I scrub my hands up and down my face.

Fuck. Just… fuck.

I sigh, sitting back in my seat, utterly dejected, and growl, "What are you doing here, Katy?"

She drops into the seat across from me at the small two-person table, all smiles and rainbows, not the least bit ruffled by my salty mood. I hate that I'm glad she's here when I shouldn't be. It was a brutal night, and simply seeing her automatically makes me feel lighter and heavier all at once. She's wearing a red, knee-length, flowy sundress with a V neckline that ties in a knot behind her neck. Her chestnut hair is down, long and thick with silky waves.

Does she have to be this fucking pretty?

Like, so pretty I can hardly stand it?

I'm slowly getting used to seeing her at work in her scrubs with little to no makeup on and her hair up. But I'm definitely *not* used to seeing her like this. Nothing is easy when it comes to this girl. It seems unfair that it had to be her of all goddamn people I'm being taunted with. But isn't that the story of my life right now?

"I was visiting my friend," she chirps. "What's your excuse, or is this where you come to hang out and read smut?" She reaches for the book and swipes it from beneath my hand. Her lips twitch in amusement, her blue eyes glowing as she reads the title. "*Surprise Baby for the Billionaire Doctor?*" Her eyebrows bounce suggestively. "Bold choice." She sets it down and places her chin on her hands, smiling sweetly at me. "Is it any good?"

I run my hand through my hair and sit up, dropping my forearms on the table. "Reading is my mother's favorite hobby, and she loves dirty romance books. She was diagnosed with non-small cell carcinoma about six weeks ago and is undergoing chemo and immune therapy. Whenever she has her treatments, I try to be there with her, and she likes it when I read these books to her. Part of me thinks she does it to bust my balls because that's the sort of woman she is, but I also know they bring her a lot of happiness. But even though I'm pushing forty, as she likes to remind me, she's still my mother and I'm still her son, and much to her chagrin, I don't love reading the dirty parts to her, so sometimes I read ahead so I know where to skip and where to restart. She fell last night. That's why I'm here now."

The smile Katy had been sporting has been completely wiped off her face, and in its place is an expression I can't read. It's serious and a little sad, but there is something else there too. It's not pity—which I appreciate—and it's not even sympathy. It's in her eyes and the way she's staring at me. It makes my heart beat faster and my skin hot and tight. It's like she can see inside me, see all the demons I'm trying to hide, and isn't afraid of them.

Katy clears her throat, blinks twice, and then reaches over and places her hand on top of mine. Just like that. "Your mom sounds like a seriously cool lady."

My chest clenches. "She is."

"How advanced is her cancer?"

"Stage three."

She squeezes my hand, and even though I shouldn't, even though I know better, I twist my wrist, intertwine our fingers, and accept the comfort she's giving me because, quite frankly, I fucking need it. Some days I'm treading water, getting through, and surviving. And then some days, some nights, I'm drowning under the weight of everything, unable to shake it off as it holds me under.

Back in Minnesota, I had a wife and a best friend. Here, I'm alone with no one to unburden myself with. My mother doesn't need my mental bullshit. She has enough of her own to manage.

"Is that why you said your life isn't so great right now when I rudely asked?"

"That's part of it."

"I heard a rumor about you."

"Oh?" My heart stops dead in my chest, and my hand tenses against hers. "What was that?"

She gnaws on her lip like she's regretting bringing it up. "Maybe I shouldn't say."

"Tell me or I'll put you on scut for a week."

She laughs. "You are a bit of a jerk. That was one of the rumors, though I didn't believe it until now. Fine, I'll tell you, but you can't hold this against me either."

I squeeze her hand again. "Promise. That's our thing now." I like that I have a thing with her.

"I heard you were forced to resign from Mayo."

I wait. I watch. Nothing else. "That's it?"

She nods.

"You didn't hear why?"

A headshake.

Well, that's a relief. "Yes, I was asked to resign from Mayo."

Her eyes narrow. "You won't tell me why?"

"Not right now." *Because I don't want you to look at me differently than you currently do.*

"Fine. I'll let it drop. But only because your mom got hurt. Is she upstairs or in the emergency room now? Is that why you're down here?"

I swallow past the thickness in my throat, silently loving how good her hand feels against mine. Warm and soft and small and perfect. "Yes. She got up in the middle of the night, felt dizzy, fell, and hit her head. Her night watch detected the incident and called nine-one-one when she didn't respond, and when she woke up in the ambulance, she had them call me."

"Her night watch?" Her brows pinch in.

"She has two Apple Watches. One she wears during the day and charges at night and one she wears at night that charges during the day. I don't live with her, and she lives alone, so I want her to always have a way of calling for help if she needs it. Which she obviously did, so I'm glad I forced her to do it."

"Smart man thinking of that. Is she doing okay?"

My lips form a flat line. "Yes. She's awake and giving the nurses and doctors hell. She has a nasty laceration on her forehead and a minor concussion. They admitted her for observation and to rehydrate her. She kicked me out and told me to go home and get some rest, but…" I trail off.

"You couldn't go home with her here," she finishes for me as if she understands exactly.

"Yeah."

We fall into silence, just sitting here, holding hands, and looking at each other. It's the nicest thing I've had in a very long time. Only Katy isn't mine to have a moment like this with. She's not mine to look at the way I am or think about the way I do.

I pull my hand away, but as I do, something occurs to me. "You don't wear a ring."

She tilts her head, studying me in confusion. "Huh? What ring?"

"A wedding band or an engagement ring."

Her head flips the other way, and a bemused sort of laugh tickles her lips. "Why on earth would I?"

Now it's my turn to stare questioningly at her. "Aren't you married?"

She's taken aback. "No. Why would you think that?"

"Because…" I trail off again. "I thought…"

"What?" she challenges when I don't follow that up.

I rub my eyebrow, nonplussed. "I saw you with… a little girl came running up to you, and well, I guess the man who I assumed was your husband embraced you with her."

She falls back in her chair and laughs, making my lips bounce in return. "You mean Owen? He's my—"

"Let me guess. He's your cousin," I interrupt, the hollow space around my heart clenching tightly. I'm much happier about this than I have any right to be.

"Yep. But Owen is also my best friend, and we have been since we were little kids. His daughter, Rory, is my goddaughter. They picked me up and we went out for dinner and then to a movie together."

"Oh." I look down at the table, hating how my lips are spreading into a relieved smile they shouldn't be. Brushing that aside, I meet her gaze again and ask, "Is your friend okay?"

"My friend?"

"The one who you came here today to meet."

A blush crawls up her face. "They're fine. They're not a patient here."

My elbows hit the table and lean against it so I'm closer to her. "You're keeping a secret again."

"Fuck," she hisses, covering her face and laughing into her hands. "I am not."

"You're a horrendous liar, Katy, but your face tells me everything."

"You're not the boss of me right now. I don't have to answer you. You didn't answer me."

I chuckle and reach over to pry her hands from her face. "Are you having a secret affair with a staff member here? It's not our hospital, and as you said, I'm not the boss of you right now, so you can tell me."

"No." She laughs harder, playfully shoving my hands away. "I'm celibate at the moment."

That pulls me up short. "Celibate? Why ever for?"

"You only get one answer. Pick your poison."

"Hmm." I tap my bottom lip, taking her in. "That's a tough one."

She rolls her eyes, playing with the long ends of her hair.

"Okay. Shit. This is hard." I sit upright. "I'll go with door number one since I'm your boss and I shouldn't be asking about your sex life." Despite how much I'm dying to know every detail. All the things that turn her on. What her hard limits are.

"Or lack thereof," she quips.

I pan a hand in her direction. "Or lack thereof." Which again, makes me happier than I have any fucking right to be. "Why are you in this hospital on a Sunday morning?"

"I sorta lied. I mean, kind of. I'm not here to see a friend per se, even though I am friendly with the person."

I raise an eyebrow, and she puffs out a breath, making her long bangs fly about her face.

"Sorry. I'm giddy and nervous so I'm rambling again. My endocrinologist came in on a Sunday to see me since he knows how hellish my schedule is. He's good friends with Owen, so he does me a solid when I need to see him."

"Endocrinologist?"

Her full, pink lips curl up into a soft smile. "We're learning all sorts of personal things about each other today, aren't we? Though I'm better at sharing than you are. I'm a type 1 diabetic, and I had some things I wanted to discuss with him, as well as renew my prescriptions for my insulin pens."

"You don't wear a pump?"

She makes a dismayed noise in the back of her throat and her hands fly out around her. "What is it with the men in my life being all about pumps?" She freezes, her eyes going round and her lips parting in an *oh shit* expression. "Not that you're a man in my life. I mean, you're a man and you're in my life, but it's different with us." She exhales a heavy breath and then laughs in a self-deprecating way. "You know what I meant."

"I do. So, no pump?"

"No pump."

I hold my hand up. "Got it. It's none of my business, and it sounds like you're on top of your care."

"I am."

"I didn't know you were a diabetic. When I knew you before, I mean."

"I didn't go around telling people. I'm not ashamed of it, and it's not a secret. But when you have something like that, a chronic condition, people can sometimes treat you differently, and I didn't want anyone going easy on me simply because I have to manage my blood sugars and take insulin. Besides, back then, I didn't have a continuous glucose monitor stuck to the back of my arm the way I do now." She twists her arm, revealing a small, round disc covered in a white protective barrier affixed to the back of her upper arm. "See. Much harder to hide this now."

"I get it. But I'm also glad I know. And no, I won't go easy on you simply because you're a diabetic."

She gives me a soft smile, and we fall into that silent staring thing again until I force myself to look away.

I clear my throat. "I should go up and check on my mom."

Katy stands. "I should get going too. I have a twenty-four-hour shift starting tomorrow morning."

Pushing away from the table, I stand, cleaning up the mess of blueberry muffin and tucking the book under my arm. Shit. I didn't realize she was doing that shift with me. "I do too, actually."

Her eyes linger on me, and I can tell she wants to say something else, but is, for once, holding back.

"What is it?" I question.

"You can tell me, you know. Not because I'm curious, though I am, but because I'm a good listener if you need someone to do that for you and I'd never say anything."

Once again, Katy has managed to knock the breath from my lungs. But Katy isn't my friend. She's a fantasy, a dangerous temptation, and I'm her boss. More than that, despite my wanting to trust her, I don't trust fucking anyone right now.

"Thank you," I say with a half-smile. "I'll keep that in mind. I'll see you tomorrow, Katy."

She comes over and stands before me, reaching up and touching what are likely purple bruises beneath my eyes. "You should get some rest, Doctor. Perhaps take your mother's advice."

I pull my face away from her touch, forcing her hand to drop to her side. Her touch is making me want what I can't have and shouldn't crave. "I will in a bit."

She smiles. "Okay."

I smile back. "Okay."

"I hope your mom feels better and gets discharged soon."

"Thank you. Me too."

She's still smiling, and so am I.

"Bye, Katy."

"Bye, Bennett." She walks off, leaving me to stare after her for a moment before I drag myself away and haul my exhausted ass upstairs.

I do need sleep. Especially if I'm going to survive my twenty-four-hour shift with her.

# Chapter Seven

## Katy

Taylor Swift blares through my headphones, and I sing along, tying my scrub bottoms and then tucking in my long-sleeve shirt and scrub top in because I'm that girl who likes to be tucked in. It's not even six in the morning, and rounds don't start until seven thirty. It's my absolute favorite time of the day to be here.

It's the quietest time in the hospital. At least for trauma surgeons.

It's also the best time of day to catch up on post-ops and labs and other things that have to get done, but you lose track of when the surgeries start rolling in.

My head bops from side to side, my hips swiveling along to the beat, and I dance and sing my way out of the women's locker room, only to bump into the last person I was expecting—or hoping—to see.

"You are shitting on my happy time," I tell Zane, the asshat from ortho I made a grave mistake with. Speaking of being that girl, I was her for about a year. The one who screws around with the guy with the bad reputation thinking they'll never be the one to get screwed over by him. Owen, Keegan, and Kenna all tried to warn me.

Hell, Owen and Kenna don't even work at this hospital but had heard stories about Zane in theirs. Talk about a freaking, blazing red flag. If a reputation is bad enough to span multiple hospitals, you should be smart enough to listen.

But did I listen?

Nope. Not this girl.

I screwed him—and I use that term deliberately—in a few bar bathrooms around the city after a few too many shots, but then, like a fool, I started listening to his lies as he told me how much he liked me and wanted an exclusive relationship—the first time in his life he ever wanted that with anyone. Swoon, right?

Naturally, I jumped in with both feet and two blind eyes because he was cute and great in bed and sweet in our private, vulnerable, post-sex moments.

I thought I had broken through to the other side of his manwhore ways, and I was the girl who changed him. We were that annoyingly cute couple who held hands in the hospital halls and threw each other sugary-sweet googly-eyed smiles that made everyone around us want to throw up. He even went out of his way to get along with my people.

After six months of being together, I moved into his place. And for another six months after that, Zane held me captive. He plied me with good sex and drugged me with swoony words of love. I thought he was it for me. We were even talking about trying for a baby—something we were both so excited for—and he was with me through my endometriosis surgery.

One evening I found an engagement ring tucked in the back corner of his desk drawer, and when he told me he made plans for us to go away for my birthday, I knew he was going to propose. Then, the night before we were set to go away, I discovered he was messing around with a nurse at Brigham and Women's and a doctor at Tufts. I had no clue. I suspected nothing. Until I came home early that night and found him having a three-way with both of them.

In. Our. Bed.

He swore it was the first time, but the women claimed otherwise. Who do you think I was smart enough to believe?

I moved out that night and into Keegan and Kenna's home office, and I never looked back.

I learned. I learned that appearances can be deceiving. I learned if something is too good to be true, it usually is. I learned that I needed to rediscover faith in my gut and to always follow it. And I decided my primary guiding force would be work, myself, my people, and nothing else.

So yeah…

"Move," I bark, my voice edged with agitation when he doesn't get the message. My elbow jabs and hits his flank. Thankfully, it provides enough breathing room for me to pass without having to touch him or get too close. Unfortunately, it wasn't hard enough to crack a rib or two.

He recovers quickly—far too quickly if you ask me—and then he's by my side again, keeping pace. "You could just talk to me," he pushes out. "You could listen to what I have to say and hear my side of this."

I laugh. Because, truly, that's a good one. His side? Only cheaters think they're entitled to have a valid side.

"No thanks." I throw him a sideways glance. "And legit, what are you doing here? You're like five months too late and well past your expiration date. Now get off my floor."

"You blocked me."

I roll my eyes. "Pathetic. Totally freaking pathetic. Of course I blocked you. What sane woman wouldn't? This is why all your fucking around will eventually lead to you being miserable and alone, nursing an incurable STI. Go spread it to someone else. I'm done with your cooties."

He grabs my arm, spinning me in place, and then walks me back into the wall. Getting right up in my face, his dark eyes blaze into mine. I shove against him, but he uses his size and weight to hold me in place.

"You won't talk to me. I've been trying to come up and see you, but you have the nurses locking me out of this side of the surgical floor and your ORs. Keegan kicked me in the nuts when I showed up at her apartment looking for you, and Kenna told the doorman to call the police on me if I showed up again."

It was funny when Keegan did that. He cried like a little bitch. And you have to love it when your girls go to bat for you, even when you didn't initially listen to them. "That's love. That's loyalty. Something you wouldn't know anything about. Now move."

I shove against him, but he pushes my hand away, pressing me deeper into the wall, his face inches from mine.

"I fucked up," he rasps brokenly. "Please, Katy. I know I fucked up. But I *miss* you. So much. You were the best thing to ever happen to me, and I ruined it by being selfish and imma-ture. All I can think about is you and the plans we were working on. I want that. I want all of that with you. So fucking badly. Please, babe. It's not too late." He cups the side of my head, holding me in position. "We can start over and still do this together."

I scoff. It's bitter as hell. I shake my head, forcing his hand away. "Save your half-baked apology for someone who actu-ally cares. You think I'd consider having a child with a lying, cheating asshole like you? I'd never intentionally poison the genetic well like that."

He growls in frustration, slamming a hand into the wall next to my head. "For Christ's sake, Katy. I've been——" Before he can finish his statement, he's dragged away from me by the back of his scrub shirt. "What the hell?" he barks.

"You better not be my new intern," Bennett snarls, releasing him and shoving him in the opposite direction of me.

"Intern?" Zane snaps indignantly. "I'm a fifth-year ortho—"

"I don't care." Bennett cuts him off, his voice sharp but not raised. He stands tall over Zane, using his extra three inches of height and fifteen pounds of muscle to his advantage. Zane doesn't back down, but he's also not stupid enough to fuck with a chief of a department either. "You're on my floor talking to *my* resident in a way I don't like. And from the looks of it, she doesn't like it either."

"This is personal between me and Katy and it doesn't concern you."

"That's where you're wrong. Dr. Barrows may have nine thousand cousins who know everyone in this building, but trust me, I'm not someone you want to mess with. Remember that. If I see you anywhere near her or if you put your hands on her again, I'll get your impotent ass kicked off your service and out of this building."

"Impotent?!" Zane squawks, and I choke on my laugh.

"I have a feeling it speaks to you on multiple levels. Now go."

Zane gives Bennett a scathing look and then shifts to me with an expression that tells me he's not done with me yet, then wisely leaves the floor.

Bennett turns to me, his features softening, his gaze all over me as if searching for signs of injury. "Are you okay? Did he hurt you?"

I shake my head. "I'd never let him hurt me again."

He considers this. "Your ex?"

"Yep." I rock on my feet.

"The reason you're celibate?" he surmises.

I shrug. "More or less. He slept with two women at the same time in our bed, but that part is sort of extra and irrelevant to the fact that he's a cheating, lying, backstabbing swine. Anyway, thank you for stepping in like that. I apologize that you had to."

He hovers over me, his eyes searching mine, something in his I can't quite read. "You don't have to thank me, and you certainly don't have to apologize. I have a persistent ex like that too."

My head bounces. "I heard you were divorced. That was another rumor."

"It seems a lot is going around about me." He sighs and looks around. "My ex is the one who got me fired."

"Oh." Because I don't know what to say to that.

"In case the rumor mill churns up the circumstances surrounding it, the reasons are bullshit, manufactured, and based purely on my ex's vengeful, vindictive nature that I didn't realize she had when I married her."

"Oh." Again, that's all I've got. Even though I'm dying to know, I won't ask what she did to get him fired. "I'm so sorry. That sounds… fucking awful," I say bluntly. "She tried to ruin your career?"

"Tried and almost succeeded."

"But you're here now," I offer brightly.

"And she's calling me here, which likely means she's trying to ruin this for me too."

"What a bitch. Maybe you just need someone to tell her to fuck off the way you just did Zane."

His lips bounce. "Are you applying for the job?"

My eyes sparkle. "Absolutely."

He grins, complete with a chin dimple and pearly white teeth. "Next time she calls the floor looking for me, I'll have the nurses put you on."

"Deal."

"I know you're not married to Owen, but were you married to that guy? I heard him mention something about you trying for children."

"No. Not married. But…" I trail off, laughing lightly and uncomfortably. This is too personal of a conversation to have with your new boss, but that seems to be what we're doing this morning. "Well, I have some reasons, let's go with that, but I want to try to have a child or children in the near future if I can. It's something he and I had talked about and wanted to try for back when we were together. Until I found him with those two women, of course."

Bennett's eyes round, and his jaw goes slack. For a long, awkward moment, he stares at me like this, as if he's too dumbstruck to respond.

"But don't worry," I quickly tack on, surprised by his reaction. "If I were to get pregnant, it's nothing that would interfere with my residency or fellowship. I promise. I'd never let that happen. If that's your concern."

He swallows audibly, licks his lips, and shakes his head as if my words aren't making sense to him. "You're trying to get pregnant? Still? Even though you're celibate?"

I look away, feeling my face heat. I can't answer him. I shouldn't have even said what I said. But after my appointment yesterday morning with Dr. Feelgood—yes, that's his actual name—things are starting to move in the right direction, and my excitement got the better of my mouth as it always seems to. Plus, Wes knew what my plans were, and as my boss, if I do get pregnant, Bennett will eventually find out, and if I keep it a secret from him, he could hold it against me when it's time to pick a trauma fellow.

He grasps my jaw and forces it back to him, his eyes fierce, and I notice his hand on my face is shaking. His extreme reaction startles me, and I'm not sure what to say or how to respond.

"Answer me, Katy. You want a child and are trying to have one on your own?"

"I haven't started trying yet," I manage to utter.

He shakes his head, blinking at me in rapid-fire, and then without a word, he walks off, storming down the hall and leaving the floor. All I can do is stare after him, at a total loss as to what just happened.

I'VE SPENT most of my shift today avoiding Bennett. After our wild encounter this morning that I still can't make heads or tails of, I'm not sure what to say or even how to be around him. But it seems life doesn't give a shit about my discomfort or nerves when it comes to my boss.

"What is it?" I call to the floor nurse as I sprint toward the elevator after getting a 911 page to the ER.

"GSW. They're rolling in with it in two minutes. It sounds pretty bad."

I throw her a wave and slam my fist into the elevator button, twisting my back to crack the tension out of it. It was a slow day, but it's been a fast-paced night. A hit-and-run had me and the ortho team—thankfully not Zane—in the OR for the better part of four hours and now a gunshot wound.

The elevator doors open, and I step on, but just as the doors start to close, Bennett comes flying on. He startles when he sees me, but quickly recovers. "They paged you too?"

"Yes."

He nods, and we both fall into an awkward silence as we descend, and I try very hard not to think about the last two times I was alone with this man on an elevator.

"You doing okay? With being on the elevator, I mean," he asks as if reading my thoughts.

"Yes. I'm trying not to think about it. How's your mom?"

He turns to me, his eyebrows raised, not having expected me to ask. "Good. She's good. She's back home and mouthing off as she likes to do with me. I had a nurse come in and check on her, so she's mad at me about that."

I smile softly. "I'm glad to hear that. Not that she's mad at you, but that she's doing better and raising hell."

"Me too. Thank you for asking."

I nod, and then we fall back into silence until the doors

open. We both take off at a sprint, following the gurney that's surrounded by ER doctors and nurses.

"What do we have?" Bennett asks as we enter the trauma room after quickly throwing on trauma gowns and gloves.

"GSW times three, two to the abdomen and one through and through to the shoulder." The ER doctor starts talking as he works on intubating the patient. "Lost a lot of blood in the field. Vitals are a mess, with a thready pulse in the one-sixties and blood pressure dropping to eighty over palp. Pulse ox sucks at eight-two, and I'm not sure why he wasn't intubated already, but he is now. Breath sounds are equal."

"Okay, good. Hang a unit of O-negative blood and open the fluids wide," Bennett orders one of the nurses. "Someone throw in a central line. I don't want to give him pressers unless we have to. Let's see if we can stabilize him a bit before we bring him upstairs. I need trauma labs sent stat. Dr. Barrows, how are those wounds looking?"

"No exit wounds for either of the abdominal entry points, and he's bleeding at a good clip despite applying pressure. We need to move him upstairs and open him up now. My guess is one of the bullets hit an artery and we're losing time."

"Alright, let's move. You heard her. Someone call up to the OR and let them know we're on our way. Dr. Barrows, are you with me? I'm going to need all the hands I can get."

"I'm with you," I tell him, and then we're locking the side rails of the gurney and racing for the elevators. The ride up is slow, and the patient is far from stable. My hands are holding pressure on one of the abdominal wounds, and the ER nurse has her hand on the shoulder wound. The elevator stops, and an intern and two more nurses immediately take the patient from us and wheel him toward the OR.

Bennett and I run over to the sinks, donning our scrub caps and masks, and then immediately start scrubbing in.

"He's a kid," I say, my voice low and my stomach in knots. I hate traumas on kids. They're the worst.

"A kid?" Bennett questions as he scrubs his knuckles.

"He looked like he wasn't a day over fifteen. Big body, but young face."

Bennett curses under his breath. "We didn't have a ton of gunshot wounds in Minnesota. I mean, I'd float up to Mayo in the Twin Cities and we'd see more there, but not that often. Not like we did when I was in Baltimore or LA."

"We don't get a ton here either."

He shoots me a sideways glance, lingers for a second, as if he's about to say something, but then thinks better of it and heads into the OR. I suck in a breath, hold it in my lungs, and then follow after him. Being around Bennett is like being on a rollercoaster, and while it's sometimes thrilling and fun, it's also spinning me through more loops and drops than I can take.

Bennett and I spend the next few hours working quickly and tirelessly to save this kid's life. We hardly speak to each other unless it's about what we're doing, and anytime we do, it's as strained as it's been all evening. Something shifted between us, and it doesn't take a brain surgeon to figure out that it's related to what happened this morning.

But the real question is, what the hell do I do about it?

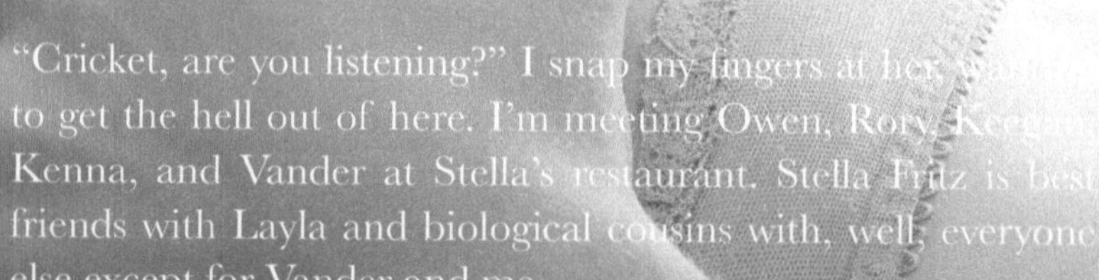

"Cricket, are you listening?" I snap my fingers at her, wanting to get the hell out of here. I'm meeting Owen, Rory, Keegan, Kenna, and Vander at Stella's restaurant. Stella Fritz is best friends with Layla and biological cousins with, well, everyone else except for Vander and me.

"Yes," she clips out, though she hasn't removed her eyes from Bennett, who is giving a report to the attending coming on. Somehow my schedule this week has been almost identical to his, but in the last five days that we've shared this floor, the ORs, and the ER together, I think we've maybe said a total of ten words to each other that weren't work-related, and most of them were good morning or good night.

I've caught him watching me several times, a serious look in his eyes, but I haven't had it in me to call him out on it. I'm terrified he'll encourage me not to try to get pregnant. That he'll tell me it'll hurt my shot at this fellowship or at finding a good attending position. Only that's bullshit.

I know plenty of doctors who have gotten pregnant or had babies and were still at the top of their game. Mason's and Owen's mothers for starters. And frankly, it's none of his business. It's mine, but… any comfort or even friendship we had been building seems to have evaporated, and I don't know what to do about it.

I shouldn't—I know I shouldn't—but... I weirdly miss him. I liked the way he talked to me and the way he looked at me, even if I knew it would never lead to another dark-corner kiss. But since Zane, Bennett is the first man to get my heart going again, and it felt fucking good. Like he was my secret. Like our past was something between us that no one else here knew, and with that, it fed into that something else.

Now that's all gone, and I've spent this week telling myself that I'm not only relieved it is, but that it's for the best, as anything else is an unnecessary and frankly unwanted complication.

"Then perhaps you should focus on what I'm saying instead of your boss."

She rolls her eyes, looks at me for two-point-five seconds, and then returns to Bennett. "He's going to give me the fellowship."

"Oh? He told you that, did he?"

My sarcasm finally manages to catch her attention, and now she's eyeing me like a cat eyeing a mouse they're about to pounce on and eat. "Wes isn't in charge anymore, so you're no longer the favorite simply because you were born into the right family."

I give her a bored look. "You know I wasn't born into the Fritz family, right?"

Another eye roll. She's famous for them. "Whatever. You know what I mean. It's an even playing field now between us, and I'm going to get that fellowship because I'm the better surgeon."

Cricket Peterson is a pain in my ass. She's been a pain in my ass for the last four years, and I know this last year of residency won't be any different. She's general surgery with a focus on trauma, same as I am, and we both want that coveted fellowship spot. And before this, I would have laughed in her face because that fellowship was all but mine. Everyone, including her, knew it.

Now nothing is a guarantee. Far from it.

For the first time since I started my residency, I'm worried about her as an actual competitor, if for no other reason than my current standing with our new chief of trauma surgery.

Only she sucks, and I'm awesome, so…

I shake my head. "I'm sorry to be the one to tell you this, Cricket, but it's never been an even playing field with us. Never." I stand. "Have fun kissing ass tonight. Dr. Iverson *really* enjoys it when you do that. Especially on a night shift." I give her a saccharine-sweet smile and then walk off. She can figure out what the patients need on her own. I've documented everything in their charts anyway.

I fly down to Keegan's floor, and then the two of us hop in an Uber and head across town to pick up Vander from his cave before we head to Stella's. This restaurant might be my favorite in the city, and it has nothing to do with the fact that Stella is my godmother. Keegan hasn't stopped talking the entire way, gabbing on about a patient with a placenta previa and one of her interns who she thinks is cute but a little brainless. Vander is doing God only knows what on his phone and has generally ignored us.

"Well, now I'm officially competing with Cricket," I inform them as we take our seats at our regular table by the end of the bar. "My boss hates me. He overheard Zane talking about the baby stuff, and then when he asked me about it, I told him. I mean, I didn't tell him I was looking into sperm donors, and I didn't tell him I was thinking of trying soon so I could have a baby between the end of my residency year and the start of my fellowship, but it didn't matter. He knows what I'm planning to do, and since then, he wants nothing to do with me. It's like I'm mommy-tracked without being a mommy yet. Plus, I think he thinks it's weird that I want kids without being married or something."

"Does he know why you want kids, even without a man as part of it?" Vander asks, rolling his tongue ring between his lips, his colorful tattoos on full display beneath his T-shirt that matches his green eyes.

I look down at my hands. "No. That's personal. I shouldn't have to tell him."

"You're right," he agrees firmly, his voice tinted with ire. "You shouldn't. And he can't mommy-track you. It's against hospital policy and, frankly, a suable offense."

"I know. It's easy to say that, but the reality is, I've worked my ass off for years to get where I am and though I really, seriously, desperately want a baby, I'm worried I'm risking everything I've built along the way to have one."

"Do you want me to look into him?"

"Noooo," I draw out, shaking my head violently at Vander. "I don't want you to do anything that you know how to do."

"Only people with something to hide should be afraid, Kit-Kat."

"I still don't know what you did to Zane to get him arrested and interrogated by the FBI." Thankfully Zane has no clue what Vander—or his father Lenox—can do with a computer and likely never suspected anything.

He smirks like the devil. "I don't know what you're talking about. All I know about Zane is that he fucked with the wrong girl and has a penchant for looking up local crime scene photos on his computer. Pretty damn creepy if you ask me and definitely suspect."

Keegan places her hand on my shoulder. "Ignore him. What does Owen say about what's going on with Bennett?"

I shrug. "I haven't—"

"What's going on with Bennett? Isn't that your new boss?"

"Nothing," I exclaim, jumping to my feet and blowing past Owen to gobble Rory up in my arms. "Hey, lovebug. How was camp today?"

"I passed swim today," she exclaims, oozing delight.

"Level four, to be exact," Owen supplies.

"You did? Level four?!" My eyes widen, and my eyebrows hit my hairline. I glance up and meet Owen's gaze before I turn back to my girl. "That's amazing! I'm so proud of you."

He chuckles, ruffling her hair. "All that time spent in the pool with her godmother is paying off."

I rub noses with Rory. "Totally, right? You're on your way to being a mermaid."

"Like you were."

I kiss her cheek. "Like I was." Because when I was her age, I had just lost my parents and I threw myself into *The Little Mermaid* for no reason other than that Ariel was beautiful and a mermaid, and I thought that was so cool. So I told my uncle Callan I wanted to be a mermaid, and he put me in swim lessons, and I swam and swam. All through grade school, high school, and college—where I got a scholarship for swimming. I still swim as often as I can, but having Rory love swimming just fills my heart with joy.

Stella comes out of the kitchen and hugs and kisses all of us. We order our usual, and then Stella takes Rory back because Rory likes to help Stella make her dinner, and Keegan goes with her, leaving me alone with Vander and Owen since Kenna still isn't here yet.

Vander fills Owen in on the discussion we had before he arrived. "Are you looking at donors?" Owen asks.

"I haven't officially started yet. I need to find a place to live first and finally move out of Keegan and Kenna's office and off their sofa bed. I just haven't had the time to really start looking and figure out what I want and what part of the city I want to be in. But I got the green light from my endocrinologist as well as my gynecologist. My endometriosis, so far, hasn't grown back after my surgery, my A1c and blood sugars are in good control, and my ovaries are cyst-free."

"So you're ready," he confirms, smiling at me in a way that tells me he's as excited about this for me as I am.

I beam. "I'm ready." And then I frown. "Except don't think my boss is too keen on me having a kid."

Vander curses under his breath, and Owen scowls in that big brother, overprotective way of his. "He's not allowed to make a decision about a fellowship based on a woman's family situation, only her skill."

"That's what I told her," Vander states flatly.

"I know."

Owen growls, and I can see he's working up a head of steam here. "If he does, he's messing with the wrong fucking army."

"No joke," Vander agrees, tossing his arm behind my chair and leaning in to speak softly. "I'd happily take him out of the picture."

"Guys." I give them a chill-out smile. "I've got this. I am a grownup despite the way I act sometimes."

"Fine." Owen holds up a consolatory hand. "But if your boss turns out to be a misogynistic dick, there are other fellowships. Brigham, Tufts, and BMC all have trauma programs, and though you haven't specialized in pediatrics, I could put in a good word for you at Children's."

I nod, taking a sip of my freshly delivered margarita. "I know, and I love you for that. We'll see. It could take a bit for me to get pregnant anyway, and I still have to fight with the bug, Cricket, for my spot."

"You're not leaving Boston, Katy," Vander tells me in no uncertain terms, sipping on his tequila.

"I have no plans to. Let's take one thing at a time. Hopefully, all of this is a non-issue." I stand and kiss the top of each of their heads. "I'm going to the bathroom before the food comes. Do me a favor? While I'm gone, both of you take some deep breaths. You're wound tighter than a nun's asshole."

I grab my purse, head around the bar area toward the

bathroom, and push through the swinging door. I do my business, wash my hands, and reapply my lip gloss. I'm freaking starving, which reminds me. Opening my purse, I pull out my phone and check my blood sugar reading from my continuous glucose monitor.

One hundred and thirty-four. Not great, but not bad. I dial up my short-acting insulin to six units, clean an area of my stomach with alcohol, and then inject myself with my pen.

I put everything away and head back out, only to nearly bash into the man standing outside the women's restroom. "What are you doing here?"

Bennett is leaning against the opposite wall, his expression firm despite his casual pose. "Coincidence. I was at the bar."

"At the bar," I parrot, mentally cringing. "So you overheard…" I raise my eyebrows, waiting for him to finish that for me.

"Everything you said to Owen and that other guy," he confirms, and my stomach plummets into my feet. Pushing away from the wall, he stands before me, his hands in his pockets, but his breathing is short and choppy, telling me there's more going on here with him. "They're very protective of you."

"Yes. They are."

His glacial eyes stay locked on mine. "I'm glad you have that, Katy, but are you sure there isn't more going on between you and either of them?"

My nose scrunches up in disgust. "Um. No. Gross. Owen is my best friend, and Vander is like a big brother, though he's younger than me by about seven years even if he looks much older. Trust me, they'd be throwing up on the floor if you asked them that. Just because we're male and female doesn't mean sex is on the agenda for us. Loyalty isn't a game we play at. It's in every pulse of blood in our veins."

He blinks, a bit startled by that declaration, but if he overheard us, he needs to know it goes both ways.

"And you haven't considered using them as donors?"

My eyebrows shoot up. "My cousins?!"

He shrugs. "They're not blood."

"No, but they might as well be for how I think of them. Owen is famous in this city as the eldest grandson of the Fritz family and that's not something I want for my child after all Rory has gone through with the media, but more than that, the thought of having a child with either of them grosses me out."

Another step, his expression is so stoic, so closed off. "I shouldn't be as happy about that as I am. I had the same reaction when I found out you weren't married to Owen."

I narrow my eyes even as I crane my neck to see his face. "What does that mean, Bennett? What are you doing right now?"

He chuckles, but there's no humor in it. "Something I know I shouldn't be doing. I'd like to talk to you about something. Would you be willing to come to my house with me? Just to talk."

"I'm here with my—"

"Family," he finishes for me. "Yes, I know. But this is… well, it's important. Potentially for both of us. But it's not for public ears or consumption, and that includes your family."

I hesitate, unsure what to make of this, but then he's practically against me, his hand on my arm and his eyes beseeching mine.

"Please, Katy. Please. I wouldn't ask if it weren't important. I have a lot to say. A lot to explain."

I search his eyes, and despite his pleading tone laced with a hint of desperation, the rest of him is shuttered up tight. It's… strange. Almost like he's forcing himself to remain detached, and it's a struggle for him.

It piques my curiosity even more. "Okay," I relent because I think he had me at hello, which isn't great, but whatever.

"But we should take food to-go. I already ordered, and I just took my shot."

He nods. "Give me five minutes and I'll meet you outside. If you would…" He releases a heavy breath. "I'd rather you not mention to your family that I'm here or that you're leaving with me. If you're okay with that?"

"Are you planning to murder me?"

He coughs, laughing at the same time, and it's like a peek of sunlight breaking through storm clouds. "Definitely not."

"I'm safe leaving here with you and not telling my family who I'm leaving with or where I'm going?"

"One hundred percent safe," he vows, placing his hand over his heart. "I'd never hurt you, Katy. Not ever."

Well then. Hard to argue when a man makes a declaration like that to you. Though, if memory serves, Zane fed me a similar line once or twice. Not to mention Bennett's my boss, and though nothing has happened between us, I already feel like we're crossing lines.

All of which means I should say no, but I think we know I won't.

"Then I guess I'll meet you out front in five minutes. But if you don't want questions, I'll get my own food to-go. You can do yours. And if my body ends up in the Charles River, you should know, you'll never see the inside of a jail cell because my grandparents, uncles, aunts, best friends, and all eight thousand of my cousins will kill you and no one will ever find your body."

A soft smile tilts up the side of his face. "Understood."

"Then go. Time is blood sugar."

His hand slides up my arm and then he's gone, leaving me here with far too many questions and a lot more nervous flutters than I want.

What am I doing?

This is crazy.

And yet I'm flying through the restaurant, heading to the

kitchen to ask Stella to put mine in a to-go box, kissing Rory goodbye, and since I can't lie for shit and I refuse to do that with them, I tell my family that I have to leave and that they can't ask why but I'm totally fine. They make me promise to explain everything later, and I tell them I will if I can.

I get looks. A lot of looks. And they all share a bunch between themselves too. But despite their protests and pushes for answers, I'm out the door in under five minutes with a to-go bag dangling from my wrist.

"You good?" Bennett questions, standing beside a Mercedes G Wagon.

I narrow my gaze as I get in his top-of-the-line ridiculous ride. "Not really, but I'm here, so let's do it."

He's still a block of ice and doesn't say anything as he drives us up a few blocks. He doesn't even have music playing, and I can't handle the tense silence, so I start to hum to myself.

"You can sing. I like it when you do that."

I raise an eyebrow in his direction. "When do you hear me sing?"

He laughs lightly. "All the time, Katy. You sing all the time. All kinds of things."

"It helps me focus, but right now, I'm only doing it because you're so quiet."

He sighs and deflates a bit. "I know. I'm sorry." That's all he offers me until he pulls into a driveway, straight back into a garage that is connected to a beautiful house on a quiet side street. He comes around and helps me down, taking the bag of food from my wrist.

"You live here?"

"I live here," he confirms.

"And the house?"

"Is all mine."

I look around as we walk from the garage to the house. The backyard is big, which is saying a lot for this part of the city. Considering the G Wagon he drove us here in runs about two hundred grand and private houses with this sort of land at least ten million, I'd say Bennett has money. A lot of money.

I stop talking after that, and he leads me inside through a back patio door that heads straight into a gorgeous freaking kitchen with dark blue cabinets, white and gray marble counters, brass hardware, and the coolest appliances I've ever seen.

"Have a seat. Would you like a glass of wine?"

"Absolutely," I tell him, not even bothering to pretend I'm cool or composed because I'm anything but. Only something occurs to me as I watch him take out glasses and silverware for us. "Is this a date?"

He pauses, his back to me, until he turns and meets my steady gaze. "No."

"Why am I here, Bennett?"

"You need to eat. I'll explain as you do."

# Chapter Nine

# Bennett

I've been thinking about it ad nauseam all week. During surgeries when I needed to be focused on the patient and what I was doing. Every second I've been in the hospital and I saw her. At night alone in my bed. When I was with my mother reading that fucking book to her and listening to her not-so-subtle comments.

It's all I've thought about.

Her. Katy Barrows. Having a baby.

Only not just any baby. *My* baby.

At first, I tried to play it off that I was happy for her and how cool and brave it is that she's doing that alone. But that didn't work. So then I took the rational approach. I don't know her well, and she's my resident and I'm her boss. There are rules. Not to mention, I don't want love or romance ever again, and I already like Katy more than I should, which would only complicate something that is already so fucking complicated further.

When none of those worked, I pulled out the big guns. I was fired for sexual misconduct—even if it was all a black-mailed lie—and asking your employee to have your baby is one hundred percent risking the same accusation, and I can't lose this job because that will be the end of my career as a doctor.

I rode those rationalizations hard. Played every single one of them on repeat.

But still, it did no good.

So then I tried adding on how Katy is looking for a donor, not a father to her child, and that she would never want to have a kid with me. She's trying to do this on her own, and I don't enter into that. Only, I knew that wasn't true since she was going to be trying for a kid with that fuckwad, nowhere-near-good-enough-for-her Zane.

All week I've been in agony.

Sleepless, restless, exhausting, pining for something I had no right to pine for agony.

I've avoided her, but I couldn't stop watching her like a goddamn creeper either. Katy is beautiful and smart and funny and fun and honest and has the biggest heart. She will be an amazing mother to her child.

And I want to be the father.

I want it so badly it's consuming me.

It's made the perpetual bitter taste that's lived in my mouth for the last few months even harder to swallow.

My problem is, and I said this before, I like Katy. She is all those things I mentioned and more. I'm not oblivious to all the ways my body wants her. But I need to get over it. I may crave her, but my heart is on lockdown, not wanting to be reopened to anyone again. But more than that, I'd have to trust her, and right now, I don't trust anyone except for my mother because she's the only person I've ever loved who didn't intentionally fuck me over.

I shouldn't have Katy here.

I shouldn't be doing this.

But sitting in that restaurant felt like fate. Seeing Katy again after all these years and knowing that she wants the same thing for her life that I do. Hearing her tonight at the table with her friends, it was as if everything fell into place for me. No more denying it or rationalizing it away. I had to take the chance, or I'd always regret it. It's delicate as sin since she works for me, and I have to see her practically every day. If this goes wrong, it'll potentially impact our work relationship, and I can't have that.

I can't lose what I just got back.

Too late now.

I acted because there was no way I could stop myself, and here we are.

I pour Katy a glass of white wine and slide it across the island to her. She's sitting at the breakfast bar on the other side, picking at some kind of creamy chicken with what looks like tomatoes and spinach with her fork as she cautiously eyes me. I pour myself a glass of wine too, and while standing, I open the lid on my pork Milanese and force myself to cut and eat a bite though I'm not the least bit hungry anymore.

I lick my lips, take a hasty gulp of wine, set the glass down, and start with, "First, I need to apologize to you for my behavior this week. When I explain everything to you, you'll understand it better, but please know my being cold or distant and possibly even a bit of a jerk was not because I think your decision to have a baby is a bad one, and it has no bearing on my thoughts or opinions of you as a surgeon."

"Okayyy," she replies softly, stretching out the word. She's visibly on edge because I'm making her so, and I don't know how to stop. I don't think I've ever been this nervous in my life, and unlike Katy, when I'm nervous, I become quiet and introspective. "Bennett, just please spit it out already. You're freaking me out."

"I want to have a baby with you."

Her fork clatters to the counter and I fall forward, my elbows meeting the marble and my head hitting my hands.

"Shit. That was not how I was supposed to say it." *Fuck.* I slap my hands on the counter and meet her startled and incredulous—and quite possibly terrified—blue eyes. "I'm so sorry, Katy. I'm doing this all wrong." I blow out a strained breath. "Please don't run. Just sit here and listen to everything I have to say."

"Um."

I hold up a hand. "I know. Trust me, I know. Just eat and I'll talk because I don't want your blood sugar bottoming out." I rest my forearms on the counter and lean against them, putting me closer to eye level with her. "I've wanted a family for a very long time. I'm an only child with no real family except my sick mother. I'll get into that more in a bit. But I want kids, I want more than just me and my mom, and the woman I was married to, well, I won't get into all the ugliness and betrayal—"

"I told you mine," she interrupts. "I told you about what Zane did. You told me you'd explain, and I want the full story. You already told me she got you fired, but you never said how or why."

Her eyes are still wide, her food all but forgotten, and I motion to it for her to start eating. The fact that she's still here, asking to hear the full story, is so much more than I could ask for.

"All right," I concede with a sigh. "I'll tell you everything. I met my wife about six months after I moved to Minnesota. We had wanted the same things. Marriage, children, our careers. All was great until she kept pushing back on me when I wanted to start a family. Eventually, I wore her down and we did start trying. And trying and trying. I'll skip ahead several months to the important part. It turns out she had a tubal ligation the year prior to our 'trying'"—I put air quotes around that—"and never told me about it. She did it in secret it because as it turns out, she had been fucking my best friend for the better part of two years."

Katy gasps, nearly choking on the sip of wine she was

taking but manages to swallow it down and not spray it across my kitchen. "Ah, wine burns when it goes up the back of your nose." Her eyes pinch shut, and she shudders before shaking it off and glaring at me in horror. "But for real? She did that?" she croaks. "*Your best friend?*"

"Yes. We roomed together all four years of college. He was the reason I moved to Minnesota. He was an admitted bachelor and didn't want any children. So he told my now ex-wife that if she wanted to continue fucking him, she couldn't try for children with me because he couldn't be sure whose kid it would be, his or mine."

"Holy shit, Bennett." Her hand covers her mouth. "God, I'm so sorry. That makes what Zane did look saintly by comparison."

I take a bite of my food. "There is no comparing being cheated on. It sucks and it hurts and feels like a knife in the back no matter what."

"So all that time you thought you were trying for a baby..." she trails off.

"I wasn't," I tell her simply, trying to ignore the omnipresent, sharp bite I feel every time I think about it. "She was simply going through the motions with me because she didn't want a divorce—she liked my money. I'll give you more on that in a minute—but she didn't want to let go of her affair either. She let me believe we were trying. She let me believe we were partners who loved each other and communicated. Instead, she went and made a major life decision for both of us without consulting me all because she didn't want to stop fucking him."

"Christ. Okay." She shakes her head bewilderedly. "I can't even with that. But go on."

I finish off my glass of wine and lick my lips. I haven't told anyone this other than Jack, who told Wes. There are rumors that I was forced to resign, but so far, no one seems to know the reason behind that.

I wipe my mouth and slide my hand until I'm gripping the back of my neck. "My dad died about three years ago and left me a substantial inheritance. Lizbeth—that's my ex—her family had a lot of money, so we had a prenup when we got married. A big one that stated she kept her money, and anything I earned or inherited would stay mine in the event of a divorce. But about a year before I found out about the cheating, Liz's family money was wiped out by shady dealings and crappy investments, taking Liz's trust and inheritance along with it. Our divorce was messy, and since we had the prenup, I didn't have to give her a dime. She didn't like this. And later, after the divorce was finalized, she promised she'd ruin my life, and she tried."

"Sounds like a peach of a woman," she deadpans. "I'm assuming this is where the firing you thing comes in?"

I nod, taking a step back and resting my hands behind me, gripping the edge of the marble. Just thinking about this, about all that she did to me has me burning up with a poisonous rage so invasive it robs the air from my lungs. She's out there, living her life, still fucking calling me just to see how much deeper she can twist the knife.

I manage a steadying breath. "She's a hospital administrator, and when I essentially told her to fuck off, she somehow blackmailed two women, one a scrub nurse and one a former resident who left the program, into saying that I sexually harassed them by making inappropriate comments, advances, threats, and physical contact. I never did anything of the sort. It was all lies."

Katy does a long, slow blink, her lips parted as she attempts to grapple with that. "That's..." She stops and shakes her head. "That's... fuck, Bennett, I'm not sure I have words for that. That's the most fucked-up thing I've ever heard in my life, and I grew up with the Fritz family and the Central Square people, who are famous and have had their share of bullshit and blackmail. Why didn't you contest it?"

"I did," I defend. "At least I tried to. The hospital put me on administrative leave and shortly after told me that they'd keep it quiet as much as possible if I resigned and walked away. I wanted away from Liz. I wanted away from Cayden, my ex-best friend. So I took the forced resignation and left Minnesota."

She runs her hands across her face and through her hair, dumbfounded. "All right. Wow. For the record, your ex is a fucking cunt and I hope her vagina shrivels up and falls off her body. I know it sounds trite, but I have to say that I think getting away from her was the best thing you ever did. But now you're here, and so am I. Tell me how that happened."

My lips curve. Only fucking Katy could get me to smile after all that.

Pushing away from the counter, I return to the island and lay it all out for her, keeping my tone flat and void of the emotions rioting inside me. "My mom, as you know, is very sick. It's always been her dream that I have children and make her a grandmother. I'd do anything to make my mom happy because her life wasn't always the happiest. It's also always been my dream to be a father. So when I heard you talking to Zane about that, about trying to have a baby with him and then without him, I…" I trail off, trying to find the right words and how to phrase this. "I was jealous, I think. You can do that. You can have a baby on your own, but it's so much harder for me to do that. But then, I couldn't stop thinking about what if I *could* do that and what if I could do that with you. A woman who wants a baby but isn't necessarily looking for love or emotional commitment from it. I tried to fight those thoughts all week, but then I heard you tonight, talking about finding a place to live and a sperm donor, and I—"

"You want to be my sperm donor?"

Her lips are twisted to the side, almost as if she's trying to hide her smile, and I can't help it, I'm so tense, so on edge, I break and start laughing.

"Yes. I want to be your sperm donor. But I want to be more than that. I want to be the father of the child. I want to be a full-time co-parent." She's silent for an eternity after that and when I can't take it another second, I allow my desperation to take over. "Say something, Katy. Please."

# Chapter Ten

## Bennett

"Say something?" she parrots incredulously. "Do you not understand all that you've just given my brain to handle? That's hardly a run-of-the-mill request or story for that matter."

"I realize that." I'm honestly terrified she's going to get up, walk out of here, and report me for misconduct. And this time, it would be warranted. But hell, I told her all of it—every piece of the ugly truth along with the bombshell of why I asked her to be here. She hasn't run out the door screaming for her life, but she's still staring at me in a way that has me sweating through my T-shirt and my skin prickling with adrenaline.

"You want to have a baby with me."

I nod carefully, even though it wasn't posed like a question.

"You hardly know me."

I swallow at the thickness in my throat, and when that doesn't work, I clear my throat and chase it with a gulp of wine, wishing it were something stronger. "I know and I know what I'm asking you for has enormous complications and considerations." I set my glass down and wipe at my tacky forehead. "And just so you're aware, because I was an idiot and didn't tell you this at the start, you can say no and tell me to fuck off and walk right out of here. It will not impact your work or how I view it or you. I mean that. I'm not the monster my ex painted me to be. I'd never ever want you to feel trapped or uncomfortable in any way."

She sighs, picking at a piece of chicken with her fork before forcing it into her mouth and chewing thoughtfully. She swallows and finishes off her wine, setting the glass down with a light *clink*. "Bennett, I don't think you're a monster, and you can take a breath. I'm not going to sue you or try to get you fired. We're adults having a conversation outside of work, and I completely understand why you're asking, me what you're asking even if it's the most insane thing anyone has ever asked me."

I blow out a breath I didn't realize I was holding. "Thank you for that."

She shakes her head as if she's nowhere close to done. "You understand having a baby together would put us in each other's lives forever. This isn't some temporary arrangement where we have to deal with each other for a year or two. A child is a lifetime of never getting rid of me."

I go about pouring us each another glass of wine. "I know that. Trust me, I've thought of nothing else but this all week."

Lifting my newly filled glass, I take a sip while I give her time to work through her thoughts. I start eating my tepid dinner, and she does the same with hers. For a few minutes, we're here, silently eating, though somehow it's not awkward. It's as if saying all that to her set me free and I feel lighter, regardless of how it turns out.

After she's finished, she sets her fork and knife down and closes the lid on her to-go container. "You don't expect a relationship from me? Like, you don't want us to get married, right?" she finally asks, her voice gentle, but her firm eyes are on me, watching my reaction closely.

"No. I don't," I tell her honestly. "After what my ex put me through, I'm not interested in falling in love or entering into another relationship like that." I swallow and rub my hand across my forehead. "Is that something you were looking for?"

She shakes her head. "No. I mean, I won't say that's not something I eventually want because it is. I want love and marriage and all of that. Zane knocked me down, but I fully intend to get back up again. Just not yet, and not while I'm going through all of this because I think that would confuse things or interfere. I don't want love or romance to be part of this equation, and I'm not looking for that with you if this is something we end up doing."

Something we end up doing. Holy shit. "Are you considering this?"

She shrugs. "I don't know. I have a lot of questions, and I need a lot more information first."

I try to tamp down my burgeoning excitement. "Ask me anything."

"What about work? My job and the fellowship?"

"I don't intend to make any final decisions about the fellowship, and that includes outside applicants, until February, as announcements begin in March. I haven't even started interviews yet. That said, as I told you before, I will only base the decision on the surgical merits of the candidate and nothing else. As for work, I'd like us to stay completely professional in the hospital and not allow any personal situation between us to interfere there."

She smiles, liking that answer. "What are your expectations with this? From me?"

My laugh is strained. "I hadn't gotten that far, Katy. I never even got as far as imagining you sitting here having this conversation with me."

We stare stoically at each other, precariously suspended in this vibrating energy as endless heartbeats stretch between us. She's waiting on me, I realize. She has her plan. She knows what she wants from this. What she's uncertain about is me.

"I think we'd need a contract," I tell her. "I have some serious trust issues, and I suspect you do too. So a contract is essential to me even though we're talking about a child, and that's a fluid thing."

"I agree."

This is where it gets tricky, and I hadn't gotten this far with my thoughts before, but listening to her talk about finding a place to stay and seeing her here in my kitchen… "I might want you to move in here. In fact, I know I would."

Her eyes go comically wide, and she shoots out of her chair, stumbling to her feet. Shit. I pushed her too far, too fast. Fuck. Her eyes snag on the back door. She's going to bolt.

I hold up my hand, slowing her down. "Katy?"

She hooks an arm around her waist, staring at me from beneath her lashes, her eyes wild and unblinking.

*"You want me to move in with you?"*

Blood pumps hot and sticky in my veins with the island separating us, but I've come too far to backtrack now, and she might as well know it all at this point. "At least during the pregnancy and maybe the first, I don't know, six months of the baby's life."

"Jesus fuck, Bennett. Are you crazy? You want me to move in here and for us to have a baby together?"

Yes. Without a doubt yes. I wouldn't be asking this of my resident and risking all that I'm risking if I weren't.

"I know how this sounds. I know it's crazy and probably a bit stupid to suggest that. But I want to be there for all of it," I tell her, gripping the counter so I don't round the island and grab her. "The pregnancy, the doctor's appointments, the delivery, the lack of sleep, the midnight feedings—all of it. I don't want to miss out on any of that, and I'd want to help you as much as I could. I'm not looking to be a weekend dad or to take the kid when it's convenient for me. I'd be a partner."

She's eyeing the back door again. Yeah, she's about to bolt, so I slow myself down and backpedal a bit.

"I appreciate that might be more than you want, especially from me, but it's what I'm looking for. Though with a contract comes negotiation, and I'm open to discussing anything and everything with you."

Her expression is glassed over, and she walks toward the back door. My heart shoots up into my throat as panic and regret surge over me, but she doesn't touch the knob. Instead, she's staring out at the deck and backyard beyond.

"You'd want me to live here with you for at least a year and a half?"

"Yes."

"That's a long time to live with someone and not be involved with them."

It is, and I honestly don't know why I'm asking for her to other than for some inexplicable reason, I want her here. I like the control of it. I like knowing I'll be the one to take care of her and make sure she wants for nothing.

"We both work long hours, and neither of us is looking for anything romantic. If it didn't work or if we felt it was too much, we could obviously discuss that and renegotiate at any point."

"You're very businesslike."

I bite down my smile. "I'm a fucking mess," I admit. "Look at me, I'm sweating like a Mafia boss in confessional."

"Good." She turns, her eyes shining against the evening sun as it casts through the glass of the back door as she studies my expression. "I'm glad I'm not the only one."

My head bows and my hands go to the back of my neck. "When I saw you in the restaurant tonight, when I heard all that you were saying…" I blow out a breath. "Fuck, Katy, I had to take this risk. I had to ask you. I've wanted this for so long and nothing in my life is right, and maybe this isn't either, but I've got nothing, and this felt like a chance at something."

"I think that's the most honest thing anyone has ever said to me."

I laugh mirthlessly. "I don't know if that's a good thing or not."

"I don't either." She laughs, and my lips reluctantly tug up into a smile. This girl's energy and life infuse my dull, empty one. "I assume I'd have my own room."

"Of course. I have four bedrooms in this house including mine. You'd have your pick."

"What about sex?" she asks bluntly, sideswiping me. "Will you be bringing women home? And what if either of us meets someone?"

A rip current of jealousy grips me by the chest and sucks me under so fast and furiously that I can't fight it or swim away from it. The thought of her meeting someone else, especially while she has my baby growing inside her has me seeing red. I don't think I could stand that. It'd drive me insane, and yet, how do I tell her not to live her life or meet someone when I'm not willing to be that man for her?

"I'd rather us not do that while you're pregnant," I manage though I grit it out through clenched teeth, and I'm sure she can hear the strain in my voice and see it across my face.

Thankfully, she doesn't comment on my strange reaction to her basic question. "So no sex with anyone else during the pregnancy? The same goes for you?"

"Yes," I say easily because I can't imagine doing that with another woman, casual or otherwise, while I have another woman carrying my child and living with me. I'll miss sex. Hell, I already do—it's been a while—but this is more important to me than sex, and hopefully, I'll have plenty more sex ahead of me once we've had the baby and things settle down.

"And how do we make this baby?"

"What?" That pulls me up short, and I stand to my full height. "I thought you were looking for a sperm donor."

"I am."

"I thought you were celibate."

"I am."

My eyebrows slant in and I tilt my head, studying her. "I don't understand then."

She laughs as if she doesn't either. "I'm looking for a donor and I'm celibate, but you're talking about going all those months to possibly years without sex. I don't know… I'm panicking, I think." She laughs again, wiping a stray tear that slips out. "This is a lot to absorb, but you were so honest with me, so I'm going to be that honest with you. I can't imagine going that long without sex. Other than surgery, sex is one of my favorite things to do. It's already been five months and eight days since Zane, and yes, I've kept track because I'm celibate, but another year and a half without it feels like a death sentence."

My cock surges with blood at hearing her say that, but I ignore it and cross the room to stand before her. "Are you suggesting we have sex?"

She shrugs. "I don't know. That seems like a bad idea. Like a really bad idea, right?"

"I have no way to answer that."

"You're my boss and we're talking about having a nonromantic kid together."

"Then I guess you're right? Bad idea?" And yes, I pose both of those as questions. Because it does seem like a bad idea, only it also seems like the best idea she's ever had.

"Definitely a bad idea." She works this through, her wheels visibly spinning. "But… what if we did, you know, try for the baby… naturally?"

"Naturally," I repeat as if the word doesn't make any sense. Like she's saying it in Polish, and I don't speak a word of Polish, only my body isn't as dense as I am. My body speaks whatever language she's speaking and it absolutely fucking *loves* it.

My cock goes from a semi to stone as lust swirls like an elixir through my veins.

The thought of fucking Katy bare, of taking her body every way I've always imagined while making a baby is easily the biggest turn-on of my life. It's taking everything—and I do mean everything—I've got not to grab her, rip her clothes off, flip her around, press her into the glass of the back door, and fuck her blind.

But after leaving my old life behind, I've come to realize I don't want anything like what I had before. If anything, this fury and unrelenting anger have awoken the beast I never allowed myself to set free. I'm not cruel, and I'd never hurt Katy in the name of anything but pleasure, but fuck, do I want to mark her body and watch her moan and writhe against my touch.

"You want that?" My voice is husky, encased in thick need, but I have to ask even if there is no hiding my obvious lust or the way I'm looking at her with so much heat my house is about to ignite and burn around us.

Her cheeks are flushed the most gorgeous shade of red, and her pupils have completely blown out. "I…" She licks her lips, and my head dips reflexively, wanting to repeat the motion with my tongue. "I don't know. You're making all these demands and stating all these things that you want, and I'm flustered and overwhelmed. Focusing on the sex or lack of sex seemed like the easiest place for my mind to go."

"You can make demands too. You can have anything you want." *I shouldn't. I shouldn't. I shouldn't. Don't fucking do it, Bennett!* "If you want to try to make the baby naturally, we can." *Fuck! Fucking asshole!* "But maybe…" *Stop thinking with your dick!* "Maybe we should put into the contract that we stop after we're pregnant."

"Just so things don't get complicated between us, and we know where we stand," she agrees, her voice low and raspy, almost like a purr, and I'm dying right now with how badly I want her. I'm so fucking drawn to this woman I can't see straight.

"Right." I inch in. "So there's no confusion."

"Exactly."

Somehow my hands are on her hips beneath her shirt, my thumbs rubbing along her hip bones over her smooth, soft skin. Despite how much I want to slide them up and cup her tits—and I seriously fucking want to—I force my hands away and make myself take a few steps back.

"I want this too much to fuck it up by making a move on you that I shouldn't be making."

I suck in a silent breath, regaining my control. Something I only seem to lose when I'm around her. Something I better get a tighter grip on now. If…

"Katy, will you consider having a baby with me?"

# Chapter Eleven



Will I consider having a baby with my boss? How did I even get here? Oh my god! I'm *Surprise Baby for the Billionaire Doctor.* The weird hysterical laugh thing I do when I'm overly nervous or anxious about something is roaring up the back of my throat, but now isn't the time for it. His mother has a sense of humor. I'll give her that.

But how do I answer that? I can't freaking answer that. Doesn't he know all he's asking of me?

I won't lie. There is something so undeniably convenient about his proposal.

For one, he's gorgeous, brilliant, a doctor, and I believe he's a good man despite all he's been through. He cares for his sick mother. He wants to be a father and not simply because he wants an heir or to have kids to check a box. He clearly has plenty of money of his own, so going after my trust fund that he knows nothing about is not at the forefront of his mind. There's also the part of him that doesn't want love or a relationship, which as weird as this sounds, is a relief.

But then there are the other massive conflicts that are telling me to say no and run for my life.

He's my boss. He evaluates my work, and in addition to

being unethical, I'm also after a coveted fellowship he presides over. If we do this and he doesn't pick me, I might kill him, and if we do this and he picks me simply because I'm his baby mama, I *would* kill him. So there's that.

Plus, how can I live with him for that length of time? Will I grow to hate him or even worse, love him? Or could we manage to stay distant, living solely as roommates and eventually co-parents? Then there's that.

Co-parenting with him.

That might be the biggest slice of this pie because that puts Bennett in my life forever. Helping to make decisions for the kid and coming in with his own expectations of what he wants for it. What if he remarries one day and my kid then has a stepmother I'll have to manage?

And, well, you know, there's also the big, fat volcano of sexual attraction that was lying somewhat dormant and is now ready to erupt all over us because I said I wanted to try to have the baby naturally. Which is nuts. Why the fuck did I say that? Because living with him won't be enough, I have to start fucking him too?

That laugh escapes, and he gives me a curious look, his lips bouncing since I do sound like a hyena as Owen so kindly put it. Ugh.

"I'm not sure what that is."

I cover my face with my hands and sigh despondently into them. "It's a weird laugh thing I do when a situation is a bit more than I can handle emotionally. You have no idea how many times I nearly did that when we were stuck in the elevator together. You'd think after thirty years of being on this planet, I'd have a better grip on it."

"Ah." He approaches me and pries my hands from my face, forcing my gaze up to his. "Take all the time you need to figure this out. I understand what I'm asking and how that's no small thing. That said, I'd greatly appreciate you giving my offer genuine consideration."

He makes it sound like a job proposal. Which I suppose in a fucked-up way it is.

Still, having a baby with Bennett is like winning the genetic lottery. At least looks wise. His personality is a bit of a cartwheel, but I think a lot of that has to do with the fact that he feels like his life is falling apart or was ripped away from him. I get that. Hell, I'd likely be worse than him if I were dealt his hand.

My hands drop to my sides, and I blink, studying him with the same focus I gave my medical boards. "You really want to do this with me? Have a baby together? You'll be stuck with me for life as the mother of your child?"

"I really want to do this with you," he says in no uncertain terms. "All of it. The making the baby, the carrying the baby, the having the baby, the raising the baby. And just to get this out of the way, I've been tested and can show you the results. I'd never touch you if I wasn't. And I'm happy to undergo any genetic screening you'd like, but off hand, I don't know of any preexisting genetic conditions in my family."

"I was tested after Zane," I tell him, since that's the weird direction this weird conversation has taken. "And he was the last person I was with. As for genetic testing, I think I'll leave that up to my OB since they'll test me for stuff. As you know, I'm a type 1 diabetic, so it seems my genetic lot is worse than yours." Wow. I'm actually having this conversation with him.

He gives me an impish grin. "Looking at you, Katy, knowing what I know, from where I'm standing, you're perfect to me."

I blush. It comes out of nowhere, but I totally freaking blush. He catches it and the way he's looking at me… the way it makes me feel…

I clear my throat and all that girlish *gah!* away. "I don't know if it's smart to try naturally with you."

He licks his lips and nods. That's it. Yeah, I started something that's a bit hard to undo. Because I want sex with him, and he wants sex with me. That much is obvious. But wanting sex to scratch an itch because the guy is sexy and it's been too long since you've gotten any, and having sex to make a baby are two totally different things, though both a minefield in their own right in this situation. I digress.

"What about the boss thing?"

He hitches up one shoulder. "For me, it's as bad as it gets. I'm not on probation per se, but the board and my boss made it very clear when they hired me that I can't have any indiscretions or I'm out, which is why I shouldn't be doing this with you at all. But here I am, and I don't want to pull back regardless of the risk. Maybe I'm nuts, but I think we could make it through the next year or two without it interfering with our work while managing to keep it a secret."

A secret. As in we live two different lives, one at work and one here in his house.

Hmm. Okay then.

I mean, I'm not sure how well things like that work out, but then again, I don't exactly hang out with anyone in the general surgery or trauma departments, and I also don't get personal with them. The only people I'm personal with are my family, and they'd never tell anyone. It's not like I have to tell people who the father is, but then again, he'd be the father, so—

"But," he tacks on, interrupting my thoughts. "I realize the tricky nature of that, and if we do manage to get pregnant and this does all work out, I will speak to the head of surgery about it and make sure if our secret gets out, it's not as scandalous as it could be. I can't have that happen. For either of us. It's more of a risk this year leading up to the fellowship. After that, not so much, especially if we're not together."

I raise an eyebrow. "You're taking the sexy, forbidden element out of this for me."

He laughs, the sound cracking through some of his stiff armor. "You sound like my mother."

"I was thinking about the title of the book I saw you reading."

"Now you know why she picked it for me to read to her. But that's fiction, Katy, and this is real life. We can keep it a secret until we have something that requires telling. And we won't fall in love with each other like they do in romance books."

Fair enough.

"I need to think about it." *A lot.* "I should go." Because even though having a baby with a gorgeous billionaire doctor sounds perfect, as he said, this isn't fiction. This is something I've wanted for a long time. Something I wasn't always sure I'd be able to have with my medical issues. So bringing someone else into my life, into my future planning, is a huge deal.

"Can I drive you home?"

Home. I don't even have a real home. I'm a thirty-year-old woman trying to be a single mother sleeping on a goddamn pullout couch at my friends' place. I'm a cliché. I also think I'm having some sort of existential crisis. Or maybe just a mental WTF.

"Sure," I utter because my thoughts are too chaotic right now, swirling in a thousand different directions and scrolling through a million different variables and scenarios. This day took an unexpected turn on me. It's making my head hurt and my stomach queasy.

I have him drive me to my uncle Callan's and Layla's house instead of Kenna and Keegan's place. Cal and Layla are away right now, staying at my uncles Oliver and Luca's place in Italy for two weeks and then floating around Europe for another month or so after that. But this is the house I came to after my parents died. The house where my uncle took me in and did everything he could to make me feel loved and wanted.

And with that, it's where I need to be tonight.

Not with my cousins seeking me out to ask questions.

I need to be alone where I can absorb and work through everything Bennett offered tonight.

Only the moment I enter the house, the freaking mass alarm sounds. In a flash, I punch in the code and then answer the person who comes through the intercom asking for the password along with my name. The alarm shuts off, but then my phone immediately rings, and I groan.

"I'm sorry," I answer Uncle Callan.

"Are you okay? We were notified the alarm went off and that you're there."

My laugh cracks in two. "No. Not even close. But I'm fine if that helps. I'm at your house. Obviously, you already know that. Sorry. I might be losing it a bit. I needed a comforting place to be tonight where I could think."

He's silent for a beat and I know it's because I just threw a lot at him and because he's half-asleep since it's the middle of the night in Italy.

"Katy my lady, talk to me."

My heart swells at the nickname he's had for me since as far back as I can remember. "It's late."

"Fuck late," he growls. "Talk to me. Do you need us to fly home? We'll be on the next flight."

"Stop being so perfect, Uncle Cal."

I hear the smile in his voice as he says, "Then talk to me and I'll try."

How I love this man.

"I got the green light for undergoing fertility stuff," I tell him, walking up the stairs and heading down the hall toward my bedroom.

"Oh, Katy," he breathes out and I hear Layla mumble something to him in the background. "It's Katy. She got the green light to try for a baby."

"Ah!" Layla screeches. "Put me on speaker."

"Is that okay, Katy?"

I smile. Feeling so grateful and loved. I think that's what

Bennett is missing. He has his mom, but it doesn't seem like he has much else. It makes me break a little for him because I'm not sure what I'd do without these people in my life.

"Of course," I say. "I want to talk to you both."

"Katy!" Layla screeches again. "Talk to me. I'm so freaking excited even if I'm like a million years too young to be a grandma."

I enter my bedroom, leaving the lights off. "I'm excited too. More than excited. It means my body is healthy and ready. And that's not something I thought I'd ever get. But…" I blow out a breath, dropping onto the edge of my bed and staring at the walls that are still painted to look like the ocean. "My boss, Bennett Lawson wants to have this baby with me."

"I'm sorry, what the fuck now?" Callan growls, and I shake my head before I launch into an account of everything Bennett and I spoke about tonight, and when I'm done, they're both silent. Too silent.

"You have to say something," I provoke. "Or did you fall back to sleep?"

"Katy." That's Callan. He clears his throat. "Christ, that's a lot. I don't even know where to start. I feel for him. I truly do. That's about as fucked up of a situation as I've ever heard. But I guess I'm wondering… you're saying he's willing to risk his new job, possibly the only one he can get with a history like that and no reference coming from Mayo to have a baby with you?"

I gulp, and then gulp again because the way he phrased that… the implications of it… the meaning behind it… "Yes. It seems he is."

"Jesus. Are you considering this?" he persists, his tone edged with incredulity and worry.

"I don't know," I answer truthfully. "I guess I am, right? Otherwise, I wouldn't be here, and I wouldn't be talking to you about it. I was going to do this with asshole Zane because I want my baby to have everything, and that includes two parents if possible. There are a lot of variables to this, and it's risking a lot for both of us."

"It is," Callan agrees. "Do you know anything about this man? Have you had Vander or Lenox look into him?"

"No. This all happened right before I walked into your place. But this isn't a relationship. It's a business deal. An arrangement."

"All the more reason you should have them do a background check."

I roll my eyes. "The hospital is required to do one, and I knew him seven years ago. He takes care of his sick mother. I was in his home today, which isn't littered with doll heads or beer cans. He's been honest, sincere, and respectful. Despite his indecent proposal." And mine, for that matter.

"So he's likely not a psycho. Good stuff. How do you feel about the business arrangement side of this?" Layla queries.

I stare sightlessly at the wall, rolling that question through my head. "On the one hand, it makes it easier. We'll have a contract, and I know he'll always be part of the baby's life and not some guy who could simply take off on me, abandoning us both. I mean, he could still do that, but it's not nearly as likely without love playing a factor. He wants the baby, badly enough to risk this, so that speaks volumes about the sort of parent he'd be. On the other hand, it's weird. We're talking about a baby. A human life. How do you write up a contract like that? Not to mention, one day, when the child is old enough, how do we explain it to them?"

"A donor is like a contract in a way," Layla offers. "You sign papers, and there are laws surrounding it. It's different in that it would be entirely on your terms that way. This way brings someone else in who will have their own set of ideas on parenting and desires for the child."

"Yes. There's that too." My elbow digs into my thigh, and I rest my forehead in my hand, putting my phone on speaker and setting it on the bed beside me.

"Let's start small," Callan suggests. "Is he a good man? A man worthy and deserving of you and your babies? Is he the sort of man you'd pick as a donor and would feel comfortable having continuously be in your child's life?"

Shit. "That's not small, Uncle Cal."

He chuckles. "Fine. Maybe not. But it might be the most important part of this."

That question knocks me sideways if for no other reason than the answer that immediately hits my brain. "Yes. He is." I blow out a breath. "At least I think he is. I haven't spent a lot of time with him, at least not in a while, but when I knew him back when I was a student, he was, and even now, I've seen him nearly every day for the last couple of weeks or so, and yeah, he is. I think he married a nasty bitch of a woman and chose the wrong best friend. I think he's had a seriously bad run of things. But I think he's a good man at his core. Wes believed the same, otherwise he wouldn't have brought him in as chief. I think he's like you, Uncle Cal."

And now my tears start coming because I think about when I was six years old and I came to live here. My uncle did everything—including risking his entire world and making Layla his fake fiancée—all for me. All so I could stay with him and not be taken from his custody. All because I was his sole priority and he loved me.

Would Bennett be that kind of dad? The one to risk everything in his life for his child? Isn't that what he's already doing by asking this of me?

"Katy, I think the question you have to ask yourself is, do you want a father to your child, or do you want to be the sole parent?" Layla's voice rings through my turbulent thoughts. "There is no wrong answer, and you know you have a network of us to help you with the child no matter what. You're not in this alone. But do you want your child to have a dad? If it's not necessary, then you don't need to risk all that comes with doing this with a man like Bennett. If you do want that, then maybe the risk is worth the means."

I flop back onto my bed, my feet still on the floor, my forearm across my forehead, and my eyes on the ceiling. "How will I know the right choice? You do understand I could be risking my fellowship for a multitude of reasons despite a contract and promises. I don't want to give up my career, but I don't want to give up on having a baby either, and I'm not sure what my window is past now to do that. Could be months, could be years."

"True," Callan agrees. "You don't know. But you don't need Bennett for this. He needs you."

"I know," I say thoughtfully.

"I took a chance that risked my career. Layla was my medical student, and I made her my fake fiancée anyway. You were worth it, Katy, and I could never have done it without Layla. She was so important to both of us. But I fell in love with her. Hell, I was halfway there before we even started with the fake stuff. So if that's truly not what you want, you either have to be in the mental headspace where he is a father to your child and nothing more. Or you do this without him, and he'll have to deal."

"Okay," I murmur, my voice absent, lost.

"When your uncle asked me to move in and be his fake fiancée, I got drunk at Stella's bar and forced Amelia, Octavia, and Stella there. They helped me work out if being fake engaged to your uncle—when it was all for him with nothing for me—was the right choice. Sometimes our people help us through it. But, Katy, in my heart and in my head, I knew it was the right choice before I dragged them along. I just needed people I trusted and loved to validate my thoughts and feelings, or at the very least listen to them. That's what you're doing now, which is great, but you don't have to rush into anything. You can take days, weeks, or even months to figure out what feels right for you."

"I know," I utter, feeling like I'm on repeat. "But the truth is, I don't want to wait weeks or even months. I was ready to start this before Bennett threw me a curveball."

"Then my best advice is to follow your heart and have faith that everything else will work out because you will do whatever it takes to make that happen. I followed my heart, and it brought me you."

Fuck. "Bitch," I sob, and she laughs, hearing the tears in my voice. "I love you."

"I love you too. It'll be okay, Katy. It will be. You know the right choice. But that doesn't always make it the easiest. The right choice is often the hardest to make."

"Thank you." I clear my throat. "I needed this so much. Now go back to sleep," I tell them, sniffling like crazy until I drag myself up and snatch a tissue from the box on my night-stand to wipe my nose. "And thank you for always being there for me."

"No matter what," Callan promises.

I hang up with them and stare up at the ceiling for hours. Crying. Laughing. Shaking my head. Speaking in gibberish because I'm not always so rational when my life gets compli-cated. I can walk into surgery and be five steps ahead, but when it comes to the personal stuff, I flounder. I don't always trust my gut or my instincts the way I do in the OR.

Maybe that's because of what Zane did to me, or maybe that's why I trusted him in the first place. I have to remember that there are the Zanes of the world, and then there are the Callans, Owens, and Vanders. I need to take myself out of the equation and focus on the baby.

Do I want my baby to have a dad, and do I want that dad to be Bennett?

But come 4:00 a.m., I'm still without sleep, still unsure what to do. The only thing I know is—oh shit. I bolt upright, hit with a dawning realization. One that almost feels too well-timed—almost like fate—to ignore.

# Chapter Twelve



It's not even dawn when I show up on his doorstep, my mind racing yet somehow determined. I'm letting Layla's words be my guiding force. I feel like my body—and not my heart—are going to drive this train, and I think that's the right way to take it. She said I'd know in my gut the right call, and I feel like I do.

At least I hope I do.

Fuck, my gut's been a stupid bitch in the past, allowing me to fall for Zane.

*You're saying he's willing to risk his new job, possibly the only one he can get with a history like that and no reference coming from Mayo to have a baby with you?*

He's not the only one risking everything, but all that means is we'll have to fight harder to keep it. But the risk is worth the reward if this all works out.

The door swings open and there is freaking Bennett, his dark hair in wild disarray, his deep blue eyes smoky and sleep-covered, and his body, well his body is a work of goddamn art. The only thing he's wearing are gym shorts, which leave plenty of smooth, golden, naked chest landscape for me to ogle. Stacked bricks of muscle and a honed chest sweep up into built shoulders, biceps, and triceps that put NFL players to shame.

I might be drooling. I might not even know how to stop. What sort of crazy bitch cheats on a man who looks like this?

"Hey," he rasps, rubbing the top of his head and making his hair stick up even more. "Are you really here or am dreaming? It's been a long night of very little sleep."

I walk straight into his house, loving that he's also suffering from a sleepless night. It tells me the talk we had last night is weighing on his mind as much as it is mine. It tells me it's everything to him the way it is to me.

"I have a few things I need to ask, and then I have to tell you something after that."

"Okay." He closes and locks the door and then leads me into the living room, offering me a seat that I decline because I'm far too worked up to sit, let alone sit still.

"You're almost naked."

He glances down at his body and then back up at me. And he smirks. A fucking devilishly delicious smirk that makes my stupid nipples harden. "Is that one of the things you need to ask me?"

"No, that was a statement and a fact."

"I'm wearing shorts," he points out.

"And no shirt."

His thumb glides along his bottom lip in a move that should be illegal for how wet it makes me. Clearly my body has made up its mind and says we're a go for launch.

"I wasn't expecting you to be on my doorstep before dawn. Or at all, for that matter. I'll run upstairs and put on a shirt."

I can't even with that. Who on the planet Earth would *ever* want him to do that?

"Absolutely not. Stay where you are, or I might lose my nerve. It just caught my attention and sidetracked me because you, well, you look like that." I wave a hand up and down his body, swirling my finger around to indicate his abs.

"Should I ask what that means?"

I throw him a look. "Don't play coy, Bennett. You know exactly what you look like."

He grips the back of his neck and lifts his shoulders in a self-deprecating way, though in doing so it makes the muscles of his arms bunch and Jesus, can he just stop it already? Maybe he *should* go and put on a shirt. Arms are my total lady porn, and he has some of the best I've seen.

"Sorry. Sometimes I can't help myself when it comes to flirting with you. And honestly, I'm so fucking nervous I can hardly breathe. The floor is yours, Katy, and I'll answer anything you ask."

I start to pace my way through his living room, which is gorgeous and expertly decorated with what appears to be expensive furniture. It's not a place where children can play without ruining or breaking something. I wonder if he's the sort of guy who cares about things like that. Like will he have forbidden furniture and rooms children can't play in and freak out when they do?

"Do you like this room?"

"Huh?" He scratches the back of his head again and wipes some sleep from his eyes as he surveys the space around him. "Uh, I don't know. I mean, I guess it's okay. I've never given it much thought. This is the longest I've ever spent time in here. Formal spaces aren't exactly my thing."

Great answer.

I turn on him. "Are you a good man? Because I told my uncle Callan, who no joke risked his entire world for guardianship of me, that you were. Are you the sort of man who would risk everything and anything for his child the way it seems you're doing to try to have one?"

He steps forward and grasps both of my upper arms, stopping my pacing. "Yes," he says unequivocally. "I swear, every accusation those women said about me was a lie."

"I believe you." I believed him before. That question wasn't even about that, and I hurt for him that he thought I was questioning that.

"I can't tell you how relieved I am that you do. I think of myself as a good man. The sort of man who would do anything for those he loves and cares about. I'd be that man for you, too. It's not just for our children." He licks his lips, his eyes flickering back and forth between mine. "I'd protect you the same way I'd protect them. And if anything came down from this, I'd make sure I take the heat for it. Not you."

Fuck. I wish he hadn't said that because my chest is inflating like a balloon and my stomach is like a bounce house on crack. But then I catch on that word…

"Children?"

He smirks and then immediately wipes at it as if he didn't mean to say that and is embarrassed that I caught it.

"You know, if that's how it ends up." His grin goes lopsided, and his chin dimple pops. "I've always sort of dreamed about twins, but I know that's my own thing and not reality."

The man not only dreams about having kids but twins?! Gah. My ovaries are punching my stomach, screaming at me to get with the program and let this man impregnate me.

My heart thrashes in my chest, but it's the good kind of thrashing. The kind of thrashing that comes with excitement and nerves and knowing you're about to embark on something that will change your life—hopefully for the better—forever. But it's also the kind of thrashing that's telling me to do this.

I'm trusting my gut. I just hope I don't live to regret it.

I have a million more questions, and we have so much more to discuss, but for the life of me, I can't think of anything else except, "Bennett, I'm ovulating."

"What?" he manages as if the words don't make sense.

"I realized I'm ovulating. It's thirteen days from my last period, and not only am I on a twenty-six-day cycle, but I always get a twinge in my lower quadrant on the side I'm ovulating on when I'm ovulating, and I felt that twinge earlier today on my left side."

"A twinge?"

I nod.

His dark eyes give a quick sweep of my body. "You're ovulating? Right now?"

Another nod.

"And that's why you're here at four thirty in the morning?"

"Yes."

"Katy, are you telling me—"

"We're doing this. I want to do this." A smile cracks clear across my face, and that balloon in my chest is so big I could burst with it as I say those words. Holy shit. We really are doing this. And clearly we're doing this naturally, otherwise why would I be here right now? I'm not only saying yes to having a baby with him, but to sex to make that baby.

Stupid or not, that's how this is going to go.

He takes a hasty step toward me, only to pull back as if he's still unsure. "I'm about to maul you right here in my living room unless you tell me to stop. I want to knock you up, Katy. But also, I seriously want to fuck you. You have no idea how beautiful you are right now. Tell me to stop or we're doing this. If you're saying yes, we're going to start trying to make a baby right now."

I don't make a sound. I'm searching for the voice that's telling me not to do this, but I can't find it anywhere.

He rushes forward, his chest against mine, his hand on my jaw, demanding my full focus. "Tell me to stop, Katy, or I'm going to fuck you. I don't even care about a contract. We can figure that out after, but you're here and you're telling me you're ovulating, and I want this and you so fucking badly I can hardly breathe or think rationally. You understand if I fuck you, if I knock you up, that baby will be mine, and you will be too."

My ovaries are legit exploding right now. Possessive caveman types are my total weakness.

"Fuck me, and let's see how you do with knocking me up."

"Oh, sweetheart." He picks me up by my thighs and presses my pussy straight against his hard cock. "You feel that? I've been hard since I set eyes on you again. Katy, I'm going to come in you so many times you'll leak me in the middle of surgery two days from now. I *will* knock you up. It's not a matter of if, but when."

I have no idea why that's so hot, but it is.

"Do you have any idea the dirty things I want to do to you? You have to tell me if it's too much or if I'm too rough because the way I'm feeling right now cannot be contained."

His delicious promise ignites a wildfire of pure, uncontained desire inside me.

My hands get lost in the back of his hair, and I stare into his blue eyes, so dark and riled with lust and determination, but also caution and possibly a touch of an apology, and my empty core clenches. God, I can already tell he's going to be so good.

My breathing grows erratic, and I slam my lips against his. "I want all your dirty, all your rough, all your unhinged. Fuck me like you need to fuck me, Bennett, and don't worry about being gentle. I can take anything you can unleash and more. Hell, I'll likely beg for it."

He groans. "You're a fucking dream, Katy. My dream."

His hands slide up and squeeze my ass as his tongue roves against mine, moving fast like he's starving for me. Urgently, he walks us around his living room, nearly tripping over a random piece of furniture I don't care enough about to open my eyes and see. He curses against my lips, but then he has me pinned against the wall. My hands roam his heated skin, sliding over honed muscles and loving how they flex and bulge under my touch.

"You're going to be such a fun secret to keep," he murmurs against me. "But the best part about right now is that we won't know if you're pregnant for another two weeks."

A ripple of fear shoots through me with that, because I know what he's saying and I know why he's saying it. We've barely started, and yet his kisses are honeyed and drugging and the thought of having a naughty secret, of sneaking around and fucking like rabbits is deliciously wicked and fun sounding. If he fucks the way he kisses—which I suspect he does—then I'll be addicted to this in no time.

But how do I stop and how do I not grow attached?

This was my idea, and I came here this morning for this exact thing. So I guess I need to put his dick where my mouth is and vagina up so to speak. I can worry about the other stuff when I have to.

He sucks on my bottom lip, and I moan, feeling the thick, hard ridge of his cock glide just the right way and in just the right spot against my pussy. I tighten my legs around his waist and hold him closer, moving my head and attacking his mouth with a voraciousness I don't know how to slow. He matches me, our tongues dueling in a fight where we both win.

Only all too quickly, I succumb to his domination, reveling in the way he controls and overpowers me.

He sets one leg on the floor, freeing up a hand he uses to rip my T-shirt up and over my head. With one leg still pinned around his hip, I grind myself forward, humping up and down in a mindless flurry as I press against him, wanting us chest to chest and groaning in frustration when I realize I'm still wearing a bra.

He laughs against me, breaking the kiss, both of us panting for dear life. "We should go upstairs."

I nod. "Definitely." I grab the back of his head and drag him back in, practically climbing him as I kiss him like he's fucking candy and cake, only better since kissing him won't kill me or require a massive insulin shot.

Pressing me back into the wall, he rips down the cup of my bra, exposing one naked breast to him. His mouth takes full advantage, closing over my pebbled nipple and sucking hard on it.

"Fuck," I hiss when he brings his teeth into the action and drives me higher with their sharp sting and the sweet bliss of his tongue when he soothes it away. I close my eyes, my back arching against the wall to give him better access. His fingers slip up through the bottoms of my jean shorts and straight into my thong, finding my pussy wet and open for him.

"Double fuck," he growls, dropping his forehead to my chest and breathing hard. He licks my nipple, then pulls back and looks up at me through impossibly dark lashes as he slides two fingers into me. "You have no idea how many times I've thought about doing this to you. What your face would look like as I did."

He slides me a sexy grin and a shiver licks my spine as the ache between my thighs, the one he's stoking, intensifies.

His fingers move in and out of me, and then he brings his thumb up, using it to rub my clit, and my eyes screw up tight.

"You're so tight, Katy. Fuck, you're so goddamn tight. Your cunt can barely handle two of my fingers. I can't wait to feel you around my cock."

My lungs empty as without warning he spins me away from the wall and over to a nearby chair where he pushes me against the back of it.

"Hold on. You're going to need it for support."

"What—"

His mouth covers mine once more as he undoes my bra, but then he's kissing his way down my jaw, over my tits, going lower down my body until he's on his knees and eye level with my pussy. "I gotta taste you." I don't know if he's talking to me or my pussy, but right now, I don't care. The button and zipper of my shorts are undone, and they slip down my legs, pooling at my feet, but my focus is entirely on Bennett, who is staring straight at the tiny scrap of lace covering me.

He nuzzles in, taking a deep inhale and licking at my panties, sucking my clit and using the fabric for extra friction.

"Fuck, Bennett." I grab the top of his dark hair with one hand, holding onto the back of the chair with the other, because now I know exactly what he meant when he said I'm going to need it for support. His hands meet my inner thighs, and he spreads them wider, forcing my feet apart, but that doesn't seem to be enough for him, and he takes one foot out of the jean shorts that were handcuffing my ankles and places it over his shoulder.

His fingers twine the hem of my panties, and my teeth sink into my bottom lip, stifling my cry as he rips them straight off, exposing me fully to him.

"Christ, you're goddamn perfect," he murmurs, almost to himself, then swirls his tongue around my opening and groans. "Fuck, Katy. Just fuck. Your cunt tastes so fucking good."

"So glad to hear it. Now eat me, Bennett. Eat my pussy till I see fucking stars." I roll my hips, punctuating my point and making him smile against my wet, heated flesh.

"Oh, sweetheart," he says sinisterly. "You have no idea all that's coming for you."

That's part of what scares me about him, but right now, I'm too turned on to care.

He smacks my clit with his wet fingers, and holy Christmas, what is that and why is it so *good*? He does it again, two more times, each time harder than the last until I'm a writhing, panting mess.

Heat blazes up my body, flushing my skin, and when he finally sucks my clit straight into his mouth, I cry out, my clit more than just a little sensitive from him spanking it. He uses the tip of his tongue to flick it and I gasp, my knees buckling. I abandon his hair in favor of holding onto the back of the chair with both hands. He flashes me a smug smirk, palming my ass and squeezing it possessively.

Two fingers slide back inside me, pumping hard and fast, and my eyes roll back in my head. He's going so hard, sucking my clit and warming me with his hot breath as he fucks me into such a frenzy, I can hardly get my bearings.

"Oh, God," I whimper as he starts dragging his tongue up and down my pussy, rolling my clit in between passes. He nudges my thighs wider, demanding I open myself up fully to him so he can kiss and bite and lick every inch of me. His fingers slide out, the sound so fucking wet, and the second I think he's about to stop, he smacks my clit and shoves his tongue inside me until I scream.

My pussy pulses, my clit throbs, and I can't think about anything else other than the burning need to come. His pace is brutal. The way he works his fingers either on my clit or inside me, switching off with his tongue until I can't keep track. All I can do is *feel* and *beg* for more. His fingers pump and plunge and fuck, taking without asking or offering mercy.

I glance down, feeling just the tip of his tongue, such a stark contrast to what he was doing seconds ago, and find him staring up at me.

His lips are wet, coated in me, and his eyes are predatory, almost primal, but also filled with awe as he watches me lose my mind. "Keep going, Katy. Show me how sexy my girl is when she loses control and gives it all to me. I want to feel you come on my fingers and tongue, and then I'm going to fuck you till you do it again on my cock."

"Yes. Don't stop. I want it. I want more of it."

He laps at my clit, swirling it with his tongue as his fingers find that spot inside me and vigorously rub. All I can do is hold onto the fucking chair as he eats me out better than anyone ever has before. I can't even speak. It's impossible to form words, only sounds.

"I'm going to fuck you here from behind. Nice and deep. I

want you screaming my name, but then I'm going to take you upstairs and watch as you ride me. I want your perfect tits to bounce as you take every inch of my cock you can."

Jesus. His mouth. His wicked, diabolical, *sinful* mouth.

His fingers dig into my ass, his grip so firm I know I'll have marks on my soft flesh. It makes me moan and rock into his face, craving more of him, as much as I can get. His lips claim my clit, and his fingers continue to hit me exactly where I need them to, and I lose it right here in his formal living room. My back bows and my hands grip the chair so tight I'm shocked I'm not cracking the wood as I come and come, all over his face, riding him to the very edge of my sanity.

My legs are mush, shaky and unsteady as I sag back, my eyes still closed and my dopey smile unstoppable. Fuck, that man did what I asked him to. He ate me out until I saw freaking stars. With one last kiss on my pussy, he stands and starts attacking my mouth. I taste myself on him, salty and sweet, and though part of me seriously wants to return the favor, that's not why I'm here. That's not why we're doing this.

I tug at the hem of his track shorts and shove them down over his narrow hips and sensational ass until his cock springs free. I grip him in my hand, loving his heady groan, but then I pull back and stare down at him, pumping him in a steady rhythm as I do.

"Bennett…" I trail off, staring at his dick in my hand, then slowly climbing up to his dusky eyes and flushed face. "Um."

"You can take it." His lips layer against mine, licking them with an arrogant smile all over his. "You're plenty wet, and I promise, not only will I fit, but it'll feel so fucking good when I'm all the way inside you."

I pant out a strained laugh. God, I hope so. I really, seriously hope so. Because he's huge. And I'm not even just saying that. He's like over ten freaking inches long, not to mention *thick*.

He spins me around, forcing me over the back of the

chair, and starts palming my ass cheeks. "Come on, Katy," he plays, his voice taunting and menacing. "How much can you take? How much of my cock can we force into your tight little cunt before you beg for mercy?"

My eyes roll, and my toes curl into his soft gray area rug. I give my ass a little wiggle because even though he is huge, I never back down from a dare or a challenge—something I get the feeling he's learning about me.

"That'll never happen." I look over my shoulder at him. "You may be big, but I'm going to take every inch of you and fuck it like a gold medalist. By the end of this, I'll own you."

He gives my ass a solid smack. One cheek and then the other. "We'll see who owns who when this is all done."

# Chapter Thirteen

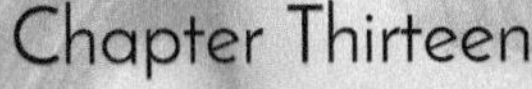



She's going to own my ass. I already know it. I can talk all the shit I want—I'm a surgeon and we're competitive by nature—but it's all bravado. Katy is going to own my ass, and she's going to own it until I get her pregnant and likely even after that because, well, she'll be pregnant with my kid. Ask any man. That's hot as fuck.

Even just the thought of it now makes my dick surge with more blood than I knew it was capable of holding. I have maybe three functioning brain cells at the moment and each one is telling me that while she may own my ass, I need to fuck her like a god and make her come at least two more times to try and make this at the very least a draw.

She likes my dirty. She likes my rough. She likes it so much she wants more of it. Yeah, she's going to own my ass for sure. And this is only our first time fucking. I get to have her again and again.

My cock thumps against my stomach, liking that idea a lot.

I grip it in my fist, give it a harsh tug, then run it along Katy's wet slit. It's heaven. This girl is heaven. The way she kisses, the way she smells, the way she tastes, the way she moves, and the way she talks—bold and unapologetic in the things she wants and how she intends to take them—are the biggest turn-ons of my life.

I haven't been with anyone since I left Liz, and while Liz was good in bed, she was timid and uncomfortable with her sexuality. She never owned it the way Katy does. She never told me what she wanted me to do to her. The one time I tried talking to her the way I've been talking to Katy tonight, she told me she didn't like it.

But Katy is so very different in the best of ways. The filthy words spilled from my lips like they've finally been set free.

Like *I've* finally been set free.

Liz used to tell me the depraved side of me was dirty and my desires were immoral. Yet something tells me that's exactly what Katy likes about sex—the dirty and immoral. As much as I hope I get her pregnant tonight, I really, seriously want to continue this until that stick shows two pink lines and I haven't even fucked her yet.

Speaking of…

"Are you ready?" I ask her, still rubbing the head of my dick up and down, getting it nice and wet.

Her head twists over her shoulder, and her bold eyes meet mine as a smile flashes across her face. "I think the better question is are you—holy, ah!" she cries as I plunge straight into her.

*Fuuuuuuuck.*

Sweat instantly coats my forehead, and I grit my teeth and clench my ass so I don't come on the spot. Tight. So goddamn tight. Her eyes pinch tight in pain, and I rub my hand up her spine, trying to get her to relax.

"You still with me, sweetheart?" My voice isn't the least bit taunting anymore. I only want her pain when it comes with pleasure. Not hurt.

She hums and pins me with a look that could make me

come on the spot. "I remember something about you making me take every inch. Is this the best you've got?"

I wheeze out a laugh, my forehead dropping to her spine, and I watch myself pull almost all the way out of her hot little pussy. She gasps, grips the hell out of the chair she's thrown over, and holds on tight as she braces for what she knows I'm about to give her. Exactly what she wants.

I slide back in, hard and deep, all the way to the hilt.

"Oh!"

I smirk, licking her skin. "Like that? Is that what you want?"

"Yes. God, yes. More, Bennett. I want more."

I start to pound into her, my hips swinging like a pendulum, pumping my cock harder and faster with each thrust. So hard I can't see straight, and the chair is dragging through the threads of the carpet, inching forward until it slams into the coffee table, rattling some stupid piece of glass my decorator picked out.

"Goddamn," I moan. "Katy." I pant out a breath, one hand grasping a full tit so I can hold her against me and the other on her hip, helping my leverage. "You feel so good." I swear, nothing has ever felt better than her slick, hot cunt. Fucking nothing.

I don't let up for a second, continuing to take her, loving how she pounds back into me with each of my forward thrusts. I want to kiss her. I want to taste her mouth and stare into her eyes as I fuck her, but that feels… intimate. Like not just sex, and as much as I want that, I also have to remember exactly what this is.

Why this has to stay just sex and why this is only temporary.

So instead, I fuck her like an animal.

Tightening my grip on her tit, my hand on her hip slides around and finds her clit, where I start to rub it in fast, furious circles. Because while I wanted her to come two more times, she feels too good, her pussy grips me too perfectly, and I'm barely hanging on. I continue thrusting with everything I've got, sweat trickling down my back, doing nothing to cool my overheated skin.

Katy squeals. "Bennett, ah, I'm so close. So close."

My eyes squeeze tight, and I pound into her, thrusting up so I hit the front wall of her pussy with every fuck I give her. I feel the moment her orgasm hits her. Feel her pussy clenching around my cock, milking it as I continue to fuck her through it. Her nails scrape at the fabric of the chair, her body spasming and shaking, her short, raspy pants filling the room.

Only I don't stop. I can't stop.

She's so wet right now—so much wetter than she was moments ago—and I can't get enough. It's too good to stop. Too good to come even. Pleasure courses through me, tightening my balls and making my stomach clench.

"Katy," I groan, dipping down and kissing her tacky skin, tasting her and smelling how sweet she is. Pulling her upright, I wrap my arms around her and give her everything I've got. I turn her head, capture her lips with mine, open my eyes, and take in the sight before me.

God, she's beautiful.

So perfect.

So... *mine*.

That thought sits with me for a very possessive moment, and I revel in it. *I'm* the one fucking her. *I'm* the one making her come. *I'm* the one who's going to get her pregnant.

Me. No one else.

Both damaged, slightly lost people who somehow found each other again at the exact right moment. And I don't allow myself to think beyond that. To wonder or question.

I'm not even tempted to.

Instead, I kiss her and hold her, and yes, I do fuck her through another orgasm before I lose my absolute mind and come inside her. My back strains, my grip bruises, my vision goes sideways, and I shoot every ounce of myself harder than I ever have in my life into her.

For a moment, I hold still, unable to move, unable to breathe, unable to think. Katy is in my arms, panting and sweaty, and I… I don't want to let her go.

On a deep inhale of her skin, my eyes close, and I shudder. It's as if the misaligned center of me is back where it belongs. *What the hell is this?* My heart starts to pound differently than it ever has before, her name a chant and a prayer and a fucking revelation in my head, her body an awakening in my arms.

She starts to squirm—likely because we're dripping cum and I'm holding her too tight—and I snap myself out of… whatever the fuck that was. Only my heart is still beating like this, and I'm not sure how to make it stop.

Slowly I slide out of her, wincing slightly as I take us both down to the carpet because there is no way I can stand a second longer, and I want my cum to stay in her for as long as it can. And hell, that thought makes my dead cock twitch back to life. Katy feels it and giggles breathlessly as she rests against me, letting me play with her mangled hair.

Can she hear how my heart is beating against her ear? Fuck, I hope not.

"We're going to ruin your rug," she warns.

I scrub a hand across my face and blow out a silent breath. "I couldn't care less. It's a rug. One I didn't even pick out. Besides, I'll have to redecorate this room if there will be a kid here eventually."

She rolls onto her back, and I roll on my side, propping my head up with my hand and taking in the woman before me. The one who has her knees bent in the air and her legs crossed at the ankles. I don't know if that's even medically a thing, and I doubt she does either, but I don't challenge it. I take in the lines of her perfect tits and muscular thighs and smooth belly. The dark hair that's fanned around her and the summer sky blue of her eyes.

*Control, Bennett. Remember why you're doing this and think of nothing else.*

"Are you moving in with me?"

She laughs. "Wow. Yeah. That." Another laugh. "I hadn't gotten that far. I realized I was ovulating and that sort of drove the train."

I reach out and unstick some of her hair that's matted to her forehead back from her face, wanting to see her eyes and read her face. "Are you having second thoughts?" *Please tell me you're not regretting this.* I couldn't take it if she changed her mind.

"Second thoughts? No." She treats me to the most breathtaking smile. "I'm excited, Bennett. More than just from the hot, hot sex."

I smirk. "Hot, hot sex?"

"Do you have a better name for what that was?"

"That was way more than hot. That was out of this world incredible." I run my fingers down the slope of her neck, tracing the bones of her shoulder, following my finger as I touch her. If I'm being honest with myself, it was the best sex of my life, but I don't tell her that. She doesn't need to know, and it wouldn't help me to say it, so I pull my hand away.

"I need to think about moving in here. It's risky. I mean, all of this is, but living here ups that ante and increases the risk of us getting caught."

She's right, of course. The risk is far greater for me than for her. It was a stupid thing to offer. A dangerous thing to offer and not just from the risk of getting caught and ruining my career for good. So why do I want her to move in regardless of all that?

She tilts her head and squints at me. "Are you okay with that?"

"Of course," I say easily. "Katy, all I want is for you to be comfortable. I realize I need you a hell of a lot more than you need me."

That thought hits me like a sledgehammer, and instinctively I sit up, finding my track shorts on the floor and hastily tugging them on. That's what's going on with my heart. That's why it's beating like this.

I swore after what I went through, I'd never emotionally put myself on the line with someone again, and though I'm not in love with Katy and have no plans to change that, I'm still vulnerable to her. I'm still handing her a huge chunk of my heart and praying she doesn't stomp all over it before shredding it to pieces.

Katy holds all the power right now, and that's why we need a contract. It's why we need boundaries. Because when I look at her, I get lost in everything amazing that she is. She's funny and beautiful and smart and so herself. She has people around her who love her, who can't get enough of her. Being around Katy is warm sunshine on your face in the middle of winter. She feels incredible, and she makes me feel incredible. She makes me feel young and alive. Like the guy who used to watch her and think about her and then one night kissed her.

Like, once again, I have possibility in my life, and she's that possibility.

Only that's not the reality for us anymore. I'm thirty-eight years old, and other than work and my mother, what do I have? When I met Liz, she was fun, smart, and exciting too. She was sweet and kind, and I thought honest. I thought she was my other half. The woman I could trust myself fully with.

So yeah, it's easy to look at Katy and want to be near her just to absorb some of her warmth and sunshine. Just to feel like I'm special enough to be on the inside of her circle. She's exactly as Wes said. You can't help but love her. But loving Katy is the last thing I want, and I know that if I don't start protecting myself now, then I'll really be in trouble.

Katy gathers her clothes and goes to find the bathroom,

and I head into the kitchen to make some coffee. The sun is just starting to rise over the eastern part of the city, and I lean against the back door, staring out at my yard. A yard I haven't been in once since I bought the place, not even to barbecue.

I have this big house full of empty rooms with only the hope of one day filling them.

"Hey," she says, her voice light, almost like she's afraid of disturbing me. I turn and look at her, at how sweet and lovely she is, and that lightness I feel in my chest every time I see her is back. It's become a thing now; I might as well get used to it.

"Hey. Coffee's brewing if you want some."

"Bennett?"

"Yeah." I twist and lean back against the glass. "What's wrong?"

She walks slowly up to me, her fingers trickling along my face. She stares at me for a very long, quiet moment, just touching me, searching my eyes, and then she smiles in a way that tells me she just worked something out.

"Do you have plans today?"

"I was going to take my mom out for brunch, but that was it."

"Do you know who Mason Reyes is?"

My brows scrunch at the change in topic. "Uh, the football player?" Then I cough out a small laugh. "He's your cousin, right? You mentioned him when we were stuck in the elevator." Only I didn't put it together at the time.

"Yep." She rolls on her feet with a triumphant smile. "He's in the middle of preseason, but he doesn't have training camp today and decided he wanted to throw a rooftop barbecue, so that's what we're doing today. There's a pool too, so it'll be fun."

"Is there anyone in this city you aren't related to?"

She gives me a cheeky wink. "Just you. But I'd like you to come with me."

"As your date?"

"No," she says, echoing what I said to her last night when she asked if me bringing her to my house was a date. "Not exactly. I want you to meet my family. I want you to make friends with them because if we're going to have a baby together, it's important to me that they know you and trust you. And also…" she trails off, licking her lips and giving me a cautious, almost apologetic look. "I think you could use some people. Some friends."

I emit a humorless chuckle. "I look that sad and lonely, huh?"

She shrugs. "Yes, you do. But they're good people, trustworthy people, and I know you'll like them. So what do you say?"

Trustworthy people. The way she says that so easily. I thought I had those in my life. I would have sworn to it. I redirect us. "You want to bring your boss to your family party?"

She rolls her eyes. "I think you're a lot more than just my boss now, Bennett."

I run my hands across her cheeks and into her hair. "I'd love to come. Thank you." I lean in and kiss her. "I'd like you to come and meet my mom."

She smiles against my lips. "I was so hoping you were going to ask me to."

My chest clenches, but I push it aside as I deepen the kiss, my cock stirring, reminding me that I only fucked her once. Her hands twist up into my hair, and somehow I have her shorts and my shorts off and I'm lying her down on my kitchen table. My mouth continues to devour hers as I hitch up one of her legs around my waist, slide her to the edge of the smooth wood surface of the table, and then thrust straight in.

And just like before, she's insanely fucking tight. And feels so unbelievably good—too good—I can hardly think about anything else other than her. It's only my second time being inside her, but I have no idea how I'll stop. Fucking Katy is the sort of thing I'll crave constantly. Especially if she's living here with me.

Why did I do that? Why did I put myself in that position?

I'm going to go from fucking her to not fucking her? How? How when she feels like this? So… perfect. So *right*.

I push all that away as I continue to slide in and out of her. Deeper, harder, to the point where I stand and hold her hips so she can't drift away from me. Her tits bounce and sway beneath her T-shirt, her eyes are shuttered tight, and I watch her. I get lost in how stunning she looks with my cock inside of her.

Her legs climb up to my shoulders and I lift her ass off the table, nailing her at the perfect angle. She comes quickly this time, and I follow immediately after, falling forward and bending her in two so I can kiss her lips as I finish shooting inside her.

"I think I'm dead," I murmur, my head on her chest, listening to her racing heart and every breath. She giggles, the sound vibrating through me, yanking a smile across my lips. Her nails scrape down my scalp, and my eyes close. A contented hum emanates from my lips, and I don't want to move. Not ever. I want to stay like this, inside her, with her hand in my hair and my head on her chest, nestled between her tits forever.

I haven't been happy in so long, but right now, I'm so fucking happy, and I don't ever want this high to die.

My cock gives a twitch—how, I have no clue—but I feel her shift against me, pushing me back.

"Nu-uh. I need to go home and shower and change before I meet your mom. And I want us to fuck like crazy tonight. Like I want to go to this party, have a few drinks with you, then come home and tear each other's clothes off because we've wanted it all day and denied ourselves."

Come home. The way she said that…

I clear my throat, pull out of her, and help her to stand. I grab her some paper towels, but I also watch as she gets dressed, and yep, hard again already. She does something on her phone, but once her clothes are back on and my shorts are too, I step into her, pressing myself against her so she feels just how hard she's gotten me. Again.

"How?" She laughs as I kiss and nibble on her neck, unable to get enough of her.

"It's you," I tell her, and then freeze because it is her. I never had the urge or desire to go more than once or twice with Liz. Even when I thought we were trying for a baby, I was never this… insatiable with her.

"I thought old men had trouble getting it up."

I pinch her nipple through her shirt and bra, making her yelp and slap my hand away.

"Obviously, I don't have that problem. I'm not going to be able to keep my hands to myself," I admit, pulling back and meeting her sensational blue eyes.

Her arms wrap around my neck, and she nibbles on my chin. "That's part of the fun. The build-up. The anticipation."

I kiss her again because I have to kiss her again. I can't get enough of kissing her.

She kisses me back with lots of tongue and a little grinding and then she slips away. "I'm going home to sleep for an hour or so." She takes a step away from me and then another, and I want to chase after her. I want to scoop her up in my arms, throw her over my shoulder, and carry her upstairs so I can fuck her in my bed. And then in my shower.

"Pick me up and we'll go have brunch with your mom."

I shake my head and step forward. "Wait. I'll drive you."

She slips her phone out of her back pocket and wiggles it at me. "My Uber is pulling up now. I'm good. See you in a couple of hours, Doctor." She winks at me and then leaves, shutting the front door behind her, and I sag back against the glass of my back door and sigh.

I'm going to introduce Katy to my mom as the woman I'm trying to impregnate. And Katy is going to introduce me to her family as her boss who's trying to knock her up. Great. Her cousins are likely going to kick my ass, and I wouldn't exactly blame them.

I scrub my hands up and down my face. This is getting complicated fast.

# Chapter Fourteen

## Bennett

The second Katy left, I emailed my lawyer and asked him if he could recommend a good family attorney to draw up the contract. Boundaries. That was the word I kept mentally repeating while I drank my coffee, took a shower, and combed through my closet. It was the same word I kept repeating even when I put on a particular blue T-shirt, knowing how it made the blue in my eyes stand out and fit my body perfectly since I'd seen women stare at me in it on numerous occasions. I had the word on my tongue when I sprayed on some cologne—cologne I hadn't worn in years—and while I packed a small bag with swim trunks and a towel knowing I'd likely get to see Katy in a bathing suit, hopefully a bikini.

But the moment Katy comes out of the building she texted me the address for, since I dropped her somewhere else last night, wearing a pink sundress with a heart-shaped neckline that hugs her chest and then flows out at the waist, stopping just above her knees, cute matching flats, pretty makeup on, and her hair up in a playful ponytail I want to wrap around my fist, that word feels like a joke. Like the universe is pointing and laughing at me for already being such a sucker and developing a real and serious crush on this woman when I absolutely should not.

It's as if the universe is reminding me that years ago, I wanted Katy Barrows more than I'd ever wanted anyone. From the moment I set eyes on her, I had to have her.

And I didn't.

I stayed within the lines as I always did—which made the sexual misconduct allegations even more ironic and harder to swallow—and I let her slip through my fingers and left her with only a kiss shared between us. Now we're in the same city again and I'm her boss—still fucking forbidden.

But this morning, I had her.

Every perfect, incredible inch of her. *Finally.*

And instead of making me want her less, instead of making me feel like I scratched a long overdue itch, it's made me want her more. The sort of more you pray has an end, or at least an enough button. Because right now Katy is all I see. My every obsessive thought is tied to her. And I want her naked and moaning my name continuously.

I could say it's a result of all those years of wondering. All those thoughts I had about her when she was just a student. Or hell, even a rebound after getting screwed over by my wife and best friend. But I'd be lying.

I'm starting to think the biggest mistake of my life was not fighting for Katy from the start.

"Hey," she chirps as she gets in, smelling like candy and vanilla as she buckles up. "Did you sleep?"

"No. I got a few hours last night, so I'm okay." *You look beautiful* nearly slips out, but this isn't a date, and I need to stop thinking of her that way.

She squirms on the seat against the cool leather and takes a deep inhale. "I got about an hour, and it was heaven. So weird how our bodies are adjusted to functioning on such little sleep, and any we get is like a bonus." Her head twists in my direction as I pull out into Boston traffic and head toward my mother's condo. "It's funny, I never asked, but I'm just realizing now, did you grow up in Boston?"

"I did. Well, I was born in Southie but grew up on the south shore about thirty minutes outside of the city."

"That's wild considering we met in Baltimore. I grew up in the house you dropped me off at last night."

"Your uncle's place?"

She nods, inhaling again without trying to be obvious about it, and I mentally high-five myself for going with the cologne, even as I mentally berate myself for the high-five. I'm so fucked.

"I should warn you about my mom," I start, twisting my hand on the wheel.

Katy pokes my shoulder with her finger, and when I glance over at her, from this angle and the way her dress is catching on her, she has an incredible amount of cleavage showing, and I hate my stupid dick for being so fucking fascinated by all things Katy that I lose every other train of thought.

"I should warn you about my cousins, but I won't. You'll just have to face them and live to tell about it." She laughs at my expression. "Don't look so panicked. They want this for me. I mean, minus you, but they'll adjust. I already called Owen this morning and told him, so he knows."

"And how did he take it?" Owen seems like someone in her life who could make or break this for me. I'll admit, I'm curious about their relationship. What the full dynamic is.

"With a lot of concern and questions, but like I said, he'll adjust. Same with your mom, right? You told me she wants you to have babies."

"She does, but—"

"But I think I'll have an easier job of winning her over, so don't worry. Moms love me. Zane's mom called me crying for weeks after I left him, telling me how much she missed me. You're the one who has to win over like ten thousand people, and half of them are overprotective males."

"Awesome," I deadpan. "Because it's not as if I come off like a dick or anything because I'm quiet and not the most social." That's always been who I am. Quiet. Reserved. More so now than I ever was before, and I definitely blame my ex-wife and ex-best friend for that. But I was always more the type of guy who had a few close people instead of a large circle, and Katy is the complete opposite of that.

She smiles, resting her arm on the center console. "You've never been a dick. At least not that I've seen. I don't know why that was a rumor about you, but I don't think it's true. You can be quiet and reserved as you said, which isn't a bad thing in my opinion. Vander is very quiet and most definitely comes off as a dick because he sort of is one. Owen is very cautious with people and also a bit of a dick, but warm and sweet once you get to know him. Mason is like his dad—wild, funny, and totally off the walls. They're the ones I'm closest with, but there are a lot of others you'll meet. Oh, and then there's Kenna and Keegan, and Owen's little sister Wren and Tinsley Monroe as well as Sorel and Selena—"

"Jesus, Katy," I interrupt, running a hand through my hair.

"Second thoughts with me?"

My face flips in her direction. "Never," I tell her. "Not for a second. I mean, it's a lot and complicated as hell, but I want to have a baby and I think you'll be great at it. We can figure it all out. And yes, my mother will love you. But she can be a lot sometimes."

She snorts. "So can I. I'm not just a lot. I'm extra almost all the time. Just wait till I'm pregnant and hormonal, sending you out for melon balls at two a.m."

"Melon balls?" I question, my brows raised in her direction before I turn back to the road.

"I don't know. I went for the most obscure thing I could think of on the fly."

"I emailed my attorney this morning for the name of a good family lawyer who could draw up—"

"I have a name," she interjects. "He's the lawyer who Uncle Cal hired when he was trying to keep me. He's one of the best in the city."

I blink, clutching the back of my neck. "Do you think we can meet with him?"

"Absolutely. I think we should. I mean"—she pokes me again—"we could already be pregnant."

I shake my head. "That's such a wild thought."

"But a cool one. And I think we should wait until I'm actually pregnant for me to move in."

I sigh. I had a feeling she was going to say that. And while part of me should be relieved at that—if for no other reason than keeping my distance and helping me keep myself in better control with her—it's not what I want. "But the trying—"

"Could take months."

We come to a stoplight, and I turn to look at her, holding nothing of myself back. "I don't care. Katy, I want this. I wanted this before I knew sex was an option, so it's not about that. If we end up having to do IUI or IVF, I'm good with all of it. I never thought I'd get here. I never thought I'd have this opportunity. I'm not looking to take over or control your life. I just want to be part of everything we're doing, and right now, if we're trying to do this naturally, then I think you living with me just makes the most sense."

"So we can fuck whenever we want," she clarifies, and I can't help it, I smile like the devil she's turning me into.

"Yes," I tell her, not even trying to hide it. "So I can fuck you whenever we want. First thing in the morning or when we come home late from a shift and are tired and hungry. When we both want a shower or it's a random Saturday afternoon and you happen to walk into the kitchen looking fucking hot and I have to have you that very second. I don't want you racing to my doorstep at four in the morning because you realize you're ovulating." My hand cups her jaw. "And if I'm on borrowed time with fucking you, then Katy, I want to fuck you as much as I can until we have to stop."

The light turns green, and I release her, driving down the street and heading for my mom's place. Katy is silent, chewing on her lip and taking in the city beyond the glass.

"I'm a little worried about that."

"Which part?"

"The fucking as much as we can until we have to stop."

My insides plummet, but I force myself to do the right thing and ask, "Would you like to keep it to only around the times you're ovulating?"

"I think so. I thought about it this morning on the drive home, and sex with you was… well, you were there so you know how amazing it was. If we're doing that constantly, that's a slippery slope."

She's right, of course. It's not what I want, but it's the smart play, and I have to stop thinking with my dick. I grip the steering wheel tighter, already feeling a weird sense of loss I shouldn't. "Then we'll start a day before you're supposed to ovulate and end a day after you should be done. We can even get those fertility sticks if you want."

"Okay," she whispers after a few minutes. "I'll move in with you. For all of those reasons. You're right. Running to your house at odd times is insane, and if we're planning to have me move in after I'm pregnant anyway, then I guess it just makes sense to do it now."

I do everything I can to hold in my excited smile, hating how my chest fucking flutters like I'm a goddamn giddy kid. "Good."

"Good," she parrots, turning to me with a taunting gleam, and I start to slip.

"Great."

"Excellent."

That smile is twitching up my lips. "You're wet, aren't you?"

"And you're hard," she throws back at me. "I can see the outline of your dick." But that's not good enough for her. My little vixen reaches over and squeezes me through my shorts until I groan and grunt and have to move her hand away.

I pull into a spot outside of my mother's building. "No more dick touching. We're here."

She pivots to look out her window. "Nice building."

"It is. I bought it for her after my dad died and left me a fortune that he never paid her in child support or alimony. Actually, he never paid her much at all to take care of me."

"Oh, that's awful. Your poor mom. Can I ask about your dad?"

"My dad was a fucking asshole who never made time for me or my mom. He cheated on her and then left us. But he had a business that did well and then another that did better. He married two more times, both to women I never met before he divorced them too. He died alone, which I'm not sad about, and I don't care if that makes me a bad human, and since I was his only living heir, everything went to me."

She flips back around. "My parents had life insurance that went to me along with the proceeds from the sale of their house. My uncle put it into a trust for me, but I haven't touched it. I'm a type 1 diabetic, and, well, I think we all know the challenges that come with that. So I've kept it as a nest egg. And that has nothing to do with my uncle Cal or my stepmom Layla's money—and trust me, they each have plenty —or what they have planned for me."

"Why are you telling me that?"

"So you know I don't give two shits about your money."

I didn't think she did, but having her say it is more of a

relief than I anticipated. "Our kid or kids will never have to worry."

She nods. "I know."

I roll my eyes because she knows that's not what I meant. I meant I'd take care of them. I know she will too, but I like knowing I can do that for my kids. I want to be the one to provide for them the way my father never did for me, and if Katy would let me, I'd do the same for her, though I know she won't.

"So, you are *Surprise Baby for the Billionaire Doctor*?"

I smirk. "I damn well hope so."

She stares at me, and I stare at her, the heat and tension between us rising. My hands twitch. My skin hums. I want to fucking maul this woman. That is until my mother knocks on the glass of Katy's window. "Is she a brunch treat for you or me?

Fuck.

Katy bursts out laughing and then flies out of the car, hugging my mother—why is she hugging my mother?!—and then tells her to take the front seat and explains how she works for me but that she hijacked my brunch with her.

My mother is glowing. She doesn't even require electricity.

The second after my mother buckles up and Katy is in the back seat and we head toward Brookline, where my mother's favorite deli is, she asks, "So, Katy, tell me, are you dating my son?"

"Mom," I warn.

"No," Katy answers evenly. "I'm not. I'm not dating right now and have no plans to."

"Why ever not?" My mother is appalled.

"Well, Paula, I'll be honest with you. Love hasn't been my bestie recently thanks to a jerk of an ex, and I have a lot of other things going on in my life at the moment, so for now, I'm not dating."

"That's too bad. Bennett has been saying the same bullshit to me since he left his lying, cheating, bitch of a wife. What is it with your generation allowing one bad burn to scar you instead of allowing it to heal and then move on as nature intended?"

"Darwinism," I quip.

"Nice try." My mother pats the side of my face as we come to a stoplight. "It's such a shame when young people stop living their lives to their fullest just because of one asshole. And interesting that despite both of you having a moratorium on dating and love, you brought your *friend* to meet me." She twists slightly, catching Katy's eyes now that she's sitting in the middle of the back seat. "Katy, dear, do you intend to never date again and does that mean you'll never want children?"

My forehead hits the steering wheel as a growl collapses my lungs. "Mom!"

"What?" She feigns innocence. "It's a simple question. She seems so young compared to you. It'd be a shame for her to give up on all facets of her life simply because she dated a dickhead of a man who didn't appreciate her."

For fuck's sake.

"I am young compared to him," Katy toys, throwing me a smug look in the rearview mirror before she reengages my mother. "Your son is not only my boss but eight years older than me," she whispers playfully. "Even though neither of us is interested in dating or falling in love, it's totally the stuff of awesome smutty romance, right?"

My mother is enthralled. "You're a reader too?"

Katy scoots to the edge of her seat, as close as she can get between us. "When I can be. I don't have a ton of time. I'm a fifth-year resident. But I won't lie and say I don't seek out the smuttiest smut with the best plotlines I can find."

"I don't care about the plot if the sex is hot," my mother

admits, and I start to vomit in my mouth. Both women ignore that.

"I love the sexy stuff, but I start to lose interest halfway through if there isn't anything else to the story."

My mother nods conciliatory. "I can see that, and since Bennett won't read erotica to me, I've had to start getting books with more plot to them to keep him reading to me. But you've done a nice job dodging my question."

Katy glances quickly over to me and then back at my mom. "Eventually, I'll date again. Just not for a while. And I have thought about having kids. I want them desperately. You see, I have type 1 diabetes, and then a few years after I was diagnosed with that, I was diagnosed with grade three endometriosis and have been treated for minor PCOS related to my diabetes. Growing up, I wasn't painted with the happiest of pictures fertility-wise. But I had a successful surgery for the endometriosis, I'm in good control of my blood sugars, and my kidney function tests are normal, and per my OB, my ovaries are clear of cysts. So, with that, I've decided to try and have a baby because who knows how long this window will be open and stay that way. Endometriosis has up to a forty percent regrowth rate. But your son—your amazing son—has agreed to help me with that."

I'm paralyzed. I didn't ask why she wanted a baby so badly and why she wanted it now. I had overheard some of what she had said to her cousins about it, but I didn't question it beyond that. Hearing her say that? The way she plays it as if *I'm* the one doing *her* the favor?

It's too much.

My mother's hand covers her lips. Her eyes—the same color as mine—are larger than I've ever seen them. She stares at Katy, who is smiling so wide all her perfect white teeth are showing, and then over at me before turning back to Katy. "Really? You and my son…"

"Are getting it on," she tells my mother plainly, and I choke. *Jesus*. Only Katy.

She smirks at my expression, throwing me a wink in the rearview.

My mother laughs, loud and full of mirth, but then grows so very serious as she stares at my profile. "You're telling me you're getting it on with this beautiful young woman, and in doing so, you're trying to make me a grandmother?"

"Yes," I finally manage, pulling into a parking spot on the street and facing her. "We are."

My mother's eyes instantly glass over, and with that, mine do too. I can't handle my mother's emotions. She knows what this means to me, and I know what it means to her. No words are necessary between us.

"But you're not dating?"

I shake my head. "We're not dating and have no plans to." I need to make that clear to her because I know how my mother is and how quickly and easily her love of love will take over and run rampant.

"But she's lovely and so full of life."

I sigh. "She is. That doesn't change anything."

"Well then. This is quite the special morning." My mother clears her throat and wipes at her eyes. "I hope they have those blintze things today. I could eat all four of them."

"I'm a big fan of the pastrami scramble," Katy offers. "But if you're game, I'll give you some of mine for some of yours."

My mother's eyes light up. "You're on. But you have to order it with an everything bagel."

"Pshaw. Is there any other bagel to order with that? And you have to order yours with strawberry preserves."

"Is there any other way to properly have a blintze?"

"Not as far as I'm concerned." Katy winks at her and then hops out of the car and heads straight into the restaurant, giving me a moment alone with my mother who is nothing but smiles.

That is, until she pats my cheeks and says, "My boy, you can say whatever you want, but you are so fucked with that one, and I don't even mean that literally."

# Chapter Fifteen



"Ladybug!" Mason shouts out, using the nickname that's never managed to die off, despite the fact that I've hit three decades of life and am a successful surgeon. He's wearing Boston Rebels red swim trunks, and an unlit cigar hangs limply from his smiling mouth.

"Ladybug?" Bennett questions with a crooked grin.

"Yep. You'll hear all sorts of nicknames for me today. Lady killer," I throw back at Mason because he pretty much is. Tall, good-looking, muscular, funny, and a famous NFL quarter-back for the Boston Rebels. Need I say more? I throw my arms around my cousin, and he lifts me high off the ground, hugging me fiercely.

"Glad you could make it, babe. And I see you brought a snack for Owen and Vander."

I roll my eyes. "Mason, this is my…" Dammit, we didn't work out what I'd call him.

"Boss, friend, and potential baby daddy," Bennett finishes for me, making my eyes go wide. "Nice to meet you, Mason. I'm a huge Rebels fan."

Mason shakes his hand automatically and then stalls mid-shake to turn back to me with a slow head swivel. "I'm sorry, did he just say potential baby daddy?"

"He did." I beam because I might as well roll with it.

Mason looks back over at Bennett, and gives him a long once-over, doing the guy sizing him up thing. "Oh shit, this is going to be a fun afternoon. I don't even have to break your fingers, brother. Owen and Vander will fuck you up so hard you'll be crying for your mama in no time."

Boys. Like, really?

"I doubt that," Bennett says confidently. "But it'll be amusing to watch them try."

"Bold. I like that. Hold onto that one. You'll need it for all the ass-beating that's about to go down."

Bennett takes a step and then Mason does too, and what in the Wide World of Sports is going on here?

"They'll love him," I state firmly as I step in between them, pushing Mason back with my hands. "I mean it, Mason. I don't want any of this macho, overprotective thing all you assholes feel the need to do to show off your dick size. Last I checked I'm a grown woman who can handle her own life without intervention." Sorta. But anyway. "You all know how important this is to me. If you scare him off, or even worse, kick the shit out of him for bullshit reasons, I'll never forgive you or make lasagna for you again."

Mason's incredulous green eyes whip over to me with the speed of a bullet. "You're threatening the lasagna over *this guy*?" He juts his thumb in Bennett's direction.

I fold my arms. "And the game-day egg casserole."

"Fuck," Mason hisses. "You're serious with this."

"As serious as my cinnamon rolls. I mean it, Mase. This isn't me bringing a boyfriend around. This isn't romantic. It's both of us wanting the same thing and nothing more. And frankly, you're all too old to act like juvenile asswipes on the playground." Especially since I'm listing the only foods I make well. Cooking is not my forte, but for some reason, Mason loves what I make him.

Mason searches my eyes, absorbing my words before he goes back to Bennett. "Welcome to the family, Bennett." He slaps Bennett on the shoulder. "As long as you swear in blood that you're going to be good to my girl here and understand that I will fucking murder you if you're not, then we're cool."

"I guess we're cool then," Bennett states, and the two of them do some sort of male stare-off, and then Mason cracks up and so does Bennett.

"It's nice to see you again, Doctor. I think we really got her with that one." He fist-bumps Bennett.

"What?!" I squawk. "You know each other?" My head volleys back and forth like a tennis ball during a match.

Mason is laughing at my appalled expression. "Do you remember when we played Minnesota last year and I got hit in the gut and they were worried I had some internal bleeding?"

"Yeah."

"Dr. Bennett Lawson was my doctor in the hospital when they brought me in. In fact, two of my guys got stuck in an elevator with him. So when Owen told me this morning that you were bringing him today, I texted the good doctor and he suggested this just to fuck with you a bit."

I turn on Bennett. "You know Mason and you never mentioned it to me?"

"I told you I got stuck in an elevator with two linemen when their quarterback got hurt."

"Uh. So. You didn't say which quarterback."

He shrugs, but there is no hiding the humor dancing in his eyes. "Patient confidentiality."

"Fuck your patient confidentiality." I smack his shoulder. "You planned this just to mess with me?"

"You told my mother we're getting it on," he counters.

Touché on that. But still!

"You're both assholes."

I start to storm off, only to swivel back around and point a finger at Bennett. "I don't care if you're my boss or potential baby daddy. You're on your own now. I'm going to change and swim with my girls. And Mason was right. Vander and Owen will fuck you up the ass. Enjoy. I hope they don't use lube. And Mason? Good luck winning your next preseason game without my breakfast casserole because I'm not making it for you." I spin back around and head for the bathroom to change. Jerks. I can't believe they did that.

"That's not fair!" Mason cries out indignantly. "I'm on your side. It was a joke."

"Tell it to someone who isn't ovulating!"

"You're not mad," Bennett throws out.

I'm not, but he can't see my smile to know that.

"You get no access until I say so, Buster!" I yell back at Bennett.

Even if he did totally get me, it was very funny and a bit un-Bennett-like. Which I like because it means he's loosening up a bit. And I like that he knows Mason and took care of him.

I change into my bikini, do a quick check of my blood sugar to make sure it's okay after the huge breakfast I had before, and then head out to the pool area that's filled with my people laughing, drinking, eating, and hanging out. It's the best, and it brings an automatic smile to my face. Glancing around, it's easy to spot Bennett with his dark, wavy hair, tall frame, and broad shoulders.

He's talking to Owen, Vander, and Stone, and seems to be in one piece. He must sense me watching him because suddenly his eyes are on mine before they dip down and take in every line of my red bikini. His lips part as if he's sucking in extra air, and when his eyes meet mine again, they're smoldering. I give him a wink that makes his lips bounce and shake his head.

That is, until Owen steals my attention. "Kit-Kat!"

Ugh. Men today. Can't a woman get a break?

"What's up?" I call back without going over to them since they're by the built-in bar area and I'm halfway to the pool on the other side.

"Tell me I shouldn't kill him," Vander says plainly to me before taking a sip of his beer, and I roll my eyes.

"You shouldn't kill him."

"I think it's kickass, Katy. Ignore them."

I blow Stone a kiss. "That's why I like you the best." I glare at Owen who is not happy.

"You didn't tell me everything there was to tell," Owen accuses, dragging a hand through his thick, brown hair.

"No?" I feign innocence. "Sucks to be you then. You don't get to hear about my sex life. BFF or not, I reserve the naughty talk for my female besties unless you want to start hearing about orgasms and oral."

Owen makes a face like he just swallowed a bug, Vander curses, Stone cracks up, and Bennett wipes a hand across his forehead, but I can tell his lips are twitching.

"Are we even yet?" I ask Bennett, and he turns and stares at me. I can tell we've drawn a bit of an audience.

"Not even close. You just upped the ante."

I smirk at him. "Looking forward to it, Doctor. Be nice to him, guys. I already threatened Mason's food, and I can come up with something for you too."

"We should talk about this," Owen calls out.

"We will. But later." Because suddenly two redheads, a blonde, and a brunette surround me. Keegan, Kenna, Wren, and Tinsley are all over me.

"Yeah, leave her alone!" Wren shouts at Owen, who is her older brother. "She's ours to get the dirt from." She turns on me, flipping her insanely long blonde hair back and leveling me with a don't bullshit me stare. "Please tell me you're screwing the hot doctor I just met before my brother came in and stole him from me. Because holy shit is he freaking delicious. A bit old for me, but for that"—she waves a finger in his direction—"I'd make an exception."

"I'm screwing the hot doctor," I tell her as I grab a Diet Coke from the table by the pool and pop the top on the can.

"I knew it!" Keegan shouts triumphantly. "I freaking knew it. That took you all of… what? Not even two weeks. We should have had a bet on it. Why didn't we have a bet on it?"

I poke her with my elbow. "Stop. I hadn't planned to sleep with him, and it's not what you think." I swallow, suddenly feeling a little nervous and shy. "We're sleeping together because we're trying for a kid."

"I'm sorry. What?" Kenna is about to shake me.

"He's going to hopefully be my baby daddy."

I get four sets of round eyes. "Your baby daddy," Tinsley parrots.

I nod. "Yep." I take a long pull of my soda.

"That beautiful man over there is going to be the father of your kid?" Wren looks like she's about to pass out.

"That's the plan."

"And you didn't freaking tell us?!" Keegan yells, only for Kenna to roll her eyes at her twin and calm her down with a hand on her shoulder.

"It all just happened last night and this morning," I explain, taking a sip of my soda and then rolling the can between my hands. "His mom is sick with cancer, and he wants to be a dad for himself and to give her a grandchild, but he just ended a horrible marriage and doesn't want a relationship. It's perfect."

Kenna snorts, eyeing me dubiously. "Uh-huh. I think I've read that book before."

"And seen the movie," Keegan follows up.

I shift my weight, some of my bravado and spunk slipping a little as I explain this to them. "It's not like that."

"Yup. Sure," Tinsley mocks. "At least not now, it isn't. But there's more. I can see it on your face. What aren't you telling us?"

I sigh because I hate that their sarcasm has a point, and if it were reversed, I'd be saying the same things to them. Only this is different. "Listen, you can't say anything to anyone. I mean it." I point a stern finger at all of them, especially Keegan since she works in the hospital with me. "This is a secret baby-making mission, and it has to stay that way."

"We get it," Wren promises.

"Good. Because I'm moving into his place."

"No wonder Owen and Vander look like they're popping aneurysms," Wren states, and I glance over to find Owen, Stone, and Vander still talking to Bennett. Owen does appear a little flummoxed, but overall, they seem to be getting along well.

"They need to get over it." I turn back to the girls. "It's just until the baby is six months old or so. He wants to be part of it. The pregnancy, the delivery, the newborn stuff. He wants to be a full-time dad without the full-time wife attached to it. He's coming out of a bad marriage, and I had a bad thing. Neither of us wants to complicate this any further."

"And yet you're moving in with your boss and having sex with him," Tinsley deadpans. "Good luck with all of that. Because your heart and your vagina aren't besties or anything."

"They're not always," I defend indignantly. "Sometimes they hate each other too and aren't on speaking terms. I messed around in college with that guy for a couple of months and didn't catch feelings." I'm getting a little huffy because I don't like the insinuation that I can't maintain a separation between sex and love.

"True," Kenna agrees, holding up a consolatory hand. "You did manage that with that guy. How'd that go with Zane since, if memory serves, you said the same thing when the two of you first started?"

I push past them and hop in the pool because suddenly it's very hot on this roof. I turn around and drop my forearms on the hardscape, setting my soda down and looking up at them. "Zane was different. He plied me with words of love and fed me every line I wanted to hear. Bennett won't be doing that. We're going to have a contract. I know it sounds bad, and if I were you, I'd be all over me about it too. But Bennett and I talked about it." Sorta. Okay, maybe we didn't talk as much as we should have. Maybe I threw myself into the deep end with this headfirst. But we can fix that. "Trust me, the sex is just, well, for sex. For procreation and nothing more, and it's only going to happen when I'm ovulating."

"So you're not enjoying it then?" Keegan folds her arms, giving me a motherly stare. "He didn't kiss you or make you orgasm? There was no foreplay? It's simple fornication and nothing more?"

I flush and stare down at my hands. "No sense in having bad sex."

"So the sex is good?" Tinsley asks, and I nod.

"How good?" Wren presses.

I glance up. "As good as your imagination, only better."

Kenna sighs and sits on the ledge of the pool, dipping her lower legs in the clear blue water. "We're happy for you, Katy. We seriously are because we know how much you want to have a baby."

Keegan comes on the other side of me, doing the same thing her twin is. "But we're also worried. He's a lot of things that a lot of women want and go for. Living with someone you're having sex with—especially really good sex—does things to people, whether we want it to or not. Plus, he's your boss and you're after a fellowship he oversees. We just don't want to see you get hurt again, or worse, seriously fall in love and then be stuck with him as your kid's father for all eternity if he's not on the same page with you."

"Not gonna happen," I promise them, only the pang of

unease I've been fighting feels like it's multiplying by the second. *That won't be us*, I silently double down on my promise. *No way*.

"Say whatever you like"—Wren smiles down at me—"but he's been watching you nonstop. Every few seconds he glances this way, knowing exactly where you are, and he lingers until he's forced to look away."

I make a dismissive sound in the back of my throat, but that doesn't stop the impossible-to-resist pull, and I turn to immediately lock eyes with him. My skin tingles, and my heart speeds up.

There are times in our lives when we can look at a situation and know that what we're doing might not be the smartest play, but we do it anyway. The lies we tell ourselves are either convincing enough that we force ourselves to believe them, or we want it badly enough that we don't care if what we're doing is wrong. That's what I'm doing now.

I don't love Bennett, and I have no plans to.

But I like him.

And I have to make myself stop that if I want a child with him.

I won't risk my heart again.

This is too important for that.

# Chapter Sixteen

# Bennett

Katy's been quiet since we left the barbecue five days ago. She was all but silent, skirting my eyes as I took her to Kenna and Keegan's apartment so she could pack a few suitcases to bring to my place. I didn't see her much at the barbecue. Her cousins Owen and Vander turned out to be everything Katy said they were, and after I swore yet another blood oath that I wouldn't hurt Katy and that if I did, they could kill me, things got better between the three of us.

Especially when Owen and I discovered we both have horrible exes and are also both friends with Jack Kincaid, Wes's son. He's actually one of Owen's best friends and the two of them grew up together, though Jack didn't mention him to me at all when he told me to get in touch with Wes. Maybe because Owen is a pediatric surgeon and not a trauma surgeon or he simply didn't come up.

That evening, Katy and I had sex—fun, hot sex, but it was missing some of the heat and spark we had that morning—and then she went to her room down the hall to sleep. That was it. By the time I got up in the morning, she was already gone, and when I got to work, we were doing more of the same dance we had the week before—avoidance.

She's friendly but distant. There but not.

It's a pattern that's continued.

Come home, have sex, go our separate ways, and then avoid each other. Wash, rinse, repeat.

At first, I rationalized that the distance between us was good. Necessary even. Important to maintain the boundaries around what we're trying to do. But the longer it goes on, the more I can't stand it. Things between us are deteriorating, and it doesn't take a genius to know that whatever her friends said to her at the barbecue is what sparked this fissure between us that's caverning into a deep chasm.

I understand her purpose with this, but isn't there some sort of middle ground? I thought that's what we had. I thought that's what we agreed upon. Hell, I thought we were in a good fucking place with each other.

But this… this is torture. Agony. I see her, touch her, taste her, but I don't feel her presence the way I did. It only makes me want her more. It's the same way I felt when I first moved to LA for my fellowship. I'd think about Katy, wonder about her, dream about her. Hell, for a long time, I regretted moving there and questioned what would have happened between us if I had stayed.

Only this time, she's right here, within my grasp, but she's also not.

I fucking *miss* her.

I miss her eyes on mine, her sweet, flirty smile, and the way she laughs and teases me.

We have sex in my bed—never hers—and then she's gone. The only proof she was ever there is her light, lingering fragrance on my pillows and sheets that I wind up burying my nose in just to keep her there with me a moment longer. I'm losing my mind.

I even went into her bathroom and replaced her bodywash with mine because I know she loves how I smell, and I wanted her to not only be forced to smell me but also smell like me. I meant it as a bit of a joke—at least that's why I told myself I did it—but she never called me out on it and I know she's using it, so now it's another thing floating unspoken between us.

I don't know what to do, and I have no one to fucking talk to about it. It's turning me into a grumpy fuck. More of a grumpy fuck than I was when I first moved back to Boston.

We have our appointment with the attorney in an hour, and Katy is in the locker room showering and changing. I've already showered and changed, but have been lingering, waiting on her. I know I need to say something to her before we put ink to paper. I need to give her an out. Even if the thought of doing that guts me.

My phone buzzes with a text.

> Katy: Just finishing up. I'll meet you at the attorney's.

I stare across the floor, taking in all the people around me, and then return to my phone, already deciding that's a totally unacceptable answer and not caring.

> Me: I'll drive you there. You can keep your car here tonight, and I'll bring you back in the morning since we both have a shift.

I watch as the three dots bounce, disappear, reappear, disappear, only to finish off with…

> Katy: I'm fine driving myself. I was thinking of sleeping at Kenna and Keegan's tonight anyway since I'm no longer ovulating.

The fuck?!

Not fucking happening.

Without thinking anything through, I storm down the hall, slipping my phone back into my pants pocket just as the women's locker room door opens and Katy emerges. Only I don't let her get anywhere before I push her back inside, shut, and lock the door behind us.

"Bennett?! What the hell are you doing?" she snaps, her voice high and loaded with shock and dismay. "This is the women's locker room."

I pin her to the closed door and get right up in her face. "Is anyone else in this locker room?"

She gulps, and I can see her mental debate. Not okay.

"Tell me the fucking truth, Katy. Now."

She swallows hard. "No. It was just me."

"Good."

In her next breath, I slide my hands to her upper thighs just beneath her ass and lift, walking her back into the locker room until we reach the space between the showers and changing areas. I slam her into the wall and press myself right into her, putting us eye-to-eye.

"What's going on, Katy?"

She makes some sort of bullshit, indignant noise like she's all upset at what I'm doing right now, but I don't give two shits. She's going to talk to me. She's going to stop hiding from me. There is only so much I can take, and I think I've officially reached my breaking point.

"I don't know what you're talking—"

"Don't," I warn dangerously. "Don't do that to me. Don't do that to us and what we're trying to do here. We have to be able to talk to each other."

She swallows and nods before slowly raising her gaze to mine. "I know."

"Tell me why you've been distant and avoiding me since the barbecue. Did I do something wrong? Did I overstep somehow or make you feel uncomfortable?"

She shakes her head. "No."

"Katy baby, you have to communicate with me. I'm going out of my mind. I have so much at stake, and I can't..." I blow out a breath, switching this up and doing what I told myself I was going to do for her. "If you need an out, you've got it. You've got it, and I won't blame you or judge you or even be angry with you. You've got that out until we know if you're pregnant, and even then, as I said, we can adjust how we do this with each other. But if you don't want a father in your kid's life or you don't want me to be that father, I need to know now."

Her arms wrap around my neck, and her blue eyes turn sheepish. "I'm not looking for an out. I want you as the father of my child."

"But?" I press because she's holding back.

"But I got spooked."

I squint. "Meaning?"

"Meaning I like you, but I don't want to love you."

Shit.

For reasons unknown and that I can't even begin to explain, that leaves me winded in the worst of ways. I don't want to love her either. I don't. But... why does it feel like there is a part of me that wants *her* to love *me*?

My throat thickens. "And you think that's a risk?"

She shrugs. "Sex confuses and complicates things. I just needed some time to get my bearings with all of this, and the distance helped."

The last thing I want right now is to stop having sex with her. I understand I will have to do that eventually, but I was, I don't know, hoping it would take us a bit to get pregnant. A couple of months. Enough time to let me have my fill of her —if such a thing is even possible. Going in, I knew the personal risk of that. I knew there was a chance I'd lose my mind and possibly a piece of my heart to her—though I did consider the latter unlikely.

I figured if the unlikely happened, it would hopefully be only temporary, and I'd learn to live with the pain if it meant I'd have her for a while and then a baby after.

But I hadn't considered her heart with that. She told me it wouldn't be an issue.

I adjust her in my hands and press her deeper into the wall so I can free a hand and cup her jaw. "Katy…" Shit. Dammit! "If you want to stop trying naturally, we can."

My chest caves in on itself at the thought of losing that piece of her. It's not even the sex per se, it's having Katy on a different level. A closer level. One of the few I have.

"I want a baby with you, Bennett, because I think you'll be an amazing father. But I don't know how to do this with you without compromising my heart or wanting yours."

What do I say? What do I do?

And why—seriously, why after all I've been through and all she's been through—does part of me want her to want my heart? I clear that away.

"So you want to stop sleeping together?"

*Please say no. Please say no.*

"No. I don't," she says after a long, tense beat. "I like having sex with you. But I need mental and physical boundaries while we're doing this part of it."

"Okay." I swallow thickly. "You've got it."

"But I want you too. That's what scares me. I don't want to stop yet. I don't even care that I'm not ovulating anymore. And that's bad, right? I shouldn't want you as much as I do."

My head slants sideways, and before I realize what I'm doing, I plow my lips directly against hers. She gasps and I take advantage, swirling my tongue with hers, groaning at the feel and taste of her like I've gone years instead of only hours without it, and this one taste is bringing me back to life.

"I want you too," I murmur against her lips. "So much. All the time. It's never enough." My hand tugs at her hair and I hold her tight, demanding full access to her mouth, demanding all of her, and not accepting anything less. Her tongue twists with mine, fighting me, angry and punishing, and yet she's so hungry she can't slow her kisses, and neither can I.

I can play this by her terms. I can force myself back and give her the space she needs. I can. I have no choice if I want this. This could be my only shot at having a baby. A baby while my mother is healthy enough to enjoy being a grandma.

There is nothing more important to me than that.

"We'll be fine," I promise her. "It's new and scary and rife with uncertainty. I get that. But we've got this. We can do this."

I start fisting at her clothes, my hand roaming, sliding over her breasts, loving how hard her nipples are for me. Katy, I've come to learn, prefers to wear dresses and skirts when she's not at the hospital and is forced to wear scrubs. And since she was set to meet me at the attorney's office, she's wearing a flowy butter-yellow skirt. I wish I could bend her over and spank her. Punish her for hiding from me, but this isn't the place, and I don't have that sort of time.

My hand dives up, and I push the center of her thong to the side so I can play with her wet pussy and pulsing clit. She wants me. She fucking wants me as much as I want her.

I continue kissing her, her hands ripping at my hair and yanking at my shirt before working the button and fly of my pants to free my cock. The moment she does, I take myself in hand, line up, and plunge in as deep as I can go.

"Fuck!" she cries. Her eyes pinch shut as her head meets the tiled wall behind her.

Her pussy convulses, gripping my cock like a fist. There is nothing like that first thrust inside her. Fucking nothing.

I hold my breath as I start to drive into her, my body desperately reacting, needing to show her that this thing between us is too good to stop or give up.

"I'm not fucking you with my heart," I tell her. "I'm fucking you with my dick. As long as we don't confuse the two, we'll be fine." I thrust deeper, panting harder. "Don't go,

Katy." *God, she feels so good.* "Please," I beg, unable to stop the words from tumbling past my lips as I continue to fuck up into her, making sure my pelvic bone hits her clit with every upward thrust. "Don't go."

She gasps, loud, and without restraint. All she can do is hold on to me, her legs around my waist, her arms around my neck. She's so fucking beautiful when she's like this—with me buried inside her making her feel good. My skin tingles, and my forehead prickles with a sheen of sweat. My hips piston, pivoting into her, moving faster, trying to outrun this… this feeling, this urgent fucking feeling that's making my chest burn.

"Tell me we can do this," I demand. I've already lost too much. I can't lose this—lose *her*—too.

Her forehead drops to mine, and our eyes cling helplessly. She licks her lips and then kisses me. "Yes," she promises, her voice barely audible. "We can do this. I want this too. I won't go. I'll stay."

I can't even begin to explain the sensation swarming like a pack of honeybees in my body. Holding her ass in my hand, my other wraps around her neck in a move so possessive and controlling I growl and nip at her bottom lip.

"Come on, Katy. Let me feel it. Let me feel how warm and tight your cunt is when it comes all over my cock." She's not ovulating anymore, I know this, but I don't care. Nothing has ever been as satisfying or felt better than coming inside her. I squeeze her neck lightly and unleash myself, fucking her with abandon. "We'll stop. When you're pregnant we'll stop."

"Ah. Bennett!"

*Yes.* There it is. "Say it again."

"Bennett," she moans, her eyes screwing up tight. "There. Oh, God, don't stop. Fuck me right there."

I do, and the second she starts to spasm around me, I let myself go and come so hard I end up pressed against her. My fingers uncurl from around her neck before I strangle her, and

I push us both into the wall for support so my legs don't give out on me.

I lick her lips, her neck, the sweet spot beneath her ear, all the while I hold her tight. And when my breathing is almost fully back under control, I rasp, "You have to talk to me. I had a wife who didn't. A wife who lied and betrayed me. I can't…" My face twists up. "I can't do that with you. Things between us have to be different than that."

"I had an ex who did the same, and you're right, we have to be different." She yanks on the back of my hair, forcing my face away from her neck so we're eye-to-eye once more. "I'm sorry. I got spooked and didn't know what to do about it."

"Sweetheart, I get being spooked. I like you too." So much more than I should. Looking at her, feeling her like this, I fucking like Katy a lot. The sort of liking that you don't want to stop or slow down because it feels amazing. It's that high you get when you've got something new and incredible and fun. But that's my own thing, not hers. "We've both been through a lot. But I have to be able to trust you and know that you'll tell me where your head is at."

She nods. "You can trust me. I'll tell you from now on."

"I'll tell you too." *That I might already be lost in you. That I might have always been.*

A fresh coat of sweat breaks out on my forehead, and my heart thunders all over again. It's the same feeling I had after I was inside her the first time. Christ, could there be anything worse?

She slides off me and gets to her feet, giving me a playful shove with a crooked smile on her lips. "Out. I have to get cleaned up now."

"Are we okay?" I check, not moving away from her until I know—until I feel it—for sure.

"We're good, Bennett. I promise."

"Are you sleeping at home tonight?" I ask.

She nods, giving me a sweet smile.

Relief floods me. "Good. Meet me downstairs in the lobby and we'll go together."

I tuck myself back in my pants, adjust my shirt, and run my fingers through my wavy hair to tame it. I made her promise to tell me where her head is, but I can't do the same with her. She'll run, and this will be over. I just have to remember my goals. Get myself back in better control. I was desperate all week with the uncertainty between us. That's all this is. Now that things are worked out, I'll settle down, and we'll settle into a groove.

It'll be fine.

I twist the lock on the door. Shit. We just did that here at work. Talk about a stupid fucking move. What was I thinking? At least no one caught us. That almost gets me out the door until I run directly into Cricket Peterson.

"Bennett?" Her eyebrows hit her hairline, understandably shocked to see me exiting the women's locker room. She's on tonight and still in her street clothes. Meaning she'll run into Katy in there when she goes to change into her scrubs.

Again, shit! Dread, along with a rush of sickly adrenaline slam through me. So. Fucking. Stupid.

"Hi, Cricket." My voice is a mess. I'm sure I am too.

"What were you doing in the women's locker room?" she asks, suspicion all over her.

"Dr. Barrows wasn't feeling well, and I brought her some water. I'm just heading out for the evening. No one else was in there but her. I made sure of it," I tack on, so she doesn't think I'm a fucking pervert trolling the women's locker room. She might not know about the rumors, but my boss does, and if she brings this up to the chief of surgery, I'm out on my ass.

"Oh." She blinks at me, taking in my weak lie and twisting it around in her head until it makes sense. At least I hope that's what she's doing. "Was it her diabetes? Because you know she has that."

*Has that?* The way she says it like it's pestilence crawling all over her and makes Katy weak enrages me. "I think she just had a hard case."

She makes a derisive noise in the back of her throat. "Pathetic, right? We *all* have hard cases. The real trauma surgeons are the ones who know how to cope with that and don't allow it to affect them."

There is no winning this in Katy's favor, and even though I want to verbally eviscerate her for being so cruel and thoughtless, I rein myself in.

"Some cases hit harder than others. I'm no different in that," I tell her simply, starting to walk away.

"Have a good night, Bennett," she calls after me, using my first name in a familiarity I don't like. It's not the name, it's her voice using it. "Will I see you tomorrow morning?"

"Likely," I throw back at her.

"Excellent. I'd love to have more time to show you my skills in the OR before we start fellowship interviews."

I freeze, my body seizing.

What am I doing? I very nearly got caught fucking Katy in the women's locker room. More than that, I have Cricket up my ass because I'm her boss and presiding over the fellowship for the trauma department.

But what's hitting me in the worst of ways is how can I pick Katy—who more than deserves it—for this fellowship? I'm fucking her. She's living with me. I'm trying to get her pregnant. If I succeed, what do I tell my boss and the board? That I'm nominating the woman pregnant with my child for a fellowship I'll be overseeing? Even if I tell them our situation beforehand, they'll never pick Katy for the position.

Moreover, they could—and likely will—fire me over this.

I told Katy this wouldn't be an issue, but someone like Cricket Peterson could and would make it one. Did I just ruin both of our careers, and what happens if our secret gets out?

I got my period. I sort of expected it when all the tests we took came back negative, but still. It sucks. On top of that, my patient died on the table this morning. There was no saving him, and I knew that, but it was just one thing on top of the other, and I still have six hours left on this bitch.

"I heard about your patient," Cricket chirps, giving me mockingly sad eyes with a stupid smirk that makes her look even more like a bug than she already is. "I guess you can't save them all. Though I'm sure I could have."

"Oh, you mean like the lady who died in your OR yesterday? The one you likely *could* have saved, but didn't?" I retort, staring at the computer screen in front of me and pretending like she's not getting to me as much as she is.

She makes an annoyed noise in her throat because there is no retort to that.

"Whatever," she snaps. "You're just upset because Bennett—"

"Delivery for you, Katy," Michelle, one of the nurses, says with a big beaming smile as she walks over carrying a cellophane-wrapped basket.

"What is it?" I ask as she sets it down before me.

"You're not allowed to have that out here," Cricket bites, her face pinched up as she eyes the large basket with derision—and likely a bit of jealousy.

Michelle and I ignore her. I'm too focused on what's before me. "It looks like a basket of goodies for you. There's a card too."

She rips the taped-on card and hands it to me. Tearing at the small white envelope, I open it, and immediately a smile spears my lips as a pack of happy butterflies fills my chest.

*Hope you're not too down, but if you are, I hope this makes you feel better. Don't stress it. We'll get there when the time is right, but, in the meantime, I can't wait to be inside you again. P.S. The baked goods are all sugar-free or sugar substitutes.*

It's in his handwriting, which means he put this together himself and had it delivered.

"Who's it from?" Michelle asks.

"A friend," I whisper, biting into my lip as I tuck the card in my pocket and then attack the cellophane with the eagerness of a kid on Christmas morning. I told Bennett—who has the day off and is going to his mother's chemo treatment to read her smut—before I left the house this morning that I got my period. He gave me a sweet kiss on my forehead, one on my nose, then wrapped me up in a hug for the ages and told me I was beautiful and perfect and that most people don't get pregnant on their first try, so I shouldn't let myself get too upset.

And now he did this.

Something so sweet and thoughtful it makes my heart pinch and my face hurt from trying to contain my smile.

Since our encounter in the women's locker room over a week ago, things between us have been great. We went to the attorney and discussed with him what we want and what we don't want, and he drew up papers we both signed. Bennett came swimming with me a couple of mornings, and I went running with him on others. We eat dinner together—healthy meals he cooks for us—when we can.

We talk. A lot. Constantly. And are so fucking honest with each other, it's insane.

I haven't slept in his bed, and we haven't had sex in mine. We're still maintaining boundaries, but this friendship we've developed feels, well, like something that is almost so much better than a friendship. Even when I'm forcing myself to remain neutral and unaffected.

So this basket is messing with that a bit, but right now, I don't care.

Inside is a small teddy bear with a pink ribbon around its neck, a candle that says *Light for Emergencies, Infused with Relaxing, Positive Vibe,* two self-packaged chocolate chip cookies, two oatmeal raisin cookies—my favorite—two brownies, two blueberry muffins—also my favorite—and a bottle of Advil that makes me laugh out loud.

He's worried I'll have cramps, which is so damn cute I could die.

I open the lid on the candle and inhale. Lavender and vanilla—my two favorite scents.

Bennett sure pays attention. I'll give him that. It makes me think about how he replaced my bodywash with his. I haven't said anything about it, but I use it and I'm positive he knows that since every time he smells my skin, he groans and growls. I like smelling like him. I like that he wants me to. And no, I don't think too closely about either of those. I also snuck a bottle of my shampoo into his shower, and though he doesn't use it, I did notice that the cap was open on it the other day so he must smell it.

"Wow!" Michelle exclaims, snapping me back. "That's some sweet gift. Whoever this *friend* is, must really care for you."

I don't take the bait, even if that makes my heart go pitter-patter faster than it already was. I know that's not how things are between us. I know he's just a good man who cares and doesn't want our first failed attempt to get me down. If nothing else, it makes me smile, thinking of what a good dad he'll be one day.

"I'm assuming it's not Zane."

I shake my head. "Not Zane." Zane would never have thought something like this up or been as conscientious about it. Even when he planned my birthday weekend away that never happened, he was taking us to Vermont so we could ski —I suck at skiing and don't love it, and he knew that.

"Katy?! Did you hear me? You can't have that out—"

"Cricket, go annoy someone else with your incessant noise. I'm moving it out of here. And because you're such a miserable, joy-sucking human, I'm not going to share my care package with you."

I give her a smug look and then take my basket toward the locker room.

When I get there, I shove it in my locker—thankfully it *just* fits—and then go to text Bennett.

Me: Thank you so much for the basket. You didn't have to do that.

Bennett: What basket?

I hesitate, squinting at the screen. Huh? If he didn't send it, then who the hell did? No one else knows—

Bennett: Ha, gotcha, didn't I?

A laugh flees my lungs, and I find myself shaking my head.

For a man who is so serious, he's becoming more and more playful.

> Me: *eye roll emoji* Ha. Very funny. Yes, you got me. Now I'm not thanking you anymore.

> Bennett: No sense of humor.

> Me: Only when things are funny.

> Bennett: If it wasn't funny, why are you smiling?

I search around, but I'm alone. My smile grows.

> Me: How do you know I'm smiling?

> Bennett: I know you, Katy baby.

The nickname is new. I've been baby and sweetheart—sweetheart is during sex, and for some reason, it's insanely hot to me—but Katy baby is when he's being fun or sweet Bennett. And I fucking love it.

> Bennett: How are you feeling though? I saw your face this morning and I wanted to do something to make you smile and feel better.

Bastard. If he's not careful, he'll make me swoon, and he's firmly in no-swooning territory.

> Me: Well, you did. I lost a patient too, so this really helped.

My phone rings in my hand, Bennett's name lighting it up, and I sigh. Perfect. Why does he have to be so freaking perfect?

I hit the green answer button. "Hey."

"Hey," he says in that gruff baritone of his that never fails to give me chills when he uses it just right. He sounds like he's walking, and then I hear a door open and shut. "I'm sorry about your patient. Are you okay?"

"Jesus wasn't even going to be able to save him. So yes. But still, that always sucks. His wife told me he likes to garden and plants her a new flower every year. I'm heartbroken for her."

"Damn. That is rough."

"Yes, but this basket is amazing."

"So are you. I hope you know that. Both as you and as a surgeon."

I blink, stare at the basket in my locker, and then slam the door shut. "How's your mom?" I ask, redirecting him. I inwardly sigh. I'm being ridiculous and need to remember to stop overthinking and overanalyzing everything. I punch in the code for my locker, remove an oatmeal raisin cookie, and then close it back up. Peeling off the foil, I shove a soft, gooey, cinnamony piece into my mouth and moan accordingly.

"Uh. She's good. Having her chemo. Um. Why are you moaning?"

"Sorry," I garble around the cookie as I swallow. "I had a bite of the oatmeal raisin."

He chuckles lightly. "Orgasmically good, huh? Since that's how you sound when I make you come."

"It is not!"

"It is too. Trust me, that sound is forever ingrained in my brain. I jerk off to the memory of that sound in the shower practically every morning."

My eyes flare, and my head whips around to make sure no one overhears that, even though I'm holding the phone up to my ear and I'm alone in here. "You do not!"

More chuckles. "I do. I even use your shampoo that somehow ended up in my shower so I can smell you as I jerk my cock. We haven't had a lot of morning sex, and I wake up hard as stone knowing you're just down the hall and I can't have you. Maybe I should start sneaking into your room and waking you up with my face between your thighs."

Heat ignites like a forest fire in my blood. "Bennett Lawson! You're fucking dirty." And getting me very wet. While I'm at work.

"Katy Barrows," he mocks playfully. "You make me that way."

I cover my mouth with my hand and abruptly stand, needing to move so I don't start squirming on the bench. "I'm riding the crimson wave. It's officially shark week in these waters."

"Next week then," he comments, unperturbed before he pauses. "Do you want me to come home tonight?"

I do. I shouldn't, but I do. So I don't even entertain it. "No. Your mom needs you tonight. She gets sick after her chemo."

"I hate the thought of you at the house alone tonight, though."

I start to pace around the changing bench. "I'll be fine, Bennett. I'm a big girl."

"I know. But I like being there when you get home."

"I'll take a bath and then watch a movie or read a smutty book."

"Without me? That's just torture. I suppose I have no choice but to get over it."

But will I?

"Are you reading to your mom?" I ask, once again redirecting us.

"Yep. Same book. We're almost at the conclusion."

"Do you think there's going to be an HEA?"

"HEA?" he questions.

"Happily ever after."

He scoffs indignantly. "I sure as fuck hope so. This couple has been through it. A surprise pregnancy, a crazy ex, some weird workplace drama, and some annoying insecurities broke them up for a bit. That was a twist my mother and I were not expecting. We thought they'd make it through without that. Why couldn't they just communicate like regular adults do?" He laughs self-effacingly. "You totally think less of me now, don't you?"

"Nope. Not even a bit." Actually, I think more of him. So much more. More than I should.

"Well, my mother is convinced they're going to have a HEA, as you put it, fuck each other crazy, and then we get the epilogue where they have the baby. She's excited to see if it's a boy or a girl."

Me too. Because I want to one day be able to tell his mom we're having one or the other. Or make Bennett's dream come true and tell her we're having twins. This thing has taken on a life of its own, but I don't have it in me to stop this train again. I'm riding it. Hell, I'm fucking conducting it.

But that doesn't mean I'm being stupid about it either.

"They better have the kid on the page."

"For real. I think that's a bit of a must. Even if the knocking-up part is my mother's favorite. Right now, with you, it might be mine too. Even if knocking you up isn't possible for a bit."

My belly swoops and my skin hums. "Bennett," I warn.

His voice drops, making delicious tingles snake up my spine. "Don't play coy, Katy. I know it's yours too."

I shake my head and bite the corner of my lip. "I'll see you tomorrow, Dr. Lawson."

I can hear the smirk in his voice when he follows that up with, "Looking forward to it, Dr. Barrows."

He hangs up, and I leave our conversation, the basket, and the fluttery feeling both have given me in the locker room. I focus on my patients and end the day with a successful surgery that was complicated and required a lot of skill and time.

With the basket in my hand, I head toward the garage.

The hot summer sun is still high in the sky, and I think I might barbecue and hang out in the backyard. I told Bennett this fall I want to plant some things back there. He hasn't done anything to it since he moved in and—

"Cricket told me your new boyfriend sent you a basket." Zane's voice comes from behind me, startling me out of my reverie.

A scowl pinches my face. Fucking Cricket. She's such a bitch, and that's not a term I throw around at women idly. She knew it would piss him off. She knew he'd come after me because Zane isn't a guy who likes to lose, and she knew that would piss *me* off. God, why do some people have to suck so badly?

"So what? You thought you'd chase after me and see for yourself?" I shake my head as I keep walking, not even bothering to look back at him. "Go away, Zane."

He grabs my arm just as I reach my car door, stopping me. "So it's true then? You're seeing someone?"

"None of your business," I tell him, shirking off his touch.

"It is my fucking business!" he yells, the sound reverberating off the concrete. "I shouldn't have to hear about it from fucking Cricket."

I laugh at his over-the-top anger because that's kind of a good one. "And I shouldn't have had to discover you were cheating on me by walking in on you fucking two women in our bed. We don't always get what we want."

"Is he going to get you pregnant? I know you're worried your endometriosis could grow back, so you're wasting time with that when you don't have to."

"I'm all set with your stud services."

He grabs my arm as I open my car door and start to get in, the basket swinging and hitting him in the stomach. He looks down at it, and fury washes over his face. "You got your period, didn't you? Either that or you miscarried."

My eyes round. "What?"

"The basket." He studies it in my hand. "I can see it all now. A teddy bear, cookies, and fucking Advil. You're trying to get pregnant, but it didn't work."

"Fuck off, Zane."

"The basket is not from your uncle or even Owen or Vander. They would have signed the card. So who are you fucking that you shouldn't be? Who is trying to get you pregnant that you don't want anyone to know about? If your new boyfriend is the real deal, why wouldn't he stake his claim by putting his name on the card?"

"What makes you think the card isn't signed?"

"Cricket told me there was no name on it."

What in the absolute fuck is going on here, and how freaking close was Cricket to me? Did she comprehend any of this too? She doesn't know about my plans to get pregnant, so I hope not.

But Zane knows.

And if he discovers Bennett is who I'm trying to get pregnant with…

"It's from Keegan and Kenna."

He gives me a mocking glare. "But we both know it's not. Who's the guy who doesn't care enough about you to tell the world you're his?"

My heart starts to pick up a few extra beats, but I do my best to keep my tone bored and my expression annoyed. "It's your brother," I retort, and it's a dig. A nasty one. One I hope is powerful and bitchy enough to push him back. He and his brother don't get along at all, and his brother hit on me relentlessly when I went to his family's house for Christmas last year just to get a rise out of Zane. It worked. They ended up in a fight—an actual fight—over it.

He turns to stone. "Fuck you with that, Katy."

I smirk. "Nope. And never again." I get in my car and

slam the door practically in his face. He steps back, his expression hard and determined, and I drive off with my heart in my throat. I have a bad feeling this could all blow up in our faces if we're not careful.

## Chapter Eighteen

*Katy*

"It doesn't matter what he thinks he knows or doesn't," Bennett says, his voice ringing through the speakerphone as I dance my way around the kitchen, listening to music on Alexa while I finish my salmon and veggie stir-fry and clean up.

Bennett called to thank me for sending over dinner for him and his mom. Comfort food from her favorite deli. Sometimes being related to big people is awesome. I made a couple of calls, and now Paula has matzo ball soup and cheese blintzes, and Bennett has a Reuben and fries, which is what he ordered that morning we went out for brunch.

"How can you say that?"

"Easy, Katy baby. He's just jealous it's not him. If he thinks you have a new boyfriend, that's great. There's no reason for him to assume it's me. Besides, he doesn't matter. His loss will forever be my gain, and that's how I'll think of this. He doesn't know I'm the man you're living with or that I'm the one who gets to be inside you. You're mine now and not his, and I protect what's mine, so you have nothing to worry about. I'll take care of him."

I huff, not allowing myself to think about the way he calls me his. It's not the first time, and I know it's just his male possessiveness speaking. *I'm fucking you with my dick and not my heart.* Ripping off my shirt, I head upstairs, flipping off the lights and going into his room without allowing myself to challenge what I'm about to do. I start the water in his mammoth bathtub—my bathroom only has a standing shower—and let it fill up.

"I don't need protection from Zane. He's an annoying bug like Cricket is. I don't want you speaking to him or getting involved. It'll only increase his suspicion. I can more than handle him on my own."

He makes a displeased noise in his throat because he knows I'm right. "I don't want him near you. I want to break his fucking fingers for even trying to be. If he comes after you again while I'm there, I'll have no choice but to respond."

"Fine." I sigh, still unhappy but knowing it's not worth the argument. I walk down the hall into my bedroom and throw my clothes in the hamper. "But I don't like it."

"You don't have to. That's how it is and how it'll be." He pauses. "Your voice is muffled, and you're moving around a lot. What are you doing?" His growl hits my ear and I shiver, smiling to myself as I go back into his bathroom so he can hear the water splashing in the tub.

"I was getting naked," I tell him simply, setting the phone on the ledge of the tub and putting it on speaker. "You see, this guy sent me a candle at work today, and I want to relax in the tub while I light it and think of him."

"Fuck. Put me on FaceTime."

I balk. But only for a second. The thought of Bennett watching me in his house while I slip into a bath in his bathroom is so hot, I can't wait to see his face. It's funny. I don't even have to remind myself anymore. He's not Zane. He's Bennett. And Bennett is so much better than Zane.

I hit the button on my phone, and Bennett picks up almost immediately, his face there on the screen, his deep blue eyes wild, only to grow frustrated as he realizes I have the phone pointed up toward the ceiling.

"Hey there." I hover my face over the phone and smile down at him. "How's your mom?"

He's not amused. "She's fine. She's already in bed and kicked me out of the house."

"What?"

"You didn't bother to look, sweetheart. I'm in the car at a stoplight. My mom called in the nurse I had hired for her, and the two of them kicked me out."

"Oh."

He chuckles. "Suddenly not so brave now that you know I'm on my way home to you?"

"I'm bleeding," I remind him.

He shakes his head. "I don't give a fuck. Your period blood doesn't scare me. I want to watch you come. At least a few times."

I wink at him and give him a peek of my boob as a bonus for that. "Good to know, but I'm not ready for that with my boss. I think my only option is to get naked in his bathroom and take a bath. Alone."

"Katy…" His voice is so dark. So dangerous.

"Yes, Dr. Lawson. Oh," I moan, sinking into the tub. "That feels so good."

"You're a fucking tease."

I lift my phone and point it at my naked body visible beneath the water since I didn't add bubbles. "I might be. But I don't care. Tell me what you would do if you were here."

"What?" He licks his lips, taking in the view I'm giving him since the tops of my breasts are very visible to him.

I cup my wet breast, pinching and rolling my nipple. "What would your hand be doing right now? Tell me and I'll do it. Fuck me with your mouth, and I'll do it with my fingers."

"Christ. You're making me sweat. Spread your legs for me, sweetheart."

Water sloshes as I spread my legs, and the angle of the camera gives him the most sinful view of me. It's making me so freaking wet and excited. Being this naked—this exposed to him—should terrify me, but for reasons I can't explain, it doesn't. What we're doing has me more turned on than I think I've ever been.

"Now what?"

He shifts around in the car, the phone down on the center console as he drives, but I can see his profile glowing against the interior lights of his car.

"Now I want you to prop your phone up in a place where I can see you and use two fingers on your right hand to start rubbing your clit and use your left hand to squeeze and play with your tits. You can't be quiet, either. I want to hear you." He makes a noise of his own. "Why don't you have a vibrator?"

I laugh at his pained expression. "I do. I just hadn't planned on the dirty FaceTime. Would you like me to go and get it?"

"What does it look like?"

"I have a few of them. One is long and thin but angled for my G-spot. One is thick and plays with my clit too. The third is a bullet and is all about my clit."

"Fuck. Christ, I'm so fucking hard for you. Go get one of them. Your choice. I'll be home in three minutes to use it on you."

"Use it on me?"

He gives me a stern look. "Is that not what I said? Go now, and you'll be lucky if I don't spank your ass red for making me wait."

I shiver and inhale my moan because, fuck, he's talked about being dirty and rough, and he has been to some extent, but I think he's been afraid to fully unleash himself on me, so he hasn't pushed it too far yet. And I haven't pushed it either because the sex with him is already so good that if he gives me something extra like that, it'll only make me crave him more. His hand around my neck in the locker room made me come so hard I was seeing stars, and he barely squeezed. I want a bit of a strong hand. Someone to force and push me places I might not otherwise go.

But after the day I had and knowing he's coming home just for me… I want this too much not to play. Hell, I think I need it.

I wink at him. "Sit tight."

Quickly wrapping a towel around myself, I scoot out of the tub and bathroom and scurry down the hall to my room, trying not to slip on the hardwood floors with my wet feet. In my nightstand drawer is my small but mighty arsenal of toys. I close my eyes and grasp the first one my hand hits—my long, thin, angled guy I've named Chris after, well, all of the Marvel Chrises—then shut the drawer and quickly pad back down the hall and into the bathroom.

"I brought a friend," I announce, climbing back into the tub.

"Show it to me."

I wave the wand back and forth, turning it on so he can hear the vibration. "Now what, Doctor? Tell me what you want me to do next."

"Now lie back and run that over your clit to get yourself nice and wet. I'm pulling in the driveway now."

I'm already there. I don't need the vibrator to make me wet, but I do as I'm told anyway. Hell, right now with the way he's commanding me, I'd do anything he asked. I've never done anything like this before. I've never had phone sex, let alone video sex, and I've never masturbated in front of anyone and certainly not while using one of my vibrators to do it.

The vibrator pulses in the water, adding an extra layer of

friction that immediately has my eyes rolling back in my head. "Fuck," I hiss.

"Tell me."

"It's a lot."

It's fucking intense is what it is, and I can't help the flush that rolls up my cheeks as I start to play with myself for his voyeuristic enjoyment. He has the phone in his hand, his eyes on the screen, and I hear the back door open downstairs and then shut. A few seconds later, the bathroom door opens, the hazy air momentarily fleeing until he shuts it behind him.

He crouches beside the tub, his eyes in the water before they dash up to my face.

"Oh, sweetheart. Look at you. You are goddamn gorgeous. Tell me how good it feels."

I slide against the tub, my eyes closing as I run the tip of the vibrator over my clit, moving it up and down and around in circles. "See for yourself."

He grunts and my eyes open, staring at him, his face above mine.

Strong lips claim me in a starving kiss, his tongue diving straight in and tasting each moan I give him. I reach up with a wet hand and tug on the back of his shirt. I want him naked. Now. I want him in the tub with me, and I want him to take control until everything else in my life fades. Zane, the fellowship, Cricket, getting my period, and not getting pregnant.

All of it.

He smiles against my lips, reaches behind his back, and pulls off his shirt. His mouth comes back to mine, his body bent in half as he works his jeans off.

I go for his hard cock, wanting to touch it, stroke it, suck it, but he pushes my hand away. "You have to come first," he pants against me.

"Are you going to jerk off?" I half-moan, glancing down at his rock-hard dick.

"Yeah. No way I can't."

"Can I watch?"

He licks his lips, his eyes blue fire as he shifts and shows me his hand wrapped around his long, thick cock. He jerks it for me, showing me exactly what this is doing to him, and I can't help it as I press the vibrator in harder against my clit.

"I wish this were you," I tell him, using my other hand to cup my breast and play with my nipple.

"Me too," he rasps, his voice hoarse. "Put it inside you now. I want you to fuck yourself with it while imagining it's my cock. Slowly at first. I like to build you up. Get you so crazy for me that you beg for more."

*Hell.* I'm panting. It feels so good on my clit, I almost don't want to move it away. "Jerk off."

"You want me to jerk off while you fuck yourself with your vibrator?"

"Yes. But I need it hard. Not soft. I'm going to make-believe it's your cock. Just as you said. I want to watch you too."

His eyes swirl the dark colors of midnight. He stares into the water as I roll the tip of the vibrator against my clit, moving it in circles and up and down until I get it just right. His jaw goes slack. "That is without a doubt the hottest thing I've ever seen in my life. Fuck, Katy. Wider. I want your thighs wider, and I want you to start fucking it."

"I'm close though," I admit, because I am. So close. "Please," I whine. "I'm so close."

"My girl needs to come?"

"Yes," I cry, my back arching and my knees hiking up and out as I move the vibrator faster. "Please, Bennett. I need to come so bad."

"Then be my good dirty girl and come for me, and after that, I want you to fuck it until you come again. I'm not going to come until you come on it, riding it the way you like to ride me."

Fuck! This man and his wicked fucking mouth. I don't stand a chance.

He grabs my tit and gives it a good, hard squeeze before turning the same attention straight on my nipple. My face pinches up as sparkles of light dance behind my eyes and I come. So. Hard. So hard with him watching me and encouraging me and telling me all kinds of things I can only half hear and pay attention to because I'm moaning so loud and splashing water around in the tub.

The moment I start to sag, he growls, "Put it in, Katy. Put the fucking vibrator deep in your cunt. You're not done yet, sweetheart and neither am I."

Sinking my teeth into my bottom lip, I slide it inside me a little at a time. In and out, going deeper each time I do it. Bennett's hand is moving briskly, and I change up the angle so he can see me fucking the toy better as I do. I'm utterly shameless as I grind against it, twisting it until it hits my front wall and G-spot so goddamn perfectly I practically scream.

I'm not going to last long, already feeling my second orgasm ready to break, and I tell him that. He starts jerking himself faster, harder, beads of precum soaking the head of his gorgeous cock, and I lick my lips, wanting to taste him. I haven't done that yet. I haven't gone down on him because I've been telling myself that going down on him is more than just fucking for making a baby. It breaks some of our boundaries, but looking at him like this, I don't care.

"I want you in my mouth."

His head falls back, and he pants out a rough breath. "I want that too. I want to do everything with you. I want to fuck and come in your every hole."

"Yes," I cry, plunging the toy in viciously. "I want this toy in my pussy while you fuck my ass."

"Jesus, Katy. You're killing me, sweetheart. I want every part of you I can get."

"Then fuck my mouth, Bennett. Fuck my mouth while I

fuck myself. I want you to feel me moan against you because this feels so good I can hardly take it."

He doesn't need to be told twice as he grabs the back of my wet head and shoves his cock straight into my mouth until it hits the back of my throat. I gag immediately and swallow, and he lets out a low, harsh groan I feel all the way down in my pulsing clit. He starts to pump into my mouth as I pump the toy into myself. His gaze volleys back and forth between my face and the toy as if he can't decide where he'd rather look.

I do my best to flatten my tongue and relax my jaw and throat, but he's so big and powerful and his thrusts have tears running down my cheeks that his thumb comes up to wipe away.

"Do you want me to stop?" he grits out, and I shake my head because no, I don't want him to stop. I want to watch him come undone, and I want to know it's because he's losing his mind in my mouth. "If you do, hold up your hand and I'll stop."

I nod against him, using my free hand to cup his firm ass, so he knows he doesn't have to stop, and I have no plans to make him.

"My filthy, beautiful girl. God, how you make me crazy. I'm getting close, sweetheart. Are you with me? I need you to come with me."

I thrust the vibrator in faster, harder, my entire body humming from the toy and the sick, twisted pleasure of it all. I've never done anything even remotely close to this before, and I fucking love it. It's a high unlike any I've experienced. My gaze flashes up to his as his mouth falls open in a blissed-out gasp, his cheeks flushed, his hair all over the place, and his rock-hard abs flexing with every pump into my mouth.

Bennett Lawson is the sexiest man I've ever seen.

It's enough to push me over the edge, and the moment he sees it, feels how I'm moaning and crying out against his cock, he starts to come, shooting straight into the back of my throat with a strangled bellow. It's so freaking hot, it steals my breath and I come again, writhing all over the toy until I practically blackout.

Before I know what's happening, Bennett is sliding from my mouth and reaching into the tub to take the vibrator from me. He shuts it off, sets it down on the ledge beside my phone, and then picks me up and out of the water, cradling me against him.

"What are you doing?"

"Making sure you don't drown," he quips, kissing my forehead. He holds me against him, his blue eyes lazy and his smile sated. "You're incredible, Katy Barrows. Every part of you." A kiss to my lips and then he's wrapping me in a towel and walking me down the hall to my room. He sets me on the edge of my bed and disappears, only to return a few minutes later wearing sweats and holding a glass of ice water. "Are you okay?"

My limbs are mush, but I'm not sure I've ever been more okay than I am now, and I refuse to think that's related to anything more than the three massive orgasms I just had. "Fabulous. Aces over kings."

"Huh?"

I giggle lightly and clear my throat before I stand up and head to my dresser to find something to put on. "That was fun," I tell him, and he nods, his eyes still on me, though he's quiet now. "I'm going to read for a bit and then go to bed."

He looks as if he wants to say more, but I don't want him to. That was… well, it was amazing, but it also played with that line. That line we continue to play with.

The dangerous one.

The one that says even though we're working to have a nonromantic, mutually agreed upon baby, what we just did was more. It was personal and intimate. He may not be Zane, but this isn't the situation to start getting in over my head with him. The more pieces of myself I hand to him, the bigger the risk this gets out of control. If I don't stop allowing myself to get lost in him, there's a risk I might never be found.

"I'll see you at work tomorrow," I tell him, dismissing him.

He's still for a long moment, his expression wrought with indecision and something else. Something I don't dare read into or name. I ignore him, setting out clothes.

Finally, he clears his throat, takes a step back toward the door, and murmurs, "See you tomorrow. Good night, Katy."

"Good night, Bennett."

▭

THE NEXT MORNING, with a heavy sigh, I step onto the elevator, twisting my body and cracking my back. I hit the button for my floor and set my hands on my hips. That was a brutal trauma. A boating accident that left two people dead in the emergency department is not how I wanted to start my day.

A tall, broad, good-looking guy with blond hair and brown eyes that are all over me steps on and I mentally roll my eyes, absolutely in no mood.

"Hi," he says, not bothering to hit any buttons.

I give him a polite, closed-mouth grin. The universal, *I'm not interested* sign.

"I don't mean to pry, but are you okay?"

Oh. So maybe he's not giving me the eyes I thought he was. I snicker. "I look that bad, huh?"

He peers down at me. "You're beautiful, but you also look like you've had a particularly tough morning."

"I have," I tell him, ignoring the beautiful comment.

"I'm sorry to hear that." The doors close, and the elevator goes up.

"Thank you."

"Do you want to talk about it with a total stranger?"

I can't help it. I laugh at that, some of the heaviness in my chest easing with it. "I'm all set, but thank you for offering."

"Do you like working here?" he questions. "Other than your tough morning, that is."

"I do." I look up at him, his eyes still all over me, his lips twisted into a hint of a smirk, though I wouldn't exactly say he's smiling. It's more mischievous than that. "Are you applying for a job here?"

"I wasn't going to, but after meeting you, I'm strongly reconsidering that."

My eyebrows bounce in surprise at how brazen he is. "Are you hitting on me?"

"Absolutely." That smirk is definitely smiling now. "Are you—"

The elevator stops, and the doors open and in walks freaking Zane. Clearly, I'm not going to catch any breaks today. He scowls, hits the button for his floor, eyes the stranger who is standing a bit too close, and then comes straight for me.

"We need to talk," he demands.

For the love of God. Can't I just get five minutes of freaking peace without a man interrupting it? Why haven't I learned by this point to only take the stairs?

"No, we don't. There's nothing to say." I give him a *shut up, we're in public* look that he either misses entirely or doesn't care enough about to heed.

"Katy, there's a lot to say and I'm going to say it since this might be my only shot. I don't know who the guy you're keeping a secret is and I don't care. Don't do whatever you're doing with him. Get pregnant with me. I'll be so good to you this time. Please, just give me a second chance."

Jesus hell. "Are you kidding me?!" I screech, my face flushing to mortified decibels.

"Hi," the stranger who just hit on me says, extending his right hand to Zane while moving in directly beside me and putting his other hand on my lower back. "I'm Cayden. I'm the guy. Well, I should probably say her guy." He bounces his head in my direction, a cocky, *she's all mine* expression on his face.

"What?" both Zane and I gasp out.

Cayden grins and looks down at me. "It's okay to tell him, honey. I know you wanted to keep it a secret, but he'll never go away unless he knows who I am and that not only are you mine, but we're trying to get pregnant."

I'm dying. Or possibly having a stroke. Or a seizure. Or some kind of drug hallucination. Is my blood sugar low? That happens to me sometimes when my blood sugar bottoms out. I see random shit that's not actually there right before I pass out. Is that what this is?

Zane is red. Like seriously freaking red. His fists ball up and he looks like he's about to attack when his phone pings with a series of texts that call his attention away from me. I glance up at the stranger—he winks at me in a way that suggests I don't rock the boat—and then the elevator stops on Zane's floor.

"Shit. I have to go."

I shrug. "Cool for you. I don't care."

He huffs. "Katy. Just…" His eyes swat over to Cayden's before returning to mine. "He won't love you the way I always will. Think about what I'm saying." And then he steps off the elevator and the doors close, and the elevator starts again.

"Whoa. That was intense. You actually dated that guy?"

I laugh as he cracks the tension with a pitchfork. "I did, but you can't hold it against me. Thank you for that. It was nice of you to step in. Even if I don't know you and that might cause more problems."

The doors open on my floor, and we step off. I throw him a wave and start off when his hand grasps my forearm, stopping me and turning me back to face him. "What do you mean it might cause more problems? I just got your ex off your back by becoming your secret boyfriend who is trying to get you pregnant."

"You did," I concede, shaking off his touch. "But now word will spread that I'm dating someone when I'm not."

"Perhaps we should change that. Now that I'm no longer your secret, I should take you out for real."

I shake my head. "I'm not dating right now."

"No, you're dating me. We just established that. How about dinner—"

Out of nowhere, Bennett comes swooping in, fist flying, and hits the guy straight in the face, knocking him to the ground in a heap of man muscle.

I blink at Cayden's slackened form and then up at Bennett, who is shaking out his fist and cursing. "Why in the hell did you do that?"

## Chapter Nineteen

## Bennett

All I see is red. Fucking red everywhere. "That's Cayden," I snap at Katy, and just what the fuck is he doing here? And how did he find her?

She stares at me as if I just lost my mind. "I know. I just met him." She tilts her head as realization creeps across her features. "Wait. How do you know him?"

I grab her with my good hand—since the one I hit him with burns like a bastard, though that hit was totally worth the pain—around her waist and growl, "He's my ex-best friend."

"The one who was fucking your ex?"

I nod.

Her face drops. "Oh."

"Yeah. Oh."

Only that's not why I hit the motherfucker. He was talking to Katy with a familiarity I didn't appreciate. More than that, he was touching her, and for that alone, I had to hit him. He shows up here out of the blue and now he's touching Katy?! *My* Katy? No. Absolutely not. Not her. Not ever.

"Help me move him," Katy demands, bending over and grabbing Cayden by the arm. He groans, his body shifting and his eyes slowly blinking open. "Now, Bennett. You just punched a man out on your floor, and if anyone sees this, deserving or not, you could get fired."

I make an aggravated noise in the back of my throat because I'd just allow Cayden to lie here bleeding like a pussy, but I grab his other arm and help her drag him toward the empty patient room across the way.

"Put him on the bed. I need to examine him."

"Forget that—"

"Now," she demands, giving me a look that says *don't argue*.

I lop the dead weight of his body on the bed, but when she moves to help him, I yank her hand away from him because as much as I don't want his hands anywhere near her, I don't want her hands anywhere on him.

"You"—she points toward the recliner in the corner of the room—"sit there and do not speak or move. You need ice for your hand."

"Katy—"

"I said do not speak or move. Who punches someone, Bennett? You're a freaking surgeon and an adult. If you broke your hand or can't operate, how will you explain that? I'll be back."

I grunt and sit in the chair as Katy leaves the room, shutting the door behind her. Cayden groans again, and I roll my eyes. "You deserved that. You deserve worse than that, actually. I should have broken your fucking nose." *No one else touches my girl, and certainly not you, you piece of shit.*

"Again you mean."

I roll my eyes a second time and lean back, flexing and clenching my fist to test it. It's not great but not terrible, and I doubt anything is broken. "I didn't break your nose that time."

"Yes, you did. When you *tackled* me during touch football."

"You're a dick. What are you doing here?"

"Nice to see you too, buddy."

I scoff and toss my ankle up on my knee. "Buddy? What are we? Six? I'm not your fucking buddy."

"You knocked me down in front of my new girlfriend."

In a flash, I shoot to my feet and start to charge when the door opens, and Katy comes in carrying two pink hospital pitchers filled with ice along with two towels. "Sit down, Bennett." She puts the pitchers on the tray by the foot of the bed and goes about making me an ice pack. "Put this on your hand and do not argue with me." She starts to grumble to herself. "Honestly. A freaking surgeon punching someone. Who does that?"

I take the ice pack from her hand and put it on my fist.

"I'm going to examine that after I check your buddy here for a concussion."

"What is it with everyone using the term buddy today? He's not my fucking buddy."

"Why are you so grumpy?"

"Yeah, Bennett. Why are you so grumpy?" Cayden is smirking. I know that taunting tone of his. He saw the rise he just got out of me about Katy, which given his track record, means he's going to try to fuck her. And since he's Cayden Craw, he'll likely succeed. He already had her smiling. His hand was on her forearm.

"Did he touch any other part of you?" I ask Katy, not even caring if I'm grumpy or even a bit psycho. As far as I'm concerned, he's lucky I didn't kill him.

"Huh?" She turns back to me.

"Did. He. Touch. You? Tell me." So I can hit him again. Harder this time.

"I touched her lower back on the elevator when I told her ex-boyfriend I was her new guy. You know, the one trying to get her pregnant."

Katy gasps, but if I thought I was seeing red before, now it's a shower of blood over my vision.

"You son of a bitch."

I fly straight for him, ready to tear him apart piece by motherfucking piece, only to have Katy intercept me. Her small body slams into mine, and her hands shove my shoulders, trying to force me back to the chair.

"Move," I order.

"No."

"So help me God, Katy. I will spank you so hard for letting him pretend to be your fake boyfriend if you don't let me kill him now."

"Promises, promises. I still have yet to get a good spanking from you." She twists my nipple through my scrub top until I wince. "Enough!" she snaps. "You're very sexy when you're all alpha male like this, but no more beating people up."

My lips twitch. Fuck, this girl just has me. "Sexy alpha male, huh?"

"Sit down, Bennett, and ice your goddamn hand."

"I thought you weren't dating," Cayden throws out, still lying supine like the pussy he is. "Isn't that what you told me when I asked you out?"

"I'm not." She pulls a penlight from her pocket and starts examining him. "Pupils are equal, round, and reactive to light."

"Oh, so then there's nothing going on with you and Bennett. All that spanking talk is just workplace banter. Good stuff. My window is still open then."

"You stupid motherfu—"

"I said enough. Jesus. It's like preschool in here." She sits Cayden up. "You're awake but stupid enough to start shit and risk getting hit again. I can't tell if that's from a head injury or you just like to run your mouth. Can you follow my finger with just your eyes?"

"Can't I just stare into yours instead?"

"Sure. You can intentionally fail your neuro exam. I have no problems sending you down to the emergency department and having all the new interns perform full neuro exams and possibly a few rectal ones on you."

Cayden chokes on a laugh and twists to meet my eyes, giving me a smug look that tells me he likes Katy. Yeah, take a number, asshole. I flip him off with my good hand.

"I'm a neurosurgeon," Cayden explains pompously to Katy, acting like a peacock. "I can do my own neuro exam."

"Goodie gumdrops for you, but I'm hardly impressed by that. Now shut up and do as you're told." Katy holds up her pointer finger in front of Cayden, and he follows her every command. "I don't think you have a concussion."

"No," he agrees. "It was a lousy sucker punch. His mother hits harder than that."

"I'll let her know you're in town and see if she can do better," Katy deadpans. "The cut on your face doesn't need stitches, which is too bad since I can't let the interns play with it." She tosses an ice pack at his face and then comes for me. "Your turn."

"It's fine," I maintain, my hard eyes on Cayden's Cheshire grin. He stares at her ass as she bends to examine me, and I'm legit going to kill him. It'll be fun. I bet if I ask nicely enough, Vander will help me get rid of his body. He seems like the sort to know how to do that.

She raises an unamused eyebrow at me. "Oh, is it there, Boxer Joe? So you not only look like Superman but have his X-ray vision too?"

"Huh?" I turn back to her.

"Your hand is swollen and red. Already. You need an X-ray."

"Not gonna happen, sweetheart. No way that will stay quiet."

"If you won't get an X-ray, then let me examine it to make sure it's not fractured, and then you better keep this ice on it."

"Fine," I grumble, leaning back in the recliner and

allowing Katy to put her hands on mine and her body between my spread legs. Now it's my turn for a smug grin.

"No fracture that I can tell," she says when she's done. "At least not an obvious one."

Katy's phone starts going off with text pages, and I stand, threading my good hand through her hair and kissing her like my ex-best friend who wants my girl is watching. I kiss Katy until she's breathless and her lips are glossed from mine.

"I'll see you tonight." Another kiss. "And I'll be sure to give you that spanking." Which she knows I won't since she has her period, but that was more for Cayden than for her anyway. I shove her out the door and fall back into the recliner, putting the ice back on my fist because yeah, it is swollen and it's definitely red, and it hurts like a motherfucker. Speaking of. "What the hell are you doing here?"

"She says you're not dating her. It has to hurt that she doesn't care enough about you to acknowledge you."

Cayden leans against the head of the bed, his feet dangling over the side, his ankles crossed. I'm pleased to say he's going to have a nice shiner by tomorrow. "Your face looks like shit."

Because he's vain, he puts the ice on his cheek.

"Funny thing… you found out I was nailing your wife behind your back for two years and all you did was leave town. You didn't even seek me out. You just left with your dick between your legs. I show up here and flirt with your new non-girlfriend in the hall, and you punch me out cold for it."

I relax back in my chair and throw my ankle back up on my knee as I stare at him, unfazed.

"I know who she is," he says, his face rife with confidence, and he follows that up with, "She's the third-year medical student girl."

My eyes widen. "How do you know that?"

"I remember her name. You whined about that girl for

over a year to me on the phone and in person when I saw you. Is Katy why you moved here? Did you know she was working here?"

I don't know why I bother answering him, but I do. Maybe because I'm shocked he remembered her name or because I hadn't realized I whined about her to him for that long. "No. It was a coincidence."

"And now you're trying to get her pregnant. That's pretty perfect for you, Bennett. To be so in love and trying for the baby you've always wanted."

My jaw clenches. "I'm not in love with her, asshole, and shut up about the baby. You, of all people, have no right."

"You are in love, my friend. It's all over your face. It's in the way you look at her. In the way you kissed her just now and came after me for putting my hand on her back, and punched me out for so much as talking to her."

I lean forward, pressing my elbows into my parted thighs while holding the ice to my hand and willing myself not to hit him again. "Why. Are. You. Here?"

"Because you never gave me the chance to explain."

I laugh acerbically and shake my head. "Liz explained everything to me. There was nothing left for you to add, and I wasn't going to let you rub salt in it just because you could."

I move to stand, but he stops me when he rushes out, "I didn't know she got her tubes tied."

That pulls me up short and I turn to look at him. "She said you told her to do it."

"No." He gives a small head shake. "She lied. I never would have told her to do that. I know what having kids means to you."

"And yet you fucked her behind my back." Liz cheating hurt like hell, and her getting her tubes tied and not telling me was a crushing blow. But Cayden was my best friend for nearly two decades. The one person—other than my mother and Liz—in my life who I felt I knew and could trust with anything.

It gutted me when I found out it was him. And when the accusations started, he kept his mouth shut. He didn't come to my defense even though he knew I'd never do any of the things they were saying about me. That was crushing.

I was alone with no one on my side, no one I could trust, losing the life I loved, the one I had built, and all the people in it. And now he's here fucking with Katy, the one good thing I have going, and I can't stand it.

He looks miserable as he admits, "I was in love with Liz. Every minute of the time you were with her, I loved her. And every minute of our friendship, I've been jealous of you. Perfect Bennett Lawson. Top of our graduating class. Teacher's pet. Amazing at any sport you tried. Flawless with women who swoon all over you. I loved you. You were my best friend, but hell, I hated you sometimes too."

I sigh, resting my forearms on my thighs and staring down at the floor. The ice is melting and the towel she wrapped it in is wet, but I hardly notice it.

"When we met Liz and she went for you like everyone else did, it killed me. I stood by and I watched the woman I loved with my best friend for years. So when she kissed me, I didn't stop it, even though I knew I should have. I tried to end it a few times because the guilt was eating me alive, and there were months that nothing happened between us. But then I'd cave, and it would start over again."

"And the baby?" I find myself asking, my voice rough like sandpaper.

"When you told me you and Liz were finally going to try for a baby, I told her we had to end it for good. She refused. She told me she'd tell you what we had been doing and I…" He licks his lips and stares off toward the window. "I didn't want to lose you."

I pause, thinking about that, my eyebrows slanting because I'm not sure how that all adds up, but then he continues, and I lose my train of thought.

"I was in love with her, but you were my best friend and I fucking loved you too. I told her I couldn't risk her getting pregnant and us not knowing who the father was, and she told me that wasn't going to be a problem. I only slept with her for another couple of months before I ended it because I saw how miserable you were that you weren't getting pregnant."

I look at him. "She had the tubal ligation over a year before that."

He shrugs. "Like I said, I didn't know that."

Interesting. He's telling the truth. This means Liz did that on her own and not at his request as she said. She's a real piece of work. Not that it matters now. I haven't thought about Liz—not beyond her incessant calling—in weeks. Funny. I hadn't realized that until now.

"And when the accusations came?"

"Liz told me not to get involved or I'd lose both of you. You were already gone to me, and I was trying for something more with her."

"Why bother telling me any of this now?" And then it hits me. "Liz left you. That's why she's started calling me."

"Actually, I left her."

Strangely, I don't care either way. I don't even care if they get back together.

I stand. "Thanks for telling me."

He stops me right before I reach the door. "I'm sorry, Bennett. That's why I came here. I wanted to tell you that I'm so sorry for hurting you and lying to you. You were my best friend, my brother, and I betrayed that in the worst of ways. I know you might never forgive me, but I hope one day you can. And as for Katy, deny it all you want, but you were in love with her seven years ago, and you're in love with her now. I know you, Bennett. You can lie to yourself, but you can't lie to me."

His words wrap around my chest and squeeze it like a vise,

making it impossible to breathe. I open the door and leave, needing to get back to work. Needing to not think about everything he just said and the possibility that he's right about Katy.

# Chapter Twenty

"This is not going to help," Keegan tells me as she sips her cappuccino and stares down at her chipping nail polish. "If anything, it's going to make it worse."

I lean against the window frame and stare into the nursery filled with all these cute, tiny new babies and sigh. "It's fine. I like being here. I like seeing them." Weirdly, every time I've come down here, it's kept me grounded and focused on my goals. Even if it does sting. "Besides, I wanted to bring you your favorite cappuccino and see you since it's been days. It's not my fault this is where you live."

"But you're off now. You should go home and rest. Get some sleep."

"Stop trying to get rid of me or I won't bring you coffee again."

She takes a sip. "I love you and your coffee. But I'm also going to nag you like your stepmother when you don't take care of yourself. Speaking of, are you having dinner with Callan and Layla tonight? They're finally back, right?"

"Yes. They just got back from Europe the other day. Actually, I think Uncle Cal is working today. I'll leave in a minute. I want to watch the babies and catch up. I feel like I haven't seen you in forever."

"Because you haven't. We've all been busy, but you're extra busy right now."

I can feel her eyebrows bouncing suggestively at me, but I pretend not to notice.

It's been a weird two months. Weird because I'm still living at Bennett's and only my family knows about it. Weird because he and I are freaking roommates who have sex constantly for procreation, though eighty percent of it is not for procreation at all, and the sex is wild and hot and occasionally a bit kinky.

We've been trying like rabbits in spring and so far, nada.

I'm set to get my period in three days, and the test we took last night before I came into work was negative. I'm sluggish to go home because if I go home, I'll be tempted, and I don't want to see another negative one. Not to mention, I promised Bennett I'd never pee on a stick without him, and he's at work now. I told him we'd do it tonight when we get home from dinner with Callan and Layla.

Things I did not tell my best friend Keegan? Bennett is meeting Callan and Layla tonight. It's not me bringing a guy to meet my guardians. It's not. It's me bringing the guy trying to knock me up to meet them. That's all.

But until then, I should go home, sleep, and not take a test. Night shifts are rough enough, and I've been battling a case of food poisoning I got from some bad fish the other night. But if I'm not pregnant this time, I'm going to move out for a bit and maybe only sleep there when we're actively trying and I'm ovulating.

Living with Bennett—roommates or not—is tempting my heart too much. Plus, it's risky. We've nearly been caught too many times. He had me pinned in an old, unused lab the other day, and a few days before that, he fucked me against the glass of the gallery over an empty OR. And then, just a couple of days ago, he dragged me into an empty patient room and finger-fucked me to orgasm twice.

Plus he watches me constantly. I feel his eyes on me all the time, and eventually someone is going to notice.

Keegan offers me some of her drink and my stomach roils. I shake my head, puffing out my cheeks as if I'm about to boot. "No thanks."

"Maybe you should eat something. Even just some crackers."

I shake my head. "I can't. I seriously can't. Tonight I'll eat something at dinner. Some plain pasta, maybe."

"You're going to dehydrate."

I pull up my sleeve and show her the IV I have capped off in my arm. When I first got sick, Bennett slept in my bed with me and took care of me all night. And when I started throwing up water, he panicked and put in an IV, making sure I got glucose and fluids.

"I don't see fluids in there now."

"I'll do another round when I go home," I promise her because I likely should. My blood sugars have been a mess since I got sick. "I had a few sips of a sports drink not too long ago."

"Fine. I'll stop mothering you. How's it going with your secret lover?"

I roll my eyes and watch as a baby starts to squirm and then cry. One of the nurses comes over and picks him up, cuddling him to her chest. I want one. "How do you not want one of these?"

"Katy," she demands. "You haven't said anything about it to any of us. What's the deal?"

I hitch up one shoulder. "There is no deal other than the deal we already have."

"Are you still sleeping together?"

Thankfully my phone vibrates with a page, so I don't have to answer her. I don't want to hear the lecture. The one where she reminds me how crazy what I'm doing with Bennett is. I like having sex with him. He's good at it and being with him that way is perfectly and undeniably convenient. It's like trying to get pregnant with a bonus I never originally anticipated.

And the moment I'm pregnant, it'll stop. Once that happens, everything will fall in line between us the way we've designed it to. We both know that. We both hope this is only borrowed time. So why not take advantage of it while we can?

It's like Bennett said, he's fucking me with his dick and not his heart, and every time he's inside me, I remind myself of that.

"I gotta go," I tell her, reading the stat page to the OR. "Some kind of construction site accident."

"But you're off," she maintains. "They shouldn't be paging you."

I shrug. "They must need me, and I only got off ten minutes ago." I pull away from the wall and head toward the stairs. "I'll catch up with you later."

"You will, because tomorrow night we're taking you out for dinner and you're having a slumber party at our place," she calls after me. "No exceptions."

"Sounds awesome. I might seriously need it. Love you, Keegs!"

"Love you too, bitch."

Someone nearby hisses at her, and I catch Keegan apologizing for her curse just as I open the door to the stairwell—no more freaking elevators for me—and fly up three flights, panting as I reach the trauma surgical floor. I have a headache and my stomach feels like a sponge someone keeps squeezing, but all that starts to fade as I enter the OR.

Holy hell.

"Great. You're still here. I'm sorry to call you back, but we need all the hands we can get at the moment. Go get gowned and gloved up, but don't worry about scrubbing in."

I blink at Bennett and then over toward the patient who

has a rusty metal rod straight through his stomach and some kind of tool stuck in his side. Bolting out of the room, I quickly throw on my scrub cap and booties, wash my hands, and then race back in. A nurse helps me gown up, and I snap on a pair of gloves even though I'm not sterile.

The patient is sitting up and intubated, and I come in beside Cricket, who is not pleased I'm here to help hold the patient upright. "What happened?" I ask. Two nurses are working on draping the patient and making the area as sterile as they can while me and another nurse hold the patient and gurney steady so he doesn't move or shift even the slightest amount.

"Construction site accident. He wasn't harnessed in, and he fell. His blood alcohol level is more than twice the legal limit, which only complicates this further."

"Damn," I mutter.

"Seriously," Cricket snarks. "What kind of moron is drunk at seven in the morning on a construction site?"

"Someone with a problem from the sound of it," I retort. "What's your plan?"

"Dr. Lawson and I are doing the surgery. You're just here to help like one of the nurses."

My eyebrows hit my hairline, and I glance over at the nurses in here who are—rightfully so—pissed at the snotty implication that nurses aren't just as important as doctors, which is absolute bullshit.

Bennett gives Cricket a hard look for that comment too, but then turns back to me. "Dr. Peterson and I are going to go scrub in, but I want you to stay with the patient and keep him as steady as possible."

Cricket gives me a bright and shiny smug grin, and I so want to tell Cricket to fuck herself with the rusty pole, but I keep my mouth shut and my jaw clenched.

"What a bitch," I mutter under my breath the moment they're gone.

"A serious bitch," Martha, the nurse helping to hold up the patient, says.

The anesthesiologist snickers. "You need to be careful, Katy. She bashes you every chance she gets and is quick to steal surgeries."

"She's like an ambulance chaser," I drawl. "A surgical bottom feeder. But for real, have you ever seen anything like this? What is that tool in his side?"

"On X-ray, it looks like some kind of pliers."

I wince. "Ouch."

The OR doors swing open, and Bennett and Cricket return along with some interns and second-and-third-year residents who are eager to watch since cases like this don't come along every day and will require a lot of moving parts to make it successful.

"Thank you, Dr. Barrows. I can have one of the interns come and spell you."

Dr. Fields comes in and takes over holding the patient up for me. "Can I scrub in?"

Bennett gives me a long look as if he's debating that but then nods. "Yeah. Go ahead, but be quick."

I catch Cricket complaining about that, but she can eat my ass if she thinks I'm not scrubbing in. I set my phone to vibrate and drop it on the table along with the others before I fly out of the OR to scrub in at light speed. In a flash, I'm back in, getting regowned and gloved up, and then coming in and going exactly where Bennett points me to.

"Katy, I want you on the other side there beside Cricket. We're going to start with the tool first since the pole is tamponading any bleeders in the chest, and it appears that the pliers are pressing right into his liver, which is bleeding profusely. Let's move fast, pack off, and cauterize what we can so we can move onto the pole and then open him up."

An incision is made, and then the three of us get to work, packing off the liver that is not in good shape. I'm shaking from the adrenaline, which is a bit odd since I never shake in situations like this, but then again, this isn't an everyday trauma.

"It's sclerosed," Cricket laments. "I don't see how we're going to be able to stop the bleeding like this."

It's true. The liver has a lot of damage from what appears to be years of alcohol abuse, and unfortunately, sclerosed livers bleed and don't clot well. It's an absolute mess. More blood is hung to transfuse and keep the patient's vitals stable —which they shockingly are—and we do what we can before the team starts in with the saw to cut the pole. We stand back while they do this, oxygen turned off as sparks fly, which is why the anesthesiologist now has to manually bag the patient to keep him breathing.

I've never seen anything like this in my four-going-on-five years as a resident. It's seriously the coolest and craziest thing ever, and I can't wait to pick Bennett's brain about it later. He throws me a side-eye, giving me a sly wink, and I feel my face heating, my skin growing clammy, and my heart beating faster.

Once the pole is cut, we jump back in, sliding it out slowly while working from behind to stop any bleeding. I'm sweating, my muscles are aching, my heart is racing a mile a minute, and… my vision sways.

The hell?

I brush that off and keep going, following Bennett's directive.

"Someone's phone is vibrating like crazy over here," the circulating nurse announces just as we finally manage to remove the pole and lay the patient down so we can open him up and fix his liver and other internal injuries.

"Is it a call or a page?"

"Neither," she says. "It looks like an app notification."

"Whatever it is can wait," Bennett growls, annoyed by the interruption.

"I thought we weren't allowed to have app notifications

going," Cricket gripes, and she's right. We're not. We're not supposed to get notifications from things like social media, weather, or any other non-essential apps. They're distracting in the OR. Clearly.

Except suddenly, I think I know what that buzzing is. I think it's my continuous glucose monitor giving me a warning. Because I'm sweating and my heart is pounding in my chest. I've got a headache, my muscles are shaky, and my stomach is still feeling like that sponge.

Shit. My blood sugar is low. Just how low I don't know—low enough to trigger the alert—but I don't want to check it in a room full of other doctors, Bennett, and most of all, Cricket.

Only as things continue, it becomes harder and harder to ignore. I can feel that it's low. Seriously low. And when my vision starts to tilt from side to side, I take a wobbly step back.

"Dr. Barrows?" Bennett questions, only his voice sounds distant. Tinny. And my vision isn't just swaying now, it's almost cartoonishly wrong. I need to get out of here. I need some orange juice or one of the glucose tabs I keep in my bag, but I put that back in my locker when I got the page.

"I..." Oh God. "I'm sorry, Dr. Lawson. I'll be right back."

I have no idea if he can understand me or if that comes out clear at all. It doesn't matter. I start to head for the door, willing myself to make it. Only I'm not sure I can.

"Katy?!" his voice calls urgently just as the room crackles and my vision is fuzzy. "Someone help her!" he cries out, but it's too late, and I feel myself start to fall just as everything goes black.

# Chapter Twenty-One

## Bennett

I'm going out of my mind. The patient on my table is bleeding as fast as we can give him new blood. His surgery is more than just a little complicated and requires my complete attention. But Katy is unconscious on the goddamn OR floor.

Adrenaline shakes me and shortens my breath. I need to get to my girl.

"Dr. Lawson, you're sterile and your patient is bleeding," the nurse on my right reminds me as I instinctively go for her. *Fuck!*

"What's going on?" I bark, my body and mind screaming at me to run to her and pick her up, but I fucking can't or my patient will die. "Someone check her vitals. What's her blood sugar?"

"We're on it, Dr. Lawson," one of the circulating nurses tells me as she and an intern are all over Katy, checking her blood pressure and her glucose. I can see from here on the vitals cart screen that her heart rate is one-thirty-eight and her blood pressure is shit at 86/52. No wonder she passed out. She's been sick with food poisoning, and I should have made her stay home again last night. She was adamant and promised to keep the IV site in her arm in case she needed fluids.

Which she likely did but didn't take the time to get them.

Goddammit! Why didn't I make her stay home with me where I could take care of her? Hell, why did I let them page her, and why the fuck did I let her scrub in when she was already on all night? I'm her boss. Her… her… fuck, what am I to her? Not her boyfriend or even her lover. I'm not casual, and I'm not a friend with benefits either. I'm simply the guy she's living with who is trying to knock her up.

But… she's more than that to me. So much more.

She always has been and seeing her like this… "I need an update," rips from my throat.

"Blood sugar is forty-one," the nurse announces with a grim expression. "We're going to move her down to the emergency department."

I nod, even as I grit my teeth behind my mask and clench the instrument in my hand a little too tight. Forty-one?! How long was she feeling that before she tried to step away? Dammit, Katy!

We were going to take another test tonight after dinner with her uncle and stepmother. I haven't met them yet, and knowing how close they are with Katy, I've been nervous about it. I invited them over and offered to cook, but Katy suggested we all go out to Stella's to make it more casual.

Her uncle is going to kill me for not taking better care of her and I won't blame him.

"Okay. Take her down and notify them that you're on your way. Thanks." I don't mean it. I'm ready to burn down the world to go with her. "Start some D10 saline. She already has a line in her left arm. She had food poisoning the other day and required some fluids for it."

One of the nurses gives me an acknowledging wave, and then they transfer a pale and unconscious Katy onto a gurney, lift the side rails up, and wheel her out. Her uncle is working down in the emergency department today. He'll take care of her. Even if I can't.

Frustration slams through me, and it's taking everything I have not to call in another attending to take over so I can go be with Katy and hold her goddamn hand and help fix her.

Except I can't.

No one knows anything about us or what we've been doing, and not only would it ruin my career, but it could be devastating to hers. She wants this fellowship—and she's earned it—and that could all be ripped away from her in the blink of an eye if I do or say the wrong thing.

*Fuck!*

I can't do this anymore. How can I keep her a secret? I want this baby with her, but now… I also want her. I told myself if it took a few months for us to get pregnant, I could fuck her out of my system. But that's a joke. So laughable I'm almost embarrassed I believed something so ludicrous.

There is no fucking Katy out of my system. She *is* my system.

Doesn't she know she has to take care of herself? That I can't lose her?

I swallow thickly at that.

I walked away from Liz without a second thought or hesitation. But seeing Katy pass out, seeing her on the ground, imagining the worst… I don't want to lose Katy. Not ever. The thought makes it feel like someone is reaching inside and slicing out my organs one by one. I survived letting Liz go, but I don't think I'd survive letting Katy go a second time.

It's been over three weeks since Cayden left. Three goddamn weeks of trying not to think about what he said to me about her. I told myself he was wrong and that he only said that to get a rise out of me and nothing more. That liking Katy as much as I do isn't the same as loving her. But the truth is, I've been lying to myself longer than that. Since Katy and I started this.

Months of pretending I don't think about her all the time. Months of pretending that she hasn't just turned my world upside down, she's become it.

But I can't pretend anymore. Not as the truth slams into me with the force of a bullet.

I love Katy. I'm totally, wildly, head over heels in love with her. She makes me want things I swore I'd never want again.

I knew Katy would own my ass. I had a suspicion I'd be in trouble if I didn't lock myself down. But I never expected this. I never expected to feel this way again. I didn't think I had it in me.

I thought Liz had ruined me, but the truth is, it's Katy who did that. Long before anyone else came into the picture. Katy, my beautiful, sweet, incredible girl, is on her way to the emergency room with a life-threateningly low blood sugar, and I need to be there with her.

"Wow," Cricket remarks, snapping me out of my thoughts and back on the patient whose life I'm here to save. "That was unbelievable."

"Yes," I say lowly, blowing out a slow, even breath.

"I can't believe how unprofessional Katy is."

"What?" I bark as I continue to work on his liver wound.

"Well, you wouldn't see me passing out from a little food poisoning. A real trauma surgeon doesn't let things like that stop them from doing their job. I don't even care that she's a diabetic. That's utterly disgraceful."

"Utterly disgraceful?" I parrot, beyond incredulous—and frankly, fucking furious, to the point where she's lucky there's a patient between us saving her ass from me. I finally start to get a good footing on the liver, and the bleeding slows. "Dr. Peterson, what is wrong with you? Are you that nasty and heartless of a person that you have to be disparaging about a fellow doctor and colleague who just passed out from dangerously low blood sugar?"

"It's not nasty and heartless if it's the truth," she defends with an insolent sniff. "Dr. Barrows doesn't have what it takes the way I do."

Rage bubbles up inside me, threatening to overtake my better sense, but I cool myself down enough to only scoff derisively at her. "Do you want to know what makes a good trauma surgeon, Dr. Peterson? Having some humanity. Something I've seen in spades from Dr. Barrows and completely lacking from you. You think it makes you look better to shit all over Dr. Barrows while attempting to boost yourself up, but it doesn't. It makes you look catty, resentful, and insecure. Now get out of my OR. Williams and Shefter." I call over to the two third-year residents who are standing off to the side sporting matching owl eyes. "Please go scrub in. I'm going to need your help."

Cricket is still standing across from me, and you could hear a pin drop for how silent this room is. I likely shouldn't have publicly berated her that way, but right now I don't care. I'm too worked up, and Cricket picked the wrong time to be a bitch. There's no way I'm not going to defend Katy when she's not here to defend herself. Katy was taken out of here unconscious on a gurney, and instead of giving two shits about a woman she's worked with for the last four going into five years, she took advantage and tried to use this as an opportunity to play chess with me, and I won't have it.

"Dr. Lawson—"

"Don't make me say it again, Dr. Peterson. I expect better from the surgeons on my service. You may not like Dr. Barrows, and you may think of her solely as your competition, but you *will* treat her with respect."

"Yes, sir," she utters, turns, and walks out with her head high, despite blatantly avoiding eye contact. I hope she's embarrassed. She should be fucking embarrassed.

I blow out a strained breath and roll my neck until it cracks. "I apologize if I made anyone uncomfortable, but there is no excuse for that sort of behavior, and I won't abide by it."

"Don't apologize." Tamara, the circulating snorts. "I'm glad someone finally said something to her. She is a mean girl, and I think I'm speaking for all of us when I say I was happy to leave that nonsense back in high school. There is no place for it here when we're working to save lives."

"I appreciate that."

"I'm texting with Margot Albright, who is the head RN in the emergency department," she continues. "She said they're working to get Katy's blood sugar up and that her vitals are stabilizing. She came around for a bit but is unconscious again. She was pretty dehydrated too. Her uncle Callan is there with her."

Dehydrated too. And I allowed her to stay and see this case because I wanted to show off in front of her and make her happy by allowing her to scrub in on a once-in-a-lifetime trauma. What is wrong with me? I should have forced her to go home. I should have made sure when I came in this morning after not seeing her all night that she had been taking care of herself.

April, the nurse on my right laughs interrupting my self-misery. "I'm sure half the hospital will be down there once word gets out. You know she has like twenty cousins, uncles, and aunts who work here in some capacity or another. That's not even an exaggeration."

My lips twitch behind my mask, and I'm relieved no one can see it.

"Let's hope Zane doesn't find out until they discharge her. That man is relentless with her."

"Yeah, I heard he stalked her to the parking garage a few weeks back."

"I heard he trolls her in the elevators."

As the nurses and techs continue to go back and forth, I go from a barely there smirk to a deep frown. Zane. I can't blame him for trying to win her back, but that doesn't mean I don't also want to kill him. Katy hasn't mentioned him to me in a while and hasn't said a thing about any of this. Though, now that I think back, Cayden mentioned something about pretending to be her boyfriend in the elevator with her ex. I was too worked up from seeing him to give it any thought.

Between my relentless ex and Katy's, we make quite the pair.

I told Zane if he didn't leave her alone, I'd ruin him, but that's the problem. He's not doing it on my floor, and I have no real jurisdiction over him. I can't fight him off as her man. This constant feeling of being stuck in between is stifling.

Katy is mine. She's always been mine.

And my heart irrevocably belongs to her.

The woman who brought sunshine back into my dreary life and made me long for everything I've been reading to my mother in her romance books.

I want us to be something real—something lasting and permanent and for more than just the baby we're trying to make—except she's nowhere close to wanting that with me. So that's where my pretending comes back into place. Because I don't think I can do it again. Not with her. I can't offer my heart up to her on a shiny silver platter and have her smash it into oblivion.

I will love the baby we make, and I'll love it more because I'm in love with its mother, but I have to learn to accept that that's where my love needs to end.

After an eternity in the OR, we finally manage to save this patient's life and tell his family that he needs to not only stop drinking but that he needs a new liver. They don't even try to play it shocked or cool. My guess is they've heard this before and know exactly how bad his alcohol addiction is.

The second I'm done with them, I race my ass down to the ER, through the back web, and after checking the board, straight to Katy's room. The door is closed, and I hesitate for only a second before I slide it open and freeze, my heart in my throat. Katy's small body is on the gurney, wearing only a hospital gown and a thin blanket, with an IV coming straight from her arm up to a bag of saline with glucose. She's pale and her hair is a matted mess, but she's still the most beautiful woman I've ever seen.

I stand here for no longer than a second or two before my gaze flickers up to the monitor, where I do a quick assessment of her vitals, and then over to the tall man sitting in the chair beside her bed. I haven't met Callan Barrows yet, but I know it's him without requiring introductions. They have the same eyes, and I wonder if her father had them as well.

Entering the room, I shut the glass door and close the curtain behind me to give us privacy.

"Hi," I say, extending my hand. "I'm—"

"Bennett Lawson," he answers for me, half-standing and shaking my hand before he retakes his seat. "Yeah, I know who you are. You're the man getting my Katy pregnant."

That pulls me up short, and I practically fall into a chair on the other side of her bed.

"Um, yes, sir, I am. But that's not—"

He holds up his hand and stops me with a chuckle. "Relax, Bennett. Call me Callan. I'm too old to kick your ass, and if her cousins haven't done it already, then there's no need for me to. Owen, Vander, and Mason are terrorizers when it comes to her. They've scared off nearly every boyfriend she's had and then honestly nearly killed Zane when he didn't heed their very direct threats about not hurting her."

"I can't blame them for that. I'd love to kill him myself."

He nods and stares thoughtfully at me. "I figured as much. Katy told me about your situation. You're taking quite the risk with her."

I wipe at my lips. "She's taking quite the risk with me too." Which is probably why I trust her as much as I trust anyone right now. Yet another realization that leaves me winded. Katy is everything lovely and selfless in this world. So different from everything I've known in the past. I don't think Katy has it in her to intentionally hurt or betray anyone, and fuck if that doesn't make me love her even more.

"Katy has always done things her way and made no apologies or excuses for it. The fact that you're still here is reassuring for me, and the wrecked and terrified expression on your face when you came in and saw Katy like this makes me think she's more to you than just a ride to a baby. Am I wrong in that assessment?"

I lean forward, my elbows digging into my thighs. I glance over at Katy, who's still asleep, and then back at him, staring him straight in the eyes, man to man. I won't lie to him. It's not who I am. "No. You're not. She is a lot more than that to me."

He tosses his ankle up to his opposite knee and leans back, throwing his hands behind his head and butterflying his elbows out.

"I'm assuming based on the way you said that, she doesn't know that's how you feel?"

I shake my head.

A wry grin hits his lips, and he sets his forearms down on the arms of the chair. "So then tell me, Bennett, what's your plan?"

My eyebrows bounce. "My plan?"

He pans a hand in my direction. "I've been where you are before. I loved the hell out of a woman who didn't want any of that with me. She too had been hurt by an asshole who didn't deserve her. It sucks, so I get it."

I let out a strange, strangled laugh, not even bothering to deny the love part. I sit up and rub the back of my head. "How'd that turn out for you?"

"One day I decided I was done giving her the choice, and I showed her that not only would I be different from the others, but that I'd never stop fighting for her until I not only won her, but she realized she couldn't live without me either."

My lips twitch. "Was she as stubborn as Katy is?"

"Every bit as much. Men like us wouldn't have fallen so hard for them if they weren't. It just depends on if you're up for the challenge she presents or not." He leaves that hanging in the air between us and I don't bother reassuring him that I am. He can see it all over my face. "I'm going to get her discharge paperwork sorted." He stands and plants a kiss on Katy's temple and then goes to leave. "Hey, Bennett?"

I glance up at him. "Yes, Callan?"

"Take care of my Katy for me."

I swallow thickly. "I intend to."

"Good. Because you should probably be the one to tell her she's pregnant."

# Chapter Twenty-Two

# Katy

I feel like total and complete trash right now. Everything hurts. And I'm tired. Like so damn tired I can hardly move, and the thought of opening my eyes feels like the effort of a lifetime. I think I remember what happened. I think I passed out on the damn OR floor, which is, well, gross and humiliating all at the same time.

Not to mention, my family will never let this go. They'll be up my ass and around the corner over it. Then there's Bennett. Ugh. He's going to be supersonically *pissed*. Rightfully so, but still. Maybe I'll just sleep for a while longer. Like another decade or so.

"Katy baby, are you awake? Your heart rate is going up a little." Bennett's soothing voice filters through my ears as he runs a soft hand over my head and through my hair.

"That depends on how mad you are," I rasp, my voice sounding like I ate a hundred pounds of cotton and washed them down with sand. "On a scale from one to a hundred."

"I'm pretty fucking mad so I'll have to go with a hundred."

"Then I'm still asleep."

His lips plant against my forehead, and he murmurs into my skin, "You scared me."

"I know—"

"No, baby, you don't. I'm not sure I've ever been as scared in my life as when I saw you pass out like that. You have to take better care of yourself. You're my baby's mommy now, and that means your health comes first."

It takes a half-second longer than it should for my sluggish brain to catch up, but when I do, I blink open my eyes, squinting against the harsh fluorescent lights, and meet Bennett's deep blue ones from inches away. "Baby's mommy?"

He smiles, his nose brushing mine as he cups the back of my head. "That's you."

"So I'm…"

"Pregnant. Yes."

"Oh my god." I start to tremble, my eyes closing as tears immediately fill them. "Bennett. Are you sure?" I can't say anything else without sobbing.

I've never cried happy tears in my life. Not when I won big swim meets or got into the medical school of my choice or landed a residency back here in Boston. I know we have a long way to go, and anything can happen, but I can't begin to explain the unadulterated joy and relief swimming through me right now. It's consuming and overwhelming and I'm so glad Bennett is here right now.

I'm so glad he was the one to tell me.

"I'm sure. Your uncle told me, and then I broke about seven thousand rules, laws, and regulations and checked your chart. But only for that. I swear, I didn't sneak or look at anything else, but I had to see for myself, so I hope you're not mad about that."

"I'm not mad about that. I'm so many things right now, but mad is definitely not one of them."

He wraps his arms around me and presses his head and

chest against me as I cry into him, no longer able to hold back my sobs. I reach behind his head and grip his scrub top. I'm trembling, and this time it has nothing to do with my low blood sugar.

I'm pregnant.

I'm fucking pregnant.

My life will never be the same again. And Bennett will always be a part of it.

My tongue thickens in my mouth, and I try to swallow past it. Everything is going to change now, and I need to be ready for that. A weird, almost panicky burning hits the center of my chest. It makes it feel like I'm inhaling a lungful of fire with each breath. I reach up to wipe it away only it's not going anywhere.

"Bennett…"

"It's okay, baby. I've got you. I know, and I've got you."

"You're shaking," I note, needing to focus on anything other than this feeling.

He holds me tighter. "I'm so fucking happy we're pregnant, but every time I close my eyes, I see you on that floor," he whispers, his voice hoarse. "I can't take it, Katy. I can't have anything happen to you. Not just because we're pregnant now. You hear me?"

I nod against him. "I'm sorry," I croak.

He kisses my head before pulling back and wiping the tears from my cheeks with his thumbs. For a long moment, he stares into my eyes, and everything starts to shift and move. Into place or out of sync, I can't tell which. He leans in and presses his lips to mine, so gently, so tenderly, so reverently it steals my breath. His hands thread through my hair, and he holds me as he deepens it, parting my lips and tickling my tongue with his.

All too soon it's done and he's pulling back, and part of me wonders if that'll be the last time he kisses me. Can I handle it if it is?

"Can I take you home now?" Another swipe of his thumb across my cheek.

"What about your shift? What time is it?"

"It's noon. I had Dr. Wilson cover my shift. I told him I had a family emergency and that I'd pick up half of his on Saturday."

"Bennett—"

His flinty gaze cuts to mine. "Don't argue with me, Katy. No one knows I'm here with you, and I'll have your uncle wheel you out, but I want to take you home."

"Okay," I relent because I'd like to go home too. I need a shower and to sleep for a hundred years. My heart quakes in my chest as more tears fall. "I'm really pregnant?"

"You're really pregnant." He puts his hand over my lower belly. "We have a lot to talk about."

We do. A lot to talk about. And a lot is about to change between us. I went from possibly planning to move out to now living with Bennett at least until the baby is six months old. That's a long time to live with him.

My gut sinks at that thought, but I don't dwell on it. Not now. Not when I'm so fucking happy, I could burst.

▭

"YOU NEED TO TALK," I tell my uncle as he wheels me out toward the ambulance bay. I remember once when I was just coming to live with him, and he brought me here, and Layla hung out with me in the ambulance bay and braided my hair because I refused to go inside the hospital. I didn't know how to talk to my uncle at the time, but Layla had been through the same hell as I had, and she understood my pain.

I remember thinking I could make it through not having my parents if I had Layla, and my uncle made it so that I did. Now I'm starting to think that I could make it through this if I have Bennett.

But what does that even mean?

Yes, I know I care a lot for Bennett. I do have feelings for him. I have all along.

I'm in a unique position where I don't have to put my child—or myself—through the tumult of heartbreak and separation of ending something romantic with their father. My baby can be born into a clean world where its parents are amicable, their relationship is solely parental and platonic, and there is no angst or resentment as part of the equation to divert focus from them.

I can do that for my kid.

And I need to.

Falling in love with Bennett isn't an option.

Even when he holds me just right, kisses my face, wipes my tears, and tells me he wants to take care of me. He's a good man, and that's the sort of thing good men do. He'll be a great dad, which fills my heart with so much warmth, I'm overflowing with it.

It'll be fine. Hell, it'll be fucking great.

"I'm happy for you. So happy, Katy."

"You're quiet."

He chuckles. "I'm always quiet."

"Not like Uncle Lenox quiet."

"No. Definitely not that quiet," he agrees. "My Katy is pregnant and making me a grandfather. It's a lot to take in. What I will tell you is that you'll be fine. You're strong and smart and resilient and more ready for this. You're going to be a *fantastic* mother, Katy, and I can't wait to see it. And no matter what, you have us, your whole family, by your side and always on it."

"Am I making a mistake with him?"

He laughs incredulously. "You ask that now?"

"No. Yes. I'm not. I know I'm not."

"I agree. You're not. So stop your brain from going down

rabbit holes it doesn't need to go down. Trust your gut. Trust your heart. Rely on your intuition. But also, I believe Bennett is going to be an incredible dad to your child."

He's right. As always, he's so freaking right. "Thank you," I mumble, crying again, but I needed to hear that now, even if he's said it to me dozens of times before. We reach the edge of the garage, and I slowly stand up. I'm feeling better, but I'm still a bit shaky. I turn and hug him, squeezing him tight. "I love you, Uncle Cal. Thank you for always being my hero."

"Thank you for always being mine," he replies softly, his voice thick.

"Okay, enough of this emotional shit."

He laughs, kissing my forehead and then releasing me. "Bennett is waiting. He seems like a good guy, but if he's ever not, let me know and we'll ruin his life."

I roll my eyes. "You sound like Owen and Vander."

He gives an unconcerned shrug, smirking at someone behind me, and I turn to find Bennett standing there, clearly having overheard since he's wiping at a smile on his lips. "Where do you think they learned it from?"

Bennett takes my hand and helps me into the car, and we drive back to his house. It feels surreal. All the months and years I've been thinking about this moment and it's here. Bennett brings me inside and then lifts me off my feet, carrying me toward the stairs bride-style.

"I can walk."

"I know."

"You're not going to be like this with me for the next nine months, are you?"

His eyes meet mine as he walks me up the steps, not even winded as he goes. "You passed out in my OR this morning, Katy. You've been sick all week. No way in fucking hell am I letting you risk getting dizzy and falling down the stairs."

Fine. I don't press it. Not even when he walks me into his

bathroom and turns on his shower, letting the water come up to temperature. His eyes lock on the bathtub and then shoot over to me, and I can tell he's trying very hard to keep them in safe, neutral territory.

"You're thinking about the last time I took a bath in here, aren't you?"

He smirks, his dimple sinking in deep. "I think about that night every time I come in here. And I mean that literally in both ways."

"I think about that night a lot too. Every time I use Chris."

He chokes. "Chris? Who the fuck is Chris?"

I shrug. "Hemsworth, Evans, Pratt. Take your pick."

He curses under his breath. "I'm going to have to buy you a Bennett vibrator."

I try not to frown at the insinuation behind that and start to undress, only to pause when I catch Bennett watching me. We've been sleeping together for a couple of months, but now everything is different. Hell, it's in our contract.

I didn't think about it the last time we had sex.

I didn't think that would be my last time with him.

He moves in behind me and reaches around me, undoing the tie on my scrub pants. They fall down my legs along with my thong that he pushes over my hips. Without a word, he gets undressed too and follows me into the shower.

"I didn't invite you to join me," I tease.

"Yes, you did. You just didn't realize it. Besides, I wasn't giving you the choice."

I shake my head at that. Such a goddamn caveman.

The warm water feels like heaven on my aching muscles, and I reach up, brushing my hair from my face and getting it wet. I grab the shampoo, but he's right there with it, massaging it into my head, the scent of him surrounding me since he used his and not mine, clinging to the steam and my senses. He does the same thing with the conditioner all the while we're silent, neither of us knowing how to start this.

He dumps a handful of bodywash into his palm and rubs his hands together, creating a foamy lather. With his eyes on mine, he starts to wash my body, rubbing, massaging, and cleaning me without lingering anywhere too long. His hands coast over my breasts, between my legs, and across my ass.

He's hard, but he's not paying any attention to that. This is about him taking care of me, as he always does, and I can't get enough of it. Of *him*. When he's done with me, he forces me to sit on the stone bench he has in here, and then he quickly washes his own hair and body before he turns off the shower, hops out to wrap a towel around his waist, and then returns with one for me.

"Can you eat anything?" he finally asks, his voice a soft purr.

"Maybe some broth. I need to check my glucose and make sure I'm not having any rebound hypoglycemia."

"Do you feel like you are?"

I shake my head, and relief swarms his features.

"Good. Come with me." He lifts me again, not giving me the choice, and then sets me down on his bed. With a quick kiss to my nose, he goes down the hall to my room and returns with a thong and a pair of sweatpants that he hands me to put on.

"I need a shirt." I laugh the words.

"I know."

He moves into his closet and comes back out with a T-shirt and sweatshirt of his.

I raise a questioning eyebrow, but he ignores it as he gets himself dressed. He wants me to wear his clothes. Probably for the same reason he put his bodywash in my bathroom and anytime I attempt to bring my own back in there, it magically disappears with only his to be found. I like being wrapped in him. I feel comforted and safe when I smell his scent on my skin.

And now, with it surrounding me in his clothes, well...

I stop thinking about it and just put them on, inhaling deeply and not even caring if he catches me doing it. I want more of this because I don't want it to end between us. But deep down, I know it has to. Even if it makes my heart hurt in the worst of ways.

# Chapter Twenty-Three

## Bennett

Katy is quiet, and I have no idea what to do with a quiet Katy. She has a lot on her mind, but when Katy is anxious or excited, she talks. Non-freaking-stop, she talks. It's a magical portal into the wild thoughts that live in her head, and I love it. So a quiet Katy is disconcerting. What happened with her today scared me. But it also shook me with a reality I no longer want to ignore.

We have a lot to talk about. A lot to sort out.

But right now, she's too lost in her thoughts for that.

Passing out at work and then learning that you're pregnant is a lot to take in.

We canceled our dinner with her uncle and stepmom because Katy is wiped from the day—and frankly, she isn't able to eat more than soup—but right now, I'm not what she needs. I pose too many complications in her head. I see it all over her face as she sips the soup I made her. I saw it when she reluctantly took my clothes to put on.

I'm not even sure why I did that other than I wanted her surrounded by me, so she'd know that I have her and that not only is she safe, but I'll always take care of her. Only instead of making her feel that way, I think I'm fucking with her head.

At least I hope I am. I hope I have her questioning and rethinking everything we wrote into that contract.

But still…

"Katy?"

She slowly lifts her chin.

"Kenna, Keegan, Owen, Vander, Stone, and Mason will be here in about ten minutes. I'm going to change and head to the bar down the block so you can have time alone with them."

She blinks at me, a slow roll of her eyes and dark lashes. "You called them?"

I rest my elbows on the counter on the other side of the island from her. The exact same position I was in when I brought her here and proposed all of this. "You look like you need them."

She puffs out a loud, exaggerated breath as if she's trying to hold herself together. A tear tracks down her cheek, but she quickly wipes it away and then breaks out into a shaky laugh. "How did you know? *I* didn't even know."

I shrug. "I know you, Katy baby. I can read you."

"You're okay if I tell them? Even though it's so soon. I can hold off on telling the others for a bit, but that won't last long if I'm not drinking. My people know me."

I grin. "They do know you, and I'm fine with telling them. We need to tell my mom."

"Can I cook dinner for her tomorrow night? We can tell her then."

My eyebrows bounce. "You want to cook?"

She shrugs. "If my stomach is up to it, yeah. I mean, it won't be much. As you know, I only know how to make like five things, but I'm sure she'll like one of them."

Hope blooms in my chest. She's starting to talk. To brighten up a bit. "She'll love anything you make her. Especially if we tell her you're pregnant. How are you feeling?"

A brilliant smile overtakes her face. "Good. Excited.

Weird. Happy. Freaking out a bit. Or a lot. I might be freaking out a lot. You?"

"Same. All of the same." I hesitate. *Fuck it.* I round the island and drop into the seat beside her, twisting her until she's facing me, and take her hand in mine.

"Katy…" *I want you to move into my room. I want you to fall in love with me. I want to be not just the father of your baby but your guy, the one you love and curl up against every night and wake up beside every morning. Fuck!* "We're having a baby together."

"That we are, my friend."

I stiffen, my insides plummeting hard and fast to my feet. Friend. Did she just call me her fucking friend? It was said off the cuff, but now she's staring straight into my eyes and she's not taking it back or talking over it the way she typically would.

She wants me to know she means it.

"Katy… I…" I don't know what to say. *I don't want to be your friend. I want to be your everything the way you are mine.*

Fuck. Just… fuck. I don't think I've ever been in as much pain as I am now, and hell, is that saying a lot. I had a father who didn't love me, a wife and best friend who betrayed me, and a mother who is sick with cancer. But one word from Katy and it feels like my life is falling apart faster than it ever has before.

Friend. A humorless, devastated laugh hits the air between us. It's funny, or not so much. Maybe more ironic in a twisted way. Her eyes are all over mine, and just as she opens her mouth to say something else, the doorbell rings. Her eyes close, and she blows out a breath.

There's nothing else to say after that anyway.

"You're sure about this?" Katy whispers through the side of her mouth.

"You mean I should turn them away?"

She opens her eyes just as a second impatient ring sounds.

"I'm just saying, gird your loins because shit is about to go down."

"Who says gird your loins? I'm not sure I even know what that means."

"It means there's an incoming invasion."

"Katy…" I trail off, stuck, fucking ruined and miserable, and yet so goddamn elated and happy, I can't make heads or tails of any of it. I lost Katy, but she's pregnant with my kid. She called me her friend. Her fucking friend.

How do I fight that?

She might as well have cut me off at the stem and tossed my dick in the trash before chucking my nuts outside for the squirrels to have. They're no longer necessary to her, and she made that abundantly clear. Purpose served, now move on.

Only I can't move on.

I'm in love with the woman carrying my child and all she wants from me is friendship. How do I change that? Is that even an option? We have a contract. She's following the rules when I'm trying to break them.

"Thank you for this," she says, giving me a half-smile and a small hip bump like the buddy I am to her as we head for the door. "They would have been relentless otherwise."

"This is your home, Katy. They're your people. Don't thank me. They're always welcome."

"I'd thank you by dropping to my knees later, but we're not doing that anymore."

Blood races like a Formula 1 race car straight to my dick and the words "We could" flee my lips before I can censure them.

"I thought we weren't doing that anymore."

"We could," I repeat.

She shakes her head and looks at me as she chews on the corner of her lip just as the doorbell rings for a third time. "Probably not a smart thing to do anymore." She clears her throat. "We should let them in before Keegan breaks down the door."

"Right." I can't even meet her eyes. Getting kicked repeatedly in the nuts hurts less than this.

Katy leaves me standing here like the chump I am and goes for the door, swings it open, and Keegan and Kenna immediately swallow her up.

"Oh my god! Are you okay?" Keegan cries, squeezing the life from Katy. "We've been worried sick about you all day and you had your phone off."

"I'm fine," Katy reassures them. "It was just low blood sugar. Not the first time I've passed out, and likely not the last."

"I told you that you should have eaten something," Keegan wails.

"Let her breathe," Owen demands, pulling her in for a hug, looking her over, and then coming over to me for a fist pound. "Thanks for calling, man."

I give him a nod because that's about all I've got at the moment.

"Yeah," Stone exclaims, giving me a bro hug. "That means a lot."

"Definitely," Mason agrees, with a slap on my back. "We've been pretty worried since we got the text earlier. Even after Cal told us she was okay and back here with you."

In the two months Katy and I have been doing this, I like to think I've grown decently friendly with these guys. I talk with them. We shoot the shit. I like them, and I believe they like me back. But they're not my people the way they are hers. I can't confide in them as she can, and once again, I'm reminded just how alone I am.

"Do you want to tell them?" Katy asks softly, her gaze on mine from halfway across the room, and I can feel everyone else's eyes bouncing between the two of us.

"Holy shit." Keegan gasps. "You're pregnant. Aren't you?"

"We are," Katy confirms, and the girls scream, hugging her again. "Stop! I haven't even missed my period yet. It's early, and you all know better than anyone that a lot can happen in the first trimester."

"Did you just find out?" That's Kenna.

Katy walks them into the family room off the kitchen and sits down on the plush leather sofa, tucking her feet beneath her.

She nods. She giggles. She exalts. "Yes. We found out when I passed out. They ran blood."

Owen and Vander—ever fucking observant Owen and Vander—take in her sweatshirt, her wet hair, and then mine. They both catch my eye and read everything I'm doing a shit job of trying to hide and frown. They both frown at me. Like poor fucking Bennett, we see you, but she doesn't get it. And for that reason, I need to go. If they see it, everyone else will, and I can't. I just can't with that right now.

I'm too furious with myself for even getting here in the first place.

"I'm going to go and give you time together," I announce.

Before Katy can say anything or I can register her expression, I'm out the door and plowing down the street. I got everything I asked for, but I feel like I have nothing at all. I slam into the bar on the corner, the swanky gay bar that's all trendy lighting, thumping house music, fantastic drinks, bar food, and thankfully no women who are interested in me. Moving to the South End has its perks.

"What can I get you, honey?" the bartender asks as I take a seat at the bar.

"Tequila. A lot of good tequila. No ice."

"How good?"

"The best you've got."

He goes for the tall, blue, and white bottle on the top shelf and uncorks it. He sets the low-ball glass on the wood and pours me a solid three fingers. "Maybe you should just call him and tell him how you feel."

I blink at the man. "Maybe I should." I pick up my phone and dial the number I've been avoiding for three weeks.

"Hey!" Cayden picks up on the first ring, shock and hope stirring his voice.

I pick up my glass and down half of it in one gulp before wiping my lips with the back of my hand. "You're an absolute motherfucker. A total piece of shit. I will never forgive you." Even as I'm mentally thanking him. If he hadn't fucked Liz, I wouldn't be here with Katy. Even if she's not mine and never will be.

We're pregnant. I'm going to be a father. My mother is going to be a grandmother. That's what I need to focus on. Not the way my heart feels like it's been run over a cheese grater.

The bartender throws me an eye as if to say, *that's not what I meant,* and I finish off my glass, pointing to it for him to refill it. He quickly does and then sets the bottle on the ledge behind the bar and goes over to help someone else down the other end.

"I know," Cayden says solemnly. "I am a motherfucker, and I don't deserve your forgiveness. I'm sorry, Ben. So fucking sorry."

I rest my forehead in my hand and stare down at my glass as I press the phone to my ear. "She's pregnant."

"What?! Liz is pregnant?"

I roll my eyes and take another sip, savoring the smooth flavor and warmth filling my stomach and veins. "No. Seriously? Are you that stupid? Katy is, you fuckass."

"Oh." He clears his throat, almost in what sounds like relief. "Okay." I hear him moving in the background. "Right. You're in love with Katy and I'm in love with Liz, so that's just how my brain worked. How do you feel about that? Katy, I mean. Forget Liz."

*I already have.* "How do you think I feel? The woman I love is pregnant with my kid."

He chuckles under his breath as muted sounds flow around him. "Ah, so you finally admit it."

"She doesn't love me back."

The bartender refills my glass even though I didn't ask him to. He gives me a look like he wants to say something but doesn't know what, other than, "You know, I totally didn't peg you as straight. Not with that curly hair, those blue eyes, and that dimpled chin despite your rugged features."

I shrug. "As long as you don't peg me, I don't care."

He belts out a laugh, and so does Cayden. "Shame. It's always the pretty ones who are the least available."

"I think that was the best joke you've ever made," Cayden says in my ear.

"That was a total Katy joke," I tell him before going back to the bartender. The hollow space around my heart grows, and I crumble. "Just keep them coming."

"Are you driving?"

I shake my head. "I live up the street."

"Then I'll keep them coming," he promises and leaves me again.

I'm a mess.

"I'm hanging up on you now," I inform Cayden. "I just wanted you to know that you're a motherfucker and I hate you."

Movement on my left stirs me, I stare blankly at Cayden as he pulls out the stool and slides casually into it. I hit the end button on my phone and set it down, annoyed he's here. He points to my drink and flashes the bartender two fingers.

"What the fuck are you still doing in Boston?"

He doesn't look at me as he lifts his glass and takes a sip. "I never left. I'm renting a place two blocks away from your house."

"Why?"

"Because I came here for you. I couldn't go until you forgave me or at least spoke to me again."

"Baby, if he doesn't take you back after a declaration like that, I will." The bartender has his hand over his heart, his eyes big and round and full of swoon.

"He fucked my ex-wife behind my back for two years and then hit on my new girlfriend."

The bartender's face sours. "Oh. Straight too, huh? And a cheater. Bitch, you can pour your own drink next time."

The bartender huffs off, and Cayden takes his words as gospel, opening the bottle and topping himself off. "Anyway, as I was saying, I came here for you, but I happen to like Boston. It's my kind of city."

Of course it is. Boston fits him better than Minnesota ever did, and if he can mess with me, he will. "How did you find me?"

"We have tracking on our phones that you never shut off."

Well, shit. No wonder Liz always knows when I'm at the hospital or home. I go into my phone and shut that feature off, blocking her—and him—out.

"Why am I happy that you fucked Liz for two years?"

"Because you're in love with the woman carrying your kid. You just said that."

I lift my glass of tequila and down it in one large, over-the-top gulp that has me wincing and wheezing ever so slightly despite its smooth flavor and expense. The bartender pours me more, but if I keep this up, I'll be crawling home instead of walking.

"Her friends and family are at my place right now. She has about a thousand of them, but she's only telling her closest people. At least for now. I have my mom, and we're going to tell her tomorrow at dinner because Katy wants to cook for her. Katy can't cook to save her life, but she wants to cook for my mom." I turn to him. "Do you feel me on that? Katy, who has a thousand people and can't cook, wants to cook for my mom so we can tell her we're pregnant."

"I feel you on that."

I'm not sure he does. "I don't have a thousand people. I only had you and maybe a couple of others because I was never good at being social or opening myself up. But then you stabbed me in the back, and I lost you, and now I have no one."

He stares remorsefully at the bar. "I know."

There's something in his tone that I'm missing, but I'm starting to get too drunk to care. I shake my head. "My mom is fucking sick. I'm in love with someone I shouldn't be. We're having a baby I've wanted for years. I've needed you." I stare down at the glass of clear liquid and sigh. "Why didn't you ever tell me you loved Liz?"

He lifts his glass to his lips and polishes off most of it before taking it upon himself to refill his glass. "Would it have stopped you?"

Would it have?

"It might have," I admit. "I liked her, but it took me months and months to fall in love even when she told me she loved me. So yeah, for you, it might have stopped me."

"You're a better man than I am. You always have been. And much like you and Katy, she didn't love me back ,so what difference would it have made?"

I swallow that for a moment. I get his heartache. In a way, I understand unrequited love. The bitterness and agony it can cause. Hell, I'm here drinking myself under the bar because the woman I got pregnant called me her friend tonight.

Love can be tormenting and unkind and doesn't give two shits if it makes you the happiest person on the planet or the most miserable.

There isn't much I wouldn't do to be with Katy, but I don't think I would have ever betrayed him. Not the way he did to me.

"Liz isn't who I thought she was," he says, pulling me away from that, and I raise my glass.

"Same."

He clinks his glass to mine and we both drink.

"But I'm so glad she's not."

"Not me," he laments. "I was hoping she was everything I always thought she was."

"You should have told me. Then you could have married her, and I could have… I don't know. I like to think I always would have found my way back to Katy."

"Does Katy truly not feel the same way back? That seems impossible. Women always love you."

"You think so, but you're wrong. My life isn't the perfection you make it out to be and it never was. Katy called me her friend tonight. After we showered together and while she was wearing my clothes. My actions today were not those of merely a friend, but that's exactly what she called me."

"Oh."

"Yeah. Oh." I finish off my drink and slide the glass away.

"So what will you do?"

What *will* I do?

"The only thing I can. Fight for her. It's not perfect, but that's life. The beautiful and the ugly. The heartbreak and the joy. What good is all this fate that brought us back together if I don't do everything I can to bend it to my will? I've been a miserable sack of unhappy shit for months and months, and I'm tired of it. I might not win her, and this might cost me everything I've got left, but Katy is worth the risk."

# Chapter Twenty-Four

## Bennett

I leave Cayden in the bar and plow out onto the sidewalk. It's been a miserably warm September. and right now, with all this tequila thrumming through my veins and guaranteeing a hangover for my shift tomorrow, I wouldn't mind some cooler weather. It's not late, but it's not early as I enter my house, hearing the sounds of Katy and her people laughing from the family room.

I make my way into my kitchen, my stomach growling since I never did get that bar food. Opening the fridge, I hang on the door and stare in for way longer than I should require before my gaze snags on leftover Thai food from the other night. I didn't cook much this week with Katy being sick because I didn't want to stink up the house and make it worse for her.

I pull out the to-go container, set it down on the counter, and then dive back in for a bottle of water. I don't bother to sit as I grab some chopsticks from the drawer and dig in with gusto. My eyes wander about my dark kitchen, my vision growing fuzzy as I start to picture what things will hopefully look like in here a year from now.

Highchairs and baby food and bottles of formula or breast milk. I picture coming down here at midnight, the baby in my arms, and me feeding it a bottle in the dark while Katy gets some sleep upstairs.

My chest swells at the image. At the others that follow it. Waking up on a Sunday morning with Katy beside me. Having her bring the baby into bed with us so we can cuddle and talk and marvel at the perfection we made. I want the baby, but I also want it all. The life. The girl. *My* girl.

"We're heading out. She's getting tired," Owen announces, snapping me out of my reverie and over the doorway where he's lingering.

"I shouldn't have let her go in last night."

"Is that why I can smell the tequila from here? Guilt?"

I crack the top on my water and drink half of it down, ducking his question even though I know Owen well enough at this point to know he won't let it slide. As if proving my point, he folds his arms over his chest and waits me out.

I press my palms into the island and twist my head. "You're her best friend. You have no loyalties to me, and I've been burned enough not to trust people right now."

He considers this. "For what it's worth, I knew it would go this way. We all did."

"Thanks," I mutter sardonically.

He makes a dismissive noise in the back of his throat and then crosses the kitchen until he's on the other side of the island from me. "You're a fool."

"Is it your habit to go into another man's kitchen and insult him?"

"Jesus, Bennett. Shut up and listen. You're a smart guy. Haven't you figured it out yet? Katy is the sort who dives into the deep end headfirst without checking for rocks beneath the surface. She leads with her heart, and when she encounters something that emotionally stirs her up, she panics a bit and retreats. Call it a byproduct of losing her parents when she was a little kid or that this is simply who Katy is. Katy gets spooked, and after what Zane did to her, I'm not surprised she's being extra cautious now. But her getting spooked doesn't mean she doesn't want to swim back into the deep end. Sometimes she just needs someone to throw her in, so she doesn't see it coming."

Spooked. Isn't that the same word she used on me once? She retreated then, and I pushed her back into the deep end with me, just as Owen said.

I meet his eyes. "Thanks for the pep talk. I was already intending to, but now I think I'll start sooner than I was planning."

"You're drunk."

I sigh. "Yeah. I am. I'm sort of regretting that now. The spicy noodles should help, though."

"I'm going to assume that means you're in this with her as much as a man can be and I don't have to plan how we'll get rid of your body."

I motion at him with my chopsticks. "Assume away."

Before he can say more, Keegan walks in. "Good night, Bennett."

I throw her a wave. "Night." I scarf down the rest of the noodles.

"Are you good?" Owen doesn't know what to do with me. I don't know what to do with me.

"Don't ask me that yet. Ask me that in a week. Maybe two or three."

"Fine. Catch you later." He gives me a fist pound and I follow him to the door where he meets everyone else.

Katy says good night and then turns on me. "That's not fair, you know."

"What's not?"

"I could have used a drink or five tonight."

I step into her. My hand drags through her hair, and I

bring her mouth to mine because fuck friends. We were never friends. I slide my tongue past her lips and straight into her mouth, forcing her to taste me. She's still, hesitantly kissing me back with her arms more or less at her sides.

I pull back. "There. You just had a drink or five. Come on. You need rest." I take her hand and lead her up the stairs, walking her into my bedroom and bathroom.

"What are we doing?"

"You're sleeping in here tonight."

Her eyes round as she watches me grab an extra tooth-brush from the cabinet and hand it to her. Defiantly, she folds her arms. "Why would I do that?"

I growl, drunk and out of patience. "Either you sleep in here with me tonight or I sleep with you in your bed. Your choice, but it's one or the other."

She huffs. "I'm fine, Bennett. I'm feeling much better."

I cup her jaw in my hand. I want to tell her, but I'm drunk, and she's spooked. So I try a different tactic, softening my features and my tone. "Please? For me? For my peace of mind? I won't be able to sleep unless I know you're okay and I won't know you're okay if you're not beside me."

She sighs and stares down at the small space between us. "Fine. Just for tonight."

We brush our teeth and silently enter my bedroom. She pulls off my sweatshirt and her leggings but stays in my T-shirt that hits her midthighs. It's unbelievably sexy, and I quickly shut out the lights before she can see how hard she's making me—clearly, tequila is not whiskey when it comes to my dick. Pulling back the covers, we both climb in, and she immedi-ately rolls on her side, facing away from me.

I lie on my back, staring up at the vaulted ceiling, my hands on my head.

She can tell me no and I'll stop, but for now…

I slide my arms around her and drag her back into my chest, tucking her against me. My hand goes to her lower stomach over her shirt, but I can feel she's not relaxing. She's too in her head. "Go to sleep, Katy," I tell her softly. "We'll talk tomorrow."

A few minutes later, her breathing evens out and she's asleep in my arms. My lips plant into the back of her head and I breathe in the scent of her shampoo, begging the universe that brought us back together to give me a second chance with the girl of my dreams.

DESPITE THE FACT that I had a vat of tequila swimming through my body and I woke up with a definite hangover after a shitty night of sleep, I got up and ran four miles. It was a hellish, dragging four miles, but I did it anyway. Sweat coats my body, drips down my face and neck, and the stench of last night's tequila emanates from my pores. I use the hem of my sports shirt to wipe at it as I enter through the back door.

Immediately, I grab a sports drink from the fridge and chug half of it down, walking through the dark and silent downstairs toward the stairs as I finish off the rest. Katy was still fast asleep when I left, her body unmoved throughout the night from its position facing away from me.

But when I enter my bedroom, I find the bed empty and made as if no one slept in it at all. I jog down the hall to find Katy's door open, her room and bathroom empty. I grit my teeth and slip out my phone as I enter my bathroom, only to pause with my finger hovering over her name on my screen.

She taped a note to my mirror.

*Woke up feeling much better. Kenna and I went swimming and then she's giving me a ride to work since my car is still there. Don't be mad. I'm honestly fine. I'm making enchiladas for your mom tonight and I can't wait to tell her. XO, Katy.*

I grab her note and ball it up in my fist, chucking it in the direction of the trash and missing by about a mile.

Goddammit, Katy. So fucking stubborn and independent. She's avoiding me as she works this through. I know that. I know she needs this time.

But fuck if it isn't driving me insane.

She might not be ready for us, but I am, and with that, I need to do the right thing for her. An hour later, I'm pulling into the garage at work, but instead of going up to my floor, I get off on the fifth and walk down the long corridor. This is part of the reason I forced myself to run this morning. I too needed to think, and with that came the realization that I'm tired of hiding. I'm tired of sneaking around.

"Good morning, Dr. Lawson." Britany greets me with a warm smile.

"Good morning. Is he in?"

"He is. Just got here. I think he has a few minutes before his first surgery if you want to pop in."

"Great. Thank you."

I rap my knuckles on the chief of surgery's door, and when his growly "Come in" rings through the air, I twist the knob, suck in a steady breath, and enter his office. Evan Masters is a general surgeon and is still considered one of the best in his field despite being in his late sixties. He hired me because of Wes and did so with a very specific threat that I'm about to test.

"Bennett. What brings you in here this early?"

"Do you have a minute?"

"Sure. But just a couple."

I don't bother taking a seat. "I'd appreciate your confidentiality on what I'm about to say."

He runs his hand across his forehead and leans back in his chair, studying me cautiously. "Of course."

"I need to be taken off the final decision-making process for trauma fellows."

His hands fold in his lap, and he stares at me as if my words aren't making sense. "How come?"

"Because I'm in a relationship with Katy Barrows."

He doesn't react. Not even a deep breath or twitch of his eye. "How long has that been going on?"

"A couple of months. It began shortly after I started here." I don't tell him Katy is pregnant. It's too new, and frankly, it doesn't matter right now.

"Jesus, Bennett. Really?"

"I know the position—"

"Do you, though?" After a long, suspended look, he sits up, resting his forearms on his desk and shuffling a few papers around. "You realize she's your resident, and we have rules about that."

"Yes. I do."

"And I take it I don't have to remind you about the condition for your hire?"

"No. You don't."

Slowly, he raises his chin, his gaze relocking with mine. "Which means this is serious enough to you to not only pull yourself out of the decision-making process for the fellowship you oversee, but you're willing to risk your position here for her?"

"Yes, sir, I am. I'm in love with her. And while I love being here and I love my work as a trauma surgeon, I won't risk her future for mine. If I kept my mouth shut and word of our relationship got out, we'd both be done. Katy deserves that fellowship. I would have recommended her for it regardless of our relationship. She's smart, thoughtful, good with students, patients, and their families, and has by far the most talent of any fifth-year in her program. But ethically, I can't recommend her for the position she deserves without compromising her integrity and my own."

Now he sighs, displeasure all over his face. "What happens if she gets this fellowship? I agree, she's earned it. I've known Katy a long time and she's incredibly talented and hard-working. She takes no handouts despite the fact that her family is all over this hospital,and the staff adore her."

I shrug. "Then she's a fellow, and I'm an attending. We certainly wouldn't be the first couple in that situation nor the last, and fellows don't require the same oversight as residents do. But I can promise, as we've done so far during our relationship, we'll keep it outside the walls of the hospital."

That's sort of a lie. I've had Katy all over this hospital in a million different ways, but no one knows about that but us.

"Bennett…" He trails off, sighs again, and then stands. "I hired you because I believed you when you told me those accusations were lies propagated by your ex-wife. Now you're telling me you're involved with a resident."

I fold my arms over my chest and lean farther into the door. "One has nothing to do with the other. But if you're going to punish anyone, punish me. Not Katy. She deserves everything she's worked for and more."

He grunts, putting his hands on his hips. "Do her uncle and stepmother know about you?"

"Yes, they do. All of her family knows."

He stares at the floor for a very long, tense minute, and then finally he says, "Okay. I'm taking you off final decision-making for fellows. You'll still be part of the interview process, but ultimately, the decision won't be yours."

"Thank you, Evan."

His gaze meets mine, sharp and inscrutable. "Don't thank me, Bennett. I'm not firing you yet, but don't give me another reason to change my mind. This hospital cannot handle a scandal, and Katy Barrows with her family connections will hit the news. I will keep this between us because once word gets out, it won't be good for either of you. Cricket Peterson especially won't let that go. Keep your home life separate from work, and I trust this will be the last conversation like this that we'll have to have."

I nod, hearing his warning or threat or whatever you want

to call it loud and clear, and leave his office. A sense of foreboding sits heavy on my chest. Katy will likely start showing around the time the fellowship decision is made, and once that happens, questions will start coming in.

But more than that, how long can a secret like this keep without it spilling?

# Chapter Twenty-Five



Today was a good day. No, today was an awesome day. I slept insanely well in Bennett's arms, woke up early after hearing him leave the house, and went for a swim with Kenna. I ate breakfast—the first time I've done that in three days—and then saved two people's lives. Oh, and I'm pregnant.

The only flip side to that is that I didn't see Bennett much all day. It was surgery after surgery rolling in for both of us, so I didn't get a chance to talk to him at all. Hell, we hardly had a passing glance in the hall. Now I'm making enchiladas—Owen's dad Carter's recipe—for Paula so Bennett and I can tell her we're pregnant.

I'm so excited for it. I realize I should cool my jets because it's still so early, but I can't seem to. Where I was an exhausted, emotional, overwhelmed mess last night, today I feel… clarity. Awake. Alive. Jubilant.

Still, I was hoping Bennett would be home early so we could talk before his mother arrives. We have so much to get worked out.

Bopping my head from side to side, I sing along to the music I have blasting from the Alexa as I pile on the cheese and set the casserole dish in the oven. The rice and beans are cooking on the stove, and Paula should be here in about twenty minutes.

Everything is set. The table, the wine—which I can't drink—the food.

I have just enough time to run up and take a super quick shower since I splattered myself—including my hair—with enchilada sauce.

"Alexa, sto—ah!" I'm swirled off my feet, spun in the air, and then plopped directly on the kitchen counter. "What in the hell?" I yell, ready to kick and scratch my feisty way out of here until I meet the dark blue eyes of the man who positions himself right in my face. "Jerk." I smack his shoulder. "You scared me. How about next time warn a girl before you attack her from behind. You're lucky I didn't take a butcher knife to your favorite appendage."

He scoots me to the edge of the counter and steps between my parted thighs. "Maybe if you didn't have the music so loud and weren't singing along at the top of your lungs, you would have heard me open and close the door and call your name."

"Maybe, but that'll never happen. You're late," I tell him, changing the subject. "I was hoping you'd be home an hour ago."

His eyes brighten. "You were?"

"Yes. We have stuff to talk about."

His hands meet the counter on either side of my thighs, and his expression grows serious. "We do. We have a lot to talk about." He licks his lips, his eyes all over me. But he doesn't say anything, and it's too silent. Too tense. And I need to tell him. I need to tell him so much, so I open my mouth and start with, "Listen," just as he spits out, "I love you."

"What?" we both say at the same time. I blink and he does the same. "You go first." "You love me?" Again, at the same time.

He growls and runs his hands over his face before dragging them through his hair and making it stick up all over the damn place. "I wasn't going to blurt it out like that, but then you were sitting there with your pretty eyes all over me and it just slipped out." His hands meet my knees and run up my thighs. "I'm not taking it back though, Katy. I know this goes against everything we agreed upon, but I don't care. Fuck the contract. I love you. And I know you don't feel the same way about me. I know that's not where—"

"Bennett—"

"Just let me say this," he cuts me off. "I didn't want to fall in love again. Not ever. It didn't matter though because I've been in love with you all along." His hands cup my cheeks. "It's always been you, Katy. From the moment I first saw you all those years ago to the moment I saw you again, it's been you. No one has ever felt right the way you do because I have never loved anyone the way I love you." Our foreheads meet, and his nose runs along mine. "You're not looking to fall back in love, and you don't trust your instincts. I get it. We were both hurt, and when your trust is broken the way ours was, it makes you call everything into question. But God, sweetheart, don't you see how perfect that makes us for each other? I'll never break your trust. I'll always protect your heart. And I'll do whatever it takes to prove to you that no two people have ever fit together more perfectly than we do."

He pulls back slightly, his hands on my cheeks holding me like he's afraid to let go, his blue eyes so intense on mine.

"Don't give up on all that we could be just because you got spooked."

I rest my palm on his cheek. "Are you done?"

He swallows hard and nods nervously.

"Good. I love you too."

He tilts his head, staring incredulously at me. "You do?"

I laugh. "Yeah."

"But..." He pauses and shakes his head, squinting at me

as if my words don't make any sense to him. "Last night you called me your friend."

I sigh, wrapping my arms around his neck and dragging him back to me. "I know. That sort of slipped out and then I didn't take it back because, well…"

"You got spooked."

I give him a sheepish look. "I did. But then I saw your face when I said it and watched you storm out of here, and then when you came home a little drunk, it got me thinking."

"*It got you thinking?* I just spilled my heart out to you."

I laugh at his wounded expression. "It was a really good speech. An epic speech."

"Yeah?"

I smile and kiss his lips. "Definitely. If I hadn't already been in love with you, I sure as hell would have been after that. But even before it, I was going to tell you I'm right there with you. All this time, I didn't allow myself to go there. For one, we've both been through it with our exes, and we have so much at stake with this situation. I was afraid to put my heart on the line again because if I fell for you and you didn't love me back…"

He presses his lips softly to mine. He gets it. He gets me.

"Last night when I slept in your bed with you wrapped around me, it was as if everything clicked into place, and all the things I had been so afraid of, all the bullshit, no longer mattered. I felt your heart beating against my back, the same rhythm and tempo as mine, and I just knew. I knew we were *Surprise Baby for the Billionaire Doctor*, complete with our own HEA in the making."

He laughs, relief dancing across his features, lighting his eyes, softening his brow, and bringing the most breathtaking smile to his face. "I was prepared to throw you into the deep end with me and force you to swim."

"Huh?" I laugh the word.

"I was going to pull out all the stops. Sweep you off your

feet. Do whatever it took to make you fall as hopelessly, endlessly in love with me as I am with you."

"Damn. That sounds pretty good. Maybe I shouldn't have put all my cards on the table so quickly. Maybe I should have played this out to see all I could have gotten from you."

He pinches my side, making me yelp and giggle. "Brat."

My fingers trail up the back of his neck and into his thick hair. "No wooing needed, Bennett. I'm already yours. It is rather undeniably convenient that not only do we both want a baby, but that we fell for each other too. Almost like we're meant to be."

"We are meant to be. There's no other explanation. I love you," he whispers against my lips, his body pressed against mine as he steals a kiss.

"I love you too," I say hungrily against him, tilting my head and deepening the exchange. "So much, Bennett."

His tongue dives in, his hands all over me, ripping at my shirt, forcing it from my jeans so he can reach beneath it. "God, Katy. You're mine. You're finally mine. Both of you." His fingers caress my lower belly, and that's it. His love is a match, but his devotion is what sets me on fire. It has me tearing at his shirt, jerking it up and over his head before hauling him back against me. My legs wrap around his waist, and his mouth consumes mine.

His searing groan ripples into me like an electrical current. There is no air I want to breathe that isn't his. Any space between us is too much space. My shirt hits the floor, and we maul each other, our mouths moving fast and frenzied, our lips and teeth clashing. I rock against him, desperate for friction even as certain things start to hit my senses. The smell of overcooked cheese, the sizzle, hiss, and pop of liquid hitting the flame on the stove.

"Bennett—"

He cuts off my plea with another devastating kiss that scrambles my mind, making it impossible to focus or think about anything other than him. That is, until the fire alarm goes off, blaring an ear-splitting siren through the air at the same time his mother walks through the back door.

Bennett and I jump apart like two caught teenagers. I tumble off the counter, dropping to the floor in a heap, scrambling for my shirt, and throwing it back on. Bennett goes after the stove first, shutting off the burner before he does the same with the oven. A billow of acrid smoke plumes into the room, coating the ceiling and dulling the lights as he waves at it with an oven mitt.

"Mom, keep the door open," Bennett commands, not seeming to care that he's shirtless and that his jeans are unbuttoned. Finally, the alarm shuts off as the smoke filters out the door, swept away by the cool night air. He removes the enchiladas and sets the burnt remains on the stove beside the charred rice and beans.

"Well, this certainly wasn't the greeting I was expecting," Paula deadpans, a gleam in her eyes and a Cheshire grin on her lips.

I sigh.

And then I laugh. Because really?

Bennett snatches his shirt from the counter and puts it back on, then rebuttons his pants. "You know you had that on broil, right?" he says to me, his lips twitching indulgently.

"No, I had it on bake…" I trail off because that's not the first time I've done that with his super fancy oven, and now that he mentions it, I don't remember putting in the temperature. "Shit. I'm sorry. That's not how this was supposed to go."

"Well, I for one am very happy it is." Paula crosses the kitchen, gives me a big hug, and then tugs on something at the back of my neck. "Katy dear, your shirt is on inside out. You might want to fix that before we go out for dinner. Unless you'd like me to leave so you can finish what you were doing when I arrived."

Bennett makes a noise. "You'll never let us live this down, will you?"

"Never." She pats his face and kisses him on the same cheek. "Where would the fun in that be?"

She has a point.

"We should go out for dinner since that's now unrecognizable," I say, pointing to my ruined masterpiece. "Bennett and I can finish what we were doing later."

He throws me a look, and I give him a wink that makes him laugh. Strong arms band around me and he kisses me again, right here in front of his mother. No tongue or frenzy this time. Just a seriously good kiss, and when he's done, he turns to his mother and announces, "Katy and I are pregnant, and I love her like crazy."

"Oh, Ben." She brings a trembling hand up to her lips and stares at him with watery eyes. "Really?"

"Really," I confirm. "He's in love with me, but I can't stand him."

We all start to crack up, and his mother embraces both of us in a warm hug and then plies Bennett with kisses all over his face that eventually has him shoving her away with a "Ma, stop it."

We take her out to dinner, but the second we get back through the door and she drives off, we can't keep our hands off each other. He whisks me off my feet and tosses me over his shoulder, taking off for the stairs.

I make a squeal of protest that ends with a hard smack on my ass, quickly followed by another on the other cheek. Everything feels different now. There is no lingering tension. No unanswered questions. No what-ifs. No we shouldn't do this. Everything is light, fun, and easy.

That is, until he gets us into his bedroom—a place I have a feeling I'll be spending a lot more time in—and lets me slide down every hard inch of him. I reach up to kiss him, but in his next move, he flips me around, throwing the front end of my body onto the mattress and forcing my ass up in the air.

With a reach around, he undoes my jeans and then slides them along with my thong down my hips, leaving me fully exposed to him and the cool rush of air from the room. I shiver, my teeth sinking into my lip as he silently stands behind me, my pussy and ass bare and at his mercy.

Large, strong hands run up the backs of my thighs and across the globes of my ass, momentarily splitting them and getting a peek of my forbidden hole.

"This is because you didn't take care of yourself when you should have."

"Wha—Ah!"

A sound *smack* lands straight across my backside, spreading fire and warmth through my muscles and making my pussy clench. My eyes flash open, and a rush of air surges into my lungs with a harsh gasp.

Before I can make sense of what he's doing, another swat hits my other cheek, equally as hard and just as deadly. My body rocks forward with the momentum of the strikes, and a moan slips past my lips. I've been spanked before, but never like this. Never as a means of punishment where the spanking is a delicious form of wicked torture. Where it's so deliberate and methodical I can't do anything other than allow him to dominate me.

But that's Bennett.

He's been holding back on me.

Scared to cross the line and allow himself to fully escape. He mentioned this side of himself—the rough side. The side that wants to play. And we did some of that in the bath and on a few other occasions, but nothing like this.

Now I have his trust.

And his trust is everything I've ever craved. It's such a potent drug—pure euphoria—knowing precisely what this means for him, for me, and for us, that I'll go as far as he wants to push me.

I might not have a limit. Certainly not one he's reached yet.

I know he'll always take care of me. My safety—and the safety of our growing child—is his castle. The walls he'll live and breathe and die to protect. So I surrender. Taking each firm strike with the devotion of a woman who can't get enough. Because his punishment is turning into my heaven. Softening my limbs and sweetening my mind.

The pain is erotic bliss.

"You're soaking," he rasps, dragging his fingers up the inside of my thighs. "You feel this. Your cunt is leaking." He bends, forcing my thighs wider, and licks up the inseam on each inner thigh, tearing a loud moan from my lips. "You have the prettiest pussy." His finger swirls around my opening, playing with my arousal before sliding straight in, as deep as it can go. "And so fucking tight. What will you do when I tie your wrists to our headboard and eat you till you can't stop coming?"

*Lose my mind*, hits me first, but my body responds before my mouth can, and I rock back into him, wanting that so badly I can't even think beyond it.

His chest crawls up my back, his hot skin sliding along my spine until his mouth reaches my ear. "Such a filthy whore, aren't you?"

Holy shit. My eyes roll into the back of my closed eyes, and I rock again, seeking, *needing* friction. No one has ever talked to me this way and I swear, I'm going to come just from that.

"The sexiest fucking woman I've ever seen. You own me, Katy Barrows. You always have. But tonight, I'm going to own every inch of you." He licks the shell of my ear. "Don't move, or I'll be forced to punish you in a way you won't enjoy as much."

"*As* much?"

Two fingers shove straight into me. "Do you enjoy that?"

I give him a jerky nod in response.

"How about this?"

He takes those two wet fingers and uses one of them to start playing with the tight ring of muscles at the back before plunging in and making my back arch and a high-pitched gasp squeal past my lungs.

It's tight and it burns, but in that good way. In a way that ignites fire in my core and wreaks madness to my senses.

I turn my head over his shoulder and meet his eyes. "That the best you've got to give?"

His hand runs along my ass, giving it a firm squeeze with his finger still inside me there. "Oh, sweetheart. You have no idea what I'm about to give you."

# Chapter Twenty-Six

## Bennett

My finger pumps in and out of her ass, and my cock jerks, begging to replace it. "Don't move," I command, my voice gravelly.

I slide my finger out of her and walk into my closet, searching for a tie to bind her wrists with. I'm so amped up, I have to take three calming breaths just to get my shit back under control. This woman. This fucking woman is finally mine. And everything I'm doing with her now, she only wants more of.

For the first time in my life, everything feels perfect.

With that, I can't help the foreboding sense of doom that follows, shaking my muscles and zapping me with a twinge of fight or flight. The notion that I don't trust that anything good in my life will keep or keep for long—since that's how it's always been—is unshakable. Still, I do my best to put it behind me and focus on what I'm here for. Katy. A silk tie.

My cock slaps my lower abs as if to say, *yeah man, get your head back in the game, and let's get this going.* I grab one of the few ties I own that I never wear and head back into the bedroom where Katy is, chest down, ass in the air, unmoved. Perfect.

I reward her by trailing tender kisses up her spine as I help her to stand. "Good girl," I whisper in her ear as I lift her once more and set her on the bed.

Crawling on, I shift her to the center and remove her shirt and bra. My eyes rove over every inch of her, and my cock gives another jerk at the thought of all the ways her body will change in the coming month. How beautiful she'll be with her belly large and swollen with our child moving around in it.

My hands slip around her wrists, and I run the cool material of the tie down one arm and then up the other. She shivers, his eyes dark and glazed in lust. "If you need me to stop or you don't like something, tell me."

"I will."

Warmth slithers around my heart and fills in all the gaps and chipped-away pieces. Her trust is a salve. Her love restorative.

Taking her wrists in the manacle of my hands, I draw them up to the slatted headboard and then go about tying her up. I've never done this before, but I can't deny the thrill racing through my blood at all the firsts and lasts I'll have with her. After checking her circulation, I capture her lips with mine, kissing her wildly and with feverish abandon.

The moment she starts to grind up into me, seeking more I pull away, giving her a warning look I know she'll never heed. Not my girl.

Shifting between her thighs, I trail down her body, licking and kissing as I go. Her nipples are hard, and her skin is covered in goosebumps. I capture one nipple in my mouth, my eyes casting up to hers as I do. She is a goddess—a fucking siren—all tied up and wanting, waiting to see what I'll do to her next.

My teeth drag along her pebbled flesh, alternating between each one, squeezing and playing with each of her fantastic tits. Just as I have her squirming on the bed, I continue lower, kissing and worshipping her belly. Holy hell. Her belly. I can't help but stare at her in utter wonder. Our baby is growing in there. I never imagined I'd have this. Not ever.

My chest clenches impossibly tight, stealing my breath. I didn't know it was possible to love someone as much as I love Katy. My lips plant into her sweet, soft skin and I kiss her lower belly over and over again. Her breath hitches and I smile against her, knowing she's as overcome with all of this as I am.

Pulling back, I sit on my haunches. "Spread your legs for me, sweetheart."

I get a raised eyebrow as her only response before she brazenly and unabashedly spreads her legs, showing me everything I'm salivating to see. My cock surges, and without the ability to stop myself, I grab her by the backs of her thighs, lift her ass, and place my mouth over her dripping cunt.

Her back arches and her arms jerk, testing the restraints. "Ah. Jesus, Bennett. Your mouth."

My tongue swirls around her opening before diving in as deep as I can go. "I want to fuck your ass tonight."

She moans, her head rolling back even as she gives a jerky nod. I know she likes anal play. She's mentioned it before.

"But first, you have to come twice."

With that declaration, I start eating her like a starved man. Like a man so obsessed with his girl that he can't hold back another second. Her smell, her taste, her sounds, the way her body moves—all of them drive me wild. I can't get enough of her, and I know I never will.

My tongue rings her clit, swirling around and around. She's so responsive, so turned on, it won't take her long to come like this. I slip two fingers straight inside, quirking them up. And then I start to fuck her. Hard. All the while I play with her clit, alternating between sucking and flicking it.

She cries out, and her thighs close, plastering themselves to the side of my head. Her body is unable to handle the pressure of what I'm doing, and it has her dripping all over me. I groan into her, licking her more ravenously. I can't wait to feel it on my cock. But first, she has to come.

She clamps down on my fingers, rocking and rolling her body, fucking up into my face, seeking that high she's so close to reaching. I take one of my slick fingers, slide it straight into her ass while I suck hard on her clit, and she comes. Her moans fill the room, her legs a vice around my head, her body a trembling, quivering mess of madness and pleasure. The headboard creaks against the turbidity of her movements.

Just as she starts to sag, I lighten the pressure, but I don't stop. She bucks, trying to shake me off. She's sensitive, and I just gave it to her hard, but she's going to come again. I don't have lube, and I need her nice and fucking wet before I can take her ass without hurting her. And I refuse to hurt my girl. Ever.

"Bennett, I want you inside of me. Please. I need to feel you."

There's no way I can deny her, so I give her clit one last lick and then kiss my way up her body until I reach her face. I hover over her, staring down into her eyes. "Hi, baby."

"Hi." She gives me a flirty smile.

I touch her cheek and kiss her forehead. "Do you want me to untie you?"

"Not a chance."

"That's my good girl. I love you so fucking much, Katy." I devour her sweet mouth as I hike her legs up onto my shoulders. She starts to move, seeking me, needing to come again. I line myself up and slide straight into her, all the way to the hilt. A low hum emanates from my lips, and Katy's eyes roll back. There is nothing like being inside of her.

I start to pump in and out in a slow tempo that leaves us both breathless.

I fuck her like this for a few minutes. Working us both up to the point of madness. To the point where we can't stand it another second and we both need more. Sliding my wet cock from her, I adjust her position and stare down briefly before my gaze casts up to hers.

I give her a wicked smile and then spit, letting it drip from my lips straight onto her puckered asshole.

"Ah! Oh, hell. That's seriously fucking dirty." She lets out a breathy laugh. "And hot."

I do it again, using my finger to move my spit around, pushing my finger in and out of her, getting her as wet and lubed as I can. And when she's ready, when she is panting and moaning and shaking against my finger, begging to be fucked, I put her knees back on my shoulders and work the head of my cock into her tight-as-sin ass.

In and out, a little at a time, pushing it slowly past the tight ring of muscles that work to keep me out. I spit again and gather some of her arousal from her pussy, making sure I'm wet and slippery. My lungs empty as I manage past her muscles and slide home, settling in deep and holding still to let her get used to me.

"You okay?" I grit through clenched teeth.

She gives me a shaky nod, and I have to kiss her. I have to hold her and touch her. In my wildest dreams, I never fathomed being with anyone like this. I had no idea all that I was missing in my life until Katy came into it. I was making do. Accepting the status quo and telling myself I was happy with not nearly enough.

But being with Katy is soul-quenching. It's fulfilling on a level I didn't know existed. Being inside her body is home, the beat of her heart is the sound I'll live and die by.

My hips slide back, and in our next breath, I start to pound. My fucks deep and endless. Our sweaty foreheads meet, and our eyes hold. It's the most intense thing I've ever experienced. Her lips part on a silent scream, and she jerks against her restraints. I grin and bite down on her lip.

"It won't be that easy, sweetheart. You're at my mercy. I

can fuck you however I want, and you can't do anything about it other than take it."

She moans, her hands gripping the slats of the headboard. "So far you're not threatening me with anything I won't beg and plead for. Now fuck me and show me how hard you can make me come with your dick in my ass."

Holy hell. I wheeze out a laugh. This fucking girl.

"Let's see how much you can take." With that, I let go. I succumb. I give into every depraved corner of my mind, knowing she can take it and then some. With her knees on my shoulders, she works her hips, meeting me thrust for punishing, pounding thrust. She's impossibly slick and hot and so goddamn tight I can hardly make sense of it.

Sweat clings to my hair and back with my exertion. I grip her ass in one hand and suck the thumb on my other hand into my mouth. Using the wet digit on her clit, I rub it in vigorous circles.

"Ah! Yes. Oh my god, please yes. Don't stop. More."

I'm not sure how much more my body can take, but I fuck her with everything I've got while I work her clit. Her body trembles, her legs tighten against me, and she starts to scream and thrash. The tight fist of her ass robs my breath, and I fuck her through her orgasm, unable to tear my eyes away from her for even a second.

The moment she starts to come down, her body relaxing, I pull out, wrap my hand around my cock, and with two jerks, I come all over her belly and tits. Low growls and grunts spill from my lips along with her name.

I collapse beside her in a heap of sweaty exhaustion. Half-dazed, I reach up and untie her wrists. Her arms drop, and she rolls her wrists to work blood back into her limbs.

Gathering her arms in my hands, I massage her flesh and check for any red marks. "Are you okay? Did I hurt you?"

"Oh yes. And I can't wait for you to do it again."

I kiss the corner of her lips as I roll onto my side and move her tighter against me. I bring my hand to the mess I made on her and start to run my fingers into it, rubbing it into her belly.

"What are you doing?" she asks, her voice tired and breathless.

"Marking my territory."

She laughs. "I think the bun in the oven already does that for you."

I smile, burying my head in her neck and pulling her against me. "Come on. Let's go shower."

TODAY IS my mom's first day of her second round of chemo. She got a six-week break after finishing her first round, and so far, the scans and blood work are promising. She's in good spirits despite lamenting over her bald head. The break was good for her, and I hate that she has to go through another eight weeks of this. Katy came with me for it, and it made my mom's otherwise miserable day better.

She took over reading duties for me, picking up where my mom and I left off in our current read. It's some sports romance both women seem to be loving, and I don't argue when Katy reads the sex scenes with exuberance. My mind is far too preoccupied to care or even pay much attention to it.

After my mom's chemo, we have our first OB appointment.

Katy is officially seven weeks along, but with her diabetes, her OB wants her to come in for some blood work and an ultrasound. Meaning we'll get to see our baby. Words can't describe the nerves and excitement swarming through me.

Katy offered to have my mom come with us, but I told her we'd have her do that with the next one. For the first ultrasound, I want it to be just us. Tonight, Katy is staying at

Owen's place so she can have a sleepover with Rory and I'm going to stay at my mom's.

Other than that, it's been an incredibly quiet five weeks since we found out we're pregnant. Liz calls with less frequency. I haven't seen Cayden, and I have no idea if he's gone back to Minnesota or if he's still here in Boston. Frankly, I don't care. Cricket was only knocked from her high horse for a few days. After that, she was back to sucking up and snarking Katy any chance she got.

Interviews start next week for trauma fellowships, and I know Katy is anxious about them. We haven't talked much about it. She's preparing, but I also know she's worried about what her pregnancy will mean for her chances of getting it. And if she does get it, what will having a newborn do to her work?

To me, it's still too early to talk about it.

So much can happen between now and then, and we'll get a firm due date today. Once we have a better sense of how her pregnancy is going and how her body is responding to it, then we can start to plan.

Dana Farber is connected to Brigham and Women's Hospital where Katy's OB is—thankfully, it's not Keegan or one of her uncles or aunts—and as we walk, Katy holds my hand as she talks to Owen. We've taken more risks with each other outside of the hospital, though we're both aware anyone could see us at any time.

"Yes, I swear," she says, and then she laughs. "A little sugar won't kill her, Owen. It'll only kill me." She laughs harder. "No, that's great. You know me, I'll eat the hell out of all the pizza tonight. No, I don't have any weird cravings. At least not yet. My usual is perfect." She pauses to listen. "Obviously, we're watching *The Little Mermaid*." She snorts. "Dude, if you want to go out and, I don't know, pick up a woman for once in your life, go for it. I've got the little lady." Another pause. "Aw, you're cute when you're clingy to me. The three of us will have an epic pajama party, but at some point, you do need to venture into the world of sex again." She laughs. "Sounds good, my brother from another mother. Love you too."

She disconnects the call just as we approach the elevator and hit the button. "Why doesn't Owen ever go out?"

Katy glances up at me. "Owen's ex was a real piece of work. You should know what those are like." She gives me a hip bump. "Anyway, he does go out on rare occasions, but only for a night if you know what I mean. He's hesitant to bring anyone into Rory's life again after what happened with them. Not even a nanny, though trust me when I tell you he needs one desperately."

"That sucks. I feel for him with that."

The elevator doors open, and we step on and hit the button for our floor. The moment the doors close and the car starts to ascend, I take Katy in my arms and kiss her like crazy.

"I'm going to miss you tonight," I tell her. "But more than that, whatever this ultrasound shows, I'll always love you and that will never change. No matter what."

Her arms snake around my neck, and she kisses me back. "I love you too. And—" Her words sharply cut off as the elevator suddenly loses power and we glide to a stop. "What in the absolute fuck?"

Oh hell. Not again.

"You've got to be kidding me!" she shrieks and smacks my shoulder. "Bennett, what did you do?"

"Me?" I point to my chest. "I didn't do anything."

"Except the elevator stopped and doesn't have power. Again. It's not even the same goddamn hospital or elevator. How does this keep happening to you, and why are you dragging me down with you?"

I throw my arms up. "I have no idea. I honestly don't. I'm clearly elevator jinxed."

"Four times! Who gets stuck in an elevator four times? Why do you even bother riding on one?"

She has a point with that. It is a bit ridiculous at this point.

She spins around and starts to pace, her breath quickening. "You are never getting in an elevator with our baby. Ever. Why is this elevator so small? It's a hospital. Elevators in hospitals are supposed to be big. No gurney could fit in here."

"This is the office wing. The elevators are normal size."

She throws me a menacing glare. and I redirect.

"Relax. It's going to be fine, baby. I'm sure it'll come back on in a moment."

"Relax?" Her arms flail about. "I'm stuck in another fucking elevator. I was just getting to the point where I didn't think about getting stuck when I got on one, and now this."

I pull her back into my chest and hug her to me. "Yes, but this time at least there's emergency lighting."

"Oh, goodie fucking gumdrops. *Emergency* lighting. There is no Keegan this time." Her eyes spark with realization. "Oh! But there is a Kenna. Kenna works here." She slips her phone from her purse and calls Kenna, who picks up quickly. "Hey lover, is the power out in the hospital?" She listens for a minute, sighs, and then throws me another one of her death glares. "Fabulous. So the man I decided to make the father of my child *is* elevator jinxed." She starts pacing again, one hand on her hip, the other holding the phone to her ear. "We're stuck in the goddamn elevator on the way to our appointment. I know! It's unreal. Yes, we're fine, if you don't take my freaking out into account. Great. Thanks, babe. We'll just sit here and wait." The last part comes out especially sarcastic and it makes my lips bounce. I have no idea why, but for some reason, I'm finding this ironically humorous.

Not to mention, as she was talking, I hit the emergency call button and texted the number on the panel. A message popped through immediately telling me that we'd be up and moving again soon. It's simply a small mechanical error that triggered the power outage for our car, but it should be fixed once they restart the system.

Katy is walking laps around the car, her hands wild and dragging through her hair as she mutters to herself.

"You doing okay over there?" I quip, my lips twitching when she flips me off. "Still love me?"

She grumbles under her breath, but I think she said something along the lines of, "Unfortunately, yes." More muttering before she stops pacing in front of me. "Admit it, you're jinxed."

I shrug. "I might be."

"I'm never doing this with you again."

"You've said that before."

She squints at me. "Yeah, well, I mean it this time, Buster. I never got stuck once until you came into my life."

My hands meet her hips. "Fair enough."

"Stop smiling at me like that. It's not funny."

It's not, and I feel bad she's panicking again, but for some reason, I can't help but find it so. "You're cute when you're panicking."

Her jaw drops. "That's seriously messed up."

I shrug again. "Possibly, but it's still true."

"Ugh." She shoves my chest until my hands fall away, and she starts to pace again. "We're going to be late for our"—the car jerks back to life and starts to move—"appointment," she finishes.

"Not anymore."

The doors open a half minute later, and I wave for her to get off first. She nudges my shoulder. "This is why people think you're a jerk, Bennett. You might want to work on that."

"Yes ma'am."

"Did you just ma'am me? Do I look old enough to be a ma'am?"

"Will I be able to say anything right?"

"Absolutely not." She sniffs. "At least not until my heart

rate and blood pressure return to normal." Her body sags dramatically. "Ugh. That's going to throw off my vital signs in there."

"I promise, no more elevators for you, and we're safe and sound. Deep breaths."

"I'll give you deep breaths," she mutters bitingly.

Katy refuses to take my hand again as we enter the office. She's hell-bent on being angry and ignoring me, which lasts her all of ten more minutes until they take about ten vials of blood and we're brought back to the ultrasound room. Her vitals were fine, by the way. Just a slightly elevated heart rate as she recounted our elevator mishap to the tech.

Only the second Katy gets situated on the table, her anger and nerves switch gears. All her focus—and mine—goes to the machine on her right and the screen in the corner of the room.

"Good afternoon. I'm Angel. I'm going to be doing your ultrasound today."

I smile politely, but for the life of me, I can't make words come out. I've imagined this moment dozens of times over the last couple of years, but not since everything with Bennett began. Maybe because it went from future fantasy to reality, and now there is so much at stake.

Bennett sets his head on the table beside mine and takes my hand, squeezing my fingers. I can feel his pulse thrashing through his palm, and something about that settles me. We're in this together, for more than just the baby now. Yes, that raises things to another level of shit that can go wrong, but I don't think that's going to be us.

We get each other.

We see each other for exactly who we are and love each other regardless. I don't need anyone else and neither does he. That's what we were missing with our exes. With everyone who came before. When I think about Bennett, I smile and my chest flutters. I realize it's new. We're only a few months in, but I don't care, and I know he doesn't either.

When something is right, it's right, and time only stands as a means to keep you apart.

I remove my leggings and underwear, donning a gown, and a few minutes later, Angel returns and dims the lights. "Ready?"

Both Bennett and I gulp and nod. Sometimes being a doctor sucks.

After a squirt of warm lubricant on the probe, she places the wand straight into my vagina and moves it around to get it into position. A swish and a crackle fill the room, and then the monitor lights up.

"Okay, let's see what we've got." Angel holds the probe with one hand and types some things onto the keyboard as she goes. She shifts it this way and that, the image nothing more than a staticky mass of tissue until she narrows it straight on my uterus and the teeny tiny blob in there. There's not much discernible except for a larger, rounded end, which is the baby's head, an oval shape, and possibly what looks like little arms.

Tears prick my eyes, and Bennett moves closer, holding me tighter.

A few more clicks of the keyboard and a small adjustment of the wand, and, "There's your baby's heartbeat."

It's nothing more than a rapid flicker inside its chest, but fuck, there's my baby's heartbeat. And it looks good. So good. At least from what I can tell.

"Bennett," I rasp, my voice hoarse as those tears start to cascade down my cheeks like Niagara.

"I know." His voice is as thick with emotion as mine.

She continues to check things—the thickness of my cervix and uterus and other details I don't care as much about but are obviously important. We can see our baby. We can see it moving inside me. It's the most miraculous, magical thing I've ever experienced.

It's real now.

I never saw a positive pregnancy test. It was simply a notation in my chart. That's not the same thing as seeing those two pink lines or the word pregnant on the stick.

This is the first real indication I have that this is happening. That there is no going back. Not with the baby or with Bennett. This is forever. This is life-changing. I'm going to be a mother, and Bennett is going to be a father.

My heart skips a beat and then breaks out into one of those ridiculous TikTok dances with all those convoluted moves.

"You're seven weeks two days pregnant, and your due date is June seventeenth."

Oh. I mean, I guess I knew that. I figured out the math of it before having it confirmed now. But that's right when my fellowship would begin. I have no idea what I'll do about that, but I suppose I have time to figure it out.

"Can I have pictures?" I ask the tech. I need to show Callan and Layla. I need to show Owen, Keegan, Kenna, Vander, and Mason. I need to show my people. All those years of never thinking I'd have this, and now here I am. I know the risks. I know we're far from out of the woods. I know maintaining tight control of my blood sugars will be a daily challenge, and I also know that my work schedule isn't the most conducive to either situation.

But I'll do it. I know I will. I'll do whatever it takes.

"Of course," the tech chirps. "Here you go." She hands me a strip of images and then some towels to get myself cleaned up and leaves. I wipe at myself up, pull on my leggings, and then swing my legs over the side of the table to face Bennett.

Before I know what's happening, he kneels in front of me and takes my hands, setting both of ours on my lap. He looks me straight in the eyes and says, "I told my boss we're a couple."

I blink at him, not having expected that at all. For a

moment, I thought… well, that's a relief, right? Not quite ready for all that yet. I digress. "Um. Okay."

"I did this weeks and weeks ago. Before we were even a couple."

My eyebrows shoot up to my hairline. "And you didn't tell me until now? Why'd you do it?"

"We had just learned you were pregnant, and I had plans to win you even if you did call me your friend."

I roll my eyes, and he leans in and kisses the inside of my wrist.

"I'm no longer part of the decision-making for fellowship applicants, but I promised him no scandals, Katy. If you're okay with it, I'd like to tell him we're pregnant."

Nervously, I lick my lips. "I wanted to wait until after my interview. Hell, I wanted to wait until after they made a decision."

His expression softens. "I know you did. And I understand why you feel like you have to do that. But I don't want to hide us. I'm tired of it. You're mine, and I'm yours, and we're having a baby." His hand cups my jaw, his other still holding mine. "I'm not saying we announce this to the world. It's still very early. But I want to tell my boss, so it doesn't appear as though I'm trying to hide anything. And with that, when you get your fellowship, I will take time off and stay home with the baby until we're all ready to put them in hospital daycare."

"You will?" I choke out as more tears start to fall. Stupid pregnancy hormones.

"Yes. And if you have to move for it, Katy baby, we'll move together. All my roads, no matter how perilous or winding, have always led me to you, and they always will."

"What about your mom?"

"If she can't or doesn't want to come with us, I'll buy a fucking plane and come in once a week to see her."

Jesus. This man. He means it.

My heart swells. I don't know if it's dumb luck or some

magical, twisted form of fate that brought us back together, but I don't care. I'll thank whatever it is until my dying breath.

"I'm getting this fellowship," I tell him sternly. "Boston is my home. My heart."

"I have no doubt you'll get it. You're the best applicant. But you have to take care of yourself and our little one while you're growing it. I can't risk your health or theirs. You got me?"

I nod shakily. "Yeah. I got you. Even if they want to try me on a pump again, I'll do it. Whatever it takes."

He smiles and stands to kiss me as he moves our joined hands and presses them against my belly. "Whatever it takes."

That night, I have the best slumber party ever with Owen and Rory. The three of us eat too much pizza—Owen gets me cauliflower crust because it has fewer carbs, which means less ingested sugar—and Owen makes s'mores. Insulin resistance can be a problem for type 1 diabetics when they're pregnant, so I don't tempt the fates with the s'mores. I promised Bennett—and this baby—that I was going to take good care of us, and I intend to. Instead, I munch on a couple of sugar-free Oreos he keeps here for me along with plenty of popcorn.

Paula slept most of the afternoon and night, and when she did wake up, she was so miserably sick that Bennett eventually gave her a bag of IV fluids into her PICC line. He's exhausted and has an early shift, but since it's my day off, I decided to make him something special now that I've figured out how to properly work his appliances.

Only, as usual with my cooking, nothing goes to plan. My chicken pot pie comes out tasting like paste, and no amount of Jesus could resurrect this from the dead. I end up ordering from his favorite Mexican place because they have the most amazing burritos and use handmade corn tortillas, which are better for me than flour. The only bummer is not having a margarita to go with it, but I'll get over it.

"How's she feeling?" I ask Bennett as I finish setting the table. He went to check on his mom before heading home.

"Better," he says in my ear. "Well, if you count her kicking me out and sending me home to you better, then I guess that's what she is."

"If she's feisty, she's better," I tell him as I dance around the kitchen to music from the Alexa in my fuzzy socks. Fall weather has finally set in, and it's perfectly cold outside with multicolored leaves scattered across the backyard.

"That's what I figure." The buzzer for the door sounds. "What's that?"

"Um. Well…"

He chuckles. "You burned dinner again, didn't you?"

"No!" I protest indignantly as I turn off the music and head for the door. "I didn't burn it. It was just a bit inedible." I swing open the door and freeze, staring in a stunned pause at the person lingering on the stoop. I'd think she was here for me if the equally shocked expression didn't immediately tell me I was wrong. "Oh, shit."

"What are you doing here?" Cricket Peterson snaps at me.

"Who is that?" Bennett barks in my ear, only I can tell by his voice he already knows but is hoping I'll prove him wrong. He growls in dismay. "What the hell is she doing there?"

"I feel a great reckoning is upon us," is my only reply to him. "See you soon." I hang up on Bennett and slip my phone into my back pocket. "I think that might be my question for you," I say to her. "What are you doing at my boyfriend's house?"

She blinks at me, nonplussed. *"Boyfriend?"*

I could have lied, but considering I opened the door in my joggers and his sweatshirt, I doubt I would have sold anything. But more importantly, why is she showing up at Bennett's front door if not to try something? No way I'm letting that go down. Plus, Bennett said he's tired of hiding us and I guess I am too, so it's game show time, folks. Let's spin the wheel and see where it lands.

"Yes. Bennett and I are together." I lean my hip against the doorjamb and fold my arms casually over my chest. "Though I guess calling him my boyfriend is prosaic for a man like him. But manfriend sounds creepy, right?"

She sputters. "What? What are you… you're really with him? How long has that been going on?"

Cricket stomps her foot like a child demanding answers, and I step outside, shutting the door behind me and wrapping my arms tighter around my chest. Why is it freaking forty-five degrees at the beginning of October?

"Have a seat." I sit my butt down on the stone step and pat the space beside me. Cricket looks like she's about to blow a gasket, but she does as I ask. Probably because she's too overwrought to fight me for once. "Let me ask you again because I think my question will kill two birds with one stone. What are you doing at my boyfriend's house?"

Her arms and legs shoot out in front of her, and for a second I think she's about to run, but then she relaxes and starts nervously playing with her neck. "I um…"

"You thought you'd come here and say something like, *I was just in the neighborhood and happened to know where you live even though it's not listed anywhere searchable and was wondering if you wanted to grab some dinner or a drink before I work you up into taking me back here for the night.* Right?"

She shifts, looking to her right, but just like me being here is obvious, so is the intent behind her showing up here. The awesome thing about this moment is that if this had been Zane, I would have been suspicious that he was having an affair, and the girl showing up didn't know about me. In Bennett's case, I know she's here unsolicited so she can try and get with our boss.

Probably for several reasons, including the fact that he's next-level gorgeous and she believes he's still the one running the fellowship. "You'll do anything to get a competitive edge," I find myself saying.

Her head whips in my direction, fury blazing in her dark eyes. "Oh, and you're not?" She harumphs. "Why are *you* here, Katy? You've obviously been keeping your affair a secret. Even his best friend didn't know about you."

My brows scrunch. "Huh? His best friend?"

"A neurosurgeon from Minnesota showed up at work today looking for Bennett, but he had just missed him. He said he was leaving town but wanted to give him this"—she pulls out something wrapped in brown paper from her pocket—"before he left."

"So he gave it to you? Just like that?"

"He told me where he lived and asked if I'd deliver it. He said he'd heard a lot about me from Bennett, and I thought…"

"You thought you'd use that as your opening."

Her cheeks flush.

There is a lot in what she's saying that isn't quite adding up. Especially about Cayden.

"Bennett and I have been together for a few months. We knew each other a while back when I was a third-year medical student, and he was chief resident. And before you start getting all Cricket on my ass, he's not deciding over fellowships anymore. Once he and I got together, he stepped back from that so it wouldn't be a conflict of interest."

Yeah, Cricket might be ready to murder me.

"Are you kidding me?!" she shrieks. "What is *wrong* with you? What kind of—"

I hold up my hand. "I'm gonna stop you there, Cricket, since your reasons for being here are far from altruistic. You could have given him whatever is in that bag tomorrow at work. Instead, you came out here to his private residence to make a personal house call. So let's not throw stones. I love Bennett. My relationship with him has nothing to do with getting ahead. But you, you give women a bad name. You wasted four years hating me and knocking me down every chance you got when we could have been friends. Competitors does not have to mean adversaries."

She sulks for a moment, dropping her elbows to her thighs and staring out at the quiet side street. The cool autumn air whips by us, rustling our hair as we fall into silence. Finally, she turns and gives me a look I can't quite read.

"Everything always comes easy to you."

I roll my eyes at her childish antagonism, resting my forearms on my knees. "Hardly. Did you not see me eat linoleum in the OR? I have a life too, Cricket. Just like everyone else does. Shit hits us all. You were always so focused on me, you never gave yourself a chance to shine."

She huffs like a brat, and I sigh. Sometimes there is no reaching people.

I stand and look down on her. "I'm going in. I'm cold." For a moment, I'm tempted to tell her I'm pregnant, but why bother? She'll see my bump eventually, and I don't owe her any explanations. "I hope your interview goes well, and no, there's no sarcasm in there. I honestly do. But I also plan to kick your ass and win that fellowship. I can wish you well and still want to win. Have a good night, Cricket."

I go inside, then shut, and lock the door since Bennett usually comes in through the back and he'll be home any minute. Cricket can do what she likes. She's no longer an issue for me. It isn't until I get inside and she's gone that I realize I never grabbed the brown bag from her.

# Chapter Twenty-Eight

# Bennett

Katy is dancing around the kitchen. This isn't new for her. She does this all the time, usually as she sings along to whatever she's listening to. But this is… different. A bit wilder. Perhaps even a little manic. The takeout bags sit untouched on the counter, the table set for us.

"Katy baby?" I call loudly so as not to startle her.

She spins around and skips over to me, a smile lighting her face. "Hey, lover boy." She jumps up into my arms, making me catch her. "Glad you're home. I'm starving."

My eyes narrow. "You okay?"

"I feel like you ask me that a lot."

"I've had a lot of reasons to ask."

"True." She gives me a sweet kiss and then wiggles out of my arms. "So Cricket was here," she says flippantly when that statement is anything but.

She starts opening to-go containers and I move in behind her, kissing her neck just beneath her jaw, which distracts her enough to allow me to make her a plate. I can smell the remains of whatever she tried to cook for us lingering in the air, and the fact that she spent her day off doing that for me and then had to deal with Cricket makes me want to hold her and never let go.

"Thank you." She takes the plate from me and goes to sits while I make my own.

"And?" I press when she doesn't follow that up. "What did she want? Why was she here?"

"She wanted to try to seduce you because you're hot. She probably likes you because who wouldn't, even if you can sometimes be a bit of a jerk, and she wants the fellowship and figured your dick was the fastest track to winning it."

My eyebrows jump. "She told you all that?"

She lifts her fork and uses the side of it to try to cut her burrito only to give up and lift it with both hands. "No. Of course not. Cricket is a bitch, but she's not stupid."

"Katy. I love you, but right now I'm having a little trouble decoding you." I take my plate and sit down.

"I know. I'm fine. I promise. I just had a lot to think through and process about it because there's more going on than her simply showing up at your door. I told her you were my boyfriend."

I nearly choke on my bite of burrito. "You did?" For some reason that makes me laugh. Maybe because Katy was so hell-bent on keeping us a secret. At least for a while longer.

She shrugs. "I opened the door in your sweatshirt. But more than that, I wasn't going to let her think you were in play. I also told her you're no longer in charge of the fellow-ship. She didn't like that." Her head tilts contemplatively. "Well, she didn't like any of it, actually. I think our being together pissed her off. She has a lot of resentment she needs to learn how to work through. But whatever. It's done and she can't say or do anything about it."

"True." I take another bite and wash it down with a sip of my water. "I'm glad you told her. Still, it was weird for her to just show up like that out of the blue."

Katy turns serious, her eyes searching mine in rapid flicks, and I wonder if her trust in me was shaken. Maybe that's why she's a bit off, almost jumpy. She's here and she doesn't seem mad, but that doesn't mean she wasn't hurt or possibly a bit worried given the pasts we've had with others. I'd fly off the fucking handle if some asshole showed up here looking to get in her pants. Katy isn't just my end game; she is my only game.

But have I done enough to prove that to her?

"Bennett, there's something we should talk about. The reason Cricket showed up here… It's something I think you need—"

Before she can finish, I rise and cut her off with a searing kiss. My hand cups her face, and my forehead melds to hers. "You know I don't want her, right? You know it's only you and will always only be you?"

"I did know that, and not simply because I couldn't see you liking a woman who's named after a bug."

I chuckle against her lips.

Her fingers comb through the back of my hair, and I shift until I'm standing. In one motion, I lift her out of her chair and drop straight up into my arms. I can't wait till I can do this and feel her belly bump against me, but we're not there yet.

"You did?" I ask, retaking my seat with her straddling my thighs.

"I trust you," she tells me, and my heart leaps in my chest. "In my heart, I knew you'd never do anything to betray me."

"Never," I swear and drag her lips back to mine, kissing her so deeply she has to gasp against me to catch air. Within seconds, our clothes are torn off, and we end up in a messy tangle of limbs and panted breaths. After that, we finish our dinner and then spend the rest of the evening wrapped around each other on the sofa while watching some Netflix show Katy's obsessed with.

Everything is perfect between us. Too good to be true. But

you know what they say when something is too good to be true…

IT STARTS with a call on my way to work. A call I'm not paying attention to because I'm stuck in traffic and running a little late, which automatically grates on me. But with cars moving at a snail's pace and cutting in and out of lanes, the road has my entire frustrated focus. Which is why I don't think too deeply about it when I answer the random phone number across my screen.

"Hello?"

"Well, look who finally picked up. I guess getting a new number was all it took."

Ice immediately slithers through my veins, hardening my grip on the steering wheel. "A new number I'm about to block. Bye, Liz."

"No! Bennett wait. Please, wait. I need to talk to you. I've been trying for months."

I grunt, running a hand through my hair before returning it to the wheel. "What do you want? Why haven't you gotten the message and left me the hell alone yet?"

"I know that's what you want. I know you hate me and feel you have every reason to do so. I'm not trying to win you back. I'm not foolish enough to believe that's a possibility. But because I love you and have never stopped, because I care about you, I also feel like I owe you."

"Owe me?"

"Yes. Bennett, I need to talk to you about Cayden."

A humorless laugh flees my lungs. "Honestly, I don't care anymore about the two of you. I've met someone else. I'm not saying that to hurt you, but I'm happy with her and—"

"Bennett, did Cayden ever tell you why he was there in

Boston? Did he tell you anything about what happened between me and him?"

That pulls me up short since that's not at all what I thought she was going to say. "Uh…" I drag a hand across my jaw as I think back. "He said he was here to apologize. To get me to forgive him. He said you forced the relationship between the two of you and he went along with it because he loved you. He claimed he had no idea about the tubal ligation and that you told him that if he didn't continue the affair, you'd tell me what was going on between the two of you and it would ruin our friendship."

She sighs. "That's what he said? That I had blackmailed him into sex with me or I'd tell you and ruin your friendship? How does that make any sense? I didn't want our marriage to end if you recall. How would telling you that have helped me? You didn't think that was odd?"

I hesitate because yeah, part of me did when he mentioned it. It just sounded… I don't know, like it didn't make a ton of sense as she just said, but I was too upset by everything in that moment to give it further thought.

"Please just listen to everything I have to say because it's important," she interrupts my thoughts. "I have no ulterior motive for doing this. Remember that. The first time Cayden and I slept together was after you and I had a fight. I left and got drunk at the bar and you called him to pick me up because you were still too pissed at me to do it yourself. Cayden came and we talked for a while, and one thing led to another. I regretted it terribly and told him it was a mistake and that it could never happen again. He disagreed and started blackmailing me."

"Blackmailing you?" I parrot, my brows raised and my eyes wide as I change lanes and inch along to a stoplight. "Cayden did this?"

"Well, threatening me is probably the better term. He told me he'd tell you about that night if I didn't continue to sleep with him." She swallows audibly. "I loved you and I didn't want to lose you, but at first, I told him no. I told him I'd come clean to you and throw myself at your mercy, but then he somehow discovered that I… I had taken a lot of money from my parents."

"You did what?"

She clears her throat, her voice low. "I knew they were losing their company, and I didn't want to lose all of my inheritance with it, so I… well, I misappropriated funds."

"Jesus, Liz. Seriously? You never mentioned this to me." I drag a hand across the back of my neck, twisting my head until my neck pops.

"I couldn't, Bennett. You know I couldn't. You never would have been on board with that."

"Of course I wouldn't have been on board," I snap. "For fuck's sake. Why the hell did you do that?"

"You grew up poor and became wealthy. You have no idea what it is to be threatened with the reverse," she sniffs defensively. "Your money wasn't my money. We had that prenup and always kept our incomes separate because of it."

I hold in my scoff and my snark because I would have given her my money. Though the *why didn't you simply purchase fewer designer things* is on the tip of my tongue. Frankly, I'm not interested in fighting with her, and my days of giving a shit about how she operates are over.

I redirect her. "So he discovered what you had done?"

"Yes, and he used that too. He threatened to turn me in to the FBI and SEC for money laundering. I would have gone to jail."

I'm having such a hard time making sense of this. Of the people I had spent so much of my life with. Liz laundering money, and Cayden blackmailing her into an affair. It's fucking madness, and it's making my head spin.

I shake my head, trying to understand everything. "So you

started sleeping with him. Fine. How did the tubal come into play?"

"I didn't want a baby with him, and he refused to use condoms. I couldn't do that. I couldn't try to get pregnant with you while sleeping with him. The risk of the baby being his was too great. And…" She trails off to clear her throat. "I didn't want children that much anyway. I had told you I did because I loved you and was willing to have them for you, but with everything spiraling out of control, I didn't know what else to do."

Finally, I reach the garage and pull into my spot. I stare straight ahead through the windshield at the concrete wall, utterly floored.

After a moment, I lick my dry lips and say, "He blamed you for everything, Liz. He said he had no clue about the tubal until after. He said he tried to end it with you several times and you wouldn't back off. Everything was you and not him. Yet he told me he was in love with you the entire time we were married and that he was jealous of me."

In fact, he said sometimes he hated me. Right? He said that. And I didn't put it together. None of it. Despite what he had done to me, I blamed Liz for most of it and was too wrapped up in myself and what was going on with Katy to care about the things he said or the things he was doing.

"God, Bennett, it's so much more than that. Cayden is sick. He became completely, terrifyingly obsessed with me. He'd follow me everywhere I'd go, sleep in the back seat of my car in our garage, and send me inappropriate texts and packages at work. He was relentless, and when you found out about the tubal and confronted me, part of me was relieved. I couldn't keep it going."

She starts to cry, heavy, wet sobs into the phone. Liz had been pulling away by that point. She'd been losing weight. Not sleeping well. After I found out about the tubal and the affair, I assumed that was the reason for all of that.

It's nearly impossible to reconcile the man I thought I knew with the man she's describing. Cayden is an actor. He's always been one. He would sit beside me and listen to me lamenting Liz not getting pregnant. He'd offer comfort and suggestions and act like a best fucking friend would.

All the while he was fucking her behind my back.

And I had no clue.

What he wants the world to see—a charming, wealthy, brilliant neurosurgeon who committed his life to being a bachelor and a good friend—is not at all who he is.

"I'm so sorry," she sniffs, emotion clogging her throat. "I told you then, but I'm telling you again now. I never meant to hurt you. Not ever. I didn't know what to do. But after everything came to light and we got divorced, I told him it was over. I had someone go into his computer and wipe all my... *transgressions* from there, as well as any financial proof that could be found. It drove him off the deep end. He thought with you out of the way, he and I would finally be together, but I never wanted that."

My hands cover my face, and I breathe heavily into them. "Liz..." I don't know what to say. This is too much.

"One of your accusers came to me, and when I heard her story—that you had all but forced a sexual relationship with her—I was furious. I felt betrayed since you had done to me exactly what I had done to you, and yet you left and blamed me for everything."

I shake my head, my ire creeping back up. "I never touched those women. You were the one—"

"It wasn't me, Bennett!" she shouts, cutting me off. "That's why I've been calling you. I thought the accusations were true, which is why I told you I was going to ruin your life. It's why I led the charge when they forced you out. I was furious. I was heartbroken."

"Except I didn't fucking cheat or coerce or behave inappropriately with anyone."

"No. You didn't." She blows out a breath, the sound crackling through the car speakers. "Shortly after you moved to Boston, it was discovered that the woman who still worked at the hospital had been doing something she shouldn't have been. She made a deal with the hospital, and in exchange for her slap on the wrist, she told them the truth. Cayden had paid both women to come forward with stories about you. They needed the money, and he took advantage. He was trying to ruin your life because I loved you and not him. And he hated you for it."

My eyes close, and my head falls back against the seat, my insides feeling like someone put them through a meat grinder.

"The hospital let him go and when I found out he came out to Boston, that's when I started calling you. I felt I owed you that much. Especially when I learned that you never did cheat on me. Cayden is a hateful, vindictive monster who's out for your blood."

I stare sightlessly up through the skylight, thinking all of this through. The timing of everything she's saying makes sense. I hadn't heard from Liz all summer, and there was a gap between when I left Mayo and came to Boston. Liz started calling me, and then a couple of weeks after that, Cayden showed up in the hospital, knowing who Katy was and exactly what floor I was on.

How long had he been watching me?

A shiver runs up my spine. He came to the bar that night. I called him and he showed up almost immediately. I told him I loved Katy. I told him she's pregnant. Fuck! And then Cricket showed up at my door last night when only Katy was there. Was that by design? Did he orchestrate that? How did she get my address, if not from him? I'm not listed anywhere because I didn't want Liz to come and track me down.

He's still trying to hurt me. But what if he's not done? What if Cricket was just the start?

# Chapter Twenty-Nine

# Bennett

I stumble onto the floor in a daze. I don't know how to make sense of everything Liz just told me. I could challenge her. I could question her. But in my heart, in my fucking soul, I *know* everything she's saying is true.

Liz isn't getting anything out of telling me this. I owe her nothing. There is no getting back together with her. But more than that, I think of Cayden. I think of what he's done. The moves he's pulled and the stories he's created. He paid women off to get me fired and ruin my name and reputation. He got fired from Mayo. How did I not know that? Nice of them to not reach out, but that doesn't surprise me.

I left angry and definitely not on the best of terms.

But then he shows up here with a sappy bullshit apology as he tries to worm his way back in, but for what? What is he up to?

Trying to break me and Katy up, or is it—

"Bennett?" A soft but firm voice comes from behind me as I step out of the locker room. I turn to find a sheepish-looking Cricket. "I wanted to apologize to you. I thought everything over, and I had no business showing up at your house last night. That was beyond inappropriate."

I clear my thoughts for a moment. "Cricket, how did you learn where I live?"

She shifts her weight, a blush creeping up her face. "Didn't Katy tell you?"

"No. We just talked about why you stopped by." And then I took her in the kitchen and after that, all talk about Cricket was over. But before I kissed her, she did say... something, right? Or started to, maybe?

She shifts again and looks off to her right before turning back to me. "Your friend Cayden came looking for you, but he had just missed you. He asked me to deliver this to you. He said he was leaving town and wanted you to have it." She hands me a brown paper bag that I reflexively take. "He asked if I could deliver it to your house, and I should have told him no. Again, I'm sorry."

I press my hand against the bag, trying to figure out what this could be. "Thank you, Cricket. It's not something we need to talk or think about again, okay? As for my relationship with Katy, it's had no impact on our work here nor will it ever. And you should know, I'm no longer in charge of fellowships."

She stares at the center of my chest. "Yes. Katy told me that."

"Are we okay then?"

Her eyes finally come up to mine. "Yes. We're okay. I was shocked and, well, assumed the worst, but like I said, I thought it over last night. You've always been fair with both of us and never showed any favoritism. I'd like us to put this all behind us and move forward."

"Good. Thank you. I'm relieved to hear that." I open the bag and freeze when I get a peek at what's inside. Thunder rumbles through my veins, and my insides shock with lightning. "Cricket, did you open this?"

"No," she says. "I had already crossed enough lines."

With that, she walks off, and I thank my lucky stars that she didn't look.

Because what the absolute fuck? How on earth did he do this? Giving a quick search, I find myself alone in the hall and pull the pictures out. I scroll through them at a rapid pace and then shove them back in the bag, crinkling it up tight.

Those are pictures of me having sex with a woman I've never seen before. A woman I've never met before. But that's my body in those images. My face. It's me on top of someone.

And Cayden handed those images to Cricket with the intent of either her seeing them, Katy seeing them, or me seeing them. Or more likely all three. My heart starts to pound in a way it never has before.

If he's been watching me, then he knows I'm with Katy. And if he showed up here right after I left, there's a chance he heard me on the phone with my mom when I told her I was stopping by before heading home. Jesus Christ. This is the most fucked-up thing I've ever experienced.

Katy is working a night shift tonight. Her plan was to sleep in as late as she could and then go swimming. I need to talk to her, but I don't want to do it over the phone. This has to be an in-person conversation.

I rub my forehead. How will I ever get her to believe me? I know how this looks and how it seems, and she has no reason to believe me other than the faith we have in each other. But is it strong enough for this? I don't know. If it were reversed, would I even listen to an explanation when pictures of her having sex with another man are right in front of me? Pictures dated last week at that. Probably not.

I can't do this. Not again. Never with her. I can't lose Katy. It's not even an option.

But I can't hide this from her either. Hiding them is worse. It looks guilty when I'm not. And I won't lie or keep things from her.

For now, I rush back into the locker room and stuff the bag in my locker. Closing it with a resounding bang, I head back out onto the floor. I text Katy, asking if she can come in thirty minutes early so we can talk. She doesn't reply, and I slip my phone back into my pocket. I do my best to shake out the restlessness that's been dancing in my limbs since Liz called and head for the nurse's station to get report from last night's staff when my boss intercepts me.

"Bennett, do you have a minute?"

Nothing good ever happens when your boss asks if you have a minute. *Fuck.*

"Of course." I force a smile and a calm demeanor despite the next round of nerves rioting through me.

"Perfect." He slaps me on the back. "Walk with me."

We start to stroll down the hall but quickly find ourselves entering an empty OR. The room is dark and cold, and I fight the urge to shiver and fidget. My skin prickles with awareness. We're alone, far from the ears of others for a reason.

"What I'm going to talk to you about is delicate."

Oh shit. "Okay." I let my arms fall casually in front of me.

"Cayden Craw came to see me yesterday evening."

My jaw automatically clenches. "I see."

"He had before, so at first, I didn't think much of it. A few weeks back he came to see me, asking about a position on the neuro team. I told him I didn't have any openings at the time, but if one popped up, I'd keep him in mind. Last week, I learned that one of our neuro staff is going to be leaving and I called him, asking him to come in for a series of interviews."

My hands climb to my hips, and I bluster out a heavy breath. "Evan, if I may—"

"Just let me finish," he interrupts, and I harden my stance as well as my expression. "He came in yesterday evening even though his first round of interviews isn't until next week to tell me that you're having a secret affair with one of your staffers and that you got her pregnant."

That filthy, slimy, weaselly motherfucker. When I get my hands on him, I will *end* him.

"He was trying to get me fired for sexual misconduct. Again."

He nods and then pauses. "Again?"

"Yes." I fold my arms over my chest. "I learned just this morning from a hospital administrator at Mayo that Cayden paid the women to come forward with false allegations against me. He was released from his position there once that truth came to light. That's been kept a secret by the hospital for obvious reasons."

He doesn't look surprised by this, which shocks me a bit. He runs his hand along his jaw. "Originally when he came to see me, he told me how close the two of you are. How he's been your best friend for years."

I shift, looking briefly down at the floor. "He was. He's also the one who slept with my now ex-wife."

He nods as if it all makes sense now. "I see. Well, yes, he came in to try to get you fired."

"Do you mind if I ask what you said to him?"

He holds up a consolatory hand. "I didn't tell him anything other than I would speak with you. What you told me was in confidence, and I don't make a habit of betraying my employees' trust to someone I don't know. Though I didn't know Katy's pregnant."

Well, that's a huge relief. And it doesn't seem as though Cayden used those pictures with him, which means the woman in the pictures doesn't work here. He was trying to get me fired for being with Katy.

"I appreciate that, Evan. Katy is only seven weeks along," I explain. "We weren't planning on announcing it until after her first trimester."

He rubs the back of his neck. "I've known Katy for a long time, as you know. I've only ever wanted the best for her. I know she's had some health issues, so I'm happy to hear that so far she's doing well. I understand your wanting to keep that bit of information to yourselves and frankly, that's personal between the two of you. And since you had already spoken with me about your relationship with her, there is no misconduct."

"And his position here?"

"His allegations made me suspicious. What sort of man calls himself close to someone and then tries to get them fired? After he left, I called around. His former supervisor told me he had been let go, though he could not tell me the reason why. Now I know. Regardless, we will be withdrawing our invitation for an interview, and he will never be a surgeon in this hospital."

"Thank you, sir. I'm very relieved to hear that."

"Bennett, I also want you to know, though I haven't spoken with the board yet, in light of everything I've learned about Cayden and everything you've told me today, I hope you know we value you and your work very highly. You've shown to be a man of honor and respect, and I, for one, am very grateful you're with us."

I'm stunned into a heavy, awed silence as gratitude shoots up through me like a geyser.

Before I can form any semblance of a reply, he takes a step forward and puts his hand on my shoulder. "Be careful with him, Bennett. He has a plan where you're concerned."

"You're the second person today who has warned me about him. Believe me, I intend to take care of it."

The moment I step out of the OR, I call Katy, and after two rings, it goes to voicemail. I try again, and the same thing happens. Is she ignoring my calls and sending me to voicemail?

I shoot her a text.

> Me: When you get this, please call. I need to talk to you ASAP.

Only as the minutes tick by, I never hear back from her.

And instinctively, I know something is very wrong.

# Chapter Thirty



With my headphones on and music blasting through my ears, I feel like a prizefighter ready to get into the ring. Or in this case, the pool. My awesome uncle Greyson has an Olympic-size indoor swimming pool, and because he loves me, he lets me come here whenever I want to do laps. One of the most important things for my pregnancy is staying fit, and since swimming is the jam to my toast, I've been upping my laps game by about three each session.

Channeling the mental game of Katie Ledecky—we have the same name even if it's spelled differently!—and Michael Phelps, I sing at the top of my lungs as I drop my old-school matching track pants and jacket poolside. My cap is clinging to my head, holding my wild locks at bay as I stare at the water, ready to make it my bitch and swim myself to pretend gold.

I never tried out for the Olympic team, nor did I swim competitively on that level. It was an extracurricular in high school, a full ride to college, and a passion that still holds my heart. But that doesn't mean I don't fantasize about that large gold coin or championship the way every athlete does, and I won't lie and say that I haven't begged Mason's mom—who won gold for figure skating—to let me wear her medal a time or fifty.

I roll my neck until it pops, swinging my elbows behind me to try and loosen up my shoulders, back, and arms. Then I remove my headphones and scream at the top of my freaking lungs when a shadowy figure moves straight in front of me. My fist comes up to strike, but Cayden's hands fly up in surrender, warding me off.

"Whoa. Slow your punch there, Ali. I'm sorry. I didn't mean to startle you. You didn't hear me call out to you."

"A chronic problem of mine," I manage, though I'm positive he can hear the wariness in my voice. "Then again, I'm supposed to be the only one here right now."

After everything that happened with Cricket yesterday—oh, hell. I never told Bennett what Cricket said about him or the bag he had her bring to him. I started to. I tried. But then he distracted me and I… I didn't think about it again for the rest of the night. And now he's here. Clearly having followed me.

"How did you get in here?"

"I watched you punch in the code. You really should be more careful about that."

My hands hit my hips, and my head twists in attitude. "Don't worry, I'll make sure it's changed before I leave here today. What do you want, Cayden?"

"To show you these. My little Cricket didn't do everything she was supposed to do last night."

Hm. "And how do you know that?"

"I was watching, of course. As I've been doing for a while now."

He slams a stack of paper into my chest, intentionally grazing my boobs, and I shove him back. But in doing so, the papers fall to the ground like snowflakes. And as they do, I catch glimpses of each one. Bennett on top of a woman. Bennett's hands interlocked with a woman's, her arms above her head. Bennett's head pulled back in the throes of passion and ecstasy.

Before I can stop myself, I bend and pick them up, noting the time stamp on the top corner. These were taken a week ago. Mentally, I do the math, thinking through dates and times. I remember that day. It was the first day I felt crummy from my pregnancy, and my stomach wasn't right. We had back-to-back traumas all day, and I remember forcing myself to eat because I was worried about my blood sugar getting too low again. I was working a shift that day, and Bennett was off.

I had texted him a picture of me eating a protein bar, and his response was, *Good girl. I'll reward you when you get home tonight.* He did. He had dinner waiting for me, and then we took a bath together. Nothing was off about him. Not one thing.

My phone rings in the pocket of my track pants, and I bend down, sliding it out. It's Bennett. Does he know about these pictures? He rarely, if ever, calls me when he's on a shift. I send his call to voicemail, only to have it ring again in my palm and do the same. I need a minute or twenty, and I'm not picking up the phone and talking to him right now.

Because I'm holding pictures of him fucking another woman and I'm trying—I'm trying so damn hard—to find the loophole in this, but I'm coming up short. My heart sinks to the bottom of my soul where it fractures into a million tiny pieces of obliterated flesh. I yank my swim cap off and chuck it across the room. My knees hit the hardscape, my eyes scouring each horrifying image that's played out before me.

"Sending him to voicemail. That's cold. Cricket must have given him the pictures. It'll be interesting to hear him try and talk his way out of this."

The only thing I have to cling to is that Bennett wouldn't do this. I couldn't say that about Zane. Zane cheating wasn't a farfetched notion for me—not to mention I caught him in the physical act. But Bennett? I just don't see it. I think about him that night. Him every night we're together. The things we've talked about and shared.

He wouldn't cheat.

It's not who he is.

More than that, I can't imagine him doing anything to risk this baby.

Me aside, that is why we started this undeniably convenient arrangement in the first place. But…

I swallow past the rock stuck in my trachea, stifling the majority of the air from my lungs. My palms turn into sheets of sweat, and the pages become rumpled middle fingers pointed directly at me. The images all blur together. Her body. His body. The dark hotel room. The silk gold curtains surrounding the window, the shades partially closed. I know that hotel. It's the Four Seasons in Boston. I've been to events there.

I look up at a supremely smug Cayden. "Why are you doing this?"

"Because I'm sick and fucking tired of everyone always loving him."

My lips twist. "You mean like his ex-wife?" I give him mockingly sad eyes. "Aw, poor Cayden. No one loves you. Tell it Dr. Phil or someone who pretends to give a shit."

His eyes flare, and I know I'm onto something there.

"You love her, right? I mean, you were fucking her for a couple of years. But she obviously didn't want you the same way you want her, which I get. Why would anyone pick you when they could have him?"

I stand, leaving the photos on the ground. I'll deal with them in a minute.

"Or is it more than that? Are you so in love with *him* that you'd take any piece of him you could get? Are you trying to ruin his life because he'll never love you back and neither will his wife?"

"Fuck you," he snarls, and I laugh caustically because that's about all I have left right now.

"Never." I shrug. "Him on the other hand…"

Rage boils up his face, hardening his features and reddening his cheeks. I likely shouldn't be taunting him like this. I'm alone in this building with a man twice my size and I'm pregnant. His hatred of all things Bennett puts me at a greater risk because he knows I'm pregnant with Bennett's child. A child Bennett has wanted for a long time.

Provoking a hungry bear fresh from hibernation never turns out well for the unsuspecting tourist. Not to mention he said he's been watching me for a while. That's the creepiest thing ever. Every woman's worst nightmare. I need him to leave, and I need him to leave now. I can deal with him after that.

"When my father died," I tell him, "I watched from the back seat, stuck and unable to move. I saw the slow, agonizing pain of his death. I hope one day you feel something a million times worse than that."

He chokes, not having expected that from me, and I'm not sure how much I mean it. I'm not one to wish death and pain on others—I'm a freaking trauma surgeon—but I hate this man with unparalleled vitriol.

"You can go now. You've done your worst."

"Not yet, Katy. I'm not sure I've done my worst yet. I've always had a fondness for ruining all the things Bennett loves."

He touches my hair, running his fingers down a thick lock of it, and I shiver at the cold malice in his eyes.

I give him a good, hard shove toward the exit, pushing all my weight into it and making him stumble a few steps, but unfortunately, he catches himself before he falls. For a second, he looks like he's about to come at me, but I point to the cameras in the corner.

"I wouldn't try it," I warn, holding his gaze and refusing to flinch. "You lay a finger on me, and I'll have you in jail for the rest of your life. That's not a threat. It's a promise. If you've done your stalkerish research, then you know exactly who I am and the pull I have in this city."

For a moment, he blinks, stunned by that, and I wonder if he has or if he's been so toxically focused on Bennett that he has no clue. I hope he doesn't.

He gathers himself and turns away from me. He knows he doesn't have to touch me to hurt me. And thankfully, his threat dies there as he notes the cameras all around this place. The central square guys don't fuck around when it comes to security. Or their families.

He gathers himself, his swagger returning. "See you around, Katy. Sorry I had to be the one to ruin your day, but sometimes evils are necessary." He chuckles at that, thinking he's so very funny.

Cayden saunters like a prideful alley cat toward the exit, and the moment he's gone, the door slamming shut behind him, I collapse to the floor. Air tumbles past my lungs only to rush back in. Thank God he left. Thank God, he didn't touch me.

My gaze drops to the images spread out before me. The cold stone beneath my ass stiffens my muscles to the point of rigor. The pages shuffle through my hands one after the other in an endless cycle as I search for something—one fucking thing—that will tell me these are bullshit.

Only I can't see beyond Bennett on top of this woman.

Leaving them where they are, I dive into the pool, starting my laps at a brutal pace. My mind swirls and tears threaten, but I can't reconcile what I know of Bennett to those pictures. I need to call him. I need to speak with him and face this head-on. I finish my lap and pull myself up and out of the water, go for my towel, and wrap it around me. The photos are on the ground beside my phone, and as I reach for it, something in one of the images catches my attention.

It's night in the photo. As in, the crack of an open shade

reveals a dark window beyond. I was home by the time it was dark out, and he was there making dinner. Lifting the picture, I examine it. I realize it's not a full time stamp, just a date, but no actual time. I spread out the images one by one and scrutinize each one carefully.

His hands holding hers are weird. It's so subtle that if you didn't look closely, you might not see it. But her fingers look almost cut off and misaligned with his.

Interesting. Hope starts to shake in my chest like an earthquake, but I'm not yet ready to scream hallelujah. I need a few more details first.

I don't call Bennett. Not yet. Instead, I make a totally different type of call.

Vander's gravelly voice crackles through my ear. "Kit-Kat?"

I fold my legs, still wrapped in my towel. "How easy is it to alter pictures?"

"Depends," he says. "What do you mean by alter?"

"Remove a person and replace their body with someone else's."

"To make it look authentic, that can be pretty difficult unless the person who is doing this reenacts the original image precisely, but far from impossible if someone has the right software."

"These aren't even the actual photographs. They're photocopies of photographs."

"Even easier," he says. "You can alter an image and print it out to look like a photo. But again, the person doing all of this would have to make the body swap almost identical to the original. What's going on?"

A weird, demented, almost psychotically giddy laugh chokes out of me and now the tears do start coming. "I need a favor. It's a big one."

"Anything. You know that."

"It's asking you to do something you shouldn't."

"Just tell me, Kit-Kat, and I'll do it. Let me worry about the rest."

God, I love my family. "I need you to run absolutely everything on a Cayden Craw. I want you to go as deep and dark and dirty as you can. I don't care how you do it, and I won't ever ask. I want every speck of dirt on the motherfucker you can find. He's made what I think are bullshit photos of Bennett with another woman to hurt me. More than that, he threatened me, Van. He said he's been following me and if I hadn't pointed out the security cameras in the corner..." I trail off on a heavy gulp.

Vander is silent for a very long moment, and I fling my legs out in front of me, folding myself in half and pressing my forehead to my knees. I hate putting Vander in this position. His father never intended to teach him how to hack, but that didn't last long. But when Vander got arrested in college during a hacking war with another top school, Lenox made him swear he'd stop. To Vander, that meant only doing clean hacks, and this is anything but.

"Can you just do this for me, Van? I wouldn't ask if I didn't need it. I need to find a reason to get rid of this guy once and for all. I'll go to the police regardless, but I want more than just a threat to get him by. But if it's too risky—"

The door to the pool area opens again and Bennett comes walking in, searching around for me, and when he sees me sitting on the ground, bent in half with the phone pressed to my ear and the pictures surrounding me, his expression crumples, all the color draining from his face, and his expression growing desperate.

"Katy, those aren't real," he says, running over to me and collapsing on his knees beside me. He takes my arm, squeezing it, almost as if he's afraid I'm going to shirk him off or run. "You have to listen to me," he implores, his voice shaky and his speech rapid. "Please hear my words. I never had sex with that woman. I swear. I've never seen her before in my life. Those images are fabricated."

"I know."

"No. You don't understand. Katy, please. I'm telling you. However these photos came to be, that isn't me. I mean, it's me, but it has to be photoshopped or something. I never in my life had sex with that woman. I don't even know who she is or where those pictures were taken, but they've been altered somehow to have me on them."

"Bennett, I know. I believe you. I realized that before you even got here."

He falls back on his haunches, staring at me as if he's never seen me before. His hand covers his heart, and then he falls forward, wrapping his arms around me and holding me tighter than he ever has. "Thank God." He pants out one breath after the other. "Thank you for believing me. Thank you for trusting me. God, Katy. I've been going out of my mind since I saw them and when you didn't call me back, I left work and ran straight here." He pulls back and cups my face, his eyes glassy. "I love you. I'd never cheat. It's what I told you last night. You're the only one I'll ever want."

I drag his lips to mine and kiss him. My phone clangs on the ground, and I jolt back. "Oh. Vander is on the phone."

Bennett's eyebrows fold in. "Why is Vander on the phone? You called him and not me?"

He looks impossibly hurt. "Uh. Well. Um."

"You can tell him, Katy," I hear Vander shout. "In fact, put me on speaker. I have some questions for both of you."

I put Vander on speakerphone, and Bennett tells him and me everything about his conversation with Liz, followed by his boss this morning. Vander asks him some questions, things I don't fully understand, until he says, "Okay, I'm in." In the background, I hear the click of the keys, and my insides shrink a bit. "I'll get back to you," he says and then disconnects the call.

# Chapter Thirty-One

Katy

It didn't take Vander very long. Within twenty minutes, he called us back and told us we needed to go to the police station and file a report. Cayden has been stalking both of us like crazy for months and has done research into which ingested poisons, chemicals, and foods could kill a fetus. Lovely.

We couldn't give the police everything because that would incriminate Vander. But we have video of him following me to the pool this morning and lurking around the building, as well as footage from Bennett's doorbell and back door cameras that show him across the street and sneaking around the house on several different occasions. We also gained access to hospital video after Bennett made a request, and he's followed Bennett and me several times in the last couple of months.

His obsession with Bennett is off the charts.

By the time we left the police station and let them know about the way he threatened me and how we feared for our safety, especially since I'm pregnant, we had a restraining order against him, and they had a warrant for Cayden's arrest. Bennett and I were assured that stalking is considered a crime in all fifty states and Massachusetts takes it very seriously. And because of our accusation of stalking and the fact that we did show them some physical evidence that he's fabricated photographs and tracked Bennett using his phone, they will confiscate Cayden's computer, phone, and other devices, which will lead them to the things Vander found.

It was a relief, but when I went to work that night, I was still feeling unsettled about it. So was Bennett, who was even more overprotective than usual. He drove me in and picked me up and had security escort me in and out of the hospital.

At least it didn't take very long to get Cayden.

Not even two days later, we got a call from the officer who took our report to inform us that Cayden had been arrested trying to break into Bennett's house—thankfully we were both at work at the time. The raid on Cayden's apartment revealed terrifying results. Weapons and video equipment and poisons. He was living a block from us. One block. We had no idea how close he was to us all that time. How deep his fixation went.

Bennett was more than just a little shaken up. After all, Cayden had been his supposed best friend for two decades and his roommate for all four years of college.

It's horrifying to think how close we came to his wrath and how lucky we were that this ended before he turned as violent as it seemed he was getting.

It got better for us from there, as two months after that, the DA informed us that Cayden made a plea deal and will be serving up to five years in prison with a chance for parole after three.

Now, with all that bullshit behind us, we've been able to focus on us, on his mom, and on the pregnancy.

These last couple of months have flown by.

I had my fellowship interview, and it went well. At least I think it did. Bennett was no help with that as he's sworn to secrecy and would not speak to me at all about the fellowship process. It's annoying and it sucks, but I understand his position on it, and I won't risk his job. Still, I won't find out until early next month.

Cricket has been a non-issue. She keeps her distance from me, and I do the same with her. I did wish her luck when I left my interview as hers immediately followed mine. She said thanks, and that was that.

Same with Zane.

Word about what Cayden did to me spread pretty quickly, and he came to check on me since he thought Cayden was my boyfriend. I told him I was with Bennett and that we were in love, and once we announced my pregnancy, I haven't seen or heard from him since. I've had offers to interview for fellowships from eight different hospitals, one of them in Boston, and I interviewed at five of them. A girl has to have a backup plan. Still, if I don't get this hospital, I'll be crushed beyond all measure.

For now, I'm not thinking about it. Well, doing my best not to think about it.

"This is a joke, right?" I ask Layla as I try to squeeze into the tight dress she brought into the dressing area for me.

"What? Why? What's wrong with it?" She blinks her pretty blue eyes at me, all innocent-like when Layla Fritz-Barrows is anything but.

"Layla! My boobs are everywhere because they're freaking pregnancy huge, and my belly is like front and center. Not to mention this dress is short. Like, if I bend even a little, not only will my ass get a blast of icy February air, but I'll be flashing everyone my naughty girl from the wrong angle if you know what I mean."

Keegan chews on a Twizzler—her favorite—and snorts, making herself nearly choke. "No one knows what you mean. And you look hot. It's Valentine's Day. You're supposed to get all fancy when you have someone to do that for."

"Right." Layla points to Keegan. "What she said. Besides,

if I had your boobage, I'd totally rock that. Pregnancy tits are sexy."

"Plus, the belly is too," Kenna agrees.

Wren tilts her head, studying me. "If you wear it with Docs, it might be kind of badass."

"I second that one," her mom, Grace says. I've gathered a girl squad for this. One mention of a hot Valentine's Day date and they all came running. I have Layla, Wren's mom, Grace, Kenna and Keegan's mom, Amelia, and Tinsley and her mom, Fallon, here. We've taken over my aunt Aurelia's—who owns a fashion house under the name of Lia Sage—design studio.

"If you don't like that one, I have three more for you to try on," Aurelia offers, examining the outfit with a critical, designer's eye. "Though I do have to say, the lines fit you perfectly, and I'm inclined to agree about the boobage."

"Ugh." I adjust the black velvet thing that calls itself a dress and turn back to the three-sided mirror in the changing area. "Why am I doing this again? I hate Valentine's Day."

"You're just worried Bennett's going to propose," Layla teases, and I freeze, as does everyone else.

I slowly spin back around, my eyes wider than a full moon. "The fuck did you just say?"

Layla blinks back at us, stunned by our reactions. "What? Like none of you thought about that. The dude literally told her he wants to take her somewhere romantic tonight for dinner."

"Uh, yeah," Amelia agrees, twirling a lock of her red hair. "I totally thought that too."

"Yep," Grace chimes in as she bites the head off a gummy worm. "But I'll be honest, if he proposes to you tonight, that's a bit cliché."

"Mom!" Wren protests. "You can't say that. What if he does?"

"He's not going to," Fallon states adamantly, always level-headed and the voice of reason. "That's too predictable, and I get the impression Bennett likes to keep you on your toes."

"But maybe he's going to propose for that very reason. He doesn't think she'll think he's that conventional, so he'll throw her off her game by actually proposing."

"Layla!" I screech. "Do you know something I don't?"

Her hands fly up. "No, I swear."

I shake my head. "No one is proposing tonight. I won't be that pregnant girl. I love Bennett, but I don't need him to marry me, and certainly not because I'm pregnant."

"Slay, queen!" they all shout, raising their glasses of champagne—which is just cruel, if you ask me—and clinking them. They're already eating all kinds of candy I can't. I appreciate the solidarity, but candy and champagne around the pregnant diabetic girl. Really?

"Okay," Aurelia calls out, snapping all the drunk and sugared-up women back to task. "Next dress. Try on the pink one."

I snort as I pull off the black one and wiggle into the pink one. "Do you think if I put this on, Bennett will know it's a girl?"

Keegan shoots to her feet so fast she nearly topples over. "You told us you didn't know."

I give her a sly grin in the reflection of the mirror. "I might have lied."

"Are you freaking kidding me?!" Layla and Kenna shout.

"You're having a girl, and you didn't tell us?!" Layla finishes indignantly.

"Or Bennett?" Fallon chimes in.

"Slow your roll. I'm just kidding. Well, sort of. I am having a girl, but I only just found out this afternoon," I admit, adjusting the pink one and twisting this way and that until it's fully on. The drapey silk neckline gives a hint of cleavage without revealing too much, and the bodice hugs the curve of my belly so perfectly I actually sigh when I see it. So does everyone else.

"I went in for more blood work and the tech asked me how my girl is treating me. It must be in my chart from my genetic screening, but we asked not to be told during our ultrasounds."

Everyone is silent, and when I turn back around, they're all the spitting image of that soft, smiling, misty-eyed emoji.

"We're having a girl?" Keegan wails. "I'm so happy it's a girl. I'm having a niece."

Instantly I'm surrounded, getting hugs and belly rubs from all sides. It's the best. It's everything I've ever dreamed of when I first imagined getting pregnant. My baby is going to be surrounded by love. By women and men who adore her.

And naturally, because I'm pregnant and a hormonal mess, I start to sob. Then again, who am I kidding? I would have been sobbing anyway.

We all decide on the pink dress paired with some awesome sparkly heels. The girls work on my hair and makeup, and by the time I leave Aurelia's studio, I'm more of a goddess than I typically am. Layla drives me across town to the address Bennett gave her, and when I arrive, it's…

"A hotel?"

She shrugs. Smiles. "Have a great night."

I roll my eyes but lean across the console of her car to hug her. "You totally know stuff."

"I know nothing, Jon Snow. For real, I love you and I'm so excited we're having a girl."

"Me too. Don't tell Uncle Cal yet, okay?" I pull back. "I want to tell him tomorrow at family dinner." That's something we've started doing. On Sundays, we have dinner with Paula, Callan, and Layla. I swallow thickly, starting to get emotional once again. "I don't remember a lot about my parents," I start, staring down at my hands. "But I want to name the baby Willow after my mom. What do you think?"

She lifts my chin with her hand. "I think that's beautiful. I never met your parents, but as a mom speaking to a future mom, I know she's so fucking proud of you, Katy. You've become an incredible woman. A brilliant doctor. And you're going to make the best mom. Just like yours was."

"Just like you are too," I sob, because even though I opened this can of worms, I didn't think she'd take this to the next level like that.

We hug again and I wipe beneath my eyes until they're smudge-free, and then I climb out of her SUV, heading into the hotel lobby. A doorman whisks me into an elevator and then shoots me up twelve floors to the rooftop that's glowing with twinkling fairy lights and candles. Bennett is standing right before the doors, wearing a goddamn charcoal gray suit with a white shirt and a black tie.

His eyes bulge when he sees me, and for a moment, he doesn't do anything other than take me in line by line, unhurried in his perusal, his gaze growing more heated with every passing second. Finally, once his eyes meet mine, he gives me a wicked grin and adjusts the bulge in his pants.

So crude but wickedly hot.

He steps forward and takes my hand, pulling me into his hard chest. "God, you're stunning." His hand runs over my bump, feeling our baby, who never fails to give him a kick whenever he touches her or speaks to her.

Speaking of… "I have something I have to tell you."

"Excellent. Tell me over dinner." He plants a kiss on my lipstick-lined lips and then walks me into the glowing room. There's a table set up in the center, complete with white linens, a vase filled with red roses, and beautiful china and crystal.

"What on earth are we doing here?" I can't help but ask with a laugh. This isn't us. We're not fancy. Yes, I love my dresses and cute shoes, but we don't typically do fancy restaurants. We—and by we, I mean him—try to cook as often as we can, and if we go out, it's someplace casual.

This hotel is a downtown swanky affair overlooking the Public Gardens, and he's rented out the entire rooftop.

"We're here because it's stupid Valentine's Day." He kisses my lips and helps me into my chair. "And because you never let me spoil you the way I'd like, this was an opportunity to woo you over a lavish, romantic dinner and then fuck you like a man obsessed down one level in the presidential suite I reserved for us for the night."

I flush and immediately take a sip of my water. In addition to far too many emotions, I am, simply put, a horny bitch. My orgasms are many and intense and so fucking splendid, I legit wake Bennett up in the middle of the night by sitting on his face. He's a good sport about waking up to a pussy suffocating him, but I can't help it. Sometimes it's like I need an orgasm and I need it now, and he's *so* good at delivering them.

"You had me at fucking me like a man obsessed."

He winks at me. "I thought I would." The waiter comes over and refills my water and then gives me some bubbly pink concoction. I throw Bennett an eyebrow that the waiter must pick up on, because he says, "It's a mocktail, miss."

"Thank you." I take a sip, and it's delicious.

He hands us both our menus and then gives us a minute while promising to return shortly with bread. Thank God! My blood sugars have been in decent control, and since this is a special night, I intend to eat all the bread. My endocrinologist didn't put me on a pump, though we did strongly consider it. Instead, he has me on a tight leash with shots, and I send him my glucose levels every three days.

So far, I'm healthy and the baby is healthy, and I can't ask for anything more.

"I know you said you have something to tell me, but I should tell you something first."

I pan my hand in his direction. "The floor is yours."

"Tomorrow we're leaving for a week."

I fall back in my seat. "What exactly does that mean? Leaving?"

"It means I've booked us at a resort in the Bahamas for a week. Sun, sand, warmth, water, bikinis."

I shake my head. "What about—"

"Well, I told Evan that since you officially earned the fellowship, I wanted to take you somewhere special to celebrate. That, and you've never taken any of your vacation days, so you're more than due."

I shoot out of my chair, the thing toppling back and smacking on the floor. "Bennett Lawson!"

He stands too, albeit slower than I did, and walks around the table to take my hands. "You got the fellowship, Katy baby. Formal announcements are coming in two weeks, but it's yours. Evan told me last week. You can't say anything to the fellow applicants, but the moment I heard, I planned all this to tell you." His arms wrap around my waist, and he pulls me against him, my belly bumping his. "I'm so fucking proud of you. Look how incredible you are. I'm in awe of you. You amaze me."

"You've been holding out on this for a week?!"

His smile lights his face. "It was worth it to see your face tonight."

Holy hell. I can't even. "I really got it?"

"You really did. But more than that, you earned it."

Tears line the bottom of my eyes before they immediately start to tumble over onto my cheeks for about the tenth time today. I collapse into him, wrapping my arms tightly around his neck. "It's a girl."

"What?" he says with a bemused chuckle.

"When I went for blood work today, the tech accidentally asked how my girl is treating me. I don't think she knew not to say anything. So, it's a girl because, unlike you, I can't hold a secret for longer than five minutes." I draw back and meet his stunned gaze. "We're having a girl."

Immediately he starts trembling. "A little girl?"

I bite into my lip and nod.

He puffs out breath after breath before he starts to wipe at the emotion on his face and then he's on his knees, talking to my belly. "Hi, sweet girl." He kisses me over my dress. "If your mommy thinks I'm overprotective of her, wait till she sees me with you." He laughs and looks up. "Thank you. I didn't care, but a girl is so perfect."

My fingers comb through his hair. "I want to name her Willow after my mom."

His eyes glitter before he turns back to my belly. "I can't wait to meet you, Willow."

I break down, losing my composure completely. God, this man. This fucking man.

He stands and peppers my lips and cheeks with kisses, wiping my tears away. "We have to feed you, sweetheart. You took your shot. So let's eat, but then I want you naked in that suite until we have to get on the plane."

"Whatever you say," I quip cheekily, ready for anything and everything with him. Especially what's to come next for us.

# *Bennett*

## Epilogue

Katy has thought I was going to propose to her half a dozen times already. She thought I was going to on Valentine's Day when I planned that romantic dinner and again when we went on our trip. I'm pretty sure even before that when we went in for our twenty-week fetal survey and again at dinner with our families.

Hell, anytime I take her hand, I feel her tense, thinking I'm about to drop down onto one knee and pull out the giant diamond ring I've been carrying around for the last three months. It's why I haven't done it yet.

Katy coming back into my life was unexpected, and even though it's not my style, I want to try to be that for her. It's funny, I went from never wanting to think about marriage again to it being the only thing I do think about. Anytime I'm with her or I take her hand or I listen as she introduces herself as Dr. Barrows and not Dr. Lawson, I think about it.

I want my ring on her finger, my name as hers. I want the entire fucking planet to know that Katy is mine. Where I was filled with nothing but uncertainty before, I have never been more certain about anything or anyone in my life. Loving

Katy meant giving up what I used to believe, but in doing so, I've found exactly where I'm meant to be.

Katy is going to take six weeks off after Willow is born, and I plan to take off three months. We have a plan. We have it all figured out. We've even slowly started doing some small things in her room. No crib yet. But I had it cleared out of furniture and painted to look like the ocean—that's what Katy wanted. We have a dresser with a changing table on top, a rocking chair in the corner, a daybed, and a small bookshelf. The bassinet is in the closet in the bedroom, assembled, but not allowed in the actual room yet because Katy is extremely superstitious.

These ten months with Katy have been the best of my life despite the crap with Cayden. Even now when I think about what he did, the lengths he went to trying to ruin my life, the obsession ruling his, I still have trouble wrapping my head around it. It turns out, those pictures of me having sex were from a camera he had planted in my old bedroom and the sex I was having was with my wife. To make it look authentic, Cayden had similar sex with some random woman he picked up.

Only, he did it at night, and that's what Katy noticed. That it was dark out and by that point, on that day, we were already together. Thank God my girl has an eye and mind for detail.

In any event, he's no longer an issue for us. He'll be in prison for at least three years, and after that, the restraining order will stand, and he won't be able to come near me or Katy or even the hospital.

Cricket has accepted a fellowship in Manhattan and has done nothing but brag about it since she secured it. I'm happy for her. But I'm also happy she's leaving.

My mom's cancer isn't in remission, and her doctor didn't seem to indicate that he believed she'd ever reach that point. He said if the two rounds of strong chemo couldn't get her there, he wasn't sure what would unless an amazing clinical trial came along, but right now, he didn't recommend that for her. The chemo seems to be doing its job well enough as it shrunk two of the tumors and stopped the third from growing.

I'll take whatever I can get with that and will never stop fighting.

They'll continue with chemo and radiation and gene therapy, and that's just how it's going to be until they find a cure.

But it's yet another reminder that life is short, time is precious, and you should always hold onto the ones you love with both hands. Speaking of…

I slide my hand around the front of Katy and cover her large belly, splaying my fingers wide, hoping Willow gives me a kick. I live for her fucking kicks. They're the beat of my heart. So is the woman in my arms. Katy stirs, but she doesn't wake, and maybe what I'm doing is cruel. It's barely four in the morning, but I can't wait another second.

"Katy baby," I whisper in her ear, her body reflexively shifting closer to mine. My chest thumps and my lips part into an automatic smile in response. I never used to smile the way I do with her. "I love you. You're everything I love."

Her hand covers mine, and her warm ass sinks against my stirring cock. She slides my hand until I feel Willow's body moving, her tiny rump rolling over like I woke her up as well.

"Are you awake?"

"No," she murmurs, but I can hear the smile in her voice. "We're sleeping."

Since Katy hit her third trimester, her body has been struggling a bit. Her blood sugars are harder to control regardless of diet or insulin and her kidneys are fighting even harder than they had to before. The plan is to induce her at thirty-seven weeks—which is in three weeks—to give her body the break it needs and keep the baby as healthy as we can.

So yeah, I should let her sleep. I should wait another hour to wake her with kisses or my face between her thighs. But when a man reaches his breaking point, waiting is no longer an option. It has to be now because now is how we'll start forever, and I can't wait any longer to have forever with her.

"I was wondering if you wanted to marry me?"

She stiffens—as I knew she would—and then slowly twists until she's on her back, but that's not a safe position for her as it compresses her vena cava, so I take my pillow and slide it under her back, so it tilts her more on her left side and facing me.

In the darkness of the room, she blinks her pretty blue eyes open and stares up into mine. "Did you just—"

"Ask you to marry me? Yes. I did. But before you say no, hear me out."

"If I must."

I try not to smirk. "Katy baby, you changed my life. When I'm with you, you see me, and I see you. We see each other, and we love everything we see. Even the not-so-great stuff, we still love because it's part of what makes us who we are. That's not something you find every day. That's rare and special and the stuff of meant to be. I've always been in love with you. You are my partner, my best friend, my lover, my heart. And I don't want to live another day without you as mine." I climb on top of her, pressing my forearms into the pillow on either side of her head. "Marry me, Katy. Not for the baby, but for us."

Her gaze flickers back and forth between mine and then she freezes, her body going stiff once more. In a heartbeat, she shoves me off and scrambles to sit—scrambles to flee—and my heart plummets. She shoots out of bed and heads straight for the bathroom.

"Katy?" It's all I've got. This is not the reaction I thought she'd have. I'll be honest. I wasn't sure she'd say yes. I mean, not a hundred percent anyway. That's part of the reason why it took me so long to get here. I've heard her say on more than one occasion that she doesn't need to be married.

That it's not an important component of her life and happiness.

"Bennett, I think my water is leaking," she calls out to me, and now it's my turn to scramble out of bed, chasing after her into the bathroom. She's sitting on the toilet, her eyes wide and her lips parted to accommodate her extra breaths as breathing has become impossibly hard.

I sink into a crouch in front of her and take her hand. "Are you sure?"

"Fluid is straight up leaking out of my vagina and into the toilet and you're asking me if I'm sure?"

*Touché.* "I'm going to call your doctor's office and let them know we're on our way to the hospital. Don't move. Just stay there and keep your body relaxed. Are you having any contractions?"

She shakes her head, her chin trembling. "It's too soon."

I press my forehead to hers. "Thirty-four weeks is early, but a lot of babies are born at thirty-four weeks and do just fine."

"Owen was thirty-four weeks."

"See. Exactly. Just breathe. It'll be okay."

She gives me a shaky nod, her eyes welling up with tears, and my heart breaks. I kiss her forehead. I kiss her lips. I don't want to leave her like this, but I have to.

"I'm going to get dressed and grab you some clothes. I'll be right back." I cup her jaw. "Okay? Are you with me, sweetheart?"

"I'll be here."

I plant another kiss on her forehead, my lips pressing in with desperation, and then I release her and fly through the bedroom like the psycho I feel like. I'm a trauma surgeon. Working under pressure is what I do best, and I typically do it without breaking a sweat.

Except I'm fucking sweating now.

It's like I've never dressed myself in my life. I don't know what to put on. What I'm supposed to wear. I end up throwing on a pair of joggers and a white T-shirt. As for Katy's clothes, I'm at a loss. I simply stand here, staring at her drawers and hanging things in her closet.

"Bennett?"

"Yeah?" I yell back as I scratch the back of my head, stranded in my indecision.

"Grab me the black dress that's hanging all the way down at the end in the closet. Beneath it on the floor is my bag. It's already packed."

My head flies left and sure enough, there's a short, black sundress that I think she's worn as a beach cover-up, and beneath it on the floor is a zipped duffel bag. This is why women rule the world and our lives. They're on top of their shit while we're still floundering, hot messes.

I snatch the dress and the bag, along with her flip-flops, from one of the shelves and then race back into the bathroom. Katy is naked, her wet underwear discarded, and I start to put her dress over her head when she smacks my hand away and snatches the dress from me.

"What are you doing? I'm in labor, not incapacitated."

I scrub my hands up and down my face. "Shit. I'm a mess."

"You are. But I love you for it. Go put on shoes and call the hospital. Also, can you please call my uncle Cal and let him know what's going on? I won't bother anyone else yet until we know more."

I cup her chin and tilt her head up until she meets my eyes. "I love you. Thank you for being you right now." I kiss her lips and then race out of the room to make the phone calls and put on shoes because I'm nearly positive I would have left the house barefoot if she hadn't mentioned that. Twenty minutes later, we're entering the hospital through the emergency department. And because Katy is essentially a celebrity in whatever hospital she goes to in this city, a team of doctors and nurses greets us.

Endocrinology, obstetrics, and emergency medicine are all geared up. Katy hasn't had any contractions yet, but the moment they wheel us into a room to do a baseline check on her before sending us up to OB, her contractions start.

"Katy, we're going to get an IV going in you immediately and give you a dose of steroids to help the baby's lungs along. But if you're already having contractions and your water is leaking, the steroids might not have enough time to do their job before you deliver."

Katy nods as she watches the nurse put in the IV. "I know," she says softly, her other hand clutching firmly to mine. They get her fluids going along with a dose of betamethasone, and after doing a quick check of the baby's heart rate along with Katy's cervix, they decide to move us straight up to labor and delivery instead of keeping us down here.

We reach the elevator, the doors open, and the moment they wheel her on, I stop, backing out. "I'm going to take the stairs."

"What?" everyone asks in confusion.

"I'm not risking us getting stuck."

Katy smirks at me. "Probably a good idea. The last thing I want is to deliver our baby in here."

"I'll see you upstairs."

She nods, and the doors start to close. "Wait! Bennett?" I shove my arm in, making the doors jar back open and the elevator ding loudly. "Before this all gets going or if I do happen to get stuck… yes."

I tilt my head, my eyebrows diving into a V.

"I'm saying yes. To the question you asked me this morning when you woke me up. My answer is yes."

I fly onto the elevator, not caring at all about the audience watching us, and take her face in my hands. "You mean it?"

"Hundred percent. I would have told you that this morning, but, well…" She trails off and points down. "We got interrupted when my vagina started leaking."

"We did. I had a lot of things planned for her this morning after I made you say yes to me."

She smiles against my lips. "Now it'll have to wait."

"I'll wait forever." I kiss her as deeply as I can, holding her as tightly as I can. "You know, I had originally planned to stop an elevator and propose to you like that, but your uncle told me when I asked him for your hand that you'd definitely say no to me if I had done that."

"He's right. I would have." She smacks my shoulder, making me laugh. "You asked my uncle for my hand?"

"Yup." I wink at her. "I'll see you up there, Dr. Lawson."

My teeth drag her bottom lip, and then I get my ass out of the elevator so she can get upstairs where she needs to be. I fly up the steps, taking them two at a time, joy like I've never experienced before coursing through me. That is, until I reach the fifth floor, get myself past the front security and into the patient area, and find Katy in a ferocious amount of pain with a new contraction.

My lungs empty, and my heart seizes. I hate seeing Katy in pain. I hate not being able to make it better for her. But God, is she fucking strong and tough. She hums through the contraction, gripping two of my fingers as they walk her down the hall and bring her straight into a room. The nurses get her changed into a gown, situated on her bed, and hooked up to monitors.

And for a little while, time seems to stand still. Contractions and taking walks down the hall and massages and helping her through the pain. Eventually, she gets an epidural, and her people come and go, offering hugs, jokes, and support.

Only then it happens. Her labor stalls and the baby starts

to go into distress. In a whirlwind of motion, Katy is whisked off to the OR, and I'm tossed a pair of scrubs and a scrub cap to put on. I change in a nanosecond, masking up and running straight for the OR.

"Stay up by her head. No watching," the doctor instructs me, but for the first time in my life, I have no interest in watching the surgery. I'm up by Katy's head, both of us silent and scared, my arms wrapped around her, my forehead resting against her temple.

I don't pray often. Hardly ever. But I'm praying, and I'm praying hard now.

Not even two minutes later, we hear it. A small, wispy little cry. It's the sweetest goddamn sound I've ever heard, and both Katy and I break down, instantly crying along with our tiny little thing.

I kiss Katy's wet cheek and stand, watching as they work on our little girl. "My heart will always love yours. My heart will always know that yours is the one it beats for."

She gasps and cries harder. "I love you so much."

"You have no idea, Katy baby. True love wasn't born before I met you."

They're bagging Willow up, giving her extra oxygen and some medications to get her heart going faster. I hold Katy's hand, unable to move or speak, when every instinct I have is to run over there and get my little girl where she needs to be.

"Five-minute APGAR is six. She's doing well, Mom and Dad. You can take a breath now."

The nurse swaddles her up, sets a pink, blue, and white hat on her head, and then she's placed in Katy's arms.

"Welcome to the world, Willow," Katy whispers, her voice hoarse. "You're everything we've always dreamed of. Who knew something that started out so undeniably convenient would turn out like this?"

. . .

WANT MORE of Katy and Bennett's HEA? You can download their bonus epilogue here. **Turn the page for an exclusive excerpt of Owen's book Undeniably Forbidden!**

# Undeniably Forbidden

Owen

> Jack: Sorry for messaging so last minute. I won't be able to make it tonight. My connection out of Newark was canceled and I can't get a flight into Boston until tomorrow. Hope you're still able to enjoy a kid-free night out without me *Devil smile emoji*

A SMIRK CURLS its way up my lips, and I wipe it away with my thumb as I read the last line of his text. As one of my best friends growing up, all through our residencies, and the birth of my daughter Rory who is now six, Jack knows if I'm not at the hospital or with my family, I'm with her. My nights out are sporadic at best. But now I find myself in the unique position of sitting alone at a bar in Back Bay completely childless since my little sister Wren has graciously taken Rory for the night.

Still, I was looking forward to seeing him tonight.

> Me: Too bad. Will you back in time to introduce me to this new nanny you're telling me is perfect for Rory?

> Jack: Asshole, it's Eddie, and you've met her like a million times. She has been working as a live-in nanny for the last seven months in London and she loves kids. Just meet with her. That's all I'm asking.

Right. I know all of this, and I do know Eddie. Well, sorta. I haven't seen Jack's little sister since she was a kid. She's about twelve years younger than us and has been living abroad for art school for the last five years.

Eddie isn't so much the problem. I'm sure she's great. I trust Jack and I trust his family, and he swears once I meet her again, I'll love her, but more importantly, Rory will love her. My problem is that I'm having a hell of a time digesting the idea of a live-in nanny, though I know at this point it's what Rory and I need.

> Me: I'll meet her and I'm sure she'll be great. Safe travels and I'll see you tomorrow.

I stare at the screen of my phone, thinking this all through. It's difficult for me to admit that I need more help but with Rory starting first grade, and my insane work schedule, she needs more consistency and routine in her life than me shuffling her around between my family members.

"Another?" the bartender asks, and I stare down at my bourbon on the rocks and debate this. I could go home and get a full night of sleep—something I rarely get—and perhaps even sleep in before I pick up Rory. Or I could call one of my cousins who I don't get to hang out with nearly as often as I'd like and see what they're up to.

Or, better still, I could stay and see where the night takes me.

Even if it won't go beyond tonight.

My mental debate doesn't take long. I slide the glass back toward the bartender and lift my chin. "Two fingers, please."

She gives me a smile, the sort of appreciative smile I'm interested in. "Sure." That smile grows as her head dips, and she gazes up at me through her thick black lashes as she dutifully fills up my glass and slides it to me. "You're Owen Fritz, right?"

And just like that, my interest dies as ice floods my veins, freezing over any warmth or possibility I had been building myself up to. That. That fucking bullshit.

You're Owen Fritz.

Yeah, I am.

It's why Rory still doesn't have a nanny even though we desperately need one for her. It's why it's been far too long since I've ventured out and sought to meet a woman even for a one-nighter. It's why the only people I surround myself with are my family. Recognition as a Fritz, a celebrity family of billionaires who more or less own Boston is a more effective cock block than my little girl.

"Not tonight, I'm not," is my only reply. One she doesn't comprehend as her eyebrows slant inward and she stares bewilderedly at me. Her lips part as if she's about to question me when mercifully the other bartender calls her name. She gives me a wistful look and then reluctantly gets back to work.

I pull out my phone, deciding maybe a night hanging out with my cousins is the better option when movement out of the corner of my eye catches my attention. A delicate hand wraps around my glass and then lifts it. I turn in my seat, staring incredulously as my glass touches the full red lips of the petite woman on my right. She drinks about half of it, licks her lips, and then sets the glass down, her focus entirely on her phone that's in her other hand.

I blink at her, stunned. "That was my bourbon you just drank half of."

Her head whips in my direction as if she had no clue someone was sitting beside her and when her large, blue-green eyes meet mine, I nearly fall off my chair. Holy hell.

"This drink?" She holds up the glass in question and examines it. "What makes you think it's yours and not mine?" she retorts with an artfully curved eyebrow and a slight upturn to her red lips. I'm having trouble breathing. And remembering basic English. I might also be having a heart attack with how my heart is suddenly racing in my chest.

"I'm sorry, what?" Inwardly, I cringe. Has it been this long since I've been in the game or spoken to a beautiful woman who isn't a patient's mother? Yes. The answer is immediate. Yes!

Except she's so much more than simply beautiful. She's exotic and wild, which is normally not my thing at all, but on her… damn. Long, brown hair, so dark it's almost black with swirls of pink and blue underneath, and aquamarine eyes with an elegant curve and fan of natural black lashes. Her petite nose, which feels like such a contradiction compared to her kissable, plump bow-shaped lips, has a diamond stud in it. She's wearing a black halter top that shows off her narrow shoulders, smooth, tanned skin, and a sexy hint of cleavage from her large tits. Her ripped jeans hug her shapely hips and thighs.

She's small but perfectly fucking curvy, and hell, am I here for it.

The slight smirk she had been giving me curls into a full smile at my blundered retort and owl-eyed mystification, and if I thought I was having trouble breathing before, that's got nothing on what her smile is doing to me now.

I used to be better at this. So much better. Hell, I was fucking good at this once. I had a smile and swagger that could get a woman's panties off without even having to touch her. Now after a shitty divorce and far too much time spent in the hospital treating sick kids or staying in with my own, I've lost my game. Thank God Jack and my cousins aren't here. I'd never hear the end of this.

"You said this is your drink," she answers my inane question. "Not possible. I ordered a Knob Creek on the rocks. That's what this is. Trust me, I know the difference in my bourbons enough to taste it." Her delicate fingers swirl my glass around in a circle, the remaining amber liquid and ice going along for the ride. "You might want to work on your material. The old, that's my drink line has been used by men the world around."

I clear my throat and get my shit back together. Especially when her bit about that as a pickup line makes me chuckle. "I also ordered a Knob Creek on the rocks. And I believe"—I reach across the bar in front of her and tap the glass near her other hand—"this is your drink."

Her head slingshots and once she sees I'm right a melodic laugh bursts from her lungs. "Well, look at that." She turns back to me, a slight flush on her cheeks. "Oops. Sorry. So… that wasn't a pickup line then?"

I shake my head. "Not a pickup line."

"Thank God." She wipes imaginary sweat from her brow. "Even though you're gorgeous, that was an automatic turn-off for me. I can't stand cliché men."

I drag my thumb across my bottom lip, fighting my grin. "You prefer unexpected men instead?"

"Always." She assures me as if that should have been a foregone conclusion. "What woman doesn't?"

My jaw tingles with a smile I'm forcing myself to contain. "Like stealing someone's drink kind of unexpected?"

Her lips twitch and her cheeks flush again and I'm utterly captivated. It's rare, if ever since Angelica walked out on Rory and me three years ago that I've been drawn to anyone, but one look and a few sharp words and that's where I find myself.

She holds up a hand, her expression earnest. "I swear, I wasn't trying to be a drink thief. I was just a bit distracted by a text that came in. Let me buy you another round since I doubt you want to finish the one I just drank half of."

She moves to signal the waitress, but the last thing I want is for the waitress to return and start hitting on me again. Not when I have this woman's undivided attention and she called me gorgeous.

I reach for the glass still in her hand and when our fingers brush, a warm shockwave zings along my skin making my palm tingle. I hear her sharp intake of breath as if she too felt that. With my eyes locked on hers, I take the glass from her, bring it to my mouth, and polish off the rest of it.

She sits back and folds her arms over her chest, appraising me. "It's going to be like that then, huh? Swapping spit with me before I even get your name."

I lean in, taking a deeper inhale when I catch the hint of her subtle fragrance. "Technically you swapped spit with me first since that was my second drink in the same glass. And who says I was going to give you my name?"

She arches a challenging brow. "I think we both know you want to give it to me." She picks up her glass, takes a sip of it, and then hands it to me to do the same. I smile, a real fucking smile that feels so rare on my lips I let it linger even as I take a sip from her glass.

"What's your name?" I ask as I hand it back to her.

"Estlin."

"Estlin. That's... different. I'm not sure I've heard it before."

"Don't ask the origin. It's not a story I enjoy telling."

I smirk, tapping my thumb against the edge of the bar. "Then I won't ask."

She brushes her hair back over her shoulders, more of the pink and blue popping out and playing with the black. "I told you mine, now it's your turn to tell me yours."

And the fact that there's no mocking or hint of recognition in her eyes or voice has me saying, "Owen."

"Nice to meet you, Owen. Do you do this often? Come to bars and pick up women with overused lines?"

I chuckle lightly. "Hardly ever actually. I'm not a man with a lot of free time. What about you?"

"I haven't picked up a woman in a bar in years."

A laugh bursts from my lungs. "Oh. Is that your not-so-casual way of saying I'm barking up the wrong tree?"

"Not even a bit." She drops an elbow on the bar and leans her head into the palm of her hand as she faces me. "But that doesn't mean I'm not already someone's date tonight?"

"Are you?" I throw back at her, liking how her eyes glitter and her nose ring sparkles in the dim lighting as she boldly flirts with me.

She dips in until our faces are inches apart. "Want to know a secret?"

My hand hits the back of her barstool and I inch in close enough that I can practically taste my bourbon on her lips. There is no stopping the conspiratorially playful note in my voice as I say, "Tell me."

"I got stood up tonight."

I pull back enough to let her see my shock. "You? Impossible. What man would be stupid enough to stand you up?"

"My brother and it wasn't quite his fault."

"I got stood up tonight too."

"Impossible," she parrots teasingly. "What woman would be crazy enough to stand you up."

"Not a woman. Just a friend."

"I guess that means we're both alone tonight."

"Not anymore." The hand on the back of her chair finds a lock of her silky hair and I run my fingers through it. She shudders ever so slightly, and I smile, moving until my knee brushes against hers. She hasn't moved away or asked me to stop. She's enjoying this as much as I am.

My mouth slides along the side of her face until I whisper in her ear, "Estlin, would you like to have another drink with me?"

She makes a noise in her throat when she feels my hot breath on her skin, and I pull back, noting the resulting flush on her cheeks again. I can't help but wonder if all of her blushes so prettily.

"Yes. I'd like that. But this round is on me since I drank your last one."

"I've never had a woman who isn't family buy me a drink before," I admit. "I'm not sure how I feel about it."

She rolls her eyes at me. "We can fight about the patriarchal and archaic notion that a man has to financially take care of a woman over the drink I'm buying you." She half stands up, waving at the bartender all the way down on the end. She holds up two fingers and points to each of our glasses. He throws her a wave of acknowledgement and then she sits back down.

"It's not me being patriarchal. I believe women rule this world and do a better job of it. It's called being a gentleman."

"You're one of those guys? Hmm." The male bartender comes over and refills both our glasses and immediately she hops off her stool and picks up her glass. "I tell you what. If you beat me at darts, I'll let you pay for my drink. If I beat you, you let me pay."

I rub my jaw, eyeing the empty dartboard she's indicating. "You sure that's fair? I'm pretty good at them."

She tilts her head, her expression taunting. "I thought you wanted to buy me a drink? Now you're tipping your hand?"

Touché.

"Okay. You're on."

"I'll be back in a few, Matty," she calls to the bartender with a wave.

The bartender winks at her and then she saunters off

toward the dart board without waiting on me, already knowing I'm going to follow her.

Who the hell is this woman? And what is it about her—other than her looks—that has me so goddamn intrigued. I honestly don't know, but something about this ocean-eyed beauty has me anxious for more. Maybe it's the smart, no-bullshit sharpness of her tongue or her boldness or youth—since I can tell she's quite a bit younger than me—or the fact that I am so very out of practice with this.

Whatever it is, she has me on my toes, making me feel that even though she's within my grasp, I'm going to have to work my ass off to get her.

I've always liked a challenge and I definitely want to keep this going so I can see where it will hopefully lead for the rest of the night. So I guess it's game on.

"Matty?" I question as I come to stand beside her about six feet from the dartboard.

"We went to high school together. Take these." She hands me three red darts while she holds the green ones.

I decide not to question it. The less I know about her the better. There is only tonight for us. No tomorrow and certainly not the next day. Not with my life.

"Have you played before?" I ask, rolling the darts back and forth between my palms.

"Once or twice, but I don't recall it being all that difficult."

"All right. Ladies first." I wave her to take the lead and she shoots me a side-eye.

"Didn't we discuss that already?"

I point to my chest. "Gentleman, remember?"

She puffs a breath but relents and throws her dart, hitting the outer ring of the nine.

"Yay. That's good, right?"

I smirk. "That's good. Go again." She throws two more times in a row, hitting just outside the bullseye and the inner ring of twenty.

I squint at her. "Why do I get the feeling I'm being hustled?"

She smiles like an angel up at me since she's a solid foot shorter than I am. "I don't know what you're talking about. Who hustles at darts?" She goes over to the board and pulls out her darts and then comes and stands right beside me.

I throw my darts and hit the inner ring of the twelve, the inner ring of the twenty, and the inner ring of the nineteen."

"Oh darn. You are good at this."

I stare down at her. "You're totally hustling me."

"You're paranoid."

I give her a dubious look. "Right. Sure, I am. You realize since I won that round, I just bought your drink."

Her hand lands on my chest and I can feel the heat of her palm seeping through the thin material of my black T-shirt. "Don't get mad at me."

I laugh. "Mad at you? Impossible."

"Good. Because I get free drinks here. Matty owes me from a thing a while back, so he simply added your drink to mine. The game was just a fun diversion."

"Hustler," I play, snaking a hand around her waist and dragging her in tighter to me. My fingers trickle up until I find the smooth, bare skin of her back, warm and soft beneath my touch. My cock starts to thicken in my jeans, and if I shift a little to the right, she'll feel it for sure.

She rocks up on the balls of her feet until her chest presses to mine, her full, soft tits squishing tantalizingly into me. "I totally am. I'm killer at darts. I let you win because I'm generous like that."

"Maybe. But maybe not." My face dips. "If you say you let me win then you won't object to upping the ante, right? How about we play for something real since you already bought me my drink?"

Amusement tilts up her lips into a fearless smile. "What did you have in mind?"

My gaze washes over her, following the lines of her body and then back up to her lips. Sweet, full lips I want to devour and hear moaning my name. I meet her eyes. "If I win the next round, you get a hotel room with me for the night."

Her hand slithers up my chest, past my shoulder, to the back of my neck where she plays with the ends of my hair. "That's rather bold of you, Owen."

I don't bother pretending otherwise. "But it's exactly what I want."

"A hotel room though, huh? Are you hiding a wife or girl-friend at home?"

"I'm as single as it gets. A hotel room is just more conve-nient." I never bring women home and I have no plans to start now.

She considers this for a moment and just when I think she's about to tell me to fuck off, she surprises me with, "And if I win the next round?"

I search around the bar, moderately crowded for a Friday night in this part of the city, and then back to her. People recognize me here. Everywhere I go in this city, people recog-nize me. It wasn't so long ago that my face was plastered over every tabloid out there. So if I kiss a random woman in public, it will end up somewhere I don't want it to be.

Somewhere my daughter could see it. Even worse, some-where my grandmother could see it and then she'll start in on me with getting married again because that's what she does.

To that end, I should go, but I'd like to take Estlin with me.

"Lady's choice." Because I have no intention of losing.

She grins wickedly. "Okay. You're on."


ARE you getting excited for Owen and Estlin's super steamy, brother's best friend, single dad, nanny romance? Grab your copy of Undeniably Forbidden now.

# End of Book Note

Thank you for reading Katy and Bennett's story. I have been so excited to start this next-generation series and Katy Barrows seemed like the perfect place to start since she is the glue between my Boston's Billionaire Bachelors series and my Irresistibly Yours series.

Plus, I was so excited for Katy to get her story. I simply loved writing her and Bennett. They were so much fun together and even though this was a new trope and a challenging one at that, I am obsessed with how it turned out.

I want to thank my betas and team for all they do for me. I wouldn't be able to do any of this without them and their help and support is everything. Danielle, Patricia, Kelly, and Joy, you are the absolute best and I love you!

I also want to thank my family who put up with me when I started to lose myself and my mind in my stories. This was a particularly challenging one for me and you stood by me every step of the way. My girls and my guy, you are the loves of my life!

And to you, lovely, amazing reader! You are the reason I do this and I am grateful beyond words for you! There is so much to come in this Boston world and I am beyond excited for it.

Enjoy!

XO,

J. Saman

www.ingramcontent.com/pod-product-compliance
Lightning Source LLC
Chambersburg PA
CBHW051301130726
47987CB00004B/1609